HAWK HUNTER WAS CONSUMED BY A BLIND RAGE!

Shooting down planes was all part of the horrible game of war. But gunning down a helpless pilot after he'd bailed out was just plain cowardly murder. Anger toward the malicious Soviet pilot burned inside him like a piece of hot metal. He yanked back on the F-16's controls, putting the fighter into a steep, near-vertical climb.

Almost immediately he was surrounded by green-yellow tracers streaming past his canopy. Somehow the Russian MiG was suddenly beneath him, and Hawk felt two dull thuds on the underside of his plane.

Now there was only one way out. But no matter what the risk, he was going to take it.

War was war. But senseless killings had to be avenged!

WINGMAN
BY MACK MALONEY

WINGMAN   (0-7860-0310-3, $4.99)

#2 THE CIRCLE WAR   (0-7860-0346-4, $4.99)

#5 THE TWISTED CROSS   (0-8217-2553-X, $3.95)

#6 THE FINAL STORM   (0-8217-2655-2, $3.95)

#7 FREEDOM EXPRESS   (0-8217-4022-9, $3.99)

ALSO BY MACK MALONEY:

WAR HEAVEN   (0-8217-3414-8, $4.95)

WINGMAN

THE FINAL STORM

BY MACK MALONEY

PINNACLE BOOKS
KENSINGTON PUBLISHING CORP.
http://www.pinnaclebooks.com

PINNACLE BOOKS are published by

Kensington Publishing Corp.
850 Third Avenue
New York, NY 10022

Pinnacle and the P logo Reg. U.S. Pat. & TM Off.

First Zebra Printing: May, 1989

First Pinnacle Printing: April, 1998
10 9 8 7 6 5

Printed in the United States of America

Part I
The Raid

Part 1
The Raid

Chapter 1

The strange-looking aircraft skimmed over the steel-blue surface of the Atlantic Ocean, intently hurtling toward its destination.

The craft was a curious hybrid — part helicopter and part fixed-wing cargo plane. Its stubby fuselage hung under a wing section that, though thin, supported two huge turbine engines. Like a conventional airplane, these engines drove massive propellers that sped the craft through the air at a respectable speed.

But this airplane had a hidden talent. . . .

Its engines, encased in bulbous nacelles on each wingtip, could be rotated a full ninety degrees. Once done, this action would almost magically transform the oversize propellers into overhead rotors. Thus, the airplane was able to take off and land vertically like a helicopter.

It was officially known as the MV-22 Osprey. The amazing tilt-rotor aircraft had been designed to be the close air support mainstay for US Marine Corps amphibious assault operations. Like the seagoing bird of prey it was named after, the Osprey was built to skim the waves and strike swiftly, delivering Marines and material to the battle. At one time, before World War III, hundreds of them had seen service around the globe.

Now there was only one. . . .

Major Hawk Hunter, the man behind the airplane's controls, was concentrating on keeping the green-and-gray camouflaged plane as close as possible to the tops of the ocean swells.

Adjusting the control surfaces with the barest flick of a wrist or the slightest pressure on a rudder pedal, he found himself continually compensating for unseen turbulence in the heavy, pre-dawn salt air. Every few seconds his eyes darted about the airplane's cockpit console, quickly monitoring its gauges. Then he would look up and, by adjusting his helmet's infra-red sighting goggles, scan the thin line of the horizon, searching for the point of land in the distance that was his destination.

Hunter had flown hundreds of combat missions in every type of aircraft, in every corner of the globe—his virtually undisputed reputation as the best fighter pilot who had ever lived led to his being known as The Wingman.

But this mission was like no other. . . .

In the Osprey's squat fuselage behind Hunter there were twenty-four commandos, all of them tensely gripping their weapons as they sat facing each other in the cramped cargo cabin. Rocking with the aircraft's motion, the soldiers—members of the elite Football City Special Forces Rangers—stared down at the floor, or up at the overhead compartments, or simply sat with their eyes closed. For them, the time before combat was always reserved for private thoughts. It would be no different on this day.

For Hunter, too, it was a time for reflection. Even as he was manipulating the controls and reviewing the mission plan, another part of him was reliving a bad-dream memory that was still as painful as if it had happened the day before.

Actually it might as well have been a lifetime ago . . . .

The nightmare started with the outbreak of World War III. Lulled by several years of *glasnost*-era peace, the world exploded in war after a massive Soviet attack—launched in complete surprise on Christmas Eve—killed millions of West Europeans, not by nuclear holocaust, but by nerve gas. A massive Soviet invasion of Western Europe followed. Eventually, China was nuked and suddenly, any country who had a dispute with its neighbor decided to have it out.

The Free World struck back. After much suffering and misery, the US and NATO forces had cleverly won the final battle of the war, soundly defeating an overwhelming Soviet war machine—and all without using nuclear weapons. Moscow pleaded for an armistice. Magnanimously, the West agreed. But then, just as it seemed that peace was at hand, the Soviets launched another devastating attack—this one a nuclear strike at the heart of the American continent. All of the country's ICBMs were destroyed in their silos, and its remaining nuclear arsenal rendered useless. Now the nation's heartland was a desolate wasteland—an ugly, festering scar that stretched from the Dakotas down to the northern border of Texas.

Now, the once-fertile fields of America's breadbasket were a nightmarish radioactive moonscape called the Badlands. . . .

Only later was it learned that the Soviets had been aided by a traitorous "mole" in the US Government. Someone, who, as part of a sinister plot, arranged to have the US President, his family and his cabinet assassinated just after the armistice was declared.

Suddenly shattered and leaderless, the US had little choice but to accept the harsh terms of the Soviet "victors," a mockery of justice known as the New Order. Under this decree, the United States of America ceased to exist. Instead, the nation was carved up into a patchwork of territories, free states, and independent republics, most led by criminal puppets of the Soviets. No sooner had the New Order been declared when these mini-countries began fighting each other, further increasing the instability of the American continent.

But the darkness of these times had not totally consumed Hunter. In the handful of years that followed, and through several full-scale wars and dozens of major battles, he and his allies—known collectively as the United American Army—had fought back to reclaim their country and secure its borders.

Months before, these democratic forces had soundly defeated the Soviet-sponsored Circle Army in a battle for control of lands east of the Mississippi. More recently, another major engagement had wrested control of the Panama Canal from a group of fanatical, nuclear-armed neo-Nazis.

Yet despite these successes, Hunter knew the battle was far from over. In fact, he believed the most difficult tasks lay ahead.

But the United Americans had gained the momentum. At the

present time they controlled most of the continent's major cities, and for the first time since the Big War, its borders were relatively well-guarded.

And as such, they knew now was the time to go after the traitor.

"There it is, Hawk, dead ahead. . . ."

The words from his co-pilot—and close friend—JT Toomey shook him out of his trance.

Toomey was pointing directly to a small speck of green up ahead that was just barely visible in the pre-dawn darkness. Hunter's infra-red enhanced eyes darted to the island on the horizon, then to the instrument console and then to his watch.

They were still on schedule.

He flicked the intercom switch on his cockpit control panel.

"Bermuda now in sight," he called back to the assault team in the cabin. "Time to put the rosaries away. . . ."

The island—their target—had served as headquarters for the notoriously corrupt "New Order" gang since the end of World War III.

Nominally headed by the traitor himself, the group of international criminals had used the lush resort as a stronghold from which to enforce the harsh tenets of the New Order. At the time of its imposition, these rules restricted virtually all forms of open communications and personal freedoms. They also forbade the display of any symbol of US patriotism—such as the national anthem and the pledge of allegiance—and even outlawed the mention of the term "United States of America."

And for anyone foolhardy enough to display the red, white and blue banner that had been the nation's flag, the penalty was death.

Hunter had made up his mind very soon after learning of the New Order's rules that he would never submit to them. Instead he vowed that he would fight back whenever and wherever he could, until he had defeated the tyranny or it defeated him. He had kept that vow throughout the darkest days of the terrible struggle, in dozens of battles on a hundred shores.

Never was the dream of America far from his thoughts.

And now he was on the verge of striking at the very heart of the beast that had terrorized his nation for so long. He felt gallons of adrenaline pumping through him at the mere thought of it. *How sweet is thy nectar, the wine of revenge!*

"I read ten minutes before we enter their airspace, Hawk," JT said, once again piercing his thoughts.

"Roger, ten minutes," Hunter acknowledged. "Better start cranking the ECM."

As he heard the reassuring whir of the Osprey's electronic counter-measures package begin transmitting, his thoughts narrowed to the mission ahead.

Even the Soviets did not evoke the same contempt Hunter had for this *ex*-American traitor and his thugs. During World War III and since, the Soviets had been the major enemy—he had fought them as a soldier, giving no mercy and expecting none. But the treachery and deceit of the turncoat had summoned a fury in him that had been boiling for years. He knew it would not subside until the betrayer was brought to justice.

And that was the object of this mission.

The real planning had started shortly after they found the Osprey.

When the United American Army reclaimed the southeastern coastal states from the hands of The Circle, they discovered most of the former US military installations in the area had been looted or destroyed. The military hardware was long gone—most of it sold on a thriving New Order American black market. There, *anything* capable of being fired was quickly snapped up by the members of the many free-lance armies that served the two dozen or so nation-states now residing on the North American continent.

But near the former US Marine base at Cherry Point, North Carolina, the Circle had overlooked a creaking container ship that had been beached on the sandy banks of the Pamlico Sound. Whether it was a supply ship on its way to the European battlefront that never left port, or a luckless privateer washed ashore as he tried to run the Circle blockade was never known. But inside its rusty hold lay the sixty-foot tilt-rotor Osprey aircraft, still packed in its factory grease.

The United Americans quickly assembled the Osprey and Hunter had flight-tested it himself shortly after returning from the campaign against the Canal Nazis down in Panama. For most pilots, it would have taken hundreds of flight hours to learn the secrets of tricky vertical takeoffs and landings, rotating engines, and combined complexities of helicopter and fixed-wing flight.

Hunter had it mastered in an afternoon.

Once their transportation had been secured, the meticulous planning for the raid on Bermuda began in earnest. Primary and secondary means of ingress and egress were evaluated. Maps were drawn up. Intangibles like weather and tides were checked. Most important, several teams of United American undercover agents were dropped on the island, spies specially trained to mix in with the Bermudan population.

Training for the strike team itself had been done quickly and secretly. The Special Forces Rangers—being the protective force for the continent's gambling mecca, Football City, formerly known as St. Louis—were everyone's first choice to carry out the strike. And there was never any question that Hunter would be the mission commander.

There were many long days and sleepless nights leading up to the mission. As D-Day approached, Hunter and the other members of the United American top echelon found themselves immersed in a myriad of last-minute details. Air cover. Refueling. SAM suppression. Landing sites. MedEvac. The inevitable unexpected contingencies.

Despite the avalanche of concerns, they were ready to go in less than three weeks. . . .

At 3AM on the morning of D-Day, the team had taken off from the short field at Cherry Point. Hidden in the darkness, at first they flew southeast, *away* from the primary target of Bermuda.

The odd flight plan was necessary because, first and foremost, the Osprey needed a disguise. This is where the American intelligence operatives came in. The spies had discovered that the Cuban Air Force routinely flew a supply mission to deliver food, fuel, and ammunition from Havana to the New Order ministers. Using a battered Soviet AN-12 Cub turboprop cargo plane, the weekly flight had been "requested" of the Cubans years before by the very mysterious military clique that had run the Kremlin since the war.

Far from an inconvenience, the weekly milk run to Bermuda was considered a plum assignment by the Cuban pilots who flew it—neither the United Americans nor the renegade Yankee air pirates had ever bothered these flights before.

On this day, however, the Cubans discovered that there was a first time for everything.

They had been 250 miles from their destination when the Cuban pilots first spotted the Osprey.

It was as if it had appeared out of nowhere, popping up from the hazy sea with its twin rotors tilted up, positioning itself just a quarter mile off the cargo plane's port side. Before the Cubans could react, a Stinger anti-aircraft missile—fired by one of the commandos stationed on the Osprey's side gunner's station—flashed in on them.

At that range, the sophisticated weapon couldn't miss. The Cuban pilot was too stunned to even key his radio before the American missile's guidance system drove its warhead home, smashing deep into the hot exhaust of the cargo plane's portside outer engine. Within seconds, a mushroom of orange flame engulfed the plane. Then there was a powerful explosion . . .

There was no need to confirm the kill—aside from a scattering of wreckage and an oil slick bobbing on the ocean surface, nothing remained of the Cuban aircraft.

The lightning-quick action had been needed to provide their disguise—the Osprey's radar signature resembled that of the Cuban cargo plane, and if all went well, it would be interpreted as such by enemy radar operators.

That had been an hour ago. Now as they closed in on the island, JT leaned over and yelled to Hunter.

"We're in their SAM envelope," he reported. "About five minutes to landfall."

Taking the Toomey's cue, Hunter quickly scanned two screens in front of him, hoping he would not see the tell-tale blips indicating that hostile radars were locking in on them. At the moment, there was nothing.

So far, the disguise was working.

Hunter was glad to see the weather was cooperating—at that moment, the weather around the usually pleasant island was miserable. Low-hanging clouds, fairly high winds, and a moderate rain had been the forecast and the United American meteorologists had been correct again.

Using a thick cloud layer to hide themselves, they were skirting the island's southernmost tip a few minutes later.

There was still no sign of alarm on the ground, at least none observable from the air. Using the NightScope goggles, Hunter could see that there *was* a large cluster of military vehicles at a tiny airport about six miles to their west. He could also make out an assortment of cargo and combat aircraft bearing Cuban, Soviet, and commercial insignia. Although heat images indicating ground personnel were evident around the base, none of the airport's intercept airplanes appeared to be on alert.

And, best of all, not a single one of the anti-aircraft batteries was manned.

Hunter took another deep gulp of oxygen from his mask, a small celebration of relief. Their intelligence proved correct once again: It appeared as if complacency *had* become the norm on the New Order's island headquarters, at least in the early morning hours.

Once they were beyond the radar sweep emanating from the airbase, Hunter knew that if they continued to be lucky, few of those awake on the ground would give the lone plane flying above the heavy layer of clouds a second thought. Upon hearing the high whine of the Osprey's engines, those in the know would just assume it was the routine "crack o'dawn" supply flight coming in from Cuba and heading for the island's only other aircraft facility, a small grass strip on the northeastern shoulder of the island.

Skirting the island to the far eastern side, Hunter decreased the Osprey's speed to a near-hovering crawl. His electronically assisted vision scanned the hilly contours that curved down to meet the ocean on this, the island's rocky side. He was looking for one patch of ground in particular—its form was emblazoned in his memory via a high altitude recon photo taken of the island just a week before. The place was ideal for their mission—it was isolated, fairly well-hidden and provided a flat place to set the Osprey down.

He checked his watch again—it was just 0600. The sun was coming up and eventually, it would burn off the inclement weather. He knew that quick action was crucial now. Although they had successfully pierced the enemy's airspace, there would be trouble if just one of the island's radar operators suddenly became alert while the strike force was still airborne.

"There it is . . ." Hunter called over to JT.

The co-pilot adjusted his own NightScope glasses then he too saw it. Off to their left, a small, flat-top mountain that broke off into a cliff. At its summit was a tall white skyscraper.

This building was their objective.

Once an ultra-luxurious resort hotel, the 25-story structure was surrounded by high walls and fronted on the seaside by a large concrete bunker. A long curving road ran from the entrance to this bunker down the sloping oceanfront hillside to the beach below, a distance of about a mile.

Halfway down, the road flattened out slightly right next to a dense grove of palm trees. This was the predesignated landing zone. In seconds, Hunter had turned the Osprey toward it.

"Hang on, gang," he called to the troops in back as he approached the LZ. Then, pulling back on the Osprey's controls and rotating the big nacelles fully skyward, he quickly put the aircraft into its hover mode. The effect was like slamming on the car's brakes at 70 mph. There was an audible screech as the airplane suddenly went true vertical and started to drop, its huge rotors scattering sand and loose brush in the downwash as it drew closer to the palm grove.

They landed with a *thump!* Hunter instantly idled the twin engines and once again called back to the Rangers.

"Welcome to Bermuda, boys."

Swiftly and silently, the Rangers lowered the Osprey's rear

ramp and scattered into the palm grove. In less than a half minute, they had secured the deserted landing zone. Thirty seconds later, the airplane was camouflaged with special netting.

At that point, Hunter keyed his microphone and set the Osprey's transmitter to "Long Range—Send."

"OK, partner," Hunter said to JT. "Let's see if we can get a clear radio shot."

Using his best *hey-mon* accent, Hunter called into the microphone: "Hello, Cousin. Hello Cousin. Fishing is fine . . . I say, fishing is fine . . ."

Five agonizing seconds went by.

He repeated the message.

"Hello, hello, Cousin. I say, fishing is fine . . . very fine . . ."

Both he and JT stared at the aircraft's radio speaker, as if looking at it would produce the needed reply.

"They might be out of range," JT offered, his tone slightly worried.

"Not if they're on time, they're not," Hunter said before repeating the message a third time.

Suddenly the speaker burst to life. " 'Allo, *'allo!* Cousin!" a strange, obviously mimicked voice on the speaker called back to them. "If fishing is fine, then we come to fish . . ."

Both Hunter and Toomey breathed a sigh of relief. The low, focused radio message had come back loud and clear, so much so it caused both Hunter and JT to shake their heads at someone else's bad imitation of a Bermudan accent.

"See you soon, Cousin," Hunter replied. "Over and out."

The all-important diversion was in motion. Now it was time for the strike team to get to work.

Hunter and JT climbed out of the Osprey and quickly took a look at the lay of the land. They were just 20 feet from the dirt road that led up to the cliff that jutted out above them about a mile away. It had stopped raining and was getting lighter. The sun was just above the horizon now, its intense gold light already burning off some of the clouds.

Once again, Hunter checked his watch. It was 0607. They had less than twenty minutes to get in position before the diversion started. But one important element was still missing. He gathered the assault team in the thicket of palms to review the plan

16

and wait.

Barely a minute later, the low rumble of a large diesel engine caught his ear. Someone—or something—was advancing up the coast road.

In a split-second the strike force dove for cover among the palms, pointing their M-16s down the open road at the advancing sound. Soon a vehicle, completely enveloped in a cloud of smoke, came into view. It was a battered, double-deck tour bus, its trail of dirty engine exhaust punctuated by staccato bursts of backfiring.

The clustered Rangers hunkered down even farther as the ancient vehicle came grinding up to the clearing. The driver, intent on jamming his balky gearshift into what seemed like every other gear, didn't see the commandos until he was literally on top of them.

Suddenly he was facing 25 M-16s . . .

The bus driver, a tall, rugged black man, slammed on the brakes, and seeing he was surrounded, nervously stepped out of the creaking bus. Two Rangers stepped up to frisk him and found nothing. By this time, Hunter and JT had moved up.

Immediately, Hunter and the driver engaged in a hearty handshake and a quick orgy of back-slapping.

"Hunter, my old friend!" the sunny black man said in an excited whisper dripping with the Queen's English. "It is good to see you well."

"Humdingo, it seems like I am always asking you for a favor," Hunter told the man. "But it is good to see you also, sir."

Though he looked and talked the part, the man, Humdingo, was not a native Bermudan at all. In fact, he was an African, and a chief of a tribe of Congolese warriors to boot. Educated in England before the Big War, Humdingo had close ties to the British Free Forces who now held some semblance of order in near-anarchic Western Europe. Hunter had met the chief a year before when the pilot helped some Brits tow a disabled nuclear aircraft carrier across the Mediterranean in an effort to stop the ruthless terrorist known as Viktor from relighting World War III. Humdingo and his men had guarded Hunter's precious F-16 at a crucial time during that mission.

Now, the mighty chief was working with the United Americans. He was the leader of one of the UA spy teams that had been inserted on the island. He had learned much. But most important, via a pocketful of bribes, he had bought a job driving non-essential New Order personnel and visitors from the center of town to the skyscraper and back.

"We have so little time to talk, my friend," Hunter told him. "Is everything going according to plan?"

"Yes," Humdingo answered quickly. "Everything is set. I suggest you have your lads hop into the motorcoach. Their clothes are bundled up in the back."

A signal from Hunter and 20 of the Rangers scrambled aboard the ancient vehicle. They immediately hid between the seats, retrieving packages of clothing they found there. As planned, JT and the rest of the commandos would stay with the Osprey.

"Good luck, Hawk," JT called out to Hunter.

"You, too," Hunter replied as he hopped into the rickety open cab of the bus. "And when you hear us holler, come a-runnin'."

Then, with a series of loud backfires and grinding of the gears, the double-decker behemoth started up the steep incline, heading to the entrance of the bunker.

Hunter looked at the time again, and peered over the cracked dashboard to see the dusty road ahead.

Only twelve minutes to showtime, he thought.

Chapter 2

Fifty miles off the western coast of Bermuda, the two brightly painted F-4 Phantoms were hugging the surface of the softly swelling Atlantic. On the flight leader's count, they turned at a predescribed point and streaked toward the island at more than 800 miles per hour.

The bold lettering on their nose sections labeled them "The Ace Wrecking Crew," the well-known free-lance air combat team that flew for Hunter and the United American Army. Their slogan, emblazoned in similar circus-style lettering on the shining fuselages, read: "No Job's Too Small, We Bomb Them All."

The owner/operator, Captain "Crunch" O'Malley, had always believed that it paid to advertise. Because these days if you had two supersonic fighters and crews who knew their business, you had a very marketable commodity in the New Order world.

But Crunch and his team weren't flying for pay now—this mission they were doing *gratis*.

The "fishing is fine" signal they had received from Hunter told them that they still had the critical advantage of surprise—no alert had been sounded at the time Hunter had called in the strike. That was fine with Crunch—his Phantoms were kick-ass jets, but any day he could avoid tangling with MiGs and the like was fine with him.

With a wing signal to his partner in the Number 2 Phantom, a captain known to all as Elvis Q, Crunch relayed the order to arm their ordnance. Each plane was carrying about ten thousand pounds of napalm bombs on hard points under the wings and fuselages of the souped-up fighter-bombers.

In the rear seat of his F-4, Crunch's navigator/bombardier snapped off the red covers over the bomb arming switches and clicked all of them up to prepare the deadly munitions. Five tons of jellied gasoline hanging from the wings made both men momentarily religious—one stray tracer round from an enemy gun and their speeding fighter would turn into a supersonic ball of fire.

Crunch turned to make the final approach, hugging the rolling wavetops as he kept his two-ship flight under radar until the last possible second. The wave-licking wouldn't last long though—they would need some altitude when they let the napalm go, or they'd be caught by the flames of the explosions.

On O'Malley's order, the Phantoms broke up off the deck together. They were now a scant five miles away from their main target: Bermuda's tiny military airport. Using his APG-65 advanced imaging radar set, Crunch was able to "see" a scattering of aircraft on the airport's runways and taxiways. The largest was a Soviet-built airborne tanker that he guessed was of Libyan origin.

All the better, Crunch thought.

His rear-seater targeted the big tanker, parked near the airport's main fuel depot. Although O'Malley knew the Soviets and their satellites were drilled in proper defensive deployment and dispersal of aircraft, that knowledge was not evident at the New Order base.

In other words, the big tanker was a sitting duck.

The two F-4s flashed over the beach, at the same instant "popping up" to 750 feet. Both pilots then immediately kicked in their afterburners, increasing their speed to an awesome 1,000 mph.

Six seconds later, they were over the target.

To the shocked gun and missile crews, many just sitting down to morning chow, it appeared as if the circus-colored F-4s had materialized out of nowhere. Before they could race to their battle stations, the first sticks of napalm bombs had been loosed from the wings of the streaking Phantoms, smashing into the clustered machines on the crowded runways.

Crunch's bombs found their mark with a direct hit on the

tanker, which, as he correctly guessed, was covered with Libyan markings. The gelatinous mixture exploded in an ugly, oily mushroom of orange-white flame as it engulfed the big plane, touching off an even bigger explosion as the contents of the tanker—several thousand gallons of jet fuel—erupted into the murky gray sky.

In Phantom 2, Elvis's bombardier had laid his deadly napalm eggs among the scattered fighter planes and helicopters along the opposite end of the runway. These, too, erupted in searing geysers of fire that grew larger with every airplane and fuel tank that was added to the angry tempest.

The two sets of fires grew in size and ferocity until they met near the center of the main runway, devouring several Cuban-marked Hind helicopters and igniting an underground ammunition bunker.

"Bingo!" Elvis cried out as he saw the tell-tale greenish-white flame of tons of rifle ammo going off.

Within seconds, the secondary explosions started successive chain reactions among the nearby fuel storage tanks, bursting one after another until the entire fuel depot was one sprawling sheet of flame.

Less than a minute after the jets had departed the area, the entire airport was engulfed in a wind-whipped firestorm, one which generated temperatures so hot, the asphalt on its runways literally melted.

Arcing his swift Phantom around to survey the scene, Crunch realized the extent of the destruction at the airport. So intense was the inferno that the fires were beginning to spread beyond the airport's perimeter and on to other parts of the island. Their mission was complete; the target was destroyed. There would be no need for a second pass.

Crunch felt a brief pang of remorse. He had visited Bermuda many years ago—on his honeymoon yet—and had always remembered it as a peaceful island paradise, noted especially for its calm and cooling ocean breezes.

Now it looked like a little piece of Hell itself.

Picking up his partner on the back side of his turn, Crunch took one last look at the towering column of flame and black smoke over the airport. Then he kicked in his afterburner and roared away to the west, leading the Phantoms of the Ace Wrecking Crew back to Cherry Point.

As it had many mornings before, the beat-up shuttle bus labored up the winding road to the skyscraper's hilltop entrance and approached a small guard station.

"Everyone stay cool," Hunter calmly called back to the Rangers. "Here comes our first potential problem."

No longer crouching in the aisle, the Rangers, now wearing long white sheets and hoods, were sitting two by two in the seats on the lower deck of the bus. The strange disguise was a key to the mission. Humdingo had found out several weeks before that a number of criminal gangs from the American mainland — neo-Nazis, Mafioso, air pirates — regularly visited Bermuda at the invitation of the New Order ministers. Provided guns, drugs and prostitutes, these gangs would eventually return to America and whip up trouble.

Now, the United Americans' plan called for the strike team to play the part of one of the more notorious racist gangs Humdingo knew were actually elsewhere on the island.

Humdingo slowed the bus as it reached the guardhouse. Inside the small building was a Vietnamese lieutenant. The chief gave the man a routine wave and handed him an envelope. The guard, who recognized the old bus, quickly read the note which authorized the Knights of the Burning Cross to proceed to the skyscraper. Hardly looking up from the dog-eared nudie magazine he was reading, the Vietnamese officer waved the bus through.

"Thank you, Ho Chi Minh," Hunter whispered as Humdingo gunned the bus past the guardhouse and into the small parking lot next to the skyscraper. They came to a stop in front of a combination blockhouse and bus stop shelter, which was right next to the entrance to the building's little-used underground parking garage.

Nearby a large closed-circuit video camera rotated monotonously back and forth across the approachway, its cold unblinking eye passing over the bus several times.

To the rear of the bus was a spectacular view of the Atlantic Ocean. On cue, the Rangers turned and let out a chorus of "ooos" and "aahs." Then several who were carrying cameras began click-ing away. Meanwhile, Hunter stood and addressed the group in mostly incomprehensible pidgin English.

To the half-dozen New Order guards—mercenaries all—sprawled around the bus stop structure, nothing about the odd scene looked unusual.

Just another busload of free-loading American terrorists, wear-ing their crazy costumes and taking tourist-type pictures. Ab-sorbed in eating a pick-up breakfast in the warm, early-morning, Bermuda sunshine, none of the guards gave the busload of sheeted people a second look.

But then, suddenly, the guards felt the ground starting to shake . . .

"Now! Go! *Go!*" Hunter screamed at the Rangers.

The robed Rangers burst out of the creaking bus, the first six men firing away with their silencer-equipped M-16s. In a matter of seconds, the startled guards were quickly—and quietly—mowed down and the strike force's sharpshooter had put a hushed burst into the Vietnamese officer in the guardhouse. At the same time, Hunter blinded the rotating security camera with a blast from his tracer-filled M-16 assault rifle, which was also carrying a silencer for the occasion.

All the while the ground continued to rumble with the force of a mini-earthquake. Off to the southwest, Hunter could see the billowing black smoke and towers of flame shooting up from the tiny airbase a dozen miles away. Once again, Crunch & Crew had been right on the money.

Now, it was up to Hunter and his gang to work quickly. . . .

The trio of South African mercenaries manning the sky-scraper's bottom floor video security system was baffled at why their rear entrance camera had suddenly blinked out. Short-circuit? Sudden drop in power? Or perhaps the slight shaking they had felt moments earlier had something to do with it.

In any case, with the early morning hour and their coffee just being poured, none of the three was too anxious to get up and check out the camera's problem. Still, it had to be done.

"I'll go," one of them, a sergeant, said finally. He was hungover from a late-night drinking bout and was hoping the fresh air would clear his head and settle his stomach.

Retrieving his little-used AK-47, the soldier drained his coffee cup and started out of the small TV security control room. But when he reached the door he was surprised to find that someone was trying to come in as he was trying to go out.

It was a man dressed in an outlandish white robe and hood. Behind him were a dozen other men, all dressed the same way. As they stood facing each other for a very long second, the South African saw that the "visitor" was holding a camera in one hand; a hand grenade in the other.

Suddenly the hooded man pushed the South African hard, causing him to reel back into the control room, tossing the grenade in at the same time.

There was a bright bolt of light and a very muffled explosion as the HE flash grenade quietly obliterated the small TV studio and everyone in it.

Hunter nodded grimly as the Ranger sapper gave him the thumbs-up signal. The first objective had been destroyed. Surveillance cameras all over the building were at that moment quietly blinking out.

No one noticed that the building's top floor camera had suddenly stopped moving. To the contrary, it was business as usual on the top floor of the skyscraper.

The ten-man nightguard was preparing to change shifts at 0630, as usual. The long-range satellite communications system—the electronic umbilical cord to the military clique in the Kremlin— was about to be switched on, as usual. The evening's retinue of high-priced call girls—having plied their trade all night long in the skyscraper's top floor penthouse—were about to be paid and dismissed, as usual.

But when the officer of the nightwatch—a Bulgarian merce-nary—drew back the suite's massive drapes to let in the morning light, he saw something very *un*usual. Instead of the routine picture postcard view, he and the others in his squad were as-tounded to see a funnel cloud of black smoke and flame rising up from the airfield, 12 miles to their south.

24

"Jesus Christ . . ." the startled officer said in a voice barely above a whisper. "What the hell is happening over there?"

He turned to tell his second-in-command to quickly inform the ministers that something was amiss at the airport. Instead his attention was momentarily distracted by five of the skyscraper's six elevators all arriving at the top floor simultaneously.

The next thing he knew, the penthouse reception area was awash in deadly, yet strangely muffled gunfire. Armed men in long white robes and hoods were pouring out of the elevators and shooting everything in sight. The New Order officer was immediately shot square in his left shoulder and, a moment later, in his right knee. He crumpled to the ground, instantly in shock, and watched as the intruders methodically blasted away the men in his squad.

In his last conscious moment, he saw two men, apparently gunmen's leaders, sprint across the foyer. They pressed themselves up against the far wall, quickly consulted a small map, then dashed off down the hall toward the First Minister's private office.

"Christ," the officer said as darkness clouded in on him. "They'll fire me for this . . ."

Hunter was the first one to reach the predesignated door, leaping into it with his full weight, nearly bursting the heavy slab of wood from its hinges.

Rolling up in a tuck, he sprang up with his M-16 at the ready, sighting it down an absurdly long conference table at the three nattily dressed men seated on the other end. The startled trio was silent as Hunter, Humdingo and twelve of the Rangers filled the plush conference room to surround them, whipping off their hooded masks to reveal their faces for the first time.

At last Hunter was face-to-face with the traitor himself.

As he stared into the man's piercing eyes, The Wingman felt his finger tighten on the M-16's trigger. The gun was on full automatic, and a three-second burst would surely be enough to dispatch the man to Hell.

But frontier execution was not his mission.

Before him was the ultimate saboteur, the man who a handful of years before had knowingly crippled America's defenses and

25

allowed the devastating Soviet missile strike to smash America's ICBMs in their silos. Twenty million casualties and a nuclear nightmare known as the Badlands had been the result.

Before him was the man who had murdered the President, his family and his cabinet. The cold-blooded but hands-off assassin whose henchmen had done the dirty work, while he jetted to Moscow and into the arms of the war-mongering Soviet military clique.

Before him was the architect of the most vile form of tyranny imaginable — the oppressive New Order that had been imposed on a dazed nation against her will. Designed to keep America disjointed and fragmented, its creators had tried to choke the very thought of freedom from ever stirring in the nation's conscience again.

But in Hunter's opinion, the worst of all the traitor's crimes was that he betrayed the nation that had given him life, wealth, and power, even while serving as the country's second-highest official. Yes, before him, like a modern-day Benedict Arnold, was the man whose kiss of death had sealed the fate of the nation.

Before him was none other than the ex-Vice-President of the United States.

A long moment of silence passed before the traitor spoke.

"Who . . . who are you?" he asked, his face absolutely white with fear. "Those robes. We weren't expecting you today."

Hunter didn't recognize the other two men sitting at the table. But from the papers scattered across the top of the table and the clatter of a nearby telex, it was apparent that the three were in the midst of some kind of review meeting when the attack came.

"What do you want?" the traitor asked nervously. *"Money?"*

Hunter almost had to suppress a laugh. As if something as petty as gold or silver served to fuel his passions.

Hunter cleared his throat and began a speech he'd been waiting to deliver for years.

"We are Americans," he said in a strong, clear voice. "And we are bringing you back to stand trial for the crimes you committed against your own people."

No sooner had Hunter made his pronouncement when the two other men began chewing furiously. Before any of the Rangers could stop them, each man had broken the seal on the tiny black

26

pill they had routinely kept in their mouths. The pills contained a deadly poison and immediately both men began choking on their own blood. One gurgled something in German and pitched forward, hitting the table with a loud *whap!* The other simply slumped in his chair, his eyes grotesquely rolling up into his head. Both were dead in a matter of seconds.

In a flash, Hunter leaped across the table and jammed the butt of his M-16 into the traitor's mouth. A moment later, Humdingo was beside him, forcing the traitor's jaws open and preventing him from chomping down on a suicide pill of his own.

A strange, almost comical 15-second struggle ensued until Hunter was able to literally rip the poison capsule from the man's mouth.

"It's not going to be that easy," Hunter yelled at the man. "In fact, I'll personally guarantee that you still have a long life ahead of you."

Their prisoner was now absolutely terrified, so much so he started babbling: "Where . . . who . . . what are you doing in those robes?"

"We're taking you back to a place you used to know," Hunter snarled at him. "Back to America."

Hunter gave a signal and two of the Rangers rushed up to bind and gag the traitor with strong duct tape. Then, just as the group started to make their way down the silent corridor back to the grisly lobby area, one of the Rangers left to guard the lobby called out to Hunter.

"We've got company, Hawk . . ." the man said, motioning him to the foyer's huge window.

Hunter ran up to the window and took a quick look down.

Coming up the road he counted four BMPs, two T-72 tanks and at least a dozen troop trucks.

"There's always someone who wants to crash the party," he said.

Then, running awkwardly but swiftly in the long white robes, he and the rest of the strike force headed for the stairs.

By the time JT had brought the Osprey into a hover over the skyscraper, the skies had cleared and the entire strike force was

27

out on the building's roof, looking absolutely bizarre in their long white body sheets.

Already, the Rangers were firing down the 20 stories at the enemy troops below. Suddenly there was a large *whump!* and smoke and flames immediately began pouring out of the first three stories of the building. Toomey would learn later that the Rangers had placed several delayed-reaction bombs onto the sky-scraper's elevators and then sent the lifts down to the bottom three floors.

Still many New Order troops were rushing into the building, while others were stomping up the open stairway on the building's east side. Another explosion went off—this time on the fourth floor—blowing out just about all the windows on the bottom half dozen floors.

Meanwhile the two enemy tanks had taken up positions in the parking lot and their gunners were trying to raise their muzzles high enough to shoot at the Rangers on the roof. Another enemy squad fired a rocket-propelled grenade from the parking lot up toward the roof, but the round fell short by about 15 feet, smashing into the side of the structure with a great burst of fiery smoke and plaster.

All the while Toomey felt that he was watching some kind of odd war movie. The plan called for him *not* to provide covering fire for the strike force, as one stray bullet was enough to screw up the Osprey's delicate wing hinges, and therefore wreck the Americans' only means of escape. So, too high for the New Order soldiers to hit him, he hovered out of harm's way and waited.

But not for long . . .

Just as another RPG round was fired off the side of the building, the Osprey's radio suddenly came to life: "JT! JT! Can you hear me, pal?"

"Loud and clear Hawk," Toomey quickly replied. "You guys ready to go home?"

"More than ready," came the answer from Hunter's walkie-talkie. "Bring that wagon down here."

"On my way."

Then, with the speed of a runaway elevator, JT put the Osprey into a gut-wrenching descent. The four Rangers manning the airplane's gun stations nearly hit the roof, so acute was the

28

aircraft's "vertical translation."

By this time the first wave of New Order troops had nearly reached the top of the building's stairway. Clustered together and pressed hard up against the building, these soldiers were in a furious gunfight with a handful of Rangers just a few feet away. To make matters worse, one of the tanks in the parking lot—its muzzle close to ideal elevation—was now ricocheting cannon shots off the very edge of the roof.

A near-to-the-mark tank shell blasted away the corner of the roof's concrete railing just as the Osprey touched down. The powerful grinding sound of the VTOL's engines and the hurricane-force winds its huge propellers caused added to the already chaotic mixture of rifle shots and heavy weapons fire.

Humdingo, who had been carrying the traitor over his shoulder the whole time, now unceremoniously dumped the man into the open passage of the aircraft and climbed aboard himself. At the same moment, Hunter was running around the roof pulling the small knots of Rangers back from their positions to urge them toward the aircraft.

Half of the 20 Rangers were inside the Osprey when the enemy soldiers finally broke through and gained access to the roof. On Hunter's yell, the remaining Rangers flattened out, and the side gunners on the aircraft opened up on the New Order hirelings with their big twin-fifty machine guns.

Momentarily stunned, the enemy fell back long enough for the rest of the white-robed Rangers to scramble aboard the airplane.

As usual, Hunter was the last one to climb aboard.

"Go! Go! Go!" he was screaming even before he was halfway through the cabin door. Hearing his command, JT immediately gunned the big engines and the Osprey shot up at a speed as nauseating as its earlier rapid descent.

Straight up it climbed, up into the heavens, until the enemy troops on the roof and on the ground below could see it no longer.

Chapter 3

Two weeks later

"Have you ever been hypnotized before, Major Hunter?"

Hunter shifted around uneasily in his chair. It was a rare occasion when he felt he actually *needed* a drink.

But this was one of them.

"Major? Did you hear the question?"

Hunter quickly looked around the bare room and then up into the face of the attractive woman sitting next to him.

"No, I've never been hypnotized before," he said finally. "At least, not that I can remember."

The woman laughed. She was about forty and was a doctor—of psychology, yet. This made him uneasy.

His eyes darted around the room once again. It was dark, with only two lamps and they were being serviced by dim bulbs. On the large wooden table next to his chair there was a bank of tape recorders, one of which was already turning. Along with the doctor's chair and his own, there was nothing else in the room.

The place gave him the creeps. Located deep within the bowels of the old CIA headquarters near Washington DC, it looked like an old "rubber hose" interrogation room from a 1930s cops and robbers movie.

"Is this really necessary?" Hunter asked, not the first time.

The traitor had been in their custody for fourteen days now, ten of which had been devoted to his interrogation. Being held under heavy guard in a former US Federal holding building nearby, the ex-VP had also been allowed to prepare for his trial, which was scheduled to commence in another week. A squad of lawyers from "neutral" Finland was given permission to fly to Washington and help the turncoat prepare his defense.

In the meantime, a number of principals in the United American Army Command Staff were scheduled to begin giving trial depositions — Hunter included. Just about everyone close to the trial knew that it would be won or lost based on the strength of testimony about the traitor's most grievous crime: his part in the starting of World War III. As such, the most detailed information about the war was necessary for the US prosecutors to present at the trial.

Still, Hunter was apprehensive about the whole procedure.

"It seems like there's a million other things I should be doing," he told the woman doctor.

Like making sure his F-16 was still in flying condition. Or like getting some long overdue R&R. Or like trying to find his lost love, the beautiful Dominique.

"I believe this exercise is *very* necessary," the doctor told him. "For you, as well as for the others.

"Your testimony will be the key element in this trial. We can't expect you or the others to have total recall of the events leading up to the traitor's crimes. That's why this session, and the others, will be crucial in presenting our case and assuring that the traitor pays for his crimes."

Hunter had heard the explanation many times before, but it didn't make him feel any better. He hated thinking about the fact that someone was going to be tinkering with his brain — his psyche. His very private subconscious.

"Listen, doctor," he said in one last valiant stab at an alternative. "Why not let me just lock myself up somewhere and I'll write it all down? The whole thing . . . The day the war started. The transit to Europe. The war itself. What happened afterward. It isn't likely I've forgotten any of it."

She straightened out her short skirt and picked up a clipboard.

"You have probably forgotten more than you realize," she

said. "This has been the case with the others. Mr. Toomey. Mr. Wa. The Soviet pilots . . .

"As you know, I'm entering all of these recollections into a computer—a Gray supercomputer. With its highly advanced word processing software, the computer will be able to interconnect all of your testimonies into a single document. It really will be quite unique. A 'white paper' they used to call it, though I prefer to think of it as a 'computerized epic,' if you will. But then again, I'm a romantic . . .

"In any case, when the computer has done its work, I believe we'll have an excellent perspective on what happened back then."

Hunter shook his head and muttered a curse under his breath.

"Whatever happened to the old judge and jury type trial?" he asked. "Just put me on the witness stand and give me an hour. I'll convict the SOB myself."

The doctor lit a small cigar and seductively blew out a long stream of smoke.

"Major, you know that General Jones and the Command Staff have approved of this method of trial," she said. "So have the trial justices. If the traitor is to be punished for his crimes, it is absolutely necessary that he get a fair hearing. Generations from now, people will look back on how we handled this. We cannot be perceived as a lynch mob, dealing with a criminal via brutish Old West justice. It is an important cornerstone to the reconstruction of our country that we afford him every opportunity within the American judicial system."

Hunter shook his head again. "Including going out and hiring some smart-ass Finnish lawyers for him? Do you know what the Finns did to us after the war was over? *They're* the ones who destroyed all of our military equipment."

"I know that, Major," the doctor cooed to him. "And if we are going to win this case, we're going to have to beat the best. That is why this computerized deposition is important."

Hunter let out a long breath of resignation. He knew she was right.

"And there's another reason for this," she continued, her hand lightly touching his shoulder. "This document will, in effect, serve as a history of what happened. It will be written as almost an 'oral history.' The reasons we chose this style of writing are too numerous to explain now; suffice to say that we will go into a lot more detail once the trial starts. But I suspect that you, Major Hunter, will play a very large role in this story. I'd like to think of it as the first chapter of the Second American Epic. Years from now the American people will greatly appreciate what we are doing here. You do want to be a part of that, Major, don't you?"

Hunter shifted uneasily in the chair again.

"I guess . . . I mean, sure I do . . ." he said finally.

She smiled again. "OK, now that's the spirit," she said, her voice positively oozing sensuality.

She touched him again, this time on the back of his neck.

"Now," she said, in a voice barely above a whisper. "Just close your eyes and relax . . ."

The next thing Hunter knew, the pretty woman doctor was massaging his shoulders.

". . . that's when I met Dominique," he heard himself saying. "It was a little farmhouse in northern France, near the shore and I had . . ."

"That's all right, Major," the doctor told him, gently squeezing his shoulders. "We've got enough information now."

He shook his head, blinked his eyes open and was instantly aware of a dull throb in his jaw. It was as if he had been chewing gum non-stop for hours. The first thing he noticed was the doctor's ashtray was overflowing with crushed out cigar butts.

"But we just started," he said, slightly unsure of himself. "Didn't we?"

The doctor laughed and lit a tiny cigar. "We've been at it for twelve hours, Major," she said, reaching over to switch off the tape recorders. "You broke the record by more than five hours."

Hunter reached up to massage his sore jaw. He felt groggy, woozy, as if he had just come out of a sodium pentothal daze with some of his teeth missing.

"I . . . I was talking about Dominique," he said, more to himself than to the doctor.

33

She nodded slowly, her eyes tightening in a slightly suspicious squint.

"You gave me everything I needed to know about the war," the doctor told him. "Your memory is incredibly complete and detailed. I find it fascinating, to be perfectly honest. In fact, I am sure now that the computer will build its text around your testimony, using the recollections of the others simply to fill in the blanks.

"In other words, Major, you're going to be a modern-day Ulysses. You'll be the hero of our story. And when it's over, you'll be even more famous than you are now."

Hunter shook his head and rubbed his jaw again. Somehow that prospect didn't appeal to him.

Chapter 4

The bartender poured out another bourbon and Hunter drained it immediately.

"Why does it seem like a million years since I've had a drink?" he asked Toomey, who along with their friend Ben Wa, had been holding down the far end of the Washington DC bar with him for the past three hours.

"It's the hypnotic session," JT answered, lighting a cigar. "I was under for three hours, but it felt more like three weeks. I can't imagine what it must have been like for you to go under for twelve hours. It's got to do a job on your Ids-ville."

"Twelve frigging hours," Hunter said, shaking his head and motioning the bartender for another shot. "Goddamn, I know a lot of stuff came up that I was sure would stay hidden inside me forever."

It was the day after Hunter's marathon session with the pretty woman psychologist. He had spent most of the daylight hours sleeping, yet still he felt mentally exhausted.

"That was the whole idea, Hawk," Ben said. He had struggled through a four-hour session of his own. "It's just kind of strange how they're planning to program the computer to mix it all together like that. Like it was a novel or something."

At that point, three ladies of somewhat-questionable repute walked into the smoky, dimly lit bar. To no one's surprise, JT knew all three.

Thankful for the diversion, Hunter was about to order a

round of drinks for the females, when another woman caught his eye.

She was sitting at the opposite end, of the bar, in a very darkened corner, talking to three other women. It was only that she had lit a cigarette and the match illuminated her face that Hunter saw her at all. And while JT's friends may or may not have been "working girls," there was no doubt that the four women at the table in question were hookers.

Is that really her? he thought.

Hunter hastily excused himself and slowly made his way down the crowded bar, attempting to get a closer look at the woman. When one of her companions lit a cigarette of her own, he was able to glimpse the mystery woman once again.

Despite the pound and a half of make-up, he could see she was very pretty, with beautiful long brown hair and what looked to be a lovely figure.

Could it really be her?

He inched his way farther through the crowd until he arrived at the very end of the bar and staked out a position just ten feet from where the four hookers were sitting.

Suddenly he felt a tap on his shoulder.

"Interested in the merchandise, pal?"

He turned slowly and faced a small, bejeweled, white-suited man.

"You talking to me?" he asked, instinctively reaching for the butt of his shouldered M-16.

"Yeah," the small man replied, his voice betraying some kind of foreign accent Hunter couldn't quite place. "I saw you eye-balling the produce. You want to buy or what?"

Once again, a cigarette was lit at the table, this one fully illuminating the face of the woman in question.

Goddamn, Hunter thought, *it is her.*

"How much?" he asked the pimp, never taking his eyes off the woman.

"One bag of gold for one," the slimy little individual answered. "Three bags for all four."

Hunter couldn't help but laugh in his face. "Sure, pal," he said retrieving a single bag of silver from his flight suit and passing it to the man. "This is for the pretty brunette. You can keep the change."

The man grudgingly took the silver. "I got rooms, too," he said. "Nearby. Only two bags of silver . . ."

Hunter pushed the man away from him and was already walking over to the table. "I won't need a room," he told him.

A few seconds later, Hunter was standing over the table, the woman looking up at him through a haze of mascara and eye liner.

Even though she recognized him right away, she showed absolutely no surprise. "Fancy meeting you here," she said, blowing a stream of cigarette smoke up into his face.

He reached down and gave her arm a slight, yet forceful tug. "Come on," he said somewhat harshly. "I just bought you."

"My dream has come true," she said, gathering her things together. She crushed out her cigarette and stood up, straightening out her black negligee-style mini-dress in the process. "See you later, girls," she said, winking at her companions.

At the other end of the bar, JT had been following Hunter's actions with almost painful curiosity. Now, as he watched Hunter lead the hooker back through the crowd and toward the front door, he turned to Ben and said: "Since when did *he* start paying for it?"

Ben turned and was about to say something when he got his first good look at the painted lady.

"I can't believe it," he said. "That *can't* be who I think it is."

Just before he reached the door, Hunter glanced back over his shoulder at his two friends, a very strange expression on his face.

It was Elizabeth.

She was the same woman who, not a month before, Hunter had tramped all over Central and South America trying to locate. She and her father had been major players in the plan the United Americans had used to prevent the fascist organization, The Twisted Cross, from destroying the Panama Canal. In fact, her father was the man responsible for building a crucial piece of equipment that helped Hunter deactivate the 52 nuclear-tipped underwater mines the Cross had placed in the Panama Canal.

During the time her father was building the deactivator and the United Americans were preparing to invade the canal, Hunter had volunteered to rescue Elizabeth from the same Canal Nazis who had kidnapped her with the intention of having her lead them to a vast fortune in hidden Mayan gold.

But even though the whole affair eventually had a successful outcome — the Nazis were soundly beaten, the mines rendered inoperable and the canal saved — the adventure had left Hunter unsettled. He was the first to admit to himself that he had become enamored with the whole idea of his playing the hero, rescuing the fair maiden from the clutches of the dastardly Nazis. And during his search for her, he had become infatuated with her — sight unseen except for a grainy photo her father had provided. This romanticizing reached the point where Hunter actually fantasized — not entirely subconsciously — that when he rescued her, they might actually . . . well, walk off into the sunset together.

But that storybook ending was a far cry from what actually happened.

She didn't melt into his arms when he first found her, despite the fact that he plucked her just in time from a band of extra-vicious Canal Nazi Skinheads. And the tearful reunion he imagined would take place when she saw her father again in actuality resulted in little more than her giving him a peck on the cheek before noisily demanding to be fed.

And the fairy tale ending he had conjured up about them actually being bonded together in eternal bliss was deflated when she sent him a rather crude, pornographic photo of herself along with a cryptic message stating that he should "surprise" her sometime. Then she had disappeared.

Until now . . .

He put her into the car he had been using to tool around Washington — an all-white, souped-up 1983 Pontiac Firebird. Climbing in behind the steering wheel, he turned to her and said: *"What the hell are you doing?"*

She laughed — *that* laugh — and lit a cigarette.

"I'm just trying to earn a living," she said, blowing a stream of smoke into his face.

Hunter couldn't remember feeling so befuddled.

"Not a month ago you were on the verge of being killed by Nazis and I fly all over half of Central America to save you," he said sternly. "And now you're running around Washington dressed like a cheap hooker . . ."

"That's because I *am* a cheap hooker," she replied. "You just bought me, remember? And for what? Two bags of silver?"

"One bag," he said, shaking his head.

She laughed again—the laugh that was tinged with no small amount of madness. "All right!" she exclaimed. "So that's what I'm worth. The cheaper the better."

With that she shifted in the car's bucket seat, intentionally letting her skirt hike up around her upper thighs. For the quickest of moments, Hunter's eyes zeroed in on the lovely form of her legs, wrapped as they were in alluring dark nylon stockings.

"For Christ's sake, you're a scientist," he said, frustration and anger rising equally in his voice. "You're probably the foremost archaeologist left in this country. Probably in the entire world."

She crushed out her cigarette and immediately lit another one. "Is this your car?" she asked.

Hunter was reaching his boiling point. He had barely settled down from the mind-blowing hypnotic tell-all testimony session. And now, in the one night he thought he could actually cool out, he runs into this.

"Look, forget about the Goddamn car," he said. "Just tell me what the hell is going on . . ."

She leaned over and kissed him on the cheek, leaving a bright crimson lip print.

"You're always so full of questions," she said. "Let me ask one: after this, are we going to go somewhere and screw our brains out?"

Hunter was so stunned by the question, he was speechless.

"That's what you bought me for, isn't it?" she asked, moving her hand to his upper thigh.

He took a deep breath and looked around. The sidewalks were crowded with the usual cast of armed soldiers and beautiful women. The street itself was busy—military vehicles from jeeps to M-1 tanks rumbled by, occasionally followed by a civilian-type car. All in all, it was a fairly normal scene for post-World War III America.

The insanity was inside the car . . .

"I'll ask you one more time," he said, reaching his limit. "What are you doing, working for a scumbag like that guy in there? Selling yourself? You don't need to do this for money. Your father is well off now. And you should be, too."

She ran her fingers through her hair and began to reapply her heavy lipstick with the aid of a compact mirror.

"You really want to know what I'm doing?" she asked, smacking her lips to even out the bright red color. "OK, I'll tell you: I'm working undercover."

"Undercover?" he said. "An undercover what?"

"I'm a secret agent," she continued, still dabbing on the lipstick. "I'm gathering information for a group of people who will eventually take over this entire country."

Hunter rubbed his eyes hard. Could this conversation get any more insane?

"We've still got some work to do," she rambled on. "but eventually, we'll have everything lined up. Then, well, we'll just move in and take control."

Hunter closed his eyes and shook his head. "You *are* crazy," he said, finally submitting to the situation.

Suddenly, she turned toward him. Her eyes had become black as coal, her mouth tight and quaking, her entire face drawn in. In an instant she looked like another person entirely.

"You bet I'm crazy," she hissed at him with a voice that sounded as if it belonged in a cheap horror movie. "And don't you *ever* forget it . . ."

With that, she yanked up on the door handle, dashed from the car and ran down the street.

She had disappeared into the shadows before Hunter could make up his mind whether to follow her or not . . .

Chapter 5

Six days later

The Flag.

Hunter stared at it through the mist of the early upstate New York sunrise, unfurling into the morning sky, proudly hailing the beginning of a new day.

"Present arms!" The Marine officer's crisp command echoed across the parade field.

Hunter snapped to attention.

A full company of Marines, their dress blue uniforms razor-creased from white hats down to gleaming patent-leather shoes, clicked as one to rigid attention, then began marching past the reviewing stand where Hunter and the others stood.

A cold wind blew across the open parade field. For some reason Hunter thought that it would be warmer than this.

They were in Syracuse. It would be here, in the city's giant domed stadium, that the ex-VP's trial would be held.

Despite the chill, Hunter knew that all things being considered, the site was a natural place for the historic event. Before the war, the huge domed stadium had been the football and basketball arena for the famous Syracuse University. Like the other major cities in the eastern United States, Syracuse had been evacuated during the chaos following the Big War. Most of the residents had either fled to Free Canada or scattered to seek the comparative safety of the small towns in rural New York.

Shortly after the war ended, a new city had sprung up around Syracuse's airport, it being a strategically-located point sitting on the crossroads of the air convoy routes for most of the Northeast corridor. Under the guidance of his friend, the enterprising Irishman Mike Fitzgerald, the Syracuse Aerodrome had become famous as a waystation and watering hole for aircraft and their pilots, dispensing cargo, fuel, and repairs to any and all paying customers.

And even though nearly two-thirds of the base had been destroyed in the second and final war against The Circle, the Aerodrome had recently gone back into operation, although on a limited basis.

But in all that time, the 50,000-seat indoor athletic stadium downtown had lain abandoned for lack of any practical uses. It too had been damaged during the Circle's brief occupation of the city. But even before that, the powerful ceiling fans used to inflate the synthetic-fabric dome had been shut off, allowing the roof to sag to within forty feet of the playing surface. The place became a dark haven for some of the shadowy figures who, for whatever reason, had chosen to stay in the old city since the war.

But when the New United States Provisional Government realized that by opening the ex-VP's trial to the public, the public might come in droves, they selected the Dome as the venue. The dome was reinflated, the insides cleaned up and prepared for the crowds to come. It was also re-lit and wired for a phalanx of TV cameras, which would be able to broadcast the trial to those areas of the country able to receive TV.

That morning Hunter, Toomey and Ben flew the fighter escort for the KC-135 aircraft carrying the traitor and his lawyers to the trial. Even as they passed over the city before the sun was completely up, they saw that The Dome was thronged with people — ordinary citizens — pouring in through its concrete passageways.

As it would turn out, although more than 50,000 people were able to get in, more than twice that number camped outside, content, it would seen, to follow the progress of the trial via the large loudspeakers erected outside the Dome.

"Command, attention!" the Marine commander shouted out, bringing Hunter's thoughts back to the flag-raising ceremony before him.

As the last of the Marines marched off the parade field, all eyes on the reviewing stand turned toward the low rumble that was building in the eastern sky. Squinting into the rising sun, Hunter could make out the swift-moving shapes, racing ahead of the sounds from their engines. The four F-4 Phantom jets streaked across the sky in a tight diamond shape and seemed to join as one to disappear into the hazy western horizon. Only the scream of their engines told those on the ground that they were making a wide turn to pass by again.

This time the Phantoms came in lower and slower, forming up in a tight chevron pattern, their leader in the center, two planes wingtip-to-wingtip, slightly behind on his right and left, and one tucked in behind him, offset just high enough to avoid his exhaust trail. As they neared the parade field, the Phantom in the number-two slot to the leader's left eased back on his stick to bring the plane out of formation, its vapor trail describing a gentle swooping arc to the heavens as he climbed out of sight.

The remaining F-4s, now with the vacant position in their tight pattern, flew on over the reviewing stand.

The Missing Man Formation. A tribute by flying men to their companions, lost in battles fought and wars won but never forgotten. Every man assembled on the stand saluted and then bowed his head, each remembering fallen comrades who had paid the ultimate price for the victory that had cost them all so dearly.

Hunter watched as the Phantoms sped away to land at the nearby Syracuse Aerodrome. As the reviewing stand emptied out, he lingered for a time to watch the flag the color guard had raised as it lofted with each burst of wind, high atop the shining flagstaff at the head of the parade field.

Almost instinctively he reached into his left breast pocket and pulled out a small, frayed cloth. Carefully folded into a tight triangular shape, it revealed only a faded blue background arrayed with pale stars. Unrolling it to its full length, he stared at the red and white stripes creased and marked from being folded too long, and fingered its tattered edges.

It was a small American flag, the same one he had taken from the body of a man he saw brutally murdered in New York City way back when Hunter first returned to America after the war. He always considered the man, his name was Saul Wackerman, as the ultimate patriot; someone who was shot simply because he was carrying the American flag.

Hunter had carried it with him ever since, an act that for the past few years under the New Order, was punishable by death. This had never deterred him though, and it had come to be an authentic good luck piece for him.

Not so the photograph he always kept wrapped inside the flag. This was the well-worn picture of his estranged girlfriend, Dominique.

As it was, he hadn't been able to look at it in two months . . .

"These proceedings will come to order!"

A hush fell over the jam-packed Dome stadium as the Chief Justice of the American Provisional Government, using an elaborate public address system, gaveled the trial open.

Hunter looked around the place, still amazed that the event would draw so many people, or that it was happening at all. In front of him, at the southern end of the Dome, a stage had been erected. The most prominent feature on it was the dark wooden jurist's bench behind which the panel of five judges would sit. Before them were two long wooden tables — one for the 12-man team of Government prosecutors, the other for the defendant and his seven attorneys.

Behind these tables was a small gallery of assistants, aide-de-camps and general go-boys. Behind them was a succession of three raised platforms, each one crammed to the max with TV cameras, wires, lights, generators, editing machines, and large, dish-like microphones. A massive spaghetti — twirled bank of wires — easily five thousand of them — stretched back from the TV platforms, up the Dome's center aisle and out the front door, where more than half of them were attached to the virtual forest of TV satellite dishes located outside next to the arena.

Back inside, over the judges' bench was a huge TV screen, once so popular with the Syracuse fans, especially those way up in the cheap seats. Now, the people in the back would look to this screen to show them what was going on.

There were security personnel everywhere. An entire battalion of the famous Football City Special Forces was on hand—600 battle-tough veterans. They were responsible for security outside the Dome. To accomplish this they were armed with everything from M-1 tanks to Roland SAM systems. No fewer than 20 of their assault helicopters were airborne at any given moment, ready to spot and deal with any kind of external problem that might disrupt the trial.

Security inside the arena would be provided by 500 members of the famous US Marine 7th Cavalry, the unit formed by the late Captain John "Bull" Dozer, and a 250-man contingent of Republic of Texas Rangers.

High above and looking down on it all would be three separate flights of fighter planes—F-20s, A-7s, and a few F-5s—providing a CAP over the entire city.

It would be a jury trial.

The 36 individuals empaneled had been picked from all over the continent by a re-charged Social Security computer. They would consider all the evidence to be given, as would the judges. They would decide on whether the ex-VP was guilty or innocent of high treason. And if the verdict was guilty, they would also decide his sentence.

Off to one side of the jury box was another small gallery. This was the witness seating, and this is where Hunter, Jones, Toomey, Wa and at least one hundred other people were sitting.

Beside this gallery, and right next to the judges' bench, was the docket in which the witnesses, and eventually, the defendant himself, would offer testimony.

"We will now begin with the prosecution's opening statement," the Chief Justice boomed over the PA system.

Dr. Leylah, the pretty woman psychologist who had hypnotized Hunter and the others, took the stand, cleared her throat and began to speak:

"The primary concern of these proceedings is the war itself, the war which the prosecution hopes to prove was a direct result of treasonous acts committed by the defendant while he held the second-highest position in this country's government.

45

"We have conducted more than two hundred interviews with veterans of the conflict. We have studied thousands of official documents as well as several personal journals. We inputted all of this data into a Gray S7-SG supercomputer and programmed it to produce a single document, one that encompasses all of the separate depositions into one, uniquely written document.

"The result we have called 'The First Book of Testimony.'

"Copies of this Testimony will be distributed to the justices and the defense team today. Tomorrow, we hope to give copies to witnesses and to those citizens who are on hand to watch this trial.

"Once you receive your copy, you will immediately notice that as I said, this testimony has been written in a very unusual way. In short, it will read like a book, or more accurately, a novel. The text was written in this narrative style by a special software designed to take many points of information and collate them into a narrative. To this end, the computer incorporated not only actual events, but also the thoughts, the opinions, and even dialogue, actual and as recalled by some of the principals involved . . ."

The doctor paused for a sip of water as she let the first part of her statement sink in to the thousands gathered.

"With the court's indulgence, I will briefly explain why we have chosen to present the testimony in this rather unusual way.

"We on the prosecution team believe that what we do here at this trial will have a long-lasting effect on our country and our people, beyond what justice is meted out to the defendant.

"We believe that this trial has given us the opportunity to produce the first History Book, if you will, of the Second American era. But we also chose to produce it in this narrative style because we like to think we are realists. The future is unknown. We have no way of knowing whether in ten years our civilization here in America will still be on the road to recovery or whether it will be thrown back to the level of the Stone Age.

"We felt it was our duty to consider all the possibilities and produce a document that, no matter what the conditions are in ten years, or twenty, or a hundred, people will be able to read it, study it, remember it and, most important, retell it, whether it be in the hallowed halls of studious research, or around a campfire.

"So, therefore, this testimony was written by the supercomputer as an oral history, because we know that throughout the entire scope of mankind's history, the oral tradition has certainly endured the longest, as the works of Plato and many others would attest."

Once again, the pretty doctor stopped and took a sip of water. Then, to his surprise, she turned and looked directly at Hunter, sitting in the witness gallery just a few feet away.

"One final note," she said. "Every classic has its hero. And this document, as programmed by the Gray supercomputer, will be no different . . ."

Chapter 6

The rest of the first day of the trial was taken up by a multitude of procedural motions — instructions to the jury, swearing in of witnesses and so on. The defense team's opening statement went particularly slowly as it had to be translated from Finnish to English. As it was, the statement was a long, rambling affair, which, if Hunter had understood it correctly, claimed that not only was the ex-VP innocent, he had actually "sacrificed" himself for the good of the nation.

The trial was adjourned at sundown that day, those gathered feeling slightly cheated at the anti-climactic tone to it all.

But the second day would prove to be more exciting.

One hour before court was to begin the next day, Hunter was draining his third cup of coffee in the cafeteria of the United American Army's temporary Syracuse headquarters when Mike Fitzgerald walked in.

Hunter had found sleep impossible the night before, due in most part to the trial, but also to his bizarre encounter with Elizabeth Sandlake exactly one week before. He just couldn't stop thinking about it, and he knew his lined face and baggy eyelids probably telegraphed his condition.

But, if anything, Fitzie looked worse . . .

He fetched a cup of coffee and sat down beside Hunter, clutching a videotape as if it contained an explosive charge.

"What the hell happened to you?" Hunter asked, not quite believing that anyone could look worse than he did this morning.

"Terrible things, Hawker," he answered, neatly slipping a pint bottle of scotch from his pocket. With magician's precision he deposited a splash of the liquor into his coffee cup, did the same for Hunter's, then returned the flask to its original hiding place—all in one smooth motion. "I've been up close to forty-eight straight hours now, and still I have a full week's work ahead of me."

Early in the planning for the trial, Fitz had been appointed as an Officer of the Court. Because he was not directly involved in the war's hostilities (he was in the hospital at the time, recovering from an airplane crash), the Irishman found himself on the court's "discovery" team, the group of men who would interrogate the ex-VP and report directly to the trial's justices. As such, Fitz had been working day and night and he looked it.

The stocky Irishman took a long swig of his coffee then put the videotape up on the table.

"This tape is part of the Vice President's testimony," Fitzgerald told him. *"His* deposition, you might say . . ."

Hunter picked up the tape cassette and turned it over in his hands. "I knew he was being questioned," he said. "But I didn't realize you were videotaping it."

"Oh, yes," Fitz answered, lighting a cigarillo. "By his attorneys' request."

"That figures," Hunter said. Just because the world had quaked through a third world war, plus five years of aftershocks, didn't mean that all the fancy lawyers had been suddenly swallowed up.

"And this is just six hours of about thirty that he gave," Fitz said, taking the cassette back.

He shook his head and looked straight at Hunter.

"Hawk, you won't believe what that bastard has told us," he said gravely.

"I'll believe anything at this point," Hunter answered.

Before Hunter could ask him again, Fitzgerald blurted out, "It's a terrible thing he's done to us, he has."

"Of course it's terrible, Mike," Hunter said. "I mean the guy's picture could replace Benedict Arnold's in the encyclopedia next to 'worst traitor.' "

"You're not getting the point," Fitz said. "I'm talking about what he told us that we didn't already know."

"Well," Hunter said simply, "just tell me . . ."

Fitz shook his head. "I can't," he said. "I'm an officer of the court in all this, remember. You're a witness. If I pass inside information on to you, it could screw up the whole trial."

Hunter suddenly felt his teeth clench. He knew that due to the intentionally strict guidelines set up for the trial, all it would take was one slip-up and the ex-VP could go free. Right or wrong, that was the American way and *that* was what the trial was really about. *Preserving* the American way . . .

Yet Hunter could tell by Fitz's demeanor that something big, something downright *explosive* was on that tape.

"I'm afraid to ask you even for a hint," Hunter said in a hushed tone.

"Of this, you don't want a hint," Fitz said, finishing his coffee and getting up to go. If anything, he looked worse than when he walked in. "You'll just have to wait until the bastard takes the stand. It will all be in the court documents they'll pass out. You'll see it right before you in black and white."

Fitz took a deep breath, then added: "But I will tell you this: We, here in America, are in worse danger *now* than we've been since the Big War."

And on that frighteningly cryptic note, Fitz walked quickly from the cafeteria.

Damn, Hunter thought. *Does it ever end?* They finally kick the Soviets and their agents out of the country, secure their southern border and water trade route, and snatched the ex-VP back to stand trial. Wasn't that enough to please the gods?

Suddenly, a strange sensation went through him. For a moment, he felt a pang of regret that he hadn't taken Elizabeth up on her amorous offer a week before.

Part II
The First Book
Of
Testimony

Chapter 7

If anything, the Dome was even more crowded than the day before.

Dr. Leylah took the stand once again, a huge document under her arm. At the same time, duplicate documents were being passed out in the witness gallery.

Of the 50,000 people on hand, no one was more surprised than Hunter when he began reading the first page . . .

Gray Interactive Testimony Project
Transcript 1-AF4, Sub-Document A
"Recollections of the Hostilities"
First Witness: Major Hawker Hunter
Additional Testimony: Major JT Toomey, Major Ben-hoi Wa, Captain Geoffrey Spaulding, Major D. Larochelle, Lieutenant B. Fitch, Captain J. O'Malley, Captain Elvis "Q," Colonel B. Davis, Colonel L. Gorshkov
Additional Information: The memoirs of General Seth Jones

The day the war began

"Captain Hawker Hunter, reporting for pilot training . . ."

The uniformed airman behind the desk executed a crisp salute and briefly scanned Hunter's orders.

"Everything seems to be in order, sir," the enlisted man said.

"We've been expecting you."

The airman picked up a phone, punched in a series of numbers and quickly reached someone on the other end. "Sir, you asked me to notify you when Captain Hunter arrived," he said. "Yes sir, he's here already."

Hunter was standing in a place called Building B, just barely containing his enthusiasm. Despite its lackluster name, the place looked like something out of a science fiction movie. Functional, yet otherwordly, with just a smattering of Christmas decorations. In actuality, the building housed what could only be described as the ultimate in pilot flight-training facilities.

So this is how it feels when your dream finally comes true, Hunter thought.

He had just arrived at the Cape Canaveral Launch Center, via a bumpy, crowded, day-before-Christmas commercial flight from Las Vegas. Although he was allowed a few hours, if not a night's sleep, before reporting for duty, he was ready—now. Ready to begin training for America's space program. Ready to learn how to fly the Space Shuttle . . .

Canaveral was everything he had imagined it to be. Launch towers. Control buildings. Miles of open area. Thousands of people. A high-tech city on the edge of the Florida coastal swamps, its atmosphere heavy with history.

An Air Force officer soon appeared and introduced himself as Colonel Neil Schweiker.

The introduction wasn't necessary—Hunter knew Schweiker was one of the NASA's best and highest-profile astronauts.

"Good to meet you, Captain," Schweiker told him, firmly shaking his hand. "We've all heard a lot about you."

Hunter was always a little uncomfortable at the extra attention he received when people realized who he was. But it was well known—courtesy of cover stories in both *Time* and *Newsweek*—that at 17, Hunter was the youngest graduate ever of MIT's aerospace engineering program. And that he had completed work on his aeronautics doctorate degree three months afterward. And that he was the youngest pilot ever to join the USAF's Thunderbirds Demonstration Team. *And* that he was the youngest pilot ever to be selected for Space Shuttle pilot training.

"You're early," Schweiker told him, checking his watch. "You can rest up awhile if you want."

"No thanks, sir," Hunter answered. "I'm anxious to get going. Also, I don't want someone to have to give me the run-through tomorrow and spoil their Christmas."

Schweiker nodded. "OK," he said. "I can give you the quick look-see. Just enough to get you somewhat situated. The real work will start the day after tomorrow."

After Hunter's gear was stowed in the pilot trainees' personal quarters, Schweiker scared up a jeep and gave him a quick tour of the immediate base.

The astronaut was a friendly, easygoing sort who insisted that the military formalities be dispensed with. As they rode along, they discussed the shuttle itself and the two-site training—from Florida to Houston—that Hunter would begin shortly. All the while, Schweiker pointed out the training classrooms, the rest facilities, the labs, the launch site, the mess hall and the officers' club. Most impressive was the monstrosity called the VAB—for Vehicle Assembly Building. This was the place where they put the shuttles together. It was a building so tall that clouds actually formed just below its ceiling.

"Hell of a time to start training," Schweiker said to him at one point. "With the holiday and all . . ."

Not that much of a problem, Hunter thought. He'd been spending his holidays on either college campuses and military bases for several years, ever since his parents were lost in a plane crash.

"Lot of guys are stuck here," Schweiker continued. "That's why the mess hall puts on a really good holiday feed. And there's always a big blow-out at the Officers' Club if you're interested."

"That's good to know," Hunter told him. He knew there was no better way to get a perspective on a new base than to make that initial prowl through its authorized saloon.

They returned to Building B, their 90-minute tour complete. After making a few phone calls, Schweiker offered to drive Hunter back to his living quarters.

"No, thanks," the young pilot told him, remembering one spot in the tour that he wanted to revisit. "I'll hoof it back . . ."

He thanked Schweiker, left Building B and walked over to a marble and bronze monument they had passed earlier. It was a memorial to the astronauts killed in the Challenger disaster.

Feeling an undeniable attraction in the place, Hunter sat down on the stone bench across from the memorial and stayed there until the Florida sun had nearly set.

It was a long shadow that Hunter cast as he walked back toward the personnel quarters, his body still awash in the near-sanctity he had felt while sitting before the Challenger memorial for the past few hours.

If not for them, he had thought over and over, *would I even be here?*

Suddenly his body started tingling with a new sensation—this one more immediate and acute. From an early age Hunter knew he had been blessed—or was it *cursed*—with a gift akin to ESP. As the sensation was ultimately indescribable, he thought of it only as *the feeling*—a finely tuned, highly reliable intuition that made him what many said was "the best pilot ever."

But this *feeling* did not just affect him in flight. In fact, it permeated his entire existence—awake or asleep, walking around, as well as flying.

And now, at this moment, it was telling him that something was wrong somewhere in the cosmos—desperately wrong.

Instinctively, he headed for the center's communication building . . .

Hunter expected that most of the CENCOM's personnel would be gone—either home with families or joining the celebration at the Officers' Club. But as he approached the white stone building, he saw that it was a hive of activity.

His inner message was confirmed. Something *was* up.

It was now the height of dusk and every light in the place was on. He walked into the main administration area and it seemed like every telephone was ringing or buzzing at once. Both Air Force and NASA personnel were scrambling around in a dance of controlled confusion—so much so, not a one stopped to question who he was or what he was doing there.

He took a set of stairs two steps at a time and found himself in the CENCOM's main control room, a facility that held no less than two hundred telephones, plus banks of telex and fax machines. Like downstairs, it seemed as if every one of these communications machines was going full-blast, knots of military types and civilians gathered around them, their faces screwed up with concern. In the cacophony of shrill ringing, insistent buzzing, and tense conversation that cascaded throughout the large room, Hunter was able to distinguish only two words: "Germany" and "casualties."

In the midst of the chaos, his attention was drawn to a small television set in the corner, all but ignored in the din. Surrounded by half-empty paper cups of eggnog left over from what had been a small office party, the slightly beat-up TV was blaring out an animated Christmas program, oblivious to the desperation in the room. Struck by the incongruity of the cartoon's carefree music in the frenzied atmosphere, Hunter's eyes were instantly glued to the TV screen.

An instant later, the cartoon stopped, the screen flickered and then was filled with the words: "Emergency Broadcasting System."

Suddenly everything stopped. The room was flooded with the nightmarish EBS tone everyone present had heard many times before. But now, for the first time, the dour-voiced announcer said: "This is *not* a test . . ."

Instead, he instructed viewers to change to another channel. One brave soul among the many in the room did so, only to find the same EBS graphic being broadcast, with the words "This is not a test," blinking rapidly.

Hunter would never know just how long he stood there, an uninvited interloper who, like the others, stared in disbelief as some unknown announcer appeared on the screen and solemnly, nervously read the bulletin for Doomsday.

In his memory, Hunter could only recall swatches and bits of the first report:

Millions of West Europeans dead . . . Soviet chemical weapons strike . . . thousands of Soviet SCUD missiles launched against civilian and military targets . . . missiles carrying nerve gas. . . . Soviet invasion of Western Europe . . . No nuclear weapons used yet . . . the President is asking Congress to convene immediately . . . war will soon be declared.

Through it all, Hunter did remember the absolute silence in the room. Then, when the screen finally went to black, the men in the CENCOM, their faces pale beyond belief, simply went back to their telephones and telexes and resumed their tasks.

Hunter's next recollection concerned his close friends from the Thunderbirds. Several days before he reported to Florida, three of them had "turned over." That was, like himself, they had been reassigned after finishing their two-year stint with the Aerial Demonstration Team. General Seth Jones, Captain JT Toomey and Captain Ben Wa had relocated to a NATO F-16 base near Rota, Spain, where Jones had taken over the job of CINCUSAFE (Commander-in-Chief, US Air Forces—Europe). Hunter would have been with them if Jones hadn't first recommended, then bullied through, Hunter's appointment to the space shuttle pilot training.

Had they, three of his closest friends, escaped the deadly gas attack?

Then, after the shock, came anger. It welled up inside of him like a boiling tidal wave. So the Soviet bastards had finally done it. . . . Millions of innocents—women and children—had undoubtedly perished along with, he assumed, many of NATO's troops.

And on Christmas Eve yet, when the civilized world celebrated a time of peace. How sinister that the Red Army's war machine let loose its first deadly volley on this day.

Suddenly, as if on cue, one of the men in CENCOM approached him.

"Are you Captain Hunter?" the man asked, probably recognizing Hunter from the previous years' gush of publicity.

"Yes, I am," Hunter confirmed.

"We have a telex here, sir, that mentions you by name," the man told him. "Formal orders, but, in light of this . . ."

The man's voice trailed off, but his meaning was crystal clear. The announcement of World War III tended to put a dent in the formalities for the time being.

The man led him to a telex machine that was clicking furiously. Tearing off a portion of a message recently received, the man pointed to one, brief paragraph that started with Hunter's name, rank, and serial number.

There were surprisingly detailed orders—in this time of crisis, some computer somewhere had tracked him down: He was immediately reassigned to the 16th Tactical Fighter Wing, as the Thunderbirds were officially listed on the Air Force's active combat unit roster. He was to report to Langley Air Force base in Virginia at once. From there he would join a "tactical escort and resupply force" and transit to Europe.

In other words, Hunter was going to war.

Chapter 8

Langley Air Force Base was a whirlwind of controlled chaos.

It seemed to Hunter that every military transport in the Air Force inventory was out on the tarmac. All around him, the cold morning was shattered by the scream of jet engines being pushed up to speed, intakes greedily sucking in the clean, crisp morning air igniting within their crucibles, driving the big turbines that in turn thrust out flaming exhausts in long fiery arrows.

At the same time, hundreds of big propellers churned, biting into the air and sluicing it behind them in a thousand rivers of wind that flowed across the airfield, whipping the collars and sleeves and trouser legs of the army of ground crews.

Forklifts, tanker trucks, and flatbeds roared across the vast expanse of concrete on hundreds of intersecting lines, crisscrossing under wings and between fuselages to deliver their loads of fuel, supplies, weapons, and ammunition, then to scurry back for more.

The scene didn't look a bit like Christmas morning.

Every one of the airplanes being loaded at Langley that day were crucial components in the massive "air bridge" that was being strung from America to Europe to deal with the emergency. Long gone were the days when ships alone could carry the tools of war to the fighting front. This new war—declared by the President that morning—demanded more immediate delivery; measured in hours and days instead of weeks and months.

Only by this air route would the vital cargo of men, machines, and material reach the already-struggling NATO forces in time.

Hunter had caught a cargo plane up from Florida just before midnight and, on arrival, was immediately ordered by one of the Langley base doctors to get at least four hours sleep. He took the physician's advice—even he needed sleep every once in a while. But now, with the dawn, he was up and anxious to fulfill his own orders. And they were to get the hell over to Europe.

Oddly though, there was very little news from the front. Other than the initial terrifying report, very little could be determined about the present situation. Communications in and around the battle area were either nonexistent or at the breaking point. All that *was* known was that the Soviets were about to advance into the areas devastated by the chemical attack and NATO was doing everything it could to stop them.

But most important, neither side had detonated a nuclear bomb . . . yet.

Now, as Hunter was being transported by jeep across the vast field to take his place in the massive air convoy, he noted its main players.

At one end of the base, supported on ramps and aprons of poured concrete many feet thick, towered the giant Lockheed C-5A Galaxy super-transports of the Air Force's Military Airlift Command. With their huge nose sections yawning open to reveal the cavernous cargo bays within, and their tail ramps descended to provide access, they looked like giant dragon being stuffed with the machines of war.

Here one was being loaded with sixteen heavy trucks, being driven into the gaping maw formed by the up-tilted nose. There another was taking on a half-dozen Apache attack helicopters. Another would carry two M-1 Abrams main battle tanks, creaking on their platforms as the grinding winches reluctantly drew their 60-ton masses into the belly of the beast.

In all, the huge transports would each be loaded with more than 260,000 pounds of cargo. And when the flight was ready to begin, each one would roll ponderously to the flight line, its four giant engines ready to defy the gravity that hugged it to the earth.

Farther on were the newer, smaller but sleeker C-17 transports. These too swallowed up vast quantities of the cargo that was being fed by the steady stream of trucks. Beyond the looming, swept-back flat tails of the C-17s were the mainstays of the air bridge, the C-141 Starlifters. Hunter counted at least four dozen of them.

Beyond were the camouflage-painted C-130H Hercules, the workhorses of the Tactical Airlift Command. Their squat bodies trundled down the runways on sturdy tires and thick landing gear struts, designed to absorb the shock of short, bumpy, improvised airstrips, many of which would be close to the front. Their four big turboprop engines, supported by long, tapering wings studded with big flaps and spoilers, were designed to bring the seventy tons of plane and payload down and to a full stop in less than 3,000 feet.

And then came the KC-135 Stratotankers, and the big KC-10A Extenders, the airborne gas stations of the sky. These flying tankers would each carry tens of thousands of pounds of the precious fuel that all the airplanes in the convoy would hungrily consume—via in-flight refuelings—on their journey over the broad expanse of ocean.

On the opposite side of the flightline, Hunter saw dozens of civilian transport planes and airliners. Every major airline and air transport company's aircraft markings were evident on the crowded runways. All around him were big overseas airliners— 757s, 747s, DC-10s, and L-1011s that were also preparing for the takeoff.

He knew that the private commercial jets had all been commandeered "for the duration" by executive order. Everywhere he looked there were uniformed men milling about on runways, pouring into the airliners. These were the reservists boarding the big jets, waiting to join their comrades already in Europe.

Hunter's driver expertly cut their jeep through the sea of men and machines that spilled out across the runways, dodging fuel trucks and airplanes alike, to reach the hangar far across the field where the fighters were being fueled and armed for the escort mission across the Atlantic.

Passing the last group of civilian transports, they approached one hangar where six planes of the 16th Tactical Fighter Wing sat poised on the runway, ground crews loading ordnance under wings and pumping JP-8 into fuel tanks. As the first few rays of sunlight broke through the cold Christmas morning mist, the F-16s appeared to be sparkling like deadly, silver daggers.

Hunter saw the F-16 that would, for an indeterminate amount of time, be his own. Unlike his Thunderbird version, this F-16 was "armed and dangerous"—a supersonic killing machine that was designed for the split-second kill-or-be-killed environment that the skies over the battlefields had become. His practiced eye ran over the lines of the beautiful airplane, its big air intake slung under the long tapered nose giving it the look of a hungry shark racing for its prey.

The F-16 was a relatively small airplane—this was one of its many advantages. The smaller the airplane, the smaller the blip on the enemy's radar screen. To further reduce the plane's already-small "signature," radar absorbent materials lined the leading edge flaps of the wing, making the F-16 that much less a target for the enemy planes and missile crews who would be searching the skies above the battlefield with their electronic SAM dragnets, hoping to lock their deadly firepower on to the speeding fighter.

The F-16 would be a difficult target for them indeed. Screaming through the sky at more than twice the speed of sound, if the luckless enemy fighter or anti-aircraft battery failed to shoot it down in the first attempt, they would face a hail of firepower from their angry target.

Hunter jumped out of the jeep, thanked the driver and immediately began inspecting his new aircraft. Four AIM-9L Sidewinder missiles protruded from under the F-16's wings, and two more capped the wingtips. These advanced air intercept missiles were tied into the F-16's fire-control radar. When an enemy airplane was trapped in its electronic web, its pilot was as good as dead. A "fire-and-forget" heat-seeking missile, the reliable Sidewinder would take its target from the on-board "track-while-scan" computer, and leap off the F-16's wing to close on the enemy at speeds in excess of 1,500 mph. As it neared the target aircraft, its own infra-red guidance system would lock on to the most intense heat source — usually the flaming jet engine exhaust — and the enemy plane would disintegrate in a fireball as the missile did its deadly work.

For closer-range engagements, the F-16 had a multi-barrel, 20-mm rapid-fire cannon and as Hunter watched, the ground crews carefully loaded the 20mm rounds into the big gun's ammo chamber. Guaranteed to blast holes in any type of airborne armor, the cannon shells would pump out of the six barrels to form a lethal hailstorm of screaming lead that would slice the designated target to ribbons.

A multi-role tactical aircraft, the F-16 also possessed an excellent ground-attack capability. The 'hard points' on each wing and under the fuselage were designed to carry heavier ordnance — Rockeye cluster bombs, Mark 82 500-pounders, napalm, or incendiaries — enough for a respectable bomb load.

Bigger air-to-ground missiles — AGMs — could also be suspended under the wing. AGM-65 TV-guided Maverick missiles, their cold camera eyes relentlessly focusing on the target, could be counted to seek out and destroy fortified ground targets. AGM-88 HARMs — High-speed Anti-Radar Missiles — could home in on enemy radar signals to wipe out the SAM sites with pinpoint accuracy. Even if the launchers switched off their gun-control radars, the HARM's onboard microelectronics processor would enable the missile to still find its mark.

And, while one set of sophisticated electronic systems sought out enemy targets and guided the weapon systems, another set was designed to protect the plane from becoming a target itself. The new AN/ALQ-165 system was installed — a defensive avionics system that was more often called the Airborne Self-Protection Jammer, or the ASPJ.

Designed to identify the frequencies of incoming threats, warn the pilot, and take electronic countermeasures, the ASPJ was just one of the hundreds of acronym-labeled offensive and defensive systems in the technological arsenal of the F-16's array. IFF, TFR, LANTIRN, FLIR, TACAN, MIMIC, VHSIC, ASPJ, GPS, APG, PSP, AVLSI, ADF, AFCE, and so on. Each one was a complex, multi-unit sophisticated electronic subsystem that formed the innards of the F-16 war bird, connected by an equally complex nerve network of electronic cables, wires, and trunks that wove between the ribs and struts of the airplane's steel and aluminum skeleton.

They were all silent now, lifeless, waiting for the spark that would bring them to consciousness once the big GE F-110 turbofan engine, the very heart of the airplane, began to throb once again.

Hunter climbed into the cockpit, reviewing the flight and weapon control systems that were now second nature to his experienced eye. He strapped the wide harnesses across his middle and over his shoulders, the belts that would keep him in his reclined seat even when the fighter was streaking across the sea at Mach 2. To other pilots they were chains that held them down, trapping them in the tiny cramped space that was separated from the world outside only by a thin canopy. To Hunter they were bonds of faith, part of his special union with the aircraft around him.

A few minutes of preparation passed, then finally, he got the signal from the ground crew chief.

"Fire it up!" the man yelled to him.

Hunter answered with an OK hand gesture and pushed the required buttons.

The engine exploded in a wail of power and fury. Then the F-16's other systems quickly rose to full power. This was a very special time for him—it was as if another part of him was coming to life. Hawk Hunter the man was receding, held in suspended animation as Hawk Hunter the pilot—"the best ever"—took over. His very essence surged into the airplane's flight systems and washed back to him again. It was as if the little fighter jet was also undergoing a metamorphosis—becoming a living, breathing thing instead of an inanimate piece of steel, rubber, and plastic.

Suddenly the man seated in the cockpit became secondary—Hunter's inner being had entered into a higher state of consciousness as it continually flowed from him into the F-16's controls and back again. The on-board computer didn't need manual inputs—Hunter's brain provided the instant data it required. The rudder and stabilizers and wing surfaces didn't have to depend on their electronic controls—they moved as Hunter's limbs moved. And when the radar and radio systems crackled with life, it was as if they were Hunter's eyes and ears and voice.

Once again that very special *feeling* entered him—the sensation that set him apart from common stick jockeys. He couldn't describe the feeling to anyone—it would have been useless to try. It flowed through him every time he was in the cockpit of an airplane—any airplane.

But it was especially acute in the F-16 that he had grown to love.

Hunter took the next few minutes to go through the pre-flight checklist and to review his flight plan.

His immediate orders called for him to take the other five F-16s and fall in with the rest of the great air armada that would transit to the NATO airbase in Rota, Spain—ironically the same place where his friends Jones, Toomey, and Wa were stationed.

Soon enough, he would know their fate, and what would have been his, had he been with them . . .

His orders told him that the air convoy was forming up in three groups: The first was composed of the big boys, the C-5A Galaxies and the C-17s, laden with tons of heavy cargo. They would be guarded by two squadrons of F-15C Eagles, the kickass air-superiority fighters that, with its two powerful engines, were the fastest strike planes in the NATO inventory.

This first flight would be led by an E-3A Sentry Airborne Warning And Control System aircraft, commonly known as AWACS. Its 30-foot rotating radar dish would scan the skies ahead and below to warn of any hostile forces within striking distance.

In the second group would follow most of the slower C-130s and C-141s, along with all the civilian air transport planes. Their escort would be provided by a flight of reactivated A-10A ground attack planes. Officially nicknamed "Thunderbolts," the men who flew these squat twin-engine airplanes had quickly dubbed them "Warthogs" because of their ungainly appearance.

Ugly or not, under the right conditions, the A-10s could chew up columns of tanks with the forward-pointing, seven-barrel, 30mm GUA-8 GE Gatling guns mounted in their noses. Plus, these particular A-10s had a deadly mixture of Standard ARMs (Anti- Radar Missiles) and Rockeye cluster bombs slung under their wings.

The problem with the Thunderbolts was that they were slow — *very* slow. The lack of speed made them chop-licking targets for any Soviet grunt armed with a portable SAM. What's more, the sub-sonic 'Bolts were true attack airplanes. In other words, they were definitely *not* dog-fighting aircraft.

Without a trace of smugness, Hunter couldn't imagine what help the A-10s could be, should the convoy run into trouble somewhere over the two thousand miles of ocean between Langley and Rota.

Bringing up the tail-end of the convoy was the third group, the KC-135s and the KC-10 airborne tankers, which would be refueling any stragglers as well as the fighters, whose fuel consumption would be higher at the relatively slow speeds they'd be traveling to stay with the big cargo planes.

Also assigned to the third group was a squadron of AC-130U gunships. The attack version of the Hercules transport, these planes were the latest incarnation of the "Puff the Magic Dragon" AC-47 gunships that served in Vietnam. Flying out of Hurlburt Field near Fort Walton Beach, Florida, the AC-130s were on their way to support Special Forces Operations in Europe and the Med. They carried an awesome amount of firepower — a 25-mm Gatling gun capable of a sustained fire rate of 6,000 rounds per minute, a 40-mm cannon, and a 105-mm howitzer on special mounts by the left rear cargo door.

And they were all wired in to a AN/APG-70 digital fire-control radar system. With their Forward-Looking InfraRed (FLIR) and Low Light-level TV (LLTV) sensors, they could pinpoint an enemy position with devastating accuracy, day or night.

Hunter had seen these planes do their deadly work before and it had definitely left an indelible impression. In a test run performed on a designated target area, one AC-130 gunship making one pass had blanketed an area the size of a football field with thousands of rounds of multicaliber shells from their Gatlings, cannon, and howitzers. When the smoke cleared away, every single square foot of earth had been hit. Nothing could survive that kind of fire control intensity.

Of course, Hunter had to once again remind himself that the gunships, like the smaller Thunderbolts, didn't have much of a defensive capability. The AC-130s slow speed and nonexistent maneuverability limited its effectiveness against heavily defended targets or targets protected by enemy fighters. Their new Kevlar lightweight armor would protect the crew against stray small arms fire from defending troops, but that was about it.

Now, as the AC-130s took off, their fuselages crammed with spare ammo for their Gatlings, cannons, and 105mm howitzers, Hunter's F-16s were to fall in behind them, lifting off last to form the trailing edge of the air bridge. By "riding drag" on the tail of the convoy, the supersonic fighters would be able to kick in their afterburners and catch up to the others if there was any trouble.

But what kind of trouble could there possibly be at 40,000 feet over the Atlantic?

Plenty . . .

"Falcon flight leader ready for takeoff. Request tower clearance . . ."

Hunter was surprised at how detached his voice was—as if he were outside himself listening to another person.

"Roger, Falcon leader," the tower's own disembodied voice replied. "Your flight is cleared for take off on runway three-niner, eastbound. Wind speed is five knots, from the east-southeast. Ceiling at fifty-thousand . . ."

Hunter then led the six F-16s down the runway, gradually building speed until they ascended into the bright December sky over Virginia. Once they were airborne and organized, he picked up the proper heading for the first leg of the journey, then rose to join up with the rest of the convoy.

He looked out of the F-16's canopy at the fading coastline of the eastern United States. The sky was clear, the sun was bright; but still his uncanny "sixth sense" told him that somehow, it would be a long, long time before his eyes would see another dawn in America.

Chapter 9

The first five hours of escort duty passed without incident. The convoy, stretched out over 75 miles, was riding smoothly, seven miles high, and so far executing a perfect chapter out of the textbook on formation flying.

The flight of F-16s, led by Hunter, traced long, lazy 'S' curves above the ponderous flock of AC-130s and airborne tankers, who plodded straight ahead. The zig-zagging was necessary to keep the speedier Falcons from racing ahead of the slower transports.

Still, the time gave Hunter the opportunity to think—not always the best thing to do when one was about to go to war. He remembered one of Jones's more famous "cause-effect-result" speeches. This one was titled: The many ways to get killed in an airplane. "Frozen fuel line—flameout—crash: Dead. Too many gs in a tight dive—blackout—crash: Dead. Electrical problem— engine fire—explosion: Dead. Lose power on takeoff: Dead. Midair collision: Dead. Pancake into the runway: Dead."

The point was that an airplane—any airplane—could turn on its pilot and the results could be fatal. Just about the only way to avoid such nastiness was for the pilot to thoroughly know the airplane and to know himself. It was this one golden rule that led to the real message of the speech: How *not* to get shot down in combat.

"If you know your airplane and you know yourself better than the other guy knows his airplane and knows himself, then you will shoot him before he shoots you."

It all sounded so simple. Too simple. But now, alone in his cockpit at 40,000 feet over the Atlantic Ocean, Hunter was finally realizing the subtle complexity of Jones's words. And their darker meaning stayed with him during the hump hours of the flight, looking over his shoulder like an unseen, uninvited passenger.

Hunter's brooding was interrupted by a static-laden radio blast from the F-15 squadron many miles in front of him. Leading the convoy with the big transports, he deduced the Eagles were somewhere over the Azores by now.

His guess was accurate, as verified by the F-15 squadron commander.

"Falcon flight leader, this is Eagle leader. We are past Checkpoint Alpha Zulu and turning for destination Ringo-Oscar-Tango. Over."

Hunter knew that Alpha Zulu was the code designation for the Azores. Ringo-Oscar-Tango meant Rota.

He responded in the flat, toneless drone born of thousands of routine radio messages.

"Eagle flight leader, this is Falcon leader. Roger your status and location. All clear back here. Over."

Hunter knew the F-15s were now committed to go for Rota— they were already across that imaginary line in the sky that marked the point that they could still turn around and have sufficient fuel reserves to reach a tanker rendezvous point should Rota not be a safe place to land.

It was time to refuel.

Hunter loitered behind the other F-16s, listening to their pilots converse via secure transmissions with the big KC-10A Extender airborne tanker crew during the complex refueling process.

He didn't know any of them except for their names: Crider. Christman, DuPont, Rico, and Samuels. Yet each one took on the needed fuel like an expert.

"They're like extras in a movie," Hunter thought, realizing in the same instant that "extras" were usually the first ones to get killed in war films.

With that sobering thought, he eased his own fighter effortlessly into a flight path just below the big aerial tanker, and after a successful hook-up, took on a belly full of fuel.

Once gassed up, Hunter and the other F-16s resumed their zig-zag patterns high above the transports. The weather was crystal clear—the ocean below a shimmering blue. The overall effect was one of peace, tranquility. Hardly the weather one would expect to see while heading into the jaws of World War III.

This irony was sweeping through Hunter when, suddenly, he was shaken with another, more sinister feeling. Something was wrong up ahead.

Dead wrong . . .

Even before his radio crackled to life with the first report, Hunter had punched in his afterburner. At the same time he relayed instructions to DuPont, Crider and Rico to do likewise and follow him.

Captain Geoffrey Spaulding didn't even know that there was a problem until the jetliner had started to fall.

Cruising with his flight of A-10A Thunderbolts high above the flight of transports and airliners, he had observed the last plane on the left wing of the convoy formation—Airplane Number 6—shake with a convulsive shudder. An instant later it started to trail flames and smoke and began to lose altitude.

Spaulding immediately grabbed his microphone. "Flight Six? What is your situation?"

There was no reply . . .

"Flight Six," he called out. "Confirm in-flight emergency . . ."

Once again, there was only silence.

Even as Spaulding attempted to reach the pilot of the stricken airliner once again, a dozen things raced through his mind. Did the 747 have an engine problem? A fuel problem? Was it electrical? All unlikely—the pilot hadn't reported anything and with mechanical failures, there usually was a warning sign—an oil pressure gauge, an engine temperature light, or any one of the hundreds of feedback and monitoring systems that checked the plane's vital signs would generally give some sort of advance notice before trouble started.

"Flight Six, Flight Six . . ." Spaulding called out. *"What is your situation?"*

There was no answer. Only static.

He watched in horror as the 747 was almost immediately engulfed in flames. Then it turned over, spiraled for the long plunge down.

The spike of fear finally stabbed him. Maybe they'd been hit by enemy fire.

As the A-10A had no long-range radar to speak of, he quickly scanned the area visually, checking his position at the same time. They were at 40,000 feet and still had more than 1000 miles to go to the mainland of Europe. Where would enemy fighters come from? Unless . . .

Suddenly his radio crackled to life.

"Thunderbolt Leader! This is 747 Flight One!" he heard the desperate, electronically distorted voice say. "We are under attack! Repeat . . . *we are under air attack!"*

Spaulding quickly calculated that Flight One was five miles ahead of his present position and a mile and a half below.

"Roger, Flight One," he replied. "We're on our way . . ."

Spaulding immediately radioed up the rest of his 'Bolts and as one they dove to catch up with the airliners.

They reached the scene just as Flight One was going down. But he could see no enemy fighters — not right away, at least.

"Where are the bastards!" he cried into his microphone.

No sooner had he said it when one of his pilots called back.

"Captain! This is Murphy! I can see them . . ." came the message. "Six miles out due north. There's eight — no, *nine* of them. I can see them clear as day . . ."

Spaulding immediately put his Thunderbolt into a wide, arcing 180-degree turn, a maneuver the rest of his flight followed. Within seconds he was able to see a handful of aircraft riding almost parallel to the flight of airliners.

"They're Soviet jump-jets . . ." Spaulding called out to his flight, surprised that his voice was so calm. He had immediately

72

recognized the uniquely ugly profile of the Yak-38 Forger, a fighter flown by the Soviet Navy.

He knew more than a few things about the Yak. One, it was equipped with AA-2 Atoll air-to-air missiles, with a range of about six miles. Two, the Yak, was a Vertical Take-off and Landing type jet, and therefore operated almost exclusively from the deck of certain Soviet ships.

In other words, there was a Soviet carrier down there, somewhere.

Spaulding knew he had to act fast. There was no doubt that when the Soviet fighters had finished shooting at the convoy with their standoff missiles, they'd probably swoop in at close range to finish the job with their guns. If that happened, the ungainly A-10s would have no chance at all to save the transports, or even themselves.

So the 'Bolts would have to dive—now, straight through the formation of enemy fighters from head-on and above. And then, well—then he'd worry about what to do next.

It only took seconds for Spaulding to first broadcast a coded "Under Attack-Distress" message to the rest of the convoy. Then he armed his Gatling and signaled his flight to do the same. The Standard ARMs and Rockeyes hanging from their wings would be useless against the airborne targets. Spaulding thought ruefully that the heavy ordnance might be good for extra weight during the first dive, but then the bombs would only be that much more high-explosive baggage to drag the 'Bolt down before the swifter enemy fighters.

But Spaulding knew the Americans had one advantage: The Soviet Forger was an absolutely terrible airplane—a poor attempt by the Soviets to duplicate the superior British-designed Harrier "jump jet." Unable to master the complex thrust-vectoring technology that allowed the Harrier to use its engine for vertical takeoffs and landings as well as level flight, the Soviets had instead stuck a big turbojet in the Forger's fuselage with adjustable nozzles, and crammed two smaller engines forward, just behind the cockpit. The resulting hybrid was a heavy, difficult-to-fly monstrosity that squatted on the decks of Soviet carriers, unable to take off without the combined thrust of all its engines, and unable to use its forward lift engines to maneuver in flight.

Spaulding also knew that the Soviets were trying to work around this disadvantage. The Forgers were obviously operating off one of the Soviets' very few aircraft carriers—he guessed it was either the *Kiev* or the *Leonid Brezhnev*. They had probably tracked the air convoy from far out, then waited until the formidable F-15 force was past. Once cleared, the Forgers swooped in on the transports, firing their air-to-airs in a cowardly stand-off attack on the helpless airliners.

And that was what Spaulding knew he had to stop.

The A-10s increased their power dive on his command. The sun was with them, and although the Forger was equipped with a standard naval aviation radar, it was notorious for breaking down. For the moment, the element of surprise was with the Thunderbolts.

Spaulding crossed his fingers and took a deep gulp from his oxygen mask . . . .

Just as the enemy airplanes were about to move in on the remaining airliners, the A-10s dove through their formation. Instantly the A-10s' combined barrage of seven-barrel GE Gatling guns raked the topsides of the Soviet fighters. The big antiarmor shells punched through their steel skins, finding a cockpit or a fuel tank or an engine. The Soviets—caught completely offguard—immediately scattered. Yet in the quick, steep pass, at least three of the Forgers went spinning into the sea.

Now the element of surprise was gone. The A-10s had bought some time for the unarmed airliners to escape, but now the six remaining Soviets appeared to be splitting off to engage the slower Thunderbolts.

Though the Forgers were nobody's idea of a dogfighter, they *were* more than a match for the A-10s, which were designed for shooting up columns of tanks on the ground, not for aerial combat. Knowing this all-too-apparent limitation, Spaulding immediately ordered his flight to break off and dive for the deck.

Much to Spaulding's dismay, none of the Forgers followed. Instead the remaining enemy fighters simply continued on their way, intent as they were on going after the undefended jet liners. The Soviet pilots, Spaulding figured, were wrapped in an obedi-

74

ence straitjacket. They had orders to shoot down as many of the airliners as possible, and to the Soviets, an order was an order, with very little room for interpretation, spontaneous thought, or individual initiative.

But he also knew that at this altitude and speed, his A-10s would never be able to catch up to the faster Forgers. Perhaps his actions had given the airliners time to escape. Then again, maybe not. But he knew he was correct in taking the risk. And in any case, he knew he couldn't help the airliners now. . . .

"This is 747 Flight Two, to Escort Commander or any escorting aircraft . . . We are under attack once again. We have just sustained near-miss damage. I have an engine fire on number one . . . Can you assist?"

The 747 pilot was disheartened when he didn't receive any immediate reply.

"Fuel line off to number one," his co-pilot reported. "Fire extinguishers are on, but as of now not effective . . ."

The 747 pilot took another look at his number one engine, then keyed his microphone once again.

"This is 747 Flight Two, to any escorting aircraft . . ." he called into the microphone loudly. "We are under attack and damaged. This is a critical in-flight emergency. *Can you assist? Over.*"

No sooner had the transmission ended than the airline pilots saw no less than a half-dozen bluish-gray jet fighters climbing toward them.

"Christ," the pilot said, trying his best to keep the big plane level. "Those guys are *not* on our side . . ."

Suddenly, the airliner's radio came to life.

"Roger, 747 Flight Two . . ." a stone-cold calm voice said. "We're on our way . . ."

Just then four jets streaked in front of the big airliner, and, as one, twisted down toward the approaching enemy aircraft.

Both airliner pilots immediately recognized the quartet of airplanes as F-16s.

"The cavalry has arrived!" the co-pilot yelled out.

"That's right," the pilot said. "Now let's get us and the rest of these covered wagons the hell out of here . . ."

On the call of the Flight Two pilot, the four remaining airliners climbed and turned slightly southward, trying to put as much distance between them and the impending dogfight as possible. The sudden ascent also served to douse the flames of the lead 747's stricken engine.

"*Damn*," the 747 pilot said through a sigh of relief. "We might make it to Spain yet . . ."

Hunter led the four F-16s through the six Forgers with surgical precision.

The Soviet pilots, knowing full well the difference between the cumbersome A-10 and pistol-hot F-16, immediately tried to break and run.

But for most of them, it was too late.

Although they had the numbers in their advantage—it was, after all, six Soviets against four Americans—the Forgers were all but sitting ducks. Weighed down by their Rube Goldberg-like engine arrangements, the Soviet aircraft suffered nearly twice the turning radius of the smaller, quicker F-16. Plus, they had greedily expended most of their air-to-air missiles on the helpless airliners.

Now, they would pay.

Hunter keyed his offensive systems in on the lead Yak, figuring correctly that the airplane was being flown by the flight leader. Aligning his fire radar and arming two Sidewinders, Hunter hooked onto the Forger's vulnerable six o'clock position and stayed there. The enemy tried to jink this way and that—but to absolutely no effect.

Coolly—maybe too much so, he would later think—Hunter aimed the first Sidewinder and let it fly. Unerringly, it sped to its target just a half mile away and obediently smashed into the rear of the fleeing aircraft.

There was a puff of smoke followed by an orange ball of flame. Then came the explosion . . .

It was silent, *oddly* silent. Hunter felt the F-16 shudder just a bit as he flew through the air ripple concussion resulting from the blast. Then, as he climbed and streaked by, all he could see was a cloud of black smoke, peppered with pieces of gray and barely flaming wreckage. Then there was nothing.

It had happened so quickly—no more than five seconds had elapsed. But, just like that, Hawk Hunter had killed his first human being . . .

Chapter 10

Captain Spaulding had reformed the Thunderbolts and wheeled them in a big arc low over the churning waves.

It was true that he had done all he could for the airliners, but still his psyche was unsettled.

What now? Hug the waves all the way to Spain? Or get back up to an acceptable altitude and risk getting caught by more enemy fighters? Or should they play it safe, wait up for the final segment of the convoy and play Last Place Looie to the tail-ending AC-130 gunships? He was certain that's what his commanders would want him to do. The whole idea, after all, was to get the A-10s to the battle zone where they were needed.

But something was gnawing at him. He knew the Forgers had iced at least two jumbo jets, if not more. That meant a minimum of 600 Americans had gone down. Could he, in good conscience, let such an act go unanswered?

His answer came as his A-10 broke through the fine ocean mist lingering just above its surface.

Dead ahead was a Soviet naval task force . . .

It was composed of an aircraft carrier (the *Brezhnev*, it would later turn out), plus a *Kirov*-class cruiser, two *Sverdlov*-class light cruisers, and a protective ring of six, *Sovremennyy*-class, guided-missile destroyers.

Their bows all pointed directly at the flight of A-10s, the big ships looked like skyscrapers looming up from the ocean surface, bristling with radars and missile launchers, and anti-aircraft guns that would soon be tracking the incoming attack planes, if not already.

Screw it, Spaulding thought. *This is war* . . .

"Okay guys," he hollered into the radio, "ARMs and guns on this pass, on my command . . . Everyone ready?"

Spaulding heard a reassuring chorus of approval from his flight.

"All right," he said, taking a quick succession of gulps of oxygen and checking to make sure his Anti-Radiation Missiles were now properly hot. "Let's get some payback . . ."

Klaxons on all of the Soviet ships were blaring by the time the nine A-10s had turned and begun their dash across the wavetops in three groups. Instantly, each ship's battle command center switched on its fire-control radars. SAM crews began sending out the searching pulses of radar waves and immediately started picking up louder and louder pings as the distance between the ships and the attacking airplanes rapidly decreased.

A ripple of panic went through the Soviet AA crews as the A-10s were coming in so low, the gunners strained to depress their guns to meet them.

"Hang in there, guys," Spaulding urged his pilots as he tightened his grip on both his missile release switches and the Gatling triggers. He was leading the first wave of A-10s and they were heading for amidships of the *Kirov*-class heavy cruiser. "Just a little bit closer, make sure they can't turn off the radars in time . . ."

The attack was crazy in and of itself—but it would be a complete disaster if their missiles didn't have enough time to lock on.

"A little closer . . ." he urged his two wingmen. Puffs of long-range AA fire were now coming up to meet them. "Closer . . ."

The AA fire grew more intense as the cruiser suddenly lurched hard to port in an effort to dodge the attacking planes. Someone on board the Soviet ship launched an anti-missile rocket which streaked about crazily and fell harmlessly into the sea.

"Closer . . ." Spaulding urged. *"Closer . . . Now!* Fire ARMs!"

He found himself squinting his eyes as the dazzling rocket plume erupted under each of the Thunderbolt's wings, sending the big white anti-radar missiles slicing through the sky toward the heavy cruiser.

The other two A-10s of his group did the same, and soon six vapor trails traced the paths of the streaking missiles, their inertial guidance system computers locking on to the cruiser's SAM radars. Now, even if the Soviets turned the radars off, the missiles' memories would home them in with deadly accuracy.

Too late, the Soviet sailors on the *Kirov* cruiser had seen the missile separations on their radar screens. Now they screamed for the fire-control officer to shut down the active radar, knowing it was a beacon for the American missiles to follow directly to them.

But it was useless.

In seconds, five of the six bulky missiles found targets on the cruiser's superstructure and around the perimeter of the deck. Powerful explosions rocked the big ship as most of their air defense radars and SAM batteries blew up within a few seconds, spreading fire and shrapnel in their death throes.

Just before the Thunderbolts flashed over the heavy cruiser, Spaulding called out for Gatling fire. Their GE GUA-8 30mm seven-barrel nose cannons whirled, spitting flame and lead from the A-10s as they raked the center of the cruiser in a coordinated strafing run. Everywhere on the ships sailors were diving out of the path of murderous stream of cannon shells that poured forth from the attacking planes.

The second wave of A-10s roared in and almost perfectly mimicked the devastating attack. This time four of the six ARMs found targets, once again rocking the huge ship with a shudder of powerful explosions.

The third wave of 'Bolts executed another textbook attack on a nearby escort destroyer, hitting it with all six missiles, five of which impacted on its bow.

"Regroup and strafe!" Spaulding called excitedly as he wheeled his own A-10 up and around the *Kirov*-cruiser.

Once again coming in low and in three waves, the Thunderbolts roared over the two ships, covering each with withering cannon fire. The destroyer had been able to turn itself hard to port, thereby offering less of a target to the third group of A-10s. But the cruiser, its elongated bow now fighting against the suddenly choppy sea, took the full brunt of six Gatling guns in the first and second wave. Its starboard side was now awash in smoke and flame.

But not all the Soviet gun crews had been neutralized and some of the anti-aircraft crews on the protected portside began finding their mark. One A-10 in the first wave exploded in midair, its fuel tank riddled by tracers. Another 'Bolt, the leader of the second wave, caught an AA shell directly on its starboard engine, virtually disintegrating it. The A-10 immediately lost altitude and skipped heavily across the waves, finally exploding on impact near the side of one of the destroyers.

Although two of his pilots were killed, Spaulding felt he still had to press the attack. Neither enemy ship was out of commission yet, but two or three more strafing runs might do it.

But then suddenly, he was aware of a new threat.

Once the attack began, the Soviet carrier had turned away from the action. But now, somewhat recovered, its captain was launching Forgers to deal with the A-10s.

At that point, Spaulding knew his Thunderbolts would have one more pass at best before the Forgers were on them. He radioed instructions to the remaining A-10s to break their formations and independently target and drop their Rockeye cluster bombs on the two stricken Soviet ships. Then it would be time to tactically withdraw.

This last run was a lesson in confusion. The independently attacking A-10s were approaching from all angles, and thus harder for the surviving SAM crews to target. But the Rockeyes weren't designed for bombing naval targets. More than a few of them fell off the mark, bracketing the pair of Soviet ships with huge geysers of sea water.

One cluster bomb, however, went off right on the foredeck of the big cruiser, sending a wall of fragments and shards into the ship's superstructure, instantly destroying its bridge and combat control center.

Spaulding was the last plane in, dropping his Rockeyes on the stern of trailing destroyer, now directly behind the looming Soviet carrier. By this time it seemed as if the air was filled with

Yaks. Spaulding looked back just in time to see one Forger on his tail, pumping away with his exterior gun pod. His A-10 shuddered as it simultaneously lost an engine and sustained heavy damage to the tail control surfaces.

Unable to climb or turn, the stricken Thunderbolt roared over the battered destroyer, and slammed into the carrier's main superstructure, neatly clipping its radar mast off at the base with its left wing.

Somehow, Spaulding was able to hit his eject button just as his A-10 tumbled into the sea beyond the carrier.

Chapter 11

The battle between Hunter's F-16s and the enemy Yak Forgers had been brief.

Three of the Soviet fighters—including Hunter's first kill—had been destroyed. A fourth was smoking heavily as it left the battle and the remaining pair were last seen fleeing to the north.

With most of the Forgers disposed of, Hunter led the flight of F-16s at full speed back toward the last reported position of Spaulding's A-10 flight. At the same time, the AC-130 gunships and the two remaining F-16s at the tail end of the air convoy were approaching the same area.

Hunter reestablished radio contact with his trailing F-16s. Minutes before, Crider had spoken to one of the six A-10 pilots that had been in Spaulding's flight. The surviving 'Bolts, their ammunition gone and their fuel critically depleted, were now attempting to make it to Rota. The A-10 pilot told Crider of the Thunderbolts' daredevil action against the Soviet surface ships and also provided him with the last known position of the enemy. Crider quickly relayed the report to Hunter.

Digesting the information, Hunter contacted the AC-130 flight, speaking to the lead ship's senior Fire Control Officer, an Air Force Reserve lieutenant named Mike Fitch.

They quickly surmised—as Spaulding had before them—that this particular Soviet task force had probably positioned itself in the sea lane beneath the likely Langley-to-Rota air route days before the sneak attack on Western Europe. No doubt other similar Soviet naval groups were scattered strategically around other parts of the Atlantic as well.

The Soviets in this group, then, had somewhat cleverly evaded the AWACS and the F-15s by leaving their active search radars switched off as the first leg of the air convoy passed over, using only the less effective, but "cooler" passive radar systems. They, like the Americans, knew very well that, in war, a "hot" radar set was like hanging a bull's-eye over one's self, especially the long-range, juiced-up "active" radars.

Yet, Hunter knew that following the Thunderbolts' attack, the Soviets had probably shut down most of their surviving active systems again—that was, until another air convoy passed over and the Forgers resumed their deadly stand-off raids. And then more defenseless air transports might be lost.

But it would take more than the cannons riding aboard the F-16s to destroy the heart of the Soviet task force.

So he quickly discussed an idea with his F-16 pilots and with Fitch on the lead AC-130 gunship. They compared current positions, timing and remaining fuel loads, and finally came to the conclusion that Hunter's plan, though risky, had a chance of succeeding.

Like Spaulding before him, Hunter knew he had to take a gamble. But this one was a double long shot. He was betting not only that all the active radar sets on the Soviet ships were switched off, but also that the shitbox Soviet passive systems couldn't tell the difference between the gunships and the regular transports, at least not until it was too late.

If the first two guesses were correct, then the third leg of the bet dictated that the Americans had to switch off their own AN/APG-70 digital fire control radar sets, as the "hot" sets would have given themselves away too soon.

The overall result would be that just about everyone involved would be shooting with one hand over one eye . . .

On board the Soviet aircraft carrier *Brezhnev,* the Soviet task force commander was feeling somewhat rattled, yet still confident.

His primary mission had been executed: his airplanes had

shot down at least two of the American airliners, and damaged several more. And, in the strange air attack that followed, three of the American A-10s had been shot down.

But his task force had also paid a price. The *Kirov*-cruiser was heavily damaged, still afloat, but all but useless. The destroyer was burning badly and would most likely have to be abandoned. As many as six Forgers unaccounted for. And his own ship was missing its main radar mast after the last A-10 had sheared it off shortly before crashing.

Two airline transports and three A-10s at cost of two battered ships and a half-dozen Yak fighters, he thought. *Who won this battle?*

He had no time to think any more about it—rather, it was time to resume his mission. Stay hidden, avoid US submarines, wait for another American air convoy, and attack again. All in all, his own ship was in good shape. The few stray bomb hits that reached them hadn't been serious. Ninety percent of his communication and command equipment was still working— and all his active radars were shut down. Even the troubling lack of the top mast radar wouldn't be a problem for too long. His damage control parties had assured him that substitute radars were already working to pick up the slack.

And even now, he could see a repair crew was climbing to the top of the superstructure in order to mount a temporary radar dish near the top of the clipped-off mast.

It was these men who were the first to see the approaching F-16s . . .

Chapter 12

Like the valiant A-10s before them, the F-16 Falcons came in just above wavetop level.

They would strike in two groups: Hunter, Rico and DuPont would go in first; a minute later, Crider would lead Christman and Samuels in for the follow-up.

"Cannon armed and powered," DuPont radioed over to Hunter.

"Ditto here, Captain," Rico confirmed.

Hunter checked and confirmed that his own big gun was ready.

"Roger, cannons ready," he called back to them. "I read twenty and two miles to target . . ."

With their radars switched off, this would be an eyeball attack. But this didn't worry Hunter—their target would be one of the biggest things afloat.

"There they are," Hunter called out calmly, spotting the silhouettes of the Soviet ships just above the horizon. Also visible were the half-dozen plumes of black smoke coming from the damaged cruiser and destroyer.

"And there's the big guy," Hunter continued, spotting the massive outline of the carrier, *Brezhnev*. "Everyone got a visual?"

"Roger," came the near simultaneous reply from his two wingmen.

"OK," Hunter said, feeling an invigorating rush of adrenaline wash through him. "It's showtime . . ."

With a kick of their afterburners, the first three F-16s were in amongst the Soviet ships within seconds. For the first wave of the attack, the carrier would be the sole target—the rest of the ships would be left alone for the time being.

Although the carrier's SAM crews were not prepared to fight, the Soviet anti-aircraft gunners saw them coming. In seconds the air was filled with AA fire. But the nimble fighters, roaring in three abreast, were able to jink around the heavy stuff with aplomb, turning wing-tip up in order to reduce their target profile. They were heading toward a point off the port side of the carrier's bow, rising above the waves ever so slightly to bring their noses level to the uplifted front ramp of the carrier's flight deck.

"Ready . . ." Hunter yelled into his radio as the airplanes approached the 500-foot-to-target mark. *"Fire!"*

Instantly their cannons spoke with one terrifying voice. Spitting 20mm shells across the crowded flight deck, the exploding rounds gashed several waiting aircraft, then walked up the side of the superstructure to pepper it with holes. Then the three fighters screamed up and over the massive ship.

It took less than four seconds, but Hunter knew all three of them had inflicted damage.

But this was just the beginning . . .

No sooner had Hunter and the others gone into their steep near-vertical escape climbs, when Crider, Christman and Samuels roared in. They too found targets up and down the front part of the ship, including a direct hit on a Soviet Ka-25 Hormone ASW helicopter.

Despite the lightning quickness of his first pass, Hunter had spotted the two Forgers warming up on the carrier's flight line. Once he, Rico, and DuPont were regrouped, he signaled them to concentrate fire on the first jet on their next pass. He would take the second jet alone.

The three of them did a tight 360-degree loop, and less than a minute later were boring in on the carrier again. The AA fire was now tripled in intensity as gunners on the surrounding escort ships were now joining the battle. Hunter knew the enemy SAM crews—their radar no doubt switching on by the dozens—would soon be back in action.

The trio of jets split up about a mile out, Rico and DuPont going for the Forger near the front of the carrier's flight deck, Hunter aiming for the one nearer to midships.

Less than a quarter-mile out, Hunter started his cannon firing on the second Forger.

Although he was going just as fast as before, it seemed to Hunter like everything had suddenly gone into slow motion. As he roared in on the carrier he could see his target—apparently a two-seat version of the Forger—just starting to lift off the carrier deck. He slammed his cannon trigger and felt the F-16 shudder as the huge gun started firing. He followed the cannons' smoke streams and watched as his shells tore open the left wing of the Soviet jumpjet, exploding its fuel tanks and spilling fire onto the flight deck.

Then, in a flash, time resumed its normal pace and he was up and over the carrier once again. Looping back and looking down through his canopy, he saw that he had completely destroyed the Forger, and that Rico and DuPont had killed their target as well. Now two major fires were sweeping the ship's flight deck, virtually insuring that no more planes could take off until the wreckage of the two Forgers was cleared, and the fires were extinguished.

At this point it seemed like panic swept through the Soviet Task force. Two of the destroyers made tight turns and obviously started to escape, whether under orders or not, Hunter would never know. Then the Soviet anti-aircraft batteries' crews started to fire blindly at the attacking fighters. With little or no radar yet operating, they were hard pressed to hit one of the speeding fighters—after all, they weren't pokey A-10s.

But still, the streams of tracers and the streaking unguided missiles made the sky around the task force look like a lethal gauntlet for the F-16s.

Hunter reformed his flight and pressed ahead with the second phase of the plan: a concerted strafing run on the starboard sides of the remaining escorting ships. If the second part of his attack plan was to work, they'd need to clear the path . . .

As the F-16s swept in from the starboard quarter at an oblique angle to the remaining light cruiser and destroyers, all the ship's guns were focused on them, blazing away at the strafing planes. Cannon fire laced the cruiser's foredeck, and more shells obliterated the bridge of one of the destroyers, tearing into the superstructure.

All eyes, even those of the carrier crew, were on the six buzzing planes . . .

None of the Soviet sailors saw the big AC-130s loom out of the valley created by the big swells as they skimmed across the ocean's surface in a long line, like a flight of birds of prey. Even when they were spotted, the Soviets failed to notice the howitzers, cannons, and gun barrels protruding from their fuselages.

That is, until they opened up with the first broadside.

In the lead gunship, Fire Control Officer Mike Fitch switched on the Hughes digital fire control radar, locking on to the big carrier deck and the Forgers still lined up to receive their payloads. The 105mm howitzer and the 40mm cannon in the rear bay tracked the carrier in unison as radar gave them target and range.

The multi-barrel Gatling gun behind the pilot was armed and ready. In their armored, soundproof battle management station in the center of the gunship, the crew monitored their weapon consoles from behind a U-shaped bank of sophisticated mission control computers.

From each station, the radar operator/navigator, electronic warfare specialist, and fire control officer could verify their target and operational status as the big airplane gained altitude and leaned over, slightly dipping its left wing toward the Soviet carrier.

"Spectre Flight, lock radar and open fire as your guns bear!" Fitch's voice rose as he mashed the gunship's fire buttons. Instantly the 25mm Gatling gun roared to life, spitting fiery death at the rate of 6,000 rounds/minute. The howitzer and cannon fired their first shots together, then in a staccato pounding rhythm as they remained locked onto the carrier's deck, relentlessly pumping high explosives into the clustered Forgers.

The Soviet fuel and bomb loading crews abandoned their planes on the vulnerable, cluttered flight deck, hoses flailing, spilling jet fuel across the deck surface. Bomb trucks rolled haphazardly as their drivers dove for the false safety of the superstructure or the perimeter passageways. Pilots, strapped into their seats, were struggling to escape their bonds as the first barrage ripped into the carrier deck.

The *Brezhnev's* flight deck was instantly engulfed in flames and violent explosions as the gunships poured their massive payloads of multi-caliber ammunition into the big target. Tracers cascaded down in dazzling streams of light, punctuated by the thumping flashes of the heavier guns. Fireballs of oily smoke mushroomed from the carrier's flight deck as one Forger after another was touched off by bombs and flash fires from the spilled fuel.

The fire followed the tiniest rivulets of fuel into cracks and crevices where it had settled, spreading to all parts of the exposed deck and starting to feed back on itself. Columns of smoke and flame roared as high as the top of the superstructure, where the radar mast repair crew was watching death erupt below them.

One by one, the AC-130s passed over the carrier's deck, pounding away with their massive firepower like great airborne Men o' War delivering broadsides to the hapless enemy. Only these broadsides were digitally controlled to keep targeted on the Soviet ship throughout the long, banking turn around the front of the Soviet task force.

Several Soviet ASW helicopters erupted in huge geysers of smoke and fire as their fuel tanks and ammunition pods exploded. Huge swatches of thick gray paint peeled off the burning ship and wafted in the sky like flaming leaves.

The stunned Soviet gunners on board the other ships began to respond with anti-aircraft and machine guns as the AC-130 flight slowly rounded the front end of the task force.

Now, just ahead of the flaming carrier lay the light cruiser and the already-battered destroyer. On board the lead gunship, Fitch quickly switched off the infrared sensors of the fire control system, realizing it would send their weapons pouring back on the flaming carrier instead of on the escort vessels.

He radioed the other ships to do the same. As he locked on to the new target, the light cruiser, he felt enemy machine gun fire rake the left side of his gunship. Even in the soundproof cocoon, surrounded by the banks of computers, he could hear the dull thud of the bullets as they struck the boron-carbide Kevlar armor.

Fitch knew the armor would hold off the smaller guns, but a big shell would blast them out of the air. Their best defense would be a good offense, he thought, suppressing the big ship's guns with a barrage of their own.

But at this point, the scales tipped slightly—and temporarily—in the Soviets' favor.

Two Forgers, survivors from the previous furball with Hunter and the F-16s, had finally made it back to the area. Quickly and uncharacteristically absorbing the situation, their pilots streaked toward the AC-130s, looped up and came back again near the center of the gunships' line.

Siting one AC-130 near the middle of the line, one Forger opened fire. Instantly the gunship absorbed burst after burst of concentrated fire from the Yak's 23mm gun pod. Within seconds its right wing shattered as both engines exploded. The big plane fell out of line and cartwheeled into the ocean in fiery slow motion, finally sinking upside down in the churning water.

Anti-aircraft fire from one of the destroyers had found its mark on a second AC-130's rear fuselage, starting a fire that threatened to engulf the entire aircraft. The opportunistic Forger, sensing another easy kill, bored in on the stricken gunship, unaware that he was crossing directly into the firing pattern of the AC-130 flight leader's Gatling gun.

"Captain, give me ten degrees up on the port wing! Just a hair closer . . . Fire . . . *now!*" Fitch roared as he hammered the fire button.

The Gatling roared to life; in less than three seconds nearly 300 rounds of 25mm ammo had perforated the Forger, which disappeared under the fierce barrage of lead from the gunship. Pieces of what had been the Soviet interceptor filtered down out of the sky as the smoke cleared. But no individual part was recognizable—the airplane had simply been vaporized.

Now there was only one left . . .

Hunter sliced through the air at Mach 2-plus to overtake the hapless Forger, who was maneuvering near the flaming deck of the *Brezhnev*, trying frantically to signal the ship to activate the autoguidance system that would link with his on-board autostabilizer to land the cumbersome jumpjet.

Another bolt of anger shot through Hunter as he watched the Soviet interceptor hovering over the carrier's burning deck, its hot exhaust gases merging with the flames and smoke, blowing them out and fanning them in a large circle around where the plane was to touch down. This was one of the guys that iced the defenseless transports, he thought. Without hesitation, he clamped down on his cannon trigger and let loose a long burst of fire.

The shells immediately tore into the length of the hovering Soviet airplane. Its forward lift engines instantly blew out and failed. The pilot, caught in the middle of the furious barrage, slumped forward on his control stick, causing the stricken Forger's nose to drop sharply. It hung there, suspended for a brief, terrible moment as the rear engine struggled to keep the plane aloft.

Then the pointed nose of the plane plunged straight through the burning deck of the *Brezhnev*, propelled by its still-firing rear engine and burrowing down to the second deck of the big ship. A muffled explosion shook the Soviet carrier as the Forger's weapon loads and remaining fuel supply blew up deep within the ship's interior.

High above, Hunter's wings were buffeted by the force of the blast as the ship's main magazine was touched off three decks below by the burning plane.

The *Brezhnev* settled back into the water now, her back broken by the powerful explosions. Flaming fuel and oil from the fires raging on deck now poured onto the sea around the ship, creating a series of floating bonfires.

At that awesome and frightening moment, all of the Soviet gunners stopped firing and all of the American airplanes stopped attacking.

It was as if someone had blown a whistle—the battle was over . . .

The surviving AC-130s turned eastward and gunned their engines. Close behind were five F-16s.

Only Hunter remained, circling the battle zone at 10,000 feet.

As he stared down at the flaming, oil-slickened water, he wasn't thinking about the destruction that had just been wrought—No, his mind was filled with thoughts of the first Soviet pilot he'd shot down earlier while trying to protect the airliners. He had destroyed the Forger—and its pilot—with such workmanlike precision it scared him.

Was that really all there was to it? Was that how easy it was to kill a man? And could the situation have been reversed? Would that Soviet flyer have blown *him* out of the sky so coldly, so efficiently? Would he have watched as Hunter plummeted downward into the frigid Atlantic waters? Would he have felt the same strange emptiness that was inside of Hunter now? Why was it okay for Hunter to kill and not the other way around?

Maybe Jones was right . . . this *was* the way it had to be: kill or be killed. Get the other guy before he gets you. Reduce it all down to numbers and technology, and guaranteed you'll factor out the human equivalent. Understand that and it gets easy—too damned easy. Jones had explained the killing all right. But he never told him how to live with it afterward.

With that thought firmly entrenched in his psyche, he booted in his afterburner and streaked off to rejoin the air convoy group as it headed for Rota.

Far below and not a half mile from the battle scene, Captain Spaulding was just hauling himself aboard his inflated life raft.

He had watched the titanic battle from a dangerously close vantage point, bobbing in the sea, not daring to inflate his raft for fear the angry Soviet sailors would try to shoot him.

Now that the battle was obviously over, he clambered aboard the raft and forced-vomited the seawater from his stomach. Then, completely exhausted, he simply let the raft drift, not quite believing that he was still alive or that he had witnessed one of the most awesome air-sea battles in history.

Two hours later, still only a few miles from where four Soviet ships lay dead and smoking in the water, he watched as the carrier *Brezhnev* exploded once again and finally slipped beneath the waves.

Chapter 13

At Rota

Rota Naval Base sprawls along the Spanish coast near the mouth of the Mediterranean.

A "home-away-from-home" port for the US Sixth Fleet in peacetime, Rota was now the choke point for incoming supplies to NATO's southern flank. The first flight of the "air bridge" had landed, and the tons of cargo, machinery and materiel that had been so frantically loaded at Langley hours before was now being just as frantically off-loaded.

Truck convoys streamed through the airfield in endless green lines of chugging diesel smoke and grinding gears, picking up supplies for the long hazardous road trip to the fighting front, hundreds of miles away. Navy trucks ferried cargo loads to the docks, where ships of all kinds from the Sixth Fleet were jammed into the harbor, filling their holds with the supplies and ammunition that would support the Navy's Mediterranean operations.

Huge containers rolled out of giant transport planes onto flatbeds, and were picked up by towering cranes that lowered them into the gaping holds of the big supply ships.

On the flight line, loading crews swarmed each plane almost before it had stopped taxiing, popping airlift doors and opening loading hatches to disgorge the big planes' hastily packed cargo to the waiting trucks.

As soon as one transport had been relieved of its burden, another would be hurried along the runway to take its place in the long line of stuffed birds waiting to be gutted. This was the first stop in the air bridge that stretched back across the Atlantic, to Langley and the mountains of supplies in warehouses and supply depots across the United States.

All the while, the sky was swarming with helicopters, shuttling in and out. Some were big workhorses like the Chinook, taking on supplies that could not wait to be driven to the front. Others were gunships, returning to this—one of the only true "rear areas" in the war—for re-arming and/or repair. Other choppers carried messengers, cameras, the wounded, doctors, even an occasional civilian casualty. Still others simply orbited the big base, watched the ground below like hawks for prey, ready to thwart any possible terrorist-like attack.

Still farther up, two E-3 AWACS planes were keeping watch for any enemy air strike or missile attack.

On other runways below, the decimated airliners had limped in to the airbase with tattered wings and shredded fuselages, burning engines trailing smoke. At least two had pancaked into the runway, snapping their landing gear as they touched down.

Streaks of foam drying on the surface traced the path of a DC-10 that had landed wheels-up and flipped over, its wreckage pushed out of the way by the ground crews. And everywhere there were ambulances and stretchers and wounded men.

The survivors of the A-10 flight had landed nearby, and the pilots looked over their planes with the ground crews, fingering the bullet holes and noting other battle damage. Each pilot, some furtively and others openly, had taken a look down the now-shortened line of Thunderbolts, and wondered how Captain Spaulding would have told the pilots' families . . .

In the cold, but sunny Spanish skies overhead, the six F-16s flew in a tight formation over the air base.

First three of the fighters peeled off and landed, then the second group mimicked the maneuver. Although in light of their decisive victory against the Soviet task force, tradition may have dictated a victory roll or two, neither Hunter nor the other pilots felt this was the time or the place. They had witnessed not just a battle but a disaster in which thousands lost their lives. As such, they had no desire for grandstanding.

Hunter set his plane down last and taxied over to where the rest of his squadron was parked. As he shut down the engine and popped the canopy, the ground crews began their work, chocking the wheels and helping him unstrap.

He climbed out onto the wing and then down to meet the rest of the squadron.

For the first time, they all shook hands and formally introduced themselves. Crider, DuPont, Christman, Rico, and Samuels. They had just been names to Hunter back at Langley. The "extras" in the unfolding war epic. Now, as he took in their faces, he felt as if they were his brothers.

After the planes were secured, the pilots made their way to the briefing room near the base's command center. It was a small auditorium, rows of chairs with small desks attached to their right armrests assembled in front of a stage where a single lectern stood in front of a series of maps hanging from the wall.

The map on top was of Western Europe, with concentric rings traced in increasing diameters around the focal point, a small dot on the south coast of Spain labeled "Rota." The rest of the maps showed the various points on the European continent where fighting had broken out.

Drained and exhausted, Hunter had shuffled into the darkened briefing room and slumped into the nearest chair. The last thing he thought he'd hear was a familiar voice . . .

"Hey, flyboy, don't I know you?"

Hunter looked up to see JT Toomey and Ben Wa, Hunter's old Thunderbird buddies, standing over him.

"Jesus Christ . . ." was all Hunter could say, standing up to shake JTs hand.

"Welcome to sunny Spain, my man," Toomey said, his ever-present sunglasses reflecting the room's subdued lights. "You'll like it here. It's just like Nellis, except that the Vegas hookers were expensive and the casino booze was cheap; Here, the Spanish hookers are cheap and the booze is expensive . . ."

Ben Wa, the so-called "Flyin' Hawaiian," was right behind JT, furiously pumping Hunter's hand and beaming.

"Glad to see you could make the party, Hawk," he said. "Can't have any fun without the Wingman."

Wingman. Hunter's nickname had been bestowed upon him the first day he'd been at Nellis, when General Jones had assigned him to fly on his wing even before Hunter had sat in the F-16's cockpit. At first the Wingman label had been uttered sarcastically, but after he had proved his unique flying abilities, the cynics had become believers, and the name was almost reverently connected with Hunter's from then on.

"It's great to see you guys . . ." Hunter said sincerely, looking around the room. "But where's the Jones Boy?"

Suddenly someone yelled: "Atten-*shun!*"

At that moment, a small, wiry but sturdy figure walked onto the stage, carrying with him a fistful of paper and an undeniable sense of drama. Setting his briefing papers down on the lectern, he stared out at the small audience.

"At ease, gentlemen," Jones said. Then he nodded toward Hunter and added: "Glad you could join us, Captain. Same for you other men. Crider, DuPont, Christman, Rico, Samuels. Glad you all made the trip in one piece . . ."

General Seth Jones was the picture of what an Air Force general officer was supposed to look like: his posture ramrod straight, blue flightsuit festooned with ribbons and wings, the trademark cigar clenched between his white teeth.

"First of all, that was top-notch work out there, men," Jones said, referring to the battle at sea. "Extraordinary, even. If and when this thing is over, you boys may be looking at some Air Medals, or maybe even something higher . . ."

With that, the accolades ended. They all knew Jones had the latest intelligence data from Supreme Allied Commander, Europe, commonly known as SAUCER, which was NATO's high command. The pilots quickly took chairs nearer the front of the room as Jones pulled down a map of Central Europe with the current disposition of forces highlighted in red and blue.

"The purpose of this briefing is to update you new men on the situation," Jones said, speaking clearly and distinctly despite the cigar in his mouth. "Gentlemen, in a word, that situation is grim. Possibly even worse than we had first imagined . . ."

He stopped to flick an ash and let his words sink in.

Then he began again: "Although the war has been on for more than twenty-four hours now, we really don't have much hard information beyond what you probably already know. According to the latest reports, West Germany was hit pretty hard. We know that major SCUD missiles hits landed here, here, here, and here in the heaviest concentrations."

His listing of the locations was punctuated by taps of his pointer at Frankfurt, Bremerhaven, Bonn, and Stuttgart.

"In Bremerhaven, they lobbed in persistent nerve agents with the SCUDs, rendering the whole damn port and city useless for months, thereby denying us a route through which we could have re-supplied the central ground units in Germany," Jones continued.

"The rest of the gas was a nonpersistent nerve agent, probably GD, which will likely disperse in forty-eight hours or less. As far as we can tell, there has yet to be any major enemy troop advance into these areas, or along any front as yet. Just probing actions so far. They are most likely waiting for the gas to dissipate at least to the point where they can send in some armor with a forward decontamination team. Of course, we are under the same limitation, with the added problem that, sorry to say, NATO troops are woefully underequipped for this type of chemical warfare.

"But our spy satellites show us that the invasion is coming—soon."

"What's the status of our operating bases in West Germany?" DuPont asked. "Is anything flying up there at all?"

Jones shook his head. "No, I'm afraid not," he said, turning back to the large map of Western Europe. "We've been forced to abandon all the forward German airfields. The main ones have been gassed, and the ground forces have been torn up so badly we weren't sure how long we could hold them even if we'd stayed.

"Fortunately, we had enough warning to fuel up the aircraft and get the gas masks and CBW gear handed out at the airfields before the strikes hit. We managed to save most of the aircraft and some of the ground and support personnel."

"What about civilians? Dependents? Service families?" Hunter asked, not really sure that he wanted to hear the answer.

"Some got out . . ." Jones said after a pause. "Some didn't . . ."

The explanation hit Hunter and the others like a ton of bricks. Certainly there had been millions of civilian deaths, many, many Americans among them.

"When do we launch our own chemical strike?" Christman asked.

Toomey and Wa were still looking down at the floor. They'd heard the answer before, and they weren't going to like it any better this time around.

"We don't . . ." Jones said. "Under direct orders of the President: We are not to counter-attack with chemical weapons. Period."

"But why?" Rico asked.

Jones cleared his throat. "Because the President does not want any more innocent civilians killed," he said.

"What about nuclear weapons?" Crider asked.

"Same order," Jones said. "The US will not be the first side to introduce nuclear weapons."

"Even low-yield neutron bombs?"

"Especially low-yields," Jones responded. "The feeling is that first nuclear use will just have a domino effect. As serious as this situation is, it is obviously a major concern that it not get completely out of hand, and end up incinerating the whole damn planet, which, at this point, I might add, is still a good possibility . . ."

"So in other words," JT said, "we're fighting another 'limited war?' "

Everyone in the room blanched at the comment. The words "limited war" made up the hated military buzz-phrase for the failure in Vietnam as well as the less-than-glorious results in Korea.

The comment turned Jones's face a slight red. JT had a bad habit of speaking his mind a little too abruptly.

Still, the senior officer maintained his cool. "We are soldiers, Captain Toomey," he said. "We are hired by the people of the United States to do a job. And right now that job is to carry out orders, no matter what we think of them."

The pilots were sobered by the general's words. They all felt as if they were one step away from either Armageddon or capitulation—Hunter included. A combination of hunger, sleeplessness, and high anxiety turned the briefing into a surrealistic episode for him. In less than twenty-four hours, the whole world had turned upside down, and now he felt as if he were caught in the eye of a hurricane.

After an uneasy pause, Jones continued with the briefing.

"Right now, the vast area of West Germany hit by the SCUDs is a no-man's-land," the senior officer explained. "But, as I said, if the satellite photos are right, we expect the Soviets to start driving as soon as the gas dissipates.

"And, believe it or not, we're going to let them do just that."

Now a wave of disbelief washed through the room.

"Unopposed?" Toomey asked, expressing the surprise all of them felt.

"For the most part, yes," Jones replied. "Some of our special rear guard troops will try to delay their progress by blowing up bridges, roads, rail stations and communications links—soft targets. But it's going to be token opposition, at least over the next eighteen to twenty-four hours . . ."

"We're just going to *give it* all to them?" Rico asked, still not catching Jones's drift.

The general nodded, then revealed another map, this one marked "Projected Situation."

"There are several reasons for this strategy," he explained. "First of all, it allows our troops to withdraw to more defensible positions.

"But secondly, if this strategy leads the Soviets *deeper* into Germany, or even right to the edge of France, it will serve to stretch out their supply lines. Conversely, it makes *our* supply lines shorter. The key is this: If we can gradually inflict casualties on the enemy's rear areas by way of ambushes and airstrikes, and hitting him at strategic chokepoints as he moves across this no-man's-land, we'll not only be buying the precious time that NATO needs to regroup, we'll also be whittling down the enemy's numerical advantage in armor, aircraft, and men. In theory, the farther west they go, the more their supply lines will be stretched and vulnerable."

Ben Wa raised his hand. "But General, if they build up a head of steam, they may be unstoppable," he said. "How long do we let them march?"

Jones let out a long breath. "As long as it takes for the armies of NATO to make a stand and stop the advance."

"*If* they can stop the advance . . ." JT added almost sarcastically.

Jones started to reply, but didn't. He knew his wise-ass pilot was right—there were a lot of *ifs* in the risky strategy. *If* the air bridge held for the short term. *If* the surface ship convoys could get through for the long term. *If* they were successful in delaying some Red Army units from reaching the front.

But there was one crucial question remaining. For the strategy to work, NATO had to at least neutralize the Soviet tactical air advantage over the next forty-eight hours.

And that's where Jones and his pilots, and the rest of the NATO air forces, came in.

"The success of all this is based on our quickly achieving air supremacy, or at least, parity," Jones said soberly. "And that is *our* challenge. And believe me, a lot of people are depending on us."

He then revealed yet another map.

"To that end, gentlemen," Jones said, through a puff of cigar smoke, "let's discuss our first mission . . ."

Chapter 14

First combat in Europe

Hunter was out on the flight line early.

In the pre-dawn shadows, the silent row of F-16s stood watch over the long stretch of runway. Unlike the Thunderbird Falcons that balanced lightly on their tricycle landing gear, the fully-armed F-16 were slung with Sidewinder missiles, wing tanks, and huge belly tanks that barely cleared the ground under the plane's fuselage.

To fly from their base in Rota, perched on the southern tip of Spain, to the target areas over Germany, they would need every drop of precious fuel those tanks could hold, and then some.

That's where the tankers would come in.

The KC-10A Extenders, flying out of the support base at nearby Moron, would rendezvous with the speedy fighters over southern France to top off the tanks so the '16s would have as full a load as possible. The tankers would also be on standby if the F-16s were returning with low fuel.

Yet the tanker rendezvous was only one tiny part of the complex plan that Jones had devised. It had been spinning around in Hunter's mind ever since the briefing. He had even dreamed about it — what could go right, what could go wrong.

The mission was appropriately code-named "Operation Punchout," and it was designed to do nothing less than neutralize the Soviets' major forward air bases in Eastern Europe.

The reason behind this rather grand objective was simple: The Soviets had at least a five-to-one advantage in tactical aircraft over NATO. But depriving the Soviets of their forward airfields and support bases would somewhat even the odds in the air, at least for the next crucial 24-to-48 hours. If the operation was successful, then Soviet airplanes would have to fly farther away, from their rear bases, just like the NATO aircraft were doing now. And once the Soviets' armies advanced westward, they would be further removed from the coordinated air support needed to sustain the advance of their overwhelming ground forces in the Central European Theater.

But for the plan to succeed, it was crucial that the split-second schedule be followed with the highest degree of precision. In order to avoid Soviet concentration of defenses, Jones had called for coordinated and *simultaneous* attacks all along the East/West border. This in itself would be difficult, considering the hundreds of NATO aircraft that were to be involved.

But beyond the attacks themselves, the plan also involved some complicated deception maneuvers—deaks and feints that the Soviets would have to fall for.

With all this in mind, Hunter climbed into his cockpit and completed his preflight checklist.

The last instrument test he performed was to touch a single heat-sensitive button on the F-16's console that activated a special radar pod the tireless ground crews had slung underneath the fighter's right wing the night before.

A small radar-emitting transponder came on, triggering a yellow LED on his ECM display.

Satisfied, Hunter clicked it off and watched the yellow dot fade out. Now, at last, they were ready. The mission could begin.

For Hunter and the other F-16 pilots, their role was just beginning. But even as they were preparing for takeoff, the first major phase of "Operation Punchout" was already underway in the dawn skies over East Germany.

As the cold fingers of first light were prying the lid of darkness off a new day, Captain Michael Francis "Crunch" O'Malley was rechecking his position for what seemed like the hundredth time in the last ten minutes.

His squadron of F-4 Phantom IIs were at that moment screaming across the West German border just north of Kassel, flying barely a hundred feet off the frozen ground. O'Malley did a quick calculation and then took a deep breath.

They were now over East Germany.

So far, everything since take-off from their base near Eindhoven, Holland to this point at the border had gone according to plan.

O'Malley relayed the time check and coordinates to his backseat weapons officer, a young lieutenant from Tennessee with the unlikely name of Elvis Aaron Pettybone.

Elvis just barely grunted "Roger," in response, his eyes riveted to the radar threat-receiver on his console. At the moment, the device was silent but alert, its electronic probes searching the skies and ground in front of the speeding fighter, looking for the tell-tale radar beams from hostile missiles and aircraft.

It wouldn't be this quiet for long, Elvis thought grimly, especially since they were just about to enter one of the densest concentrations of SAMs in the world. At least Crunch had been there before, Elvis thought. He knew what it was like to have to fly through the gauntlet of SAMs, each one a radar-guided explosive javelin hurled from below.

Elvis had only been through the simulations they'd practiced endlessly, and he wondered how he'd react when the console warbled out a real warning—a real SAM, controlled by real radar, fired by a real enemy crew, trying to kill them for real.

Crunch was thinking about the SAM belt, too; and about the Soviet fighters he knew were up ahead somewhere, waiting to pounce. He kept the Phantom's airspeed at just under 700 mph, the maximum possible without the fuel-greedy afterburners. They still had almost a hundred miles to go to reach the target, and he had to save the speed and fuel for when he needed it.

They streaked across the snow-covered land into the rising sun, having left the comparative safety of West Germany for the decidedly unfriendly skies of Soviet-controlled East Germany.

Eleven other Phantoms followed him across, all rising on toward the same target.

Crunch looked out across his wings at the planes to his left and right. Despite its age, the Phantom II was a mean-looking fighter.

In its heyday, the F-4 was in use as a fighter and attack plane by the Air Force, Navy, and Marines as well as a dozen other countries' air forces. But now the aging fighter-bombers were used for special purpose strikes, rigged as a jammer in the "Wild Weasel" configuration for detecting and nullifying enemy radars, or as a RF-4 reconnaissance plane for aerial surveillance.

Crunch checked his position again. Forty miles inside the border and still no enemy radar acquisition.

Either the Soviets were sleeping or . . .

"SAM! SAM! SAM! Two o'clock!" Elvis hollered into the intercom, his voice loud enough to override the suddenly pulsing shrill tone of the missile warning indicator. "Break left!"

"Damn!" Crunch swore as he realized how close the SAM was—they'd been flying low, and the Soviet crews had shot on visual sighting only, without lighting up their radars.

He rolled the plane in a tight circle and pulled the stick up sharply, pumping his chaff dispenser to confuse the missile by scattering half a pound of aluminum shavings into the cold air.

He prayed the missile's radar guidance would take the bait. What seemed like an eternity later, he saw the SA-2 missile pass the Phantom well behind and to the left. The pulsing tone of the radar warning was fading now, as the missile sped away.

Another F-4 wasn't so lucky. The Soviet SAM crews had bracketed him with a pair of missiles, and he'd turned directly into one's path while trying to avoid the other.

The Phantom was shredded when the SAM's proximity fuse detonated the missile a mere thirty feet from the airplane. Crunch and Elvis both swung their heads around, looking for parachutes.

There were none . . .

Now the radar warning began a new, insistent blaring. More SAMs had been launched behind them, and their powerful missile-control radar signals had been picked up by the F-4's threat indicator.

"One launched—check that, *two*—at our six o'clock!" Elvis began excitedly. "No guidance signals yet . . ."

The young weapons officer knew that the first stage of the SA-2 was unguided, directed only by pinpointing it in the general direction of the attacking aircraft. When the first stage fell away, its second stage received signals from its ground crew.

So now they would have to wait—wait until the enemy ground crews had committed themselves.

The steady, high-pitched whine told Elvis the missiles were screaming toward their tail at 2,000 mph, and every instinct told him to run—to bellow at Crunch to floor it and try to escape. But his training told him differently—he had to rely on that training to overcome his instincts and to give Crunch the signal for the right time to break away.

The seconds were agonizingly slow . . .

Crunch, too, felt the tension building, his hands sweating on the stick as he listened to the screeching warning signal. He had to watch the altimeter, the airspeed, and the sky in front of him; and he had to rely on the young lieutenant behind him to tell him when to start evading the two explosive arrows that were slicing mercilessly through the air toward him.

"Steady . . ." Elvis called ahead, his eyes glued to the small radar screen in his rear cockpit that showed the position of the two SAMs as tiny, fast-moving blips glowing directly behind them. "Steady, sir . . ."

When they started flashing and blinking, he knew the missiles' radars were hot, and—the whine of the threat indicator changed to a higher-pitched warble, assaulting their ears with its relentless cries.

"*Now!* Dive and pull right!" Elvis yelled over the threat indicator's soprano whooping.

Crunch pushed the stick down and then yanked it over, feeling the g-forces push against him as the Phantom sliced around in a hard diving break.

The SAMs couldn't make the turn, and streaked off into the distance, finally detonated by their crews when they realized they were too far off course to correct.

Normally Crunch would have continued the roll-out, angled the plane down, and fired off a Shrike anti-radar missile at the offending SAM crews, hoping the missile would home in on the anti-aircraft battery's radar. But he needed every missile the F-4 was carrying for the mission ahead; now was not the time for taking on the SAM crews below.

Now was the time for extra speed.

Crunch kicked in the afterburners and immediately he and Elvis were slammed back in their seats as the Phantom's twin engines shot the plane forward at nearly twice the speed of sound. They gained some altitude to provide more maneuvering room if they needed it.

Crunch checked his time and position again. The evasive action had cost several precious minutes. Now they would have to make up for time with speed and that meant using the fuel-sucking afterburners. The more fuel they used the less they'd have to get back.

But right now, Crunch knew their survival was secondary. Because if they didn't get to the target area at the right moment, there might not be any point in trying to get back.

Their objective for Operation Punchout was the Soviet air base at Neurippin, East Germany, headquarters of the Soviet Central Air Army. More specifically, the force of Phantoms was aiming to knock out as many enemy SAM sites around the base as possible.

That's why timing was so important. If they arrived too soon, the crews of the SAMs ringing the airfield might not have their search radars activated and thus the radar-busting missiles the F-4s were carrying would be useless. But, if they were too late, the sky would be full of Soviet interceptors waiting to pluck the aging Phantoms out of the skies like marauding hawks.

Several tense minutes passed until Crunch checked his position and made visual contact with the target.

"OK, boys," he called out to the others in the strike. "There's the bull's-eye . . ."

As the flight of F-4s bore down on the Soviet base, Crunch could see that they were almost too late: several groups of Soviet fighter aircraft were already on the flight line, ready to begin taxiing down the runway.

He quickly assembled his Phantoms for the attack.

"Weasel Strike, Code Bravo!" Crunch said crisply into the microphone in his oxygen mask.

In one fluid motion, four Phantoms to his left peeled out of formation and dived toward the airfield, leveling out barely forty feet from the ground. Within seconds they were screaming along parallel to the main runway.

These F-4s were rigged as "Wild Weasel" SAM-suppressors, their specially designed electronic countermeasure jamming systems emitting powerful signals to confuse the Soviet radars.

As they roared overhead, cannisters on their wings spewed huge clouds of aluminum chaff that hung suspended over the airfield, further frustrating the Soviet crews as their radar screens first went white from the jamming, and then locked on to the huge concentrations of chaff overhead.

"Commence attack! Lock and fire!" Crunch shouted into the mike as he shoved his throttle further forward.

He and the other Phantoms were exactly ten seconds behind the Weasels. In their rear seats, each weapons officer armed the six large AGM-88 HARMs (High-speed Anti-Radar Missiles) hanging under each Phantom's wings.

The pilots were just the drivers now—it was all up to the men sitting behind them. In the lead Phantom, Elvis fired his salvo of missiles toward the Soviet base. The Soviet SAM crews, in an effort to "burn through" the Weasel's jamming, had cranked their radar outputs to maximum, and, of course, that was just what Elvis had wanted them to do.

Now the HARM's own on-board sensors identified and locked onto the pulsing SAM radar signal. The sophisticated microwave circuit boards inside the missile's guidance system processed the incoming signals in complex flight-control algorithms—semiconductor chips made thousands of decisions in a fraction of a second as the HARMs raced off the Phantom's wing, following the radar pulses like a homing beacon.

The other Phantoms had unleashed their missiles at nearly the same time, each warhead's relentless electronic brain keying in on the radar sites they had pinpointed.

Too late, the SAM crews saw the brilliant flashes under the attacking planes' wings. Now the lightning-quick HARMs were burning toward them at more than 3,000 miles per hour. Some of the crews abandoned the launch vehicles, frantically diving for cover as the missiles bore down upon them.

Others tried to desperately launch their own missiles before the HARMs struck.

Both tactics proved to be futile . . .

The HARMs found their mark with deadly accuracy. The foremost SAM site was struck simultaneously by three of the big missiles, and it was vaporized instantly. The same fate fell upon the sites on either side of it.

Then, within seconds, all around the perimeter of the airfield, missiles were boring into the big SAM launchers, destroying crews and machinery in deafening, earth-shaking explosions.

One HARM, impacting on a SA-2 site close to the flight line, ignited spare missiles stacked next to a launcher. They erupted like huge sticks of dynamite, sending their deadly debris in a flaming circle that engulfed one of the Soviet fighters taxiing down the runway.

In the confusion of the lightning raid, the Soviets had only been able to launch a handful of SAMs, most of which were decoyed by the chaff clouds or evaded by the swooping Phantoms. Their vaunted air defense batteries were now scattered piles of smoking junk that marked the SAM sites that had formed the base's defensive perimeter.

Crunch looked back over his shoulder at the pillars of smoke rising up from the Soviet base, then he checked the time again. The attack had lasted only fifty-seven seconds, and almost all the Soviet anti-aircraft missiles had been wiped out.

Crunch clicked on his radio switch to the predetermined channel and made his report.

"Ringside, this is Phantom leader. Right Cross delivered. Maximum effect. Over."

The radio crackled with static as he listened for the reply from the mission coordinator in faraway Belgium.

Crunch knew that his part of the Operation Punchout, "Right Cross," had gone well. But he also knew that it was only the first part of a major operation.

"Phantom Leader, this is Ringside," his radio crackled back. "Roger your report on Right Cross. It's your call on continuation; Left Jab still en route. Over . . ."

The coordinator's voice was tense but formal as he relayed the information to the F-4 squadron leader.

They were giving Crunch the option of additional strafing attacks on the Soviet fighters still lining the runway. The burning wreckage of the airplane that had been touched off when the SAMs had exploded had pinned the remaining jets on the ground, but the flight crews were already trying to clear the burning wreck and at the same time turn some of the fighters around to take off in another direction.

Crunch weighed the options. None of the Phantoms had taken hits, but their fuel was near the minimum safe limit for the return flight. Still, if they could nail a few of the fighters, it might give the next phase of the operation a better chance.

He was on the verge of ordering the F-4s to form up for a strafing run with their cannons, when he heard Elvis and the radar threat indicator scream at the same time, both in high-pitched insistent tones.

"Atolls launched! Six o'clock! Climb and break left!" the weapons officer hollered over the now-wailing threat warning. Two Atoll AA-2 air-to-air missiles had been launched at very close range behind them, but from where?

The Soviets hadn't been able to launch any fighters yet. There was no time for analysis now; first they'd have to shake the missiles.

Crunch yanked the stick back and hauled it over to bring the Phantom up in a sharp, climbing turn, once again pumping the chaff dispenser and launching a pair of small but intense flare decoys, whose brightly burning infrared signatures he hoped would lure the missiles off his tail.

Only one of the Atolls took the live bait, swerving away to meet the flare in a fiery explosion. The other detonated in one of Crunch's chaff clouds, close enough to pepper the side of the Phantom with shrapnel.

"Damage report!" Crunch snapped into the intercom microphone, as he, too, scanned his instruments for signs of engine or control failure.

"All systems normal. Cannon armed. Read three bogies at our four, low altitude, stationary." Elvis had identified the Soviet aircraft that fired the missiles — three of their HAVOC attack helicopters had managed to lift off and unload their air-to-airs at close range!

Two ugly, billowing clouds of black smoke marked spots in the sky that had just been occupied by F-4s, and the HAVOCs were maneuvering for a second volley.

Crunch made his decision. There was no point in waiting around for the whole Soviet fighter wing to get airborne, even though the Phantoms could have certainly made short work of the helicopters.

"Phantom flight, this is Phantom leader," Crunch called to the others in the flight. "Head for the lockers. Repeat, head for the lockers. Rendezvous plus-sixteen at Point Blue . . ."

They'd already lost three of the F-4's, and they'd completed their part of Operation Punchout. Crunch wanted no part of the angry Soviet pilots behind the throttles of the Su-27 Flankers that had just begun their takeoffs on the now-cleared runways below. That was a job for the seond wave.

He punched the afterburner for a quick burst of speed out of the target area, and the F-4s of Right Cross disappeared over the western horizon.

Chapter 15

Soviet Wing Commander Pavel Osipovich Gorshkov angrily gunned his throttles forward as the big Su-27 interceptor sped down the runway, past the wreckage of his unfortunate wingman's aircraft that smoldered in a charred heap near the SAM site whose explosion had engulfed it.

Damn the Americans and their electronics! he cursed.

The F-4's missiles had annihilated nearly every defensive battery around the big air base. And not a single SAM had claimed a victim. . . .

He wanted desperately to lift his plane off and give chase to the speeding attackers. His planes could easily overtake the older F-4 attack planes with Mach 2.3 speed supplied by the newest jet engines in the Soviet air force. And their look-down/shoot-down radar would make short work of the Phantom intruders.

But he had his orders: They were to let the F-4s escape.

He knew the Americans would not have launched such a strike — one targeted against their anti-aircraft defenses only — if they had not planned to follow it up with heavier bombers. And that was surely a higher priority — to intercept those bombers before they could finish the destruction of his air base.

That would be the best revenge.

The Soviet fighters had all lifted off the ground now, assembling on Gorshkov's order into a tight formation. They'd received a preliminary fix from one of their forward radar operators on what had to be the flight of American bombers, heading toward them at high altitude, and just now crossing the French border.

The Americans are either desperate or foolish, Gorshkov thought. The radar blips indicated that they were flying the ancient, hulking B-52 strategic bombers—hardly a match for the Soviet "Flanker" interceptor he was piloting.

Even if the bombers carried the new sophisticated cruise missiles, Gorshkov knew his interceptors would reach them long before they were in a position to fire.

Radioing instructions to his squadron to follow, Gorshkov punched in his afterburners to close in on the approaching American bombers.

At 47,000 feet, high over the French border city of Strasbourg, Hunter had just switched on his specially installed radar transponder, and watched the yellow indicator blink on.

One hundred and eighty feet on either side of him, Toomey and Wa had done the same, as had General Jones and the rest of the F-16 pilots of the 16th TFW.

They were flying high in loose formations of threes, their spacing duplicating that of the mammoth B-52 bombers whose radar signatures the special emitters were mimicking. Whereas most NATO aircraft carried electronic gear to mask their presence or interfere with the Soviet radars, the devices on the small fighters were designed to broadcast to the Russians the exact location and type of aircraft they wanted to believe were on the way to bomb them.

The F-16 pilots already knew that Right Cross had been a success—SAM sites surrounding several Soviet bases had already been attacked. So far, Jones's plans for Operation Punchout had worked. Now if only their part of it, Left Jab, could go according to schedule . . .

But that depended on the Soviets' taking the bait.

Hunter knew the principle of the radar emitter/decoy was sound enough. But the key in this gambit was convincing the Soviets that NATO would *really* send the creaking B-52s on a tactical strike. Even with stand-off cruise missiles and electronic countermeasures, the big bombers would still be sitting ducks for almost anything the Russians threw up to intercept them.

Still, Hunter knew that his side was holding some pretty high cards. One ace in the hole was the fact that the night before, NATO had virtually erased the Soviet airborne radar capability. From all reports, Operation Warm-up had gone like a dream. A squadron of shadowy near-radar-proof F-119 Stealth fighters — airplanes still so secret, Hunter had never even seen one yet — had claimed as many as ten of the Soviet's AWACS-like Mainstay converted transports, both in the air and on the ground. Deprived of their eyes in the sky, now the Soviet fighters would have to be right on top of Hunter and the others to realize the phony B-52 deception.

Of course, once they made visual contact, the Soviets would know that they'd been fooled by an F-16 squadron. What would happen then?

They'd know the answer soon enough.

Suddenly, the NATO forward radar station reported a squadron of Soviet interceptors was heading toward the F-16s at Mach 2 plus. Hunter took a deep breath and looked across the wide expanse of sky in front of him, searching for the Soviet fighters.

Wing Commander Gorshkov was scanning the skies in front of his squadron also, searching in vain for the multiple contrails that the American bombers would leave in the sky.

Where were they?

He could still pick them up on radar, maintaining their high-altitude formations. Hadn't they spotted the Soviets yet? Surely the B-52s' powerful search radars could identify them by now. Either the Americans were more foolish than he thought, or something was wrong. Very wrong.

Still his instruments told him the American bombers were continuing on course. The Soviet interceptors were closing the distance at better than Mach 2, trying to reach the flight of high-flying aircraft before they could launch their Tomahawk cruise missiles.

The Su-27s were equipped with the new AA-10 air-to-air missiles, perfect for launching from medium range at bulky airborne targets like the B-52. All Gorshkov and his pilots would have to do is to get close enough to give the missiles a radar lock, then it would be as simple as flipping a switch.

Now they were well inside West German airspace. Suddenly a light came on in the center of Gorshkov's cockpit weapons console, turning the glass cover lens a brilliant blue.

He waited until the blue light began blinking. Then a low beeping tone began to fill the cockpit.

Gorshkov instantly barked a command at the rest of his squadron as he reached down for the missiles' arming switches. He pressed the launch button on his control stick and watched his four AA-10s streak off his wings toward the bomber formations, their own radar guidance systems locking on and tracking the signals they received from the planes ahead.

More than sixty deadly airborne torpedoes raced through the sky, searching for their targets.

Hunter was the first to acquire the AA-10s visually.

The F-16s' threat warning radars had shown the missile separation from the Flankers, each big radar blip giving birth to four speeding, lethal baby blips. In all the F-16s' cockpits, radar warnings sang their piercing, one-note songs of alarm, reminding the increasingly uncomfortable pilots of their unaccustomed role as bait.

The F-16 was not accustomed to being the hunted, he thought metaphorically. Usually, the warning signal meant instantaneous evasive action—diving, climbing, jinking, turning—anything to avoid the relentless pursuit of the deadly missile.

But on orders from Jones, the planes of the 16th were holding course, transponders broadcasting a homing beacon for the Soviet missiles. It was a nerve-wracking game of chicken, and more than one pilot looked down at the small yellow dot that glowed remorselessly on their consoles, wanting to reach out and squelch the signal, breaking away.

But none did. Sweating and tense, they waited for Jones.

The general felt the pressure, too, and more. The lives of his pilots and the weight of command was riding with him in the F-16's small cockpit. Like all aspects of the operation, he had to time this exactly right. If he gave the order too soon, the Soviets would realize what was happening. Yet, if he waited too long, he'd lose most of his squadron to the oncoming missiles.

Timing is everything, he thought.

Hunter looked through the HUD at the sky in front of him, barely able to pick out the enemy missiles from the surrounding cloud base. His radar had no such trouble, however, and was blaring out its warning with fierce urgency.

Surely Jones wasn't going to wait much longer . . .

Suddenly the general's voice came on the line: "Falcon Flight, commence Left Jab! Repeat, commence Left Jab! Gloves off *now!*"

Jones was making his move, his voice crackling through the radio speaker with the command the F-16 pilots had been anxiously awaiting.

They all breathed a collective sigh of relief into their oxygen masks, then silently hoped that the general had not waited too long.

Hunter's quick hands had reached for the transponder switch even before Jones's order had been concluded. The yellow LED blinked off as he punched the switch down and simultaneously jammed his control stick forward to put the F-16 into a gut-churning power dive. Using full afterburners to charge *under* the incoming missiles, the extreme maneuver immediately served to close the gap with the Soviet fighters that had launched them.

Hunter didn't look around until the F-16 had leveled after the dizzying plunge from the thin air of 47,000 feet where they'd flown, trying to imitate the high-flying B-52 Stratofortresses. Now at 35,000 feet, the g-forces relaxed their enveloping fingers from his body. He swiveled his head to see the Soviet missiles pass above and behind him.

Their radar homing signals abruptly cut off, the Soviet AA-10s lost their guidance fix and began looping randomly, unable to re-establish a solid radar contact. Some collided, exploding in midair, and the rest sped off into the clouds or fell to the earth harmlessly.

Except for one . . .

Hunter was surprised and dismayed to see a single F-16 still flying at a dangerously higher altitude.

It was DuPont . . .

Hadn't he gotten the word to switch off the transponder and dive? Was something the matter with his radio? Or had something gone wrong with the radar emitter?

"DuPont! Gloves off!" Hunter bellowed into his oxygen mask microphone. "Throw the switch, guy, and acknowledge!"

"I can't . . . I tried . . . It must be jammed . . ." DuPont replied anxiously.

He had punched the heat-sensitive switch on and off half a dozen times with no effect. The yellow light still glowed on his console like a panic button. A single power switching transistor had failed short, bypassing the console switch and keeping the radar signal beaming out from the F-16's wing pod.

In his frantic efforts to kill the signal, DuPont had delayed his dive with the rest of the squadron by a critical few seconds. Now, as he was in mid-plunge, one of the Soviet missiles was hungrily homing in on him.

"Jettison the pod, DuPont . . ." Hunter called to the stricken pilot.

He would never know if the man heard him or not.

The Soviet AA-10 slammed into the F-16 just forward of the right wing root, roughly the position of the transponder pod. The resulting explosion ripped the small fighter in two, disintegrating the right wing and forward fuselage section.

The shredded wreck hung in the thin air for an agonizing moment before it spun down in an ever-increasing spiral on its left wing, until that too, was torn off by the force of the free-fall. The shattered nose of the Falcon plunged straight downward toward the earth, a blunted, broken arrow.

Hunter felt paralyzed, watching the stricken F-16 fall, powerless to help the young pilot who had the misfortune to be stuck with the faulty transponder switch.

Why? Why had DuPont been the one? What cosmic crapshoot had rolled his unlucky number that particular day? It could have been any one of them, Hunter thought. But why DuPont?

Suddenly, Jones's voice brought Hunter out of his brief stupor.

"Falcon Flight," the voice crackled over the cockpit radio. "We've got bogies dead ahead at twenty-seven thousand. Read

117

sixteen Flankers in formation and closing fast. Engage on first pass only.

"Repeat, engage on first pass only . . . Over."

Hunter could see the Flankers below him now, streaking toward the squadron of F-16s. With no small amount of anger welling up inside him, he armed both his cannon and Sidewinders and took aim at the rapidly approaching enemy fighters.

If he only had one pass, he was sure as hell going to make it count . . .

At first, Wing Commander Gorshkov was stunned, not wanting to believe his own radar.

Although better than most of the Soviet systems, the Flanker's radar was still quite susceptible to sudden, unexplained failure. But this glitch was very bizarre. The blips from the big B-52s they had been tracking had vanished just moments after he and his flight fired their long-range missiles at them. Certainly the missiles couldn't have reached the targets and destroyed *every* one of them so quickly.

He immediately radioed his wingman to confirm the loss of contact. His scope too showed no blips.

It was then that an awful fear began to creep up on Gorshkov. Had the Americans fooled them?

A moment later his wingman called and informed him that he was getting readings indicating that one enemy target *was* hit.

Gorshkov quickly pushed the Reset button on his target acquisition radar and confirmed what his wingman had reported.

At least they'd hit something. But just what it was he had to find out.

Gorshkov punched in his afterburner and brought the Su-27 interceptor up to full speed. Suddenly three pilots in his flight were urgently calling him and reporting new targets were appearing on their radar screens. Within seconds, Gorshkov saw them too—smaller, speedier blips were popping up all over his screen.

"Fighters . . ." he whispered, suddenly putting the pieces of the puzzle together and realizing his worst fear had come true. The Americans and their gadget-happy Air Force *had* tricked them, using fighters to decoy them, thus leaving their main base back in East Germany virtually unprotected.

He looked up through his plexiglas canopy to see the large group of enemy fighters cruising high above them. He could tell immediately by the enemy planes' small profile that they were F-16s.

Suddenly his pilots were radioing him for orders. Were they to engage the enemy, or return to base? Like good Soviet pilots, they wouldn't proceed without his authorization.

He mentally reviewed his own orders—to engage and destroy the enemy bombers before they could launch their cruise missiles. But there were no bombers . . . And he knew the F-16s carried no cruise missiles—they were flying too fast.

But he could not return to his base with this blunder hanging over him. No—if his radar said the planes above him were bombers, then he would shoot them down as bombers.

"Engage!" he called out to his flight. "Bogies are ten or more F-16s! Keep high and watch your fuel consumption!"

At the same moment he was giving the orders, Gorshkov knew that his twin engine plane would use a lot of fuel dog-fighting the swift Falcons.

But it was too late to worry about that now. All that mattered to him now was shooting down at least some of the Americans to make up for the colossal mistake of having been lured halfway across Germany with a false radar signal.

He armed his cannon while he coaxed more speed out of the big engines, angrily rising to meet the F-16s above him.

Chapter 16

Hunter saw the big Flankers climbing up toward the rapidly descending Falcon squadron.

Instantly he sized up the impending engagement. The smaller F-16s had the advantage of speed because they were power diving. But the quickly shortening distance between the opposing forces would make it impossible to use their Sidewinders against the Soviets — the missiles would have to make too tight a turn.

However, Hunter knew their angle on the larger Flankers provided the F-16s with a big target for their powerful 20mm Vulcan rapid-fire cannons in their noses, a thought that Jones confirmed a second later.

"This will be a gunfight," he called out to the Falcon flight as now barely a mile separated the two forces. "One pass and back to the ranch."

Seconds later, staccato bursts of cannon flame thundered out as the two formations of fighter planes collided in the German skies.

Hunter deliberately held off firing until the range was so close he could see the Russian pilots' helmets in their forward-perched canopies.

Coming down from a steep angle, he targeted one of the Flankers in the second wing of the Soviet squadron. As enemy tracers whizzed by on either side of his canopy, he sighted through the HUD, then squeezed the trigger in three sharp bursts.

Hunter's first burst tore into the flat topside of the third Flanker's midsection, walking cannon shells back toward the twin tails, shattering the right engine and neatly slicing off the right rudder and stabilizer.

The fatally wounded Soviet plane yawed crazily across the sky before plummeting earthward in a death dive.

Just behind and to Hunter's left, Rico was furiously pumping cannon shells into another Flanker's cockpit. The big Soviet interceptor exploded in flames and Rico had to spin out to avoid flying through the debris that scattered through the formation.

Further to his right, Jones had made short work of another Soviet fighter, nearly carving it in two with successive bursts of cannon fire.

"Okay, flight, form up and withdraw," Jones called into the radio as most of the diving F-16s leveled off and regrouped up on his wing. The sharp, quick engagement had been picture perfect from the Americans' point of view. Jones knew that they didn't *have* to fight this batch of Soviet airplanes any longer—with the Flankers' fuel reserves all but gone, and their being way beyond their bingo point for return to their base in East Germany, the Soviet planes were as good as shot down already.

As one, the Falcon flight turned and were headed south-southwest at better than Mach 2, and Jones was waggling his wings at the frustrated Soviets, daring them to follow.

"See you later, suckers," he thought.

Wing Commander Gorshkov was nearly choking with rage.

He'd been caught too low, and the American fighters had torn through his squadron like wildcats, flaming three of his pilots without taking a single hit themselves. The Flanker's speed and size advantage was nullified by the steep climb they were forced to make to intercept the F-16s, and the smaller Falcons had accelerated right through and past them, streaking off to safety.

The fact that his own plane had been hit, and that he was losing fuel from his left wing tank was almost secondary. There was no way he and the others could return to their base anyway. He checked his other gauges, did some rapid mental calculations, and grimly made his decision.

Ordering the rest of the fighter wing to turn east and try to bail out over their own lines, he pointed his plane at the disappearing Americans and kicked both engines to full afterburner, rocketing through the skies toward the F-16s, his left wing trailing a steady vaporous wisp of raw fuel.

Within a minute he had caught up with the Americans. Sighting one of the F-16s trailing the main formation, Gorshkov tightened his grip on the stick and edged his finger around to the fire control button of his cannon. Another half mile, and he'd tear the American right out of the sky. His radar acquisition signal started chirping, flashing the information he needed to complete the attack.

Just a few more seconds . . .

It was his special intuition that had kept Hunter from rejoining the F-16 flight right away.

And now he knew why.

He had sensed the danger seconds before his radar beeped out the warning of one of the Flanker's relentless pursuit. Now, he was already pulling up and around to get a clean shot at the Soviet before he had a chance to fire at the trailing F-16.

Hunter watched the big Soviet jet close the distance until the F-16 pilot—Hunter thought it was Samuels—finally snap-rolled his airplane out of harm's way and back under his attacker.

As the Flanker tried to make the turn with the Falcon, Hunter saw the radar target-finder light up through his HUD. It flashed twice and glowed steadily. Quickly he armed a Sidewinder. This was his one and only shot—if he waited too long, the dogfighting planes in front of him would be too close and the 'Winder's infrared seeker might select either one of the speeding planes' hot exhausts.

Hunter took a gulp of oxygen and squeezed the missile release. Instantly, the AIM-9 roared off his wingtip toward the Flanker's tail, covering the distance in less than five seconds.

The Soviet pilot had just opened fire when Hunter's missile disappeared up into his left engine exhaust and exploded. The left side of the plane erupted in a blinding flash and poured out black smoke as flame devoured the entire left wing, spreading fire from the leaking fuel back along the length of the Flanker's fuselage.

The stricken Soviet shuddered, pushed through the sky by the billowing clouds of black smoke and flame behind it. Then it fell off on its left wing, spinning downward in a near-vertical dive.

Gorshkov had hit his eject button just in time. Propelled by small explosive bolts under his seat, the Soviet pilot was literally blown out of the Flanker's shattered cockpit. Spinning violently through the air, he was surprised his chute deployed at all.

Just barely conscious, the next sound Gorshkov heard as he floated to earth was the thunderclap of the impact as his plane buried itself in a German soybean field and burst into flames.

With his luck, the Soviet pilot thought, he would land right in the middle of the raging fire his downed aircraft had created.

Far below and circling around the black column of smoke that rose up from the burning Flanker, Hunter heard Jones report to the mission coordinator back in Belgium.

"Ringside, Ringside, this is Falcon leader," Jones intoned. "Left Jab is concluded. Repeat . . . Left Jab concluded. Confirm three—no, four kills. One friendly down. Bandits heading east, but we believe they are past their bingos."

"Roger, Falcon flight," came the clipped reply.

"Please advise appropriate elements to commence Roundhouse," Jones continued. "Repeat, cue Roundhouse! Advise results on completion. Falcon Flight leader returning to base. Over and out."

Hunter had joined the F-16 formation just as Jones had finished his report. Taking up his usual position on the general's wing, they led the victorious Falcons back toward Rota.

Chapter 17

The US Air Force FB-111s were already circling over friendly airspace in West Germany when the order from Ringside came through on the designated channel.

Cranking their tapered wings in toward their narrow fuselages, the big tactical bombers dashed across the East German border, their powerful turbofan engines pouring out more than 50,000 pounds of thrust and moving plane, pilots, and payloads at Mach 2.5 toward their destination.

A truly schizophrenic aircraft, the F-111 was either a very big combat fighter or a very small heavy bomber, designed to do both jobs for the Air Force in the late '60's. The first of several swing-wing supersonic planes, some pilots swore by it while others swore *at* it. The complex variable-sweep wings gave it enormous flexibility in its combat mission capabilities: With wings spread out it had the lift necessary for take-offs, landings, and low-level bombing runs. With the wings swept back, it could penetrate enemy airspace at high levels doing more than twice the speed of sound to deliver a nuclear payload.

But the "Aardvark," as it was called with varying degrees of affection, was also a tough plane to handle in spite of the tons of sophisticated flight control computers that assisted the pilot.

A complex terrain-avoidance radar system would keep the plane down on the deck—usually at an altitude of 200 feet or lower—automatically maintaining a constant height over mountains, trees, hedgerows and buildings. A pilot could kick in the terrain-avoidance gear and be treated to a dizzying roller coaster ride through the treetops—very effective for coming in under an enemy's radar defenses. Not so diligent in settling one's stomach.

The FB-111s streaking toward Soviet Air Wing headquarters at Neurippin were the tactical bomber variants, carrying a massive dual payload of special runway-cratering blockbusters and incendiary cluster bombs on their wing points.

Crossing the East German border, the Aardvarks switched over to their terrain-following radar flight control and dropped to the terrifyingly low altitude of 200 feet, still doing Mach 2. Their high speed and tree-top level would bring them in low and fast enough to avoid Soviet fighters.

But there was another threat to be wary of: there was a possibility that the Soviets might have already rushed in mobile anti-aircraft radar units to replace the SAM launchers destroyed by the Wild Weasels.

To counter this threat, a specially configured EF-111A "Raven" flew slightly ahead of the main flight of F-111s. Bulging at the seams with radar detection and suppression equipment, should the Soviets light up their active search radars, the Raven's powerful jammers would fill the enemy's screens with a blizzard of electronic "snow," thus giving the bomber flight a clear shot at the target.

Meanwhile, the Soviet base commander at Neurippen was facing a tough decision.

He had long ago lost all contact with the flight of Flankers that had been launched to stop what had been thought of at the time to be a massive force of cruise-missile-toting B-52s. The last of the surviving Flankers had gone down 150 miles short of the base, empty of fuel, its pilot reporting the

Americans' masking deception before ejecting. The base commander cursed that there were no Soviet in-flight refueling aircraft available to him to save the Flankers, although he knew that these airplanes were a rare commodity even in the best of times.

Now, the commander had two critical points to consider. Another flight of Flankers—these belonging to the Polish Air Force—were coming in from a rear base near Warsaw and were due to land at his base within minutes. Meanwhile, he had sixteen aircraft of his own lined up on the runway, ready to take off for an aggressive patrol just west of the demarcation line between the Germanys. This flight, originally scheduled for earlier in the morning, had been delayed by the American F-4 attack.

But now the Soviet commander was about to disobey one of the tenets of warfare; that was, exposing the majority of his forces at one time. In peacetime, it would be routine for them to launch the 16-airplane patrol flight and recover the Polish Flankers all at once.

But in wartime, it was a gigantic risk.

By allowing the fighters—both those taking off and those landing—to cluster on the open runways, he would leave himself wide open for disaster should the enemy strike.

Standing in the huge base's control tower, he glanced out at the crews struggling to mount a temporary radar antenna for the base's single mobile SAM launcher. This was another point of contention with him. How could he be expected to defend such a critical base with only a single, back-up SAM?

He blew his nose and yearned for a glass of vodka. The lack of reserve SAMs was more evidence that Moscow had been ill-advised if not downright insane to start this campaign—this entire war—when it did. Although he was certain that NATO wasn't quite aware of it yet, the massive chemical strike on Western Europe two days before had been as much a surprise to the Soviet forward commanders as it must have been to the NATO commanders themselves. None of the advance Soviet military units in Europe had had any indication that their government was about to launch World War III. And as such, none of them was prepared for the struggle.

Why did they do it? the commander had asked himself over and over again. More importantly, how could they possibly win a war that had started such as this one?

He shook away the disturbing thoughts and looked back at the SAM crew. The anti-aircraft battery would be operational in moments—when it was, he could take the chance and land the incoming Polish fighters, while at the same time launching the long-delayed 16-airplane patrol.

It would turn out to be the most disastrous decision of his long military career.

The FB-111s descended on the Soviet airfield just moments after the last of the Polish Flankers had landed.

With no SAMs operational, the Soviets were trapped, horrendously exposed on the runways. The first wave of Aardvarks thundered over the cluttered base, dumping thousands of incendiary bomblets in wide patterns among the grounded planes. Explosions erupted across the entire width of the main runway as the firebombs did their deadly work, touching off hundreds of separate fires that quickly joined forces, engulfing planes, fuel storage, hangars, and dozens of ground personnel with yellow-orange sheets of flame.

The mobile SAM launcher that the Soviets had counted on to defend their base was one of the first victims of the raid. Even while its screens were being jammed by the EF-111 Raven, a Rockeye cannister, dropped by one of the lead Aardvarks, impacted squarely on it, killing the radar crew and destroying the battery.

The FB-111s swept around for another pass at higher altitude, this time loosing their special runway-cratering bombs on the base's now-flaming airstrips. The weapons tumbled off the wing points of the FB-111s and began a swift free-fall as their pointed steel noses aimed straight down at the burning mess below.

As they accelerated toward the ground, a spinning airspeed sensor tripped a small charge in the tail of each bomb, which fired a rocket to propel the explosive lances downward at more than 2,000 miles per hour.

The speeding darts struck the burning runways and burrowed almost ten feet into the hard concrete before their warheads detonated, sending huge chunks of concrete flying through the air. Flaming planes reared up as the heaving runways snapped and buckled beneath them, leaving giant craters jagged with rusted ends of snapped reinforcing rods to mark the bombs' devastating handiwork.

The final blow was delivered with Mk 80 500-pound conventional bombs, laser-sighted in directly on the base's two control towers, repair hangars, and barracks complex. Multiple explosions shook the ground as the bombs were detonated shortly after impacting their targets.

Survivors raced to escape the flames and destruction that tore through the shattered air base, once the proud headquarters of an entire Soviet Air Wing.

Scampering back over the horizon from which they had come, the FB-111s cranked in their wings and floored their powerful engines to race for the border and the comparative safety of their base in Belgium.

Hunter heard Jones receive the terse preliminary report from Ringside, the mission coordinator.

It was almost noon now and they were well on their way back to Rota. The three-pronged raid on Neuruppin had been a smashing success. Similar, though lower-scale, missions carried out by combined US and other allied air forces, had also gone off well. In a little more than six hours, hundreds of NATO aircraft had been carefully choreographed to inflict a heavy toll on the Warsaw Pact's forward airfields and strike planes.

But they would have to wait until they were back at Rota to get the full results—and casualty reports—over secure communications channels.

Casualties. Hunter thought about DuPont again. What bothered him most was the guy never had a chance to shoot back. The big Soviet air-to-air missile, with enough explosive power to smash a strategic bomber, had obliterated the F-16 in a split-second.

And worst of all, it wasn't supposed to happen—they were just decoys . . .

Why DuPont? Why today? How many other pilots had cashed in their tickets in this first full engagement of the war? How many more before it was over? Indeed, Hunter knew that DuPont was just a small part of the war's horrifying toll.

On the return trip, the pilot they called the Wingman surveyed the devastated West German countryside, ravaged by the ghastly Soviet chemical munitions that rained down on it two days before. Looking down from his aerial vantage point, Hunter could just imagine the attack that had laid waste to this once-fertile land. The poisonous Valkyries, riding down on their winged SCUD missile steeds, had brought death everlasting in a cruel mockery of the promised land.

Now here there was only death, pitiful and agonizing, for warriors and innocents alike.

Dead livestock dotted the snow-covered hills, dark spots that stained the quiet white blanket. Likewise, the autobahns were crammed with cars, some twisted into huge, still smoking pile-ups caused as their drivers, fleeing the poisonous gas, died in agony at the wheel. Here and there bodies were strewn outside the smashed cars, victims flung out by the force of the collisions or propelled by their last dying gasps, trying to escape the very air that carried death.

Safe but not secure in the artificial bubble world of his F-16 cockpit, Hunter saw masses of bodies littered around the city of Frankfurt. The streets were clogged with carnage, spilling out beyond the city limits in straggling dry rivers of corpses that marked the futile attempts of the denizens to escape the gas attack.

Only death as far as the eye could see. No motion, no life, just death. Once again the Black Spectre had visited Europe. Centuries before it had come in the guise of the plague and had wiped out more than a quarter of the population. Now it needed no natural mask—man had invented terrifying new means to improve on nature's destructive powers.

"Vengeance is mine," thought Hunter as he flew over the

grisly tableau of pestilence below. He looked over at Jones, who was scanning the countryside too, undoubtedly thinking much the same thoughts.

There would be vengeance enough to go around . . .

Chapter 18

Back at Rota, Hunter landed directly behind Jones, bringing the F-16 in for a flawless three-point landing.

He taxied off the main runway onto a cross-strip, waiting as a long stream of C-17s and C-5As trundled across his path, lining up for their takeoffs back to the States on a parallel strip.

He felt their jet wash rock his plane from side to side as their big engines pushed them along at faster and faster speeds, finally heaving the groaning behemoths into the air near the end of the runway. Hunter watched, thinking how improbable it must seem to those less familiar with aerodynamics to see more than a hundred tons of metal machine become airborne.

The transports went past, and he slowly maneuvered the fighter toward the specially constructed hardstands that now housed the aircraft of the 16th TFW.

Inside the gray caverns were fueling stations, munitions loaders, and repair facilities for the F-16s. The thick concrete walls were designed to withstand almost anything the Soviets could throw at them, short of a nuke. And if it got to that point, Hunter reminded himself, it wouldn't much matter where the hell the planes were if they were still on the ground.

Oddly the hardstands and hangars still carried the markings and insignia of the US Navy, and their overlarge dimensions bore testimony to the fact that they were actually designed for the big P-3C Orions of the Navy's anti-sub patrol. When the war broke out, a flight of Orions had been shuffled around to provide a home for the 16th TFW's smaller F-16s.

Originally the F-16s would have been based up north at the NATO base in Torrejon, near Madrid. That sprawling airfield and support facility had been constructed at great expense by the Air Force, and it was virtually dedicated to the F-16 fighters which had been its primary residents. The 16th would have shared the base with the 72 Falcons that formerly comprised the 401st TAC Air Wing, joining in their defense of NATO's vulnerable southern flank with close air support and interception missions.

But several years before, politics had reared its ugly head to deny NATO the use of the base. The Spanish government at the time thought the bases were too "provocative." So the F-16s were stuck on the "ass-end of Europe" instead of being hundreds of miles closer to the battle.

Hunter forced himself not to dwell on the stupid political decision that had forced the F-16s to fly out of Rota. He wasn't a politician—he was a soldier. As such, he was supposedly trained to fly and fight anywhere.

After turning the F-16 over to the ground crew, Hunter quickly headed for the briefing room to get the lowdown from Jones on their recent mission.

He found the small room nearly overflowing with pilots. The general was already there, analyzing the communiques and trying to evaluate the results of the surprise anti-airfield strike they'd just conducted. Still in his flight suit and puffing on a fresh cigar, the senior officer was sifting through a mountain of paper, poring over the coded messages coming through from airbases around Europe, and from the mission coordinator in Belgium. Finally, he made some notes, tapped a few numbers into a small handheld calculator, and turned to the pilots who were buzzing around in small groups or talking to the debriefing officers at tables around the room's periphery.

All eyes turned toward the small podium as Jones approached it, paper in hand.

"Gentlemen," he begun formally, "it gives me great pleasure to report the preliminary results of Operation Punchout, our strike against the Soviets' forward air bases. We won't be able to verify all the data for some time, but the indications are that we did considerable damage to most of their forward airfields."

Spontaneous cheering erupted from the tired pilots, elated to know their mission had been a success.

"Intelligence estimates that most will be inoperable for at least two weeks," Jones continued. "Some even longer . . ."

There was another round of cheers.

"We also have a preliminary report that states we took out more than three hundred enemy aircraft during the operation, most of them on the ground."

More cheering.

Then Jones's voice took on a sobering tone.

"NATO losses," he said gravely, "were thirty-seven aircraft. Ten Weasels went down either over the SAM belt or the Soviet airfields. The biggest single loss involved a squadron of twelve Luftwaffe Tornados coming in for Roundhouse. They were jumped by MiGs that managed to get off the ground early. All were lost. A dozen decoy planes in all were shot down, including DuPont here of the Sixteenth."

An awkward hush fell over the roomful of pilots, remembering their comrade who would never return. Jones quietly explained that a NATO search and rescue team had been sent to the crash site minutes after it happened, but there was nothing that anyone could have done.

The mood only got worse as Jones revealed another map of the battle zone, this one indicating the latest intelligence on the ground fighting.

Despite the vast success of Operation Punchout, it was clear to everyone in the room that the situation on the ground was getting worse for NATO. Judging from the spreading red arrows on Jones's briefing map, it was apparent that Soviet armor, obviously equipped with CBW decontamination gear, had began pouring into desolate, lifeless West Germany like an iron tidal wave. All indications were that the main force of the Red Army was driving fast and furiously toward cities like Frankfurt, Mannheim, Karlsruhe and Bonn.

And the only thing in between were the scattered NATO rear guard ground forces.

Even before the Red Army had made its move into West Germany, SACEUR (Supreme Allied Commander, Europe) ordered most of the NATO heavy armored units to fall back as planned in a measured withdrawal to more defensible positions, behind the Rhine. Within 12 hours of the Soviet attack, most of these NATO units were in motion, moving deliberately westward through the chemical-contaminated wasteland that Germany had become.

But not everyone was taking part in this dreary, strategic retreat.

Someone had to stay behind and slow the Red surge. In one area—it being designated by several blue dots on Jones's map—this unenviable task fell to several US and German artillery units both equipped with big 155mm self-propelled howitzers, some US Army Armored Cavalry forces, and a brigade of German national guard forces, the *Landwehr*. With little more than sheer guts, this delaying force would stay behind and set up ambushes for the Soviets advancing on roadways in central West Germany.

The cluster of blue dots was labeled NATO Blue Force Charlie. Jones pointed to their position on the map and said grimly: "Of all the rear guard groups, these guys are going to get hit the worst—almost point-blank. But they're buying precious time for the armored units, who are going to need every second of it to establish positions west of the Rhine."

Poor bastards, Hunter thought. He knew the projected casualty rate for the lightly armored anti-tank units was more than ninety percent, and that was under a normal battle scenario.

And there would be nothing normal about this . . .

But he also realized that their nearly hopeless stand might make the critical difference between the clash of armored titans that would surely follow. Without their rear guard effort, the Soviets might catch up and overwhelm the retreating NATO armor before it had a chance to establish a defensible position behind the Rhine, and that would seriously affect NATO's "strategic withdrawal" plan.

So the artillerymen and the Armored Cav and the German national guardsmen would all have to be thrown to the sacrifice. It was a grim fact of war, but that didn't make giving the orders any easier.

"Now, depending on the results of their initial encounter, we're going to give these guys in Blue Force Charlie as much help as possible," Jones said. "We'll be taking off soon to provide close

134

air support for the main armor counterstrike.

"Of course, other air units will be doing the same all up and down the line, and, judging from our success against the enemy forward air bases, enemy air activity should be scattered at best."

Jones took a puff of his cigar, then continued: "Now if we're successful, we can stall the main Soviet thrust and the Army boys will have some breathing room to set up some better defensive positions behind the Rhine."

"And if we fail?" JT asked. "What happens if the whole front collapses?"

Jones didn't so much as wince. "Then," he said soberly, "the Soviets will reach Paris in less than two weeks."

In the cold sunlight of the central German plain, the first steps of the deadly dance had already begun.

Oberleutnant Gunter Wessel of the *Bundewehr's* Second Artillery Battery shivered inside his parka as he stood beside his massive 155mm self-propelled gun and watched the empty stretch of road before him through his powerful Hasselblad binoculars.

He knew that very soon a torrent of Soviet armor would be moving down this particular section of rural roadway. And with the pullout several hours before of the last of the other NATO armor units, he and his men and their six big guns were alone against the Red Army.

Wessel checked his watch, then barked out a command to his gunnery sergeant. The sergeant yanked the lanyard of the M-198 155mm howitzer and a deafening report echoed through the woods where Wessel's mobile guns had dug in. The howitzer leaped back a few feet from the recoil of the shot and spat a long cylindrical projectile out into the frigid afternoon sky.

At precisely 200 feet over the spot they had aimed, the howitzer shell opened, allowing nine small parachutes to escape and float to earth. The chutes gently deposited their loads onto the hard-packed frozen road surface some three kilometers in front of Wessel's emplacement.

The German officer did some quick calculations, then called out another order to fire. Another explosion shook the ground beneath his feet. This time the small parachutes came to rest just

135

beyond the first set, slightly off to the side of the road.

Four more shells, 36 more parachutes. Five minutes later, Wessel was confident that the road was adequately sewn with the deadly, air-delivered mines.

He nodded curtly at the gunnery sergeant and gave a new order to train the howitzer's long barrel down at the highway a few hundred meters beyond the spot where the mines were laid. Satisfied with their preparedness, he climbed up on his 155mm self-propelled gun, directing the driver to move the clanking artillery piece to a position further forward and to the left. Now all they had to do was wait for the enemy armored column.

It seemed like an eternity, but actually only forty minutes went by before they first heard the sound.

It was faint at first, but relentlessly, it became louder and louder. While the tanks were still unseen in the distance, the German artillerymen almost had to block their ears, so deafening was the remorseless squeaking, clanking, and grinding of hundreds of tracked metal monsters rolling down the road in front of them.

The tension was maddening as they waited for the advancing armored column . . .

Finally the enemy armor came into view on the narrow road. In the lead was a Soviet T-80, their newest main battle tank. Like the rest of the column, the leader's tank was completely "buttoned-up"—hatches sealed to protect the crew inside. The column stretched out behind him in a seemingly endless green line, a traffic jam of weaponry, dwarfing the country road and even the forest around it.

Closer and closer the lead T-80 came, nearing the spot in the road where Wessel's artillery had lobbed their lethal surprise. But the Soviets were moving too fast to see the thin wires projecting up from the flat discs on the roadbed.

Evidently, they had been ordered to make a rapid advance, and that was exactly what they were doing, though not as cautiously as the situation dictated.

Wessel's grip instinctively tightened on the binoculars.

"Just twenty-five meters more, and for you, the war will be over," the young German officer thought darkly, his eyes on the lead enemy tank, hoping it would continue its blind advance.

It did. The lead T-80 made contact with the first artillery-scattered M718 mine, pushing the thin detonating wire forward until it triggered the powerful explosive charge contained in the shallow conical disc.

The force of the mine's explosion was directed upward at the heavily armored belly of the T-80, punching a hole in the tank's armor just underneath the driver. The driver never heard the exploding mine, since a jagged piece of shredded armor plating tore through his head, entering just under his chin and exiting through the back of his helmet.

The driver collapsed on the tank's controls, lurching the vehicle across the highway until it struck a second mine, which tore its left tread to pieces.

The serpentine track flattened itself out as the roller wheels and sprockets continued to spin, ratcheting more of the steel tread through the one-way cycle until the torn end escaped the last wheel and the fifty-ton metal monster ground to a halt.

A second tank, moving at the same speed, had attempted to go around the leader's stricken vehicle on the right. But it too struck one of the artillery-scattered mines and exploded in an ugly black cloud. The third tank in line slammed into the leader's lurching, track-thrown T-80 as it plowed around to the left.

The rest of the tanks and armored personnel carriers came to a shuddering stop, blocked by the three wrecked tanks in front of them, and penned in by the thick woods on either side of the road.

A Soviet infantry squad, clad in bulky anti-chemical winter gear, burst forth from one of the BMP-2 armored personnel carriers that was traveling with the tank column. Moving clumsily in the heavy, protective clothing, the Soviets didn't see the thin detonation wires of the M692 anti-personnel mines laid by the German artillery battery.

Their squad leader tripped the first mine.

Instantly, the explosive charge shot a lethal circle of metal fragments into the hapless Soviet soldiers, killing most of them, including the squad leader, whose legs were completely severed by the blast.

Wessel watched the scene through the powerful binoculars, quietly relaying new coordinates to the artillerymen in his battery, who in turn were adjusting the position of the M109's big 155mm gun by slight degrees. At the same time, the other five artillery crews were coordinating their fire control with Wessel's, each targeting a different section of the roadway that was now jammed with Soviet armor.

The young German officer took a deep breath and raised his arm once more, knowing that both his gunnery sergeant and radio operator were riveting their attention on his gloved hand, waiting for the signal.

Exhaling a cloud of vapor into the cold air, he dropped his hand and shouted the order to fire. The six big guns spoke with one, terrifying thunderclap that rolled into the sky. Puffs of black smoke emerged from their muzzles as the heavy M483 shells roared away toward the enemy.

At the precise moment, each warhead sprouted eighty-eight bomblets which rained down on the enemy armor and infantry. More than two thirds of these were anti-armor shape charges that landed on the tops of several Soviet tanks and detonated with a downward-directed explosion, blowing holes in the thin top armor and randomly killing crews with shrapnel and flames.

The rest were anti-personnel fragmentation bomblets, which exploded among the infantry who were dismounting from their BMP-2's to clear the wreckage from the front of the column. The deadly metal shards tore through the crowded groups of Red soldiers, literally and horribly shredding them. The narrow roadway was quickly a mixture of blood and black smoke, columns of which were rising from the wrecks of burning tanks.

The shells continued to fall, creating a chaos which raged through the Soviet column. Wessel had given the order for independent fire to each artillery crew, as the billowing smoke and burning tanks made it difficult to identify individual targets. His own M109 self-propelled gun was continuing to pump shells into the forward end of the column, trying to disable more tanks in the crowded roadbed that cut through the deep forest.

But soon enough the Soviet armor began to fight back.

The T-80s' 125mm main guns answered the shots as they tried to pinpoint the muzzle-flashes of the German artillery pieces. Shells began to whistle through the trees around Wessel's position as the Soviet gunners searched for the range. A huge explosion behind him and to the right told Wessel that one of the enemy tanks had found part of his ammunition supply.

Then, from farther back in the Soviet column, several big self-propelled assault guns raised their 203mm barrels skyward. Though they were well behind the front end of the Soviet column, their range was being provided by the forward tank crews. Soon the huge projectiles were landing with deadly accuracy on the NATO positions.

Wessel saw two fixed gun emplacements explode under the heavy barrages, and reluctantly decided to give the order to withdraw. The remaining M109s could still drop back to safer positions and keep pouring indirect fire from longer range.

Wessel crisply relayed the order, but he would never know if it was carried out.

As he put down the radio handset, a Russian 203mm high-explosive shell struck the top of his M109 self-propelled artillery piece, piercing the thin armor before it exploded within the gun's belly. A convulsive explosion shook the big tracked vehicle, lifting its thirty tons into the air as a firecracker would a tin can. Fire and shrapnel ripped through the crowded interior of the gun, setting everything inside aflame and exploding the stored ammo in a huge fireball that blew the barrel clear off the tracks and left jagged, charred edges of metal curling outward from the flaming hull.

Even before Wessel could utter a short prayer that he and his comrades would not have died in vain, he perished in the raging inferno along with his crew.

Chapter 19

For the second time that day, the F-16s of the 16th took off, grouped up somewhere over central Spain and, as one, headed for the war zone.

During the flight, Hunter reviewed the main points of Jones's briefing.

The 16th's mission to aid Blue Dog Charlie seemed like a routine ground support operation—the kind they'd practiced endlessly back at Nellis.

The F-16 itself was better than average at close air support. But for this mission, the 16th's primary concern would be to provide air cover for a flight of A-10A Thunderbolts. It was the 'Bolts mission to destroy Soviet armor as the recently reactivated airplane had been designed and built specifically for that purpose.

What was definitely *not* routine was Jones's revelation that a B-52G Stratofortress would be joining them while the mission was in progress. Its payload was classified, the general had explained, but . . .

"When you guys hear that bomber crew call out for 'Copperhead strike,' " he had told them, "make damn sure you clear the battle area immediately—and I mean a good three-mile clearance."

Hunter had guessed that Copperhead had something to do

with a new anti-armor weapon, but he kept his speculation to himself. If Jones had wanted them to know, he'd have explained it in the briefing.

He filed the codeword away in his mind and continued his mental preparation for the mission.

US Army Colonel Keith LaRochelle looked through his field glasses again, peering at the black column of smoke rising up from the eastern horizon.

Burning tanks, he thought. He could almost *smell* them.

Climbing up through the hatch of his own Abrams M1A1 tank, he reviewed the defensive positions his unit—the 1/32 Armored Battalion of the US Army Armored Cav—had just taken up a few hours ago.

On either side, his squad of armored beasts lay in their defiladed lairs, silent but alert, waiting for the enemy.

Just north of his position were the Leopard IIs of the German Sixth Panzer Division, dug into the soil of their homeland, awaiting the desperate battle with the invading Soviets.

LaRochelle didn't pause for longer than a moment to consider the possibility that in the upcoming German-Soviet face-off, perhaps, among the two armored armies, were men whose grandfathers had faced each other in the Second World War at places like Kursk or Stalingrad.

No, he was not in the mood for historical irony today. The armored spearhead of the Red Army was driving relentlessly forward, apparently straight toward his position. His last intelligence report indicated that he would soon be facing an enemy tank column containing at least sixty times the armored vehicles that he and the defending Germans could muster at the point of attack.

It was by no choice that he and his men were part of the rear guard action. The Germans were defending their homeland—he and his men were just simply following orders.

Their line of defense was an open field about 60 kilometers east of Frankfurt, close by a bend in the Main River. As overall commander of the allied force, LaRochelle had arranged the tanks in a ragged crescent arching around the edges of the field.

The deployment was thin at some points, but at least his tanks would have some cover. They would need every advantage that their technology and tactics could offer them against the oncoming Soviets and their superior numbers. Before the war broke out, NATO critics often said that the West didn't need to match the Red Army weapon-for-weapon because their quality would triumph over the Soviet quantity. LaRochelle knew, however, that in an armored clash like this, quantity had a quality all its own.

As was always the case, he heard the approaching tanks before he saw them. Their incessant clanking and grinding forewarned of their appearance like the dragging chain of an intruding ghost—an army of intruding ghosts.

It won't be long now, he thought.

He theorized that the unit of German self-propelled guns that had dug in five klicks from his present position had slowed up the Soviets as planned, and bloodied them in the process. But he also knew that the German artillerymen were most likely wiped out for their effort and that their action—just like this one—had been nothing less than suicidal.

With this dire thought in mind, LaRochelle slid through the Abram's open top hatch and pulled it shut behind him, dogging the heavy hatch cover. Whatever else happened, he and his crew would be inside the belly of their armored beast for the duration.

The American officer had eased his tank up against a shallow rock formation at the edge of a stand of trees. The gray, flat shapes rose just high enough to allow the long 120mm barrel of his tank to rest almost on top of the table-like slab. The granite-like mass would protect them against almost anything but a direct hit.

He now turned his attention toward the battlefield before him.

As the TC (Tank Commander), LaRochelle was in charge of target acquisition. Five minutes later, his first target came into range.

It was a Soviet tank platoon—three T-80s—moving across the vast field at high speed in a wedge at his 11 o'clock. Obviously a scouting unit from the main column, the trio of tanks were approximately one and a half kilometers away.

"Gunner!—Sabot!—Three tanks at one and half clicks, eleven o'clock!—left tank first!" LaRochelle shouted, grasping his turret override handle and slewing the big turret to the left.

"Identified!" the young gunner called back in reply, seeing the Soviet tank appear in his Thermal Imaging Sight (TIS), glowing brightly against the background color of phosphorescent green.

LaRochelle immediately released the override. The third man in the turret, the loader, slammed a 120-millimeter sabot armor-penetrating round into the breech, yelling excitedly as he threw forward the gun-safety switch.

"Round up, sir!"

It was the same routine they performed endlessly in training. But as this was the real thing, apprehension hung heavy in the cramped turret. The gunner manipulated his Cadillacs—the big control yokes that bore the Cadillac-Gage inscription were the primary turret rotation control handles—and centered the Soviet tank in the crosshairs of the TIS reticle. He pressed the range-finder button with his thumb, activating the M-1's laser sighting fire control system.

Meanwhile, the loader had pressed against a bar switch with his left knee, sliding open the blast door to the ammo compartment at the rear of the turret. He reached up for another round lying snugly in the stowage rack. Grasping, twisting, and pulling the retaining handle with one fluid motion, the loader slid the bullet-like round out of its stowage tube and into his arms. Firmly cradling the round, he pressed the knee-switch again, and the blast door slid shut. The entire process took perhaps three seconds.

The gunner peered into the rangefinder sight again, in time to see the number "1450" appear below the TIS reticle, indicating the distance to the target in meters.

"Round ready, sir!"

"Gun ready, sir!"

"*Fire!*" LaRochelle's voice rang in the crew's earphones.

Scarcely was the word out of his mouth when the gunner responded.

"*On* the way!" he hollered, squeezing the trigger-like firing switches on the Cadillacs. Instantly the turret reverberated with a dull thud as the gun breech jerked backward, absorbing the recoil.

Watching intently through the eyepiece of his TIS extension,

LaRochelle saw the speeding shell heading right for the left side enemy tank, in the process shedding the shoe-like bushing that held the armor-penetrating rod in the center of the cartridge. A second later the Soviet tank disappeared behind a brilliant flash, followed by a shower of sparks as the round hit home.

The pyrophoric effect of the M-829 round's depleted-uranium penetrator turned the T-80's turret into an instantaneous inferno. The stricken vehicle lurched to a stop, giant blowtorches of flame shooting out of its blown-open hatches as its stowed ammunition began to ignite.

"Hit!" the American officer yelled out, almost unconsciously adding: "Jesus, we actually hit the Goddamn thing . . ."

Meanwhile, the cartridge-case stub of the spent round fell out of the breechlock and into a bag dangling below. The tank was filled with the acrid smell of the round's burnt gases. Still the loader was ready, anticipating the next shot as he shoved the new round into the still-smoking breech and threw the safety-switch with a yell.

"Round up!" He then turned back to the ammo compartment to begin the whole reloading process again.

"Next target!" LaRochelle shouted exultantly, watching as another shell from his wingman's tank blew up the rightmost enemy tank.

"Next tank — fire and adjust!" he announced.

Taking out the last of the three Soviet scout tanks was now totally in the hands of the gunner-loader team. Their confidence boosted by the first-shot, first-hit, the pair of American enlisted men fired the next shell with ruthless efficiency, blowing the T-80's engine to bits in just under 40 seconds.

LaRochelle was already searching out new targets. Scanning through the split-shaped vision blocks ringing his turret cupola, he saw a Soviet BMP-2 infantry fighting vehicle behind a low earthen berm. Prone Soviet infantrymen were clustered in front of the vehicle. Two of the infantrymen were kneeling; one was holding an RPG-16 anti-tank rocket launcher.

It took LaRochelle a moment to realize the enemy soldiers were aiming the missile directly at him. . . .

"Damn," he hissed.

Frantically, he twisted the turret's override controls, at the same instant yelling: "Gunner—HEAT—RPG squad!" into the inter-com.

"Round up!" The loader screamed as he whipped an M830 HEAT—high-explosive anti-tank—round into the breech. As the turret slewed right, the gunner bellowed his acknowledgment and switched the main gun selector switch to COAX.

"Load co-ax!" LaRochelle yelled to the loader, who reached forward and yanked the charging handle of the 7.62mm M240 machine gun mounted coaxially with the main gun.

"Co-ax up!" the loader screamed in reply, confirming the rapid-fire machine gun was armed and ready to fire.

There was no time for the tank crew to use the sophisticated laser rangefinder. The Russian RPG squad would be firing in less than ten seconds and the powerful rocket-propelled grenade could disable the tank, if not destroy it. They had to eyeball the range, hoping that any close shot in the general vicinity of the Soviets might make the RPG gunner's aim a little less deliberate, giving the American tank the split-second it needed.

Normally, it was not possible to fire the tank's main gun and the coaxially mounted machine gun simultaneously, but LaRo-chelle had an experienced crew, and he had taught them well.

Squeezing the Cadillacs' triggers, the gunner sent a stream of machine gun tracer rounds arcing over the heads of the stunned RPG team. At the same time, he twisted the manual firing handle near his left knee—this was the "master blaster," an electrome-chanical firing mechanism for the tank's 120mm main gun.

Charged by the master blaster's spark, the big gun roared again, sending a bright orange tongue of flame out of the end of the Abram's barrel. The shot screamed over the heads of the clustered infantry but plowed smack into the BMP, which erupted in a mushroom-shaped orange fireball. Still fingering the Cadil-lacs, the gunner adjusted his aim down one half-mil and once again pressed the machine gun triggers.

This time the tracers streamed directly into the kneeling form of the RPG gunner, cutting the forward Soviet infantryman in two at the waist. His partner, wounded as well, looked up from his own bloody legs to see the revolting scene, then passed out.

LaRochelle was too busy to watch the RPG crew die; and he had no time to congratulate his gunner on the shot. In a treeline at nine o'clock from a range of just two thousand meters, he saw a peculiar flash and a cloud of smoke. A shudder ran through him — he'd seen enough training films to identify it as an anti-tank guided missile, probably a Soviet AT-4 "Spigot."

"Sagger! Sagger! Sagger!" he yelled, keying the microphone in his Combat Vehicle Crewman (CVC) headgear to the "transmit" position. It was the universal NATO warning for an anti-tank missile attack. Instantly all the tanks on CVC frequency began to move. Abandoning their hiding places, the tanks began driving evasively, jinking back and forth crazily in an effort to give the Soviet missileers tougher targets to hit.

Their turbine engine whined as LaRochelle's driver reacted to the implied command, moving the tank backward out of its battle position snug against the rock formation.

Looking through the vision blocks, LaRochelle estimated that they would have another twenty meters to cross before they were screened from the missile's path.

"Driver! Jink for you life! Go! Go! Go!" the tank commander hollered into the intercom.

The driver needed no further encouragement. He wheeled the tank madly to the left, hoping to present a more difficult target while also shifting to a forward gear to make a faster getaway.

It was too late. Instantaneously the sixty-ton tank was shaken by a terrific blast. Each crewman rose out of his seat as flakes of paint showered down from the turret walls and roof. Dust rose from every nook and cranny, filling the air inside the turret. Wiring-harnesses, binoculars, kit-bags, notebooks, ration-packs, and other equipment were torn loose from retaining brackets, stowage trays and hiding places.

LaRochelle's head was filled with a loud ringing. Were it not for the hearing protection provided by their CVC headgear, the whole crew would have been completely deafened.

"Driver!" he yelled above the reverb echoing in his ears, hoping that the stricken tank could still maneuver. Through the vision blocks the TC saw the smoking hulk of his wingman's tank to the right. He reached for the keying switch on his radio microphone, issuing the orders for the unit to withdraw to the next line of battle positions. When he heard no static, he realized that the hit had knocked out the tank's radio.

"Driver—Move out—Position Bravo—Route Blue!" he yelled. He said a silent prayer that the surviving tankers would begin their withdrawal once the word was passed. He saw other Abrams throwing rooster tails of fine snow behind them, and he knew they'd gotten the word. He hoped that the Soviets would not be able to get any shots at them en route to the next position. That last hit had been too close for comfort.

"Crew report!" LaRochelle announced over the intercom—at least *that* was still working.

"Gunner up! Computer inop—turret power up," said the man just below and in front of the tank commander.

"Driver up—engine's hot," answered the unseen driver from his position in the forward belly of the big tank.

"Loader up! Ammo door's jammed!" the loader called out from the depths of the still-smoky turret interior.

LaRochelle realized then that the Soviet missile must have penetrated the auxiliary ammunition compartment at the turret's left rear corner. The terrific explosion that had rocked them was caused by several rounds of main gun ammo detonating simultaneously.

Fortunately, the blast door had prevented the explosion from entering the turret, instead causing it to exit through blow-out panels in the top of the ammo compartment. Had their vehicle been an old M60 "Patton"—which lacked such a sealed compartment—the missile would almost certainly have killed everyone in the tank.

He was never more glad that he was riding in an M1A1 Abrams.

Momentarily just thankful to be alive, LaRochelle soon realized that he and his crew were still in a jam. They were still facing the large Soviet column in a tank with no communications, an inoperative fire-control system, and all they had to throw at the enemy were three HEAT rounds that were stowed in the ready rack next to the main gun.

The American commander knew that his tank force had taken out several enemy vehicles—certainly more than they'd lost themselves. But the Soviets were still rolling forward across the open field with waves of armor.

LaRochelle looked at the three meager shells in the ready rack, and at the grime-streaked faces of the other two men in the turret. He cursed the silent radio, wondering how they could hope to stop the Red Army's juggernaut.

He thought it would take nothing less than a miracle to save them all. . . .

Chapter 20

Hunter was the first one to see the long green streams of Soviet armor.

It looked just like a flood. The enemy tanks and BMPs were spilling out onto the German countryside, emptying into a two-mile-wide field like a river delta meeting the sea. On the near side of the field were the rear guard NATO armored units, withdrawing from what had been a thin defensive line.

Black scars in the earth with jagged metal centers marked the graves of both Soviet and NATO tanks. Though there were more smoking hulks on the Soviet side—Hunter counted about a dozen or so—the American tank company on the southern flank was particularly close to being overrun. Even as he approached the area, he could see the big Abrams tanks racing to their back-up positions, the Soviet T-80s in hot pursuit.

Flying in the lead, Jones, too, took one look at the deteriorating NATO situation and knew what had to be done. Keying his microphone switch, he called back to the A-10 Thunderbolt flight commander, who was leading a squadron of sub-sonic ground support aircraft a few miles behind the F-16s.

"Tango leader, commence attack immediately!"

"Roger, Falcon Leader," came the reply.

The message had been received loud and clear by the A-10 flight leader, Captain Marcus A. Powers. Instantly he ordered his airplanes to peel off out of formation and drop to four hundred feet.

Captain Powers armed his GAU-8 30mm Gatling gun, the rotary cannon nestled in the Thunderbolt's fat nose. With the touch of the trigger, a full load of heavy, depleted-uranium slugs would pour out of the big gun, punching through the relatively thin armor on the tops of the Soviet tanks. For good measure, underneath their stubby wings, the A-10s carried Rockeye cluster bombs packed with anti-armor bomblets.

One pass over the battlefield and Powers was able to select his targets. Dividing his squadron into four flights of three, he assigned each flight to one of the main columns of Soviet armor rolling down the roads into the battle area. Then dropping further still to just two hundred feet, he and his two wingmen lined up on the southernmost column of enemy tanks.

The surprised Soviets didn't have enough time to get off the road when the Thunderbolts swooped in for their first pass. Their mobile radar unit had disintegrated under a direct hit by the German artillery ambush a few miles back, and they hadn't had time to bring up a replacement. The orders were to advance, prepared or not, and that's just what they had done. The price for this adherence to orders was the blind-siding they received from the American attack planes.

Captain Powers squeezed off several long bursts from his nose cannon into the stream of green Soviet armor on the roadbed below him. Bright flashes appeared under the A-10's chin as the spent uranium slugs pumped out of the whirling barrels, lancing downward in cascading arcs toward the Soviets. His first volley struck a T-80 directly behind the turret, exploding the tank's engine in a fireball. The torrent of heavy slugs walked back to the next tank in line, ripping jagged and flaming holes in its thin top armor as the deadly effects of the uranium burst the turret at its base, killing the crew in a fiery explosion.

One of the Thunderbolts to Powers's right found a Soviet fuel truck in the column, and its content erupted in a yellow-orange mushroom of flame that engulfed several surrounding vehicles.

At the same instant the A-10 on Powers's left caught a burst of anti-aircraft fire from a mobile Soviet Gatling-type battery. Spouting flame and smoke from under the wing, it staggered out of the battle area, engines missing sporadically, until a gray-black column of smoke could be seen rising from the horizon where he had plowed into the frozen ground.

Powers suddenly found himself gulping oxygen from his mask like there was no tomorrow. It was his first taste of combat and he imagined he could feel his heart beating right out of his chest.

"God help me," he whispered to himself. "God help us all . . ."

On the next pass, Powers ordered his Thunderbolts to dump their Rockeye clusters over the stalled Soviet columns. With morbid precision, literally hundreds of the armor-shredding bomblets rained down onto the enemy tanks, BMP armored personnel carriers, and other vehicles that made up the Soviet assault force.

With a quick glance down and back from his high speed vantage point, Powers estimated that one in every three of four enemy vehicles were being hit by the deadly downpour.

By their third pass, Powers could see the roads were now clogging up with the burning wreckage of many armored vehicles. But still the Soviet battle tanks poured out onto the open field — from the woods, from dry river beds, from smaller roads — roaring across open space to chase the retreating NATO armor. A fierce counter-volley from the M-1s and Leopards — coincidentally fired at the same time as the A-10s' first pass — had momentarily stopped the advance in some places. But at the same time, more Soviet T-80s and T-72s were approaching on the main roads, maneuvering around the hulks of their less fortunate comrades' tanks and joining the fray.

Worse, two more of the attacking Thunderbolts were hit by ground fire on their bombing run and went down in side-by-side fiery crashes. At that point, Powers reluctantly gave the order to withdraw.

Immediately Jones keyed his microphone and sent out an order to his F-16s: "Falcon Flight, first unit, commence ground support ops."

Instantly half the F-16s peeled off, leaving their eight counterparts to watch the skies for enemy fighters. The first unit pilots, led by Jones and Hunter, armed their 20-mm cannons while diving down to 200 feet.

"Spread out wide on four," Jones called back to his pilots.

With aerial show precision, the eight airplanes lined up in two rows of four across. Now down to just 50 feet, the two quartets streaked over the covering forest on the southern edge of the plain and across the open field, their cannons roaring. The spontaneously combusted cannon shells found targets every few feet — tanks, BMPs, troop trucks and armored cars. The Soviet vehicles caught in the wall of cannon fire below tried desperately to zig-zag their way out of the aerial assault. But for many, it was too little too late.

Hunter was purposely seeking out and firing at the enemy's fast-moving mobile guns. Keying in on the tracked vehicles' distinctive outline, he sent fiery tongues of flame shooting out from the cannon muzzle on the left-hand side of his F-16's fuselage, propelling a stream of shells aimed at the vehicles' ammunition supply. Each time a unique, greenish fire burst forth from the tracked vehicle like a clustered fireworks display gone awry as dozens of rounds whizzed off in all directions.

But still the Soviets came forward . . .

There were now four hundred tanks deployed in the open field, rolling toward the sparsely populated line of NATO armor. If they got across the three-kilometer expanse of open ground, they would easily overwhelm the outnumbered American and German forces. And they would be across in less than ten minutes, even under the withering fire they'd received from the Thunderbolts and the F-16s.

Pulling up and out of the long strafing run, Jones knew it was time to play his trump card.

Punching in a pre-selected radio frequency, the general made a quick call to the orbiting B-52. Once its pilot assured him that he had been following the situation and that everything was "green," Jones keyed his mike to the F-16 squadron's channel.

"Copperhead strike!" he shouted into his oxygen mask microphone. "Clear it out! *Repeat.* Copperhead!"

Jones glanced back over his shoulder at the other F-16 pilots as they punched their afterburners, pumping raw JP-8 into their engines to give them an extra jolt of speed. With one eye on them, and the other on the dark speck above him that he knew was the B-52, Jones kicked his own afterburner and started orbiting in a high, wide circle over the battlefield, leaving lots of space between him and the open field full of Soviet armor.

The huge bomb bays of the B-52 yawned open. Instantly

hundreds of cylindrical projectiles came tumbling out of the big bomber's belly and started plummeting to the ground, all the while spinning rapidly. Once clear of the B-52's jetwash, each cylinder sprouted a small ram-air parachute to stabilize its descent.

As the heavy cylinders plunged to three thousand feet, they discharged six submunitions, each of which blossomed with their own smaller vortex-ring parachutes. The submunitions spun in a slow, collapsing circle, suspended by the specially designed chutes that rotated them eight times per second. As they descended, the sensor heads activated their own infrared and millimeter-wave detectors which scanned the terrain below, seeking the hot exhausts and solid shapes of the Soviet armor.

The sky above the large open field was black with pinwheeling parachutes, each cradling a warhead that was dangling at a 30-degree angle, sweeping in an ever-narrowing spiral to pick out a target for its lethal payload. Monolithic microwave integrated circuits fashioned from gallium arsenide sped through thousands of complex algorithms that separated their armored prey from the snowy background of the German field, homing in on the tanks.

One by one, the sensors selected their victims. Once confirmed and "entered," each projectile fired an explosive charge at the top of a Soviet tank. Each explosion propelled a metallic liner—a copper disk about the size of a dinner plate—directly down at its target with a velocity of ten thousand feet per second.

The force of the explosion transformed the specially-shaped liners into elongated rods of white-hot molten copper, traveling at speeds faster than six thousand miles per hour. Like fiery thunderbolts flung from the heavens by angry titans, hundreds of the molten javelins flew down at the crawling green beasts with the red stars on their turrets. They found their mark with deadly accuracy, piercing the Soviet turret tops and boring through steel armor plate like hundreds of high-speed drill bits.

The Soviet tanks quickly became armored coffins for their hapless crews. The white-hot rods punched through the steel plates to release bursts of fire and shrapnel inside the turrets. Hundreds of tanks lurched to a halt as the lethal darts found their mark in the metal, as turrets, engines, and ammunition erupted in huge geysers of fire and smoke.

Dozens of T-80s were hit in their ammo compartments, detonating the shells and blowing the big turrets completely away from the tank bodies in brilliant explosions. Everywhere on the battlefield were wrecked tanks—burning, smoking hulks of torn metal whose shattered black shapes melted into the snow-covered field.

Up along the roads leading into the battle area, more wreckage and carnage littered the roadways as the tanks had been pinned in long ribbons, making it possible for one explosion to destroy two or more armored vehicles at a time.

The violent combined attack had lasted less than seven minutes, but it had broken the back of the Soviet armored assault, and allowed the surviving NATO armor to escape.

Hunter and Jones were flying parallel above the smoking scene, surveying the weapons' devastating effects.

Hunter radioed to Jones to inquire about the nature of the air-launched missile.

"That, Captain Hunter, was the first combat test of a SADARM—Sense and Destroy Armor—anti-tank smart munitions," Jones answered. "I think the Soviets will have to agree that it was a complete success."

Jones was impressed with the destructive potential of the previously well-guarded top secret weapon. They had substantially accomplished their mission—to block this, probably the largest Soviet armored advance. But at the same time he knew that the secret SADARMs were at a premium—only a half dozen were thought to be in Europe at the moment. Plus, the weapon's awesome destructive force could only be used under a very specific condition: that was, when the enemy massed his armor in a fairly wide open area. Jones was certain that once the word of the "Copperhead" strike made it back to the Red Army's High Command, orders would be struck preventing such an open massing of Soviet armor again.

Jones was about to sweep the area once more, when his radio suddenly crackled to life.

"Bogeys at ten o'clock!" he heard Hunter's distinctive Boston-accented voice call out.

Jones quickly checked his cockpit radar, and initially saw nothing.

But in the F-16 off to his right, Hunter wasn't relying on electronic means to cue him of the threat. He had received the message through other channels.

The *feeling* was washing over him, setting off the multiple alarm bells in his mind that always signaled imminent danger. A split second before the radar warning went off, Hunter already felt the presence of the enemy.

Now, even before Jones's own radar rang out the warning, Hunter had kicked in his afterburner and was climbing fast.

Chapter 21

The flight of Soviet fighters had appeared in the eastern sky above the battlefield.

Coming to the belated defense of their now-smoking armored columns, the Russians had sent 16 of their new MiG-29 Fulcrums to intercept the American attack planes.

The Soviets had almost caught the Americans unaware, still loitering over the battlefield to survey the effects of the SADARM strike. Only Hunter's premonition had provided them the precious split-seconds they needed to gain speed and altitude to engage the Soviet fighters.

Two of the speedy Fulcrums peeled out of the Soviet formation and rose to chase the B-52G, whose pilot had already shrewdly assessed the situation and was pouring the coal into all eight engines to hasten his departure from the battle area. Dropping high-tech ordnance on Soviet armor was one thing—tangling with a Mach 2 enemy fighter was something else entirely, and he wanted no part of it.

Four more Fulcrums set out after the low-flying A-10s, who were already hugging the ground and hightailing it back to the south-west. The Soviets had a speed advantage, but they would have to fly between the trees to catch the hedge-hopping Thunderbolts.

The remaining Fulcrums headed straight for Hunter and Jones at better than Mach 2. But thanks to Hunter's quick action, the F-16s had now gained enough altitude to meet the Soviets at their level.

Reacting quickly, Jones hollered into the microphone and crisply dispatched orders to the 16th.

"JT! Take Crider and save that B-52's butt! Rico and Samuels, go cover those 'Bolts. Hawk, Ben and Christman, stay with me!"

The general's orders were answered with a ringing chorus of "Roger!" and the F-16 formation split into three groups.

Jones looked over at Hunter through the scratched plexiglas canopy. He and his wingman were in the lead, with Ben and Christman following a half mile behind.

Keying the squadron's frequency, Jones gave the order to hold formation right through the oncoming enemy flight.

"Falcon flight, this is Falcon leader," he called out calmly. "Let's hold this pattern and turn fast. Hawk and I will go at them straight on. Ben, you and Christman pick up any bandits that break formation. Cannons only. We'll all break independent after the initial pass."

Absorbing the engagement orders, Wa and Christman pulled back on their throttles and increased the distance between them and the Jones-Hunter flight to about a mile and a half.

At that point, Jones called to Hunter and said: "Think these guys are ready to play a little Chicken Kiev, Hawk?"

"First time for everything, sir," Hunter replied tightly. He had a suspicion of what Jones was planning and he was more than willing to trust the experienced man's judgment, even if it did mean flying head-on into the oncoming force of Soviet MiGs.

That was exactly what Jones had in mind.

The general had guessed (correctly as it turned out) that the Soviet flight leader had ordered his pilots to hold their eight-plane formation, waiting for the Americans speeding headlong toward them to break away first and thus give them a clean shot. Now, Jones was hoping his surprise would be enough to rattle the superior Soviet force.

As the distance closed between the two flights of speeding fighters, their combined approach velocity was greater than Mach 4. Holding their positions as ordered, the Soviets were dismayed to see the Americans fail to break off, depriving the Fulcrums of the opportunity to fire their AA-10 air-to-air missiles at the broad undersides of the F-16s. While the moments ticked off, the Soviet pilots tightened their hands on the control sticks in their cockpit, desperately wanting to flick the twin-engine planes off to avoid the oncoming pair of F-16s, but unwilling to do so without orders.

Hunter's right hand rested lightly on the side-stick controller, since he knew from experience that the slightest pressure could dart the speeding plane off course by several hundred yards in seconds.

Moments flashed by. In little more than a split second, the two groups of airplanes would be upon each other, perhaps even colliding in mid-air.

Hunter re-armed his 20mm rapid fire cannon and looked through his Head-Up Display at the oncoming Fulcrums. They were dangerous-looking airplanes — their twin tails seemed to knife through the sky guiding their sleek bodies. But looks alone weren't enough to impress Hunter, or any of the other F-16 pilots, for that matter. Little did the Soviets know that the two F-16s which were at that moment hurtling right at them were being flown by members of the elite Thunderbirds aerial demonstration team.

Now *that* was impressive . . .

Hunter's HUD showed target acquisition for the cannon. He pressed lightly on the fire button, not enough to engage the cannon, but just enough to make his reaction a fraction of a second quicker when the time came to shoot.

The gap between the two adversaries was almost gone now, and Hunter could only imagine what was going through the minds of the enemy pilots. Head-on maneuvers were commonplace for the Thunderbirds team.

He couldn't believe the Soviets were as skilled.

His radio came to life with Jones's voice. "OK, Hawk, initiate Big Squeeze formation."

Hunter knew immediately that Jones was telling him to rotate his wings to almost vertical in order to squeeze between the closely spaced Soviet fighters. As one, the two F-16s flipped up on their wings, at last convincing the eight Soviet pilots that the F-16s were in fact committed to flying straight into them.

It was too much for the Red pilots to take. Two of them in front suddenly started to break formation.

But it was too late. Hunter flicked his control stick once and depressed his fire button in one fluid motion, rocking the airplane over on its wing and pouring a stream of cannon fire into one of the leading MiGs.

The Soviet airplane seemed to stagger in midair as the heavy cannon shells exploded on its nose, wingroot and, finally, its cockpit. Three shells in all pierced the canopy glass, shattering it, and puncturing the Soviet pilot's chest, killing him instantly. The fighter immediately spun out of control, lost altitude and began a rapid spiral down. Hunter watched as it quickly slammed into the ground and exploded on impact.

Jones had taken out the Fulcrum flight leader in similar fashion, pumping a stream of cannon shells in the intake of his right engine, exploding it in a cloud of debris that the F-16s had to fly through as they passed the startled Soviets.

In a flash, Jones and Hunter were through the Soviet formation, still speeding away at full AB. At the same time, Wa and Christman dove to pursue two of the Fulcrums that had broken rank just seconds before.

Twirling around in his seat to get a visual fix on the enemy, Jones signaled to Hunter for a two-plane formation Immelmann turn — one of the countless moves from their old Thunderbird repertoire.

The maneuver was one of the oldest in fighting aviation history, originally developed by World War I German ace Max Immelmann. A half-loop brought the planes around, and a half-roll brought them upright again; it allowed a pilot to gain altitude and reverse direction to face an enemy on his tail. Now Hunter and Jones would use the same move to fire missiles at the still-speeding Fulcrums.

As if they were images in a mirror, the two F-16s gracefully executed the move as one, bringing their fighter planes up and around to face the tails of the Soviet MiGs. Hunter and Jones each released a Sidewinder, and the two missiles roared off their wingtips and zeroed in on separate Fulcrums. The deadly darts raced through the sky, vapor trails corkscrewing behind them. Each found its mark in the exhaust nozzle of one of the Russian MiGs, and two powerful explosions shook the air as the enemy fighters were enveloped in violent fireballs.

Warned too late for reaction by their radar threat indicators, the remaining Fulcrums broke off to engage the F-16s in a wide-ranging dogfight. Hunter was struck by the surprising maneuverability of the Russian MiGs — a turn radius and climb rate comparable to the F-16's, although the Fulcrum required two engines to equal the performance of the big GE turbofan that the Falcon boasted.

Making their turns, the MiGs sent a volley of AA-10 air-to-air missiles at the two American planes. The F-16's threat warning alerts began sounding as the big Soviet airborne daggers sped for their targets. Hunter rolled his plane over and over in a dizzying sideways spiral, not allowing the missile's guidance systems to lock on to the wildly revolving jet. Missing Hunter's plane, the missile spent its remaining fuel and plunged harmlessly to the ground.

Jones had also evaded the two missiles fired at his plane, as did Ben Wa, who with Christman, had pulled up closer to Hunter and Jones by this time.

The battle raged for another full minute. Then suddenly, Christman ran out of luck.

Flying behind Hunter, he had attempted to imitate a corkscrew roll that would protect him from the Soviet missiles. But he had pulled out too soon, completing only three complete spins before he dove, upside down, out of his orbit and directly into the path of one of the big enemy arrows.

The deadly missile struck his F-16 near the tail section and sent the fighter staggering downward, losing altitude in a death spiral. Unable to control the plane, Christman knew the control links must have been severed. His only hope now was to eject himself out of the stricken plane.

Remembering the training program at Nellis, he quickly tightened the shoulder straps of the harness that held him to his seat. Then he reached down to his left-hand side and pulled the ejection seat release handle, instantly firing the charge that blew off the canopy, sending it flying backward into the plane's slipstream.

The wind buffeted his facemask and helmet visor for the longest second he'd ever lived through. Then the main explosive charge fired under his seat, rockets propelling him straight up and away from the smoking, out-of-control fighter. As the seat's trajectory neared its peak, the spent rockets and seat platform fell away and his pilot chute deployed.

The small parachute stabilized Christman's fall rate and used the wind's energy to pull the main parachute out of its carefully folded resting place.

The big nylon circle bloomed in the sky, its spiderweb of lines cradling the dazed F-16 pilot, still shaken by the force of the ejection blast. The cold wind and shock of the chute's opening brought him around, and his vision had just started to re-focus when he saw his plane spinning crazily below him, several miles away.

The swirling dogfight was still going on above, and Christman found himself strangely fascinated at being so close an eyewitness to the battle.

This is why he didn't see the Fulcrum closing on his drifting parachute until it was too late.

Not content with shooting the plane down, the Soviet was going to try and kill the helpless pilot. Christman turned and immediately went into shock as he watched the MiG's nose cannon open up. Hearing and feeling the heavy cannon shells whizzing through the air around him, he was powerless to defend himself against the cowardly attack—an attack that had long been condemned by flying men of every air force in every war.

Hunter saw the Soviet bearing down on Christman, but it was too late.

Three rounds tore through the thin nylon chute and sliced several of the control lines. Then one cannon shell struck the dangling pilot full in the chest. The heavy shell tore through his torso, destroying several vital organs before exiting Christman's lower back. The stricken pilot grasped the chute lines in one last desperate act, then fell limp as his bullet-ridden parachute descended rapidly.

In a final gesture of contempt, the Fulcrum pilot passed close by the chute, near enough to fully collapse it with the powerful jet wash. Hopelessly entangled in its own rigging, the chute fell in on itself, wrapping around the lifeless form of Christman and carrying it down the several miles to the earth.

A blind rage consumed Hunter as he pushed the throttle forward to pursue the malicious Soviet pilot. Shooting down planes was all part of the horrible game of war. But gunning down a helpless pilot after he'd bailed out was just plain cowardly murder.

The anger which burned inside him like a piece of hot metal, radiated its heat in short pulses up into Hunter's brain. The fire indelibly branded a mark on Hunter's senses.

War was war. But senseless killings had to be avenged.

The Wingman had swooped in on the twin-tailed Fulcrum and fired his cannon from close range. But his raw anger had interrupted his usual concentration and the tracer shells went wide, just past the Soviet's canopy. Hunter cursed as the MiG dove away.

The MiG pilot realized the close call he'd just had, and he knew he had to get this American off his tail and fast. His best defense would be a strong offense, he thought, diving away in a fast loop.

In seconds, the agile Fulcrum was able to twist around and rise slightly, its pilot attempting to maneuver behind and beneath Hunter's F-16. At the same time, another MiG was drawing in close to Wa's Falcon in a separate action nearby. Thinking quickly, Hunter swerved and fired his cannon straight into the guts of the MiG keying in on Wa, ripping away the enemy's right wheel undercarriage and perforating its mid-fuselage fuel tank.

No sooner had he fired when Hunter felt the hair on the back of his head stand straight up. Purely on instinct he yanked back on the F-16's controls, putting the fighter into a steep near-vertical climb. Almost immediately he was surrounded by green-yellow tracers streaming past his canopy from below. The first Fulcrum was beneath him and only his extra-sensory sixth sense had saved him from taking the entire burst right in his belly. As it was, he felt two dull thuds on the underside of his plane, small explosions that staggered the Falcon as Hunter slammed the throttle forward. In saving Ben, Hunter had been caught by the other Soviet pilot, and now he only had one way out.

No matter what the risk, he was going to take it.

Hunter picked up speed as the Fulcrum's cannon volley ceased, and he nosed the F-16 over at full speed to pull a full outside loop. With an inside loop, the pilot and plane are *inside* the imaginary circle drawn in the sky, and centrifugal force presses down, sometimes inducing the pilot blackout by forcing blood from his brain.

An outside loop, however, puts the plane and pilot *outside* that circle, and causes a "red-out" by pumping *too* much blood to the pilot's brain. In extreme cases, the resulting g-forces can actually burst a pilot's eyes and cause bleeding from his ears.

Hunter knew all this, but he also knew he needed to get behind the Fulcrum. He wouldn't have time to twist around for a normal loop—the nimble MiG would be able to get away while he maneuvered.

So he had to do it the hard way. Hunter felt the pressure building as the F-16 strained to complete the loop, wings flexing. He was committed to the move now — there was no flipping out of it at this point. He was directly upside down, at the bottom of the loop, and he could see the red veil start to rise behind his vision as the blood pressed against his retinas.

Now his ears were popping, warning him of the pressure building inside his head. His feet and lower legs were tingling, deprived of the blood they needed. His vision became narrower, a small tunnel surrounded by a sea of crimson. He tasted blood in his mouth as a small amount oozed through his gums around his back teeth. He felt himself straining against the g-forces, desperately trying not to pass out before he completed the loop.

It was near the breaking point for him, and the loop might have killed an average pilot.

But Hawk Hunter was no average fighter pilot . . .

He swept through the bottom of the loop, his vision still a reddish haze as the F-16 rose on the outside edge of the invisible circle. The pressure began to subside, and his head started to clear. He had done it . . . He was flying upright now, and he was above and behind the homicidal Fulcrum pilot.

For his part, the MiG pilot was nothing less than bewildered. Moments before he saw the American nose over, and thought he dived away from the battle, or turned off in a wide bank to circle around. But then there was no sign of him in the sky below or to the sides.

Where had he gone?

His answer came from behind as Hunter laced the Fulcrum's tail section with cannon fire from point-blank range. A relentless stream of 20mm shells poured into the wide, flat valley between the Soviet fighter's rudders, igniting both engines and severing most of the tail section. Instantly half the Soviet airplane was engulfed in flames. It began breaking up and started to fall out of the sky in a ragged, fiery spiral.

Hunter watched the pilot fumble for his ejection mechanism, and the rage burned hot within him. He changed his angle on the Russian slightly, re-aiming and firing his cannon so that the shells traced a straight path across the Fulcrum's right wingroot, amputating the flat appendage like a surgeon's scalpel.

Deprived of more than half its lift, the stricken MiG fell off on its now-wingless right side in a tight spin. The rapidly increasing g-forces pinned the Russian pilot's arms at his sides, as they suddenly became too heavy to move.

Unable to reach his ejection handle, he realized his doom in a silent scream that lasted all the way down to the hard-packed ground, three miles below.

Hunter followed the MiG's wreckage down, making sure the Soviet pilot was truly finished. There was no parachute, and Hunter allowed himself a split second of unrewarding satisfaction as he watched the MiG impact into the side of a small mountain.

The feeling of revenge didn't last long, however. Hunter knew the Soviet pilot's death wouldn't bring Christman back.

That was the problem, he thought. In war, eventually everyone loses . . .

With that, he climbed back up, hoping to join the air battle that was still raging above.

By this time, JT had doubled back to join the dogfight, assured that the B-52G was safely out of harm's way. Working together, he and Jones had just picked off a Fulcrum that had tried to latch on to Ben Wa's tail, as the Hawaiian was in turn flaming another MiG with his cannon.

The surviving Russians broke off their attack at this point and headed for home, unwilling to stay and provide more ducks for the 16th's shooting gallery.

Hunter, still seething at the cold-blooded murder of Christman, was game to pursue the MiGs. He moved to engage his afterburner.

But then, he suddenly stopped.

He had never quite felt the eerie sensation on the back of his neck before, but in a split-second he knew what it meant.

Something was wrong with the F-16.

He quickly scanned the gauges and displays in the cockpit, searching their mute, numbered faces for a clue to the nature of the problem. A blinking red LED light confirmed Hunter's suspicion: his airplane was about to experience a major electrical system failure.

While loss of power was a serious problem in any aircraft, it was especially critical in the fly-by-electrical-wire F-16. He had a re-dundant flight control system and back-up computer, but it would now require his full attention and strength to bring the plane back home.

Jones pulled alongside Hunter's cruising fighter, sensing Hunter's problem. He looked at the young pilot through the canopy and keyed his microphone.

"What's the problem, Hawk?" The words were casual, but there was an underlying tension to the voice. Jones knew only too well the many of things that could bring a plane down.

"Not certain, sir," Hunter answered calmly. "I'm getting an electrical failure indication. I thought I felt some iron in my tail. Can you take a look?"

Swooping low to scan the plane's underside for damage, Jones immediately saw the source of the trouble.

Indeed, the MiG had nailed Hunter's airplane with at least one cannon round, blowing a large, jagged hole in the underside of his fuselage toward the tail. Jones let out an involuntary gasp, sucking in air through his oxygen mask, and glad his microphone was still not keyed.

"Where did he get me?" Hunter asked.

"Let me put it this way, Hawker, old boy," Jones replied. "If your plane was a bird, it would never have chicks again. . . ."

With that, Jones relayed a damage report in full. The bottom line was that the aircraft was still intact, but the afterburner and the stabilizer controls were heavily damaged.

"Lucky you didn't punch in your AB," Jones told Hunter. "You'd be flying a pair of angel wings instead of a ruptured duck."

Hunter closed his eyes and sent a big *thanks* out to the ethers, grateful that his own internal warning system had prevented him from lighting out full afterburner after the fleeing Soviet fighters.

Meanwhile, Jones ordered JT and Wa to head back to Rota as quickly as possible. After initial protests, both pilots reluctantly agreed. Because of their extra mileage action before the Fulcrum dogfight, both were low on fuel. Escorting Hunter's stricken fighter back, at such a slow speed and low altitude, would burn their reserves and possibly cause them to crash as well.

Instead, Jones would stick by the damaged F-16.

Hunter watched as the two F-16s roared off, their outlines growing smaller until they disappeared into high cloud cover toward the south. His own F-16 was acting very sluggish, plowing through the air instead of slicing it: he had to coax it to maintain altitude and level flight. Without stabilizers, every odd gust of wind threatened to buck the airplane over. He was lucky the stabilizers had been jammed in the straight position—if they were up or down, he would never have been able to control the airplane.

And so the two F-16s flew on, Jones dropping altitude periodically to check the underside of Hunter's plane, and Hunter wrestling with the heavy controls of his damaged fighter. The two pilots didn't speak, except to exchange airspeed and altitude information, or indicate fuel status. It would be tight, but they would have enough to make it back to Rota.

What was of more concern to Hunter was the landing gear controls.

His cockpit instrument panel showed his landing gear as inoperative, and he didn't dare test it while still en route. If by some miracle of electronics it did engage and lower his wheels, he might not be able to raise them again, and the plane couldn't stand the extra drag with the critical fuel situation.

Of course, if the landing gear couldn't be lowered at all, . . . well, he'd worry about that when he got back to the base.

If he got back to the base . . .

Chapter 22

As was usually the case when a stricken airplane was coming in, activity at the airbase at Rota slowed to almost a standstill.

Aircraft that could were diverted to other fields. Emergency vehicles—foam-spreading tankers and fire trucks—were lined up along the edge of the runway. All the other base aircraft were moved into their hardstands, or taxied to the opposite side of the field. No one liked to think about it, but they had to protect the remaining planes from any crash that might result from the damaged plane skidding out of control.

Further behind were the ambulances, grimly dubbed "the meatwagons." Their second-place status was a concession to fatalistic reality—pilots rarely survived unsuccessful crash landings. If a plane augered into the field and there was a fire, the best they could hope for was to remove the body parts after the flames were out.

The rescue crews stood by nervously, waiting for the signal. The 16th's ground crew chief, a Louisiana Cajun named Blue, was out on the tarmac also, clad in an asbestos fire suit and gloves. The heavy hood was pushed back to accommodate the binoculars he was using to search the deepening shadows in the northern sky.

Somewhere up there was a pilot and an airplane in trouble— Blue had nightmares about such things.

The long minutes of anxious waiting ended when they heard a low rumble vibrate across the field. A buzz rippled through the men clustered on the runway. Fingers pointed skyward. Voices rose. Two specks appeared on the horizon—one of them smoking heavily.

The roar of the engines built steadily as the two outlines developed into a pair of F-16s that began a wide circle over the base. Jones was doing all the talking with the base's air traffic controllers, as Hunter was busy trying to keep the plane aloft without benefit of the broad stabilizer flaps.

He formally cleared his own landing with the tower and then turned his attention to the damaged plane.

"Rota tower, this is Falcon leader. Confirm clearance and emergency landing prep on runway two-niner, over?" Jones's voice was steady as he flew past the slender tower with the glass-enclosed cupola.

The clearance was confirmed speedily, and the foam trucks quickly sprayed out a thick blanket of glistening white across the surface of the designated runway. The bubbly carpet was designed to prevent sparks in the event the aircraft had to make a wheels-up landing.

Inside Hunter's cockpit the temperature was hovering near the 100-degree mark. He had switched off the airplane's cockpit air conditioner, along with almost every other auxiliary system, in order to save fuel, and he was paying the price as his flight suit was now soaked through with sweat.

He circled the base two more times, using up the last of his fuel reserves. All the while Jones stayed right behind him, ready to tell him any change in his airplane's condition.

When Hunter saw that his fuel was down to the bare minimum, he knew the moment of truth had finally arrived.

Now it was time to see if the landing gear would work . . .

He pressed the undercarriage console button and crossed his fingers. A yellow light began to blink, telling him the gear could not be lowered. He quickly punched in a computer override command, but still the cursed yellow light continued to blink. One last try was the flip of the manual override switch above the blinking indicator light on his panel. He tried it a dozen times, but still the yellow light stayed on. That settled it: the landing gear was definitely *no go*.

Jones and the tower confirmed the gear's failure to lower, but Hunter had already resigned himself to landing the plane without the benefit of wheels. This was something they'd never practiced at Nellis. As he brought the fighter around for the final approach, Hunter heard Jones's reassuring voice talking him through each step of the forced landing.

He found himself mechanically performing the normal landing drill, trying not to concentrate on the thought that there would be nothing normal about this landing. Without the stabilizer flaps to guide the F-16's tail section, it would be harder than ever to bring the plane in gently enough to avoid disaster.

And, he had only enough fuel for one attempt.

"Okay, Hawk, ease back on the throttle a bit more," Jones called to him. "That's it . . . Okay, give it a little more wing flap . . . No, not that much . . . just a goose . That's the ticket. Okay, a little less throttle . . . Watch the airspeed now . . . Bring her down a little bit more . . . Watch your drift. Steady . . . That's it . . ."

Jones was flying right beside Hunter now, over the runway, his own landing gear extended to slow his airspeed to match the crippled bird's. Hunter was gradually decelerating the damaged airplane, reducing altitude by a few feet at a time, struggling with the now-balky control surfaces. Still Jones was beside him, coaching and watching.

"Okay, Hawk, you're almost there . . . A few more feet . . . Just try to stay on the foam . . ." At this point, Jones was forced to push his throttle forward and gain altitude as his plane threatened to stall out at the low altitude.

Hunter was only ten feet above the runway now, perfectly level. A hundred feet forward was the foam path the crews had sprayed for him.

"Miss that foam," Hunter thought to himself, "and it'll be a short funeral."

He breathed in sharply and let the plane drop a few more feet. Directly over the foam now, he edged the plane down until the ventral flaps were slicing through the whitecaps on the foam's surface. A little lower, and they made contact with the runway itself, sending a grating vibration through the airframe as Hunter used the thin metal plates like curb feelers to guide the plane down. Now the big air intake below the fuselage was beneath the surface of the foam, sucking in the white froth to the engine's flaming core and spewing the smoky vapor out the exhaust nozzle.

Then came the scraping sound of metal on concrete as the intake's underside made contact with the runway.

The plane sluiced through the foam on its belly, wings rippling from one side to the other as Hunter struggled to keep its nose pointed straight forward. With no brakes to control his landing, he had to rely on full wing flaps, applied gradually as the plane lost speed.

But it wasn't enough . . . The end of the foam was approaching too quickly.

He burst past the CO_2 blanket, sending a shower of sparks and metal fragments behind him as the scarred plane screeched down the bare asphalt runway. Suddenly he was spinning and his eyes were filled with lights. There were sprays of sparks—some bouncing off the canopy, others seemingly ricocheting inside the cockpit itself. Around and around he went, the sparks being as bright as flames from a welder's torch. He was sucking on the oxygen mask like never before, as if the air would save him from the conflagration of sparks.

At some point, he was thrown forward so violently that the crash helmet was yanked right off his head. Then he was thrown up and backward, a motion which caused him to crack his head against the top of the hard canopy glass.

He lost consciousness at this point. It seemed as if he was out for an hour, but looking back on it, it was probably only a few seconds.

Yet in that time, a very strange thing happened.

He found himself in a state which he could only describe as a "wide-awake dream." He was back in the States, standing on a huge pier. There were a few big gray Navy ships around, indicating the place was a military port. He felt older, bigger, more bulked up and his hair was nearly to his shoulders. He was wearing a black flight suit and carrying a battered flight helmet and talking to people he didn't recognize about an upcoming flight.

Yet, at some later point, he began to climb down into a submarine.

Then a rather pleasant darkness began to settle in on him.

Blue was first to reach the burning airplane.

Breathing heavily in the cumbersome fire gear, he leaped onto the wing of the smoking fighter and heedless of the danger, fumbled inside the heavy gloves for the canopy release handle located on the fuselage on either side of the cockpit.

Popping the emergency cover off, he yanked the handle out several feet to blast the clear canopy away from the tiny cockpit.

It launched off the plane, landing with a clatter several feet away. Reaching into the narrow compartment, he tugged at Hunter's restraining straps, trying to release the dazed pilot even as the clouds of black acrid smoke closed in.

The fire crews had already rushed up to the burning airplane and were drenching it with chemical foam and CO_2 extinguishers in an effort to quell the fire. But they knew they were fighting a losing battle.

Hunter was vaguely aware of the activity churning around the outside of his cockpit. His head felt light, and his feet seemed frozen to the rudder pedals. Everything had happened so fast, but now it seemed to be thrown into slow motion. The sparks were still in his eyes and he felt even hotter than before.

It took him more than a split second to realize that he was surrounded by fire.

Suddenly two massive hands reached down and literally yanked him out of the cockpit. Next thing he knew he was flat-out on the wing, his flight suit actually smoldering. Then he was yanked again, off the wing, to the ground and dragged for what seemed like a mile or two.

Finally all the nonsense stopped and he was stationary again. Flat out on his back, facing the clear but cold Spanish sky.

He tried to look at the crowd of faces around him, but the bright sun was in his eyes. Finally, he recognized Ben and Toomey, in the gaggle of people kneeling over him.

"How's the plane?" he asked thickly, his throat dry.

Despite the tension, those around him couldn't suppress a relieved laugh at Hunter's question.

Toomey and Ben gently raised him up by his shoulders and pointed him toward the runway.

His eyes cleared enough to see a huge pile of blackened metal surrounded by a raging fire so intense even the fire crews had backed off.

His head still spinning, he nevertheless began to realize that he had just come very close to being killed.

"Who . . . who pulled me out?" he asked shakily.

The crowd of people parted slightly to let a tall young man walk through and kneel beside him. It was Blue.

Hunter opened his mouth but could not speak. Blue relieved him of the difficult moment by saying: "Just buy me a drink sometime, Captain."

"You're on!" Hunter said, weakly shaking the man's hand. "Your drinks are on me for the rest of your life!"

Then he looked over at the charred mess that was once an F-16.

"Can you fix it?" he asked, still woozy.

Once again the crowd around him let out a laugh.

"Fix it?" Blue asked. "Damn, Captain, I can heal the sick, but I can't raise the dead. That there airplane is permanently Humpty-Dumpty city, my friend."

At that point, the medical people arrived. A doctor gave Hunter the quick once-over and determined that he had suffered no serious trauma, save for the nasty crack on his head.

Nevertheless, the medic gave him a sedative injection before he was loaded onto a stretcher and into an ambulance.

Within seconds, Hunter was asleep and dreaming once again about submarines.

172

Chapter 23

The flightline was deserted.

Hunter paced along its length, following his dim shadow being cast by the nearly full Spanish moon. It was close to midnight and an absolutely eerie calm had enveloped the air base.

The place was so quiet in fact, that if it weren't for the memories of the past two days, it would have been hard to guess that there was a war on.

The sedative knocked him out for just four hours and once he woke, he had found it impossible to get back to sleep. He spent two hours of tossing before finally getting out of his cot. His back and neck were just a little stiff from the crash, but his nerves were working overtime and he knew he had to expend some of the energy. And the fresh air would be a welcome relief to the mechanically pumped oxygen it seemed he'd been breathing since arriving in Europe.

He finally reached the spot where his F-16 had come to a flaming, screeching halt earlier that day. What debris was left of the fighter had already been hauled away — all that remained now was a blackened streak where he'd run past the anti-flame foam.

In all his years of flying — both civilian and military airplanes — it was the closest he had come to buying the farm. Looking at the black, burnt scar on the runway, he felt a change come over him. Not a revelation or a religious experience. Just a very subtle shift in his psyche.

He knew if he were a cat, he would only have six lives left. Pulling out of a crash like his in one piece wasn't something he could expect to happen too often. In fact, he knew he might never be so lucky again. That is, unless he worked on it. So right then and there he decided he would do just that: use his special gift—his extraordinary sixth sense—to its fullest extent. Use it to stay alive. Never doubt it. Always trust it.

And remember to buy Blue all the drinks he wanted for the rest of his life.

He was on the verge of heading back to his quarters when he noticed a light burning in the base's combat information center. After talking to the security guard, he walked into the CIC and found Jones there, analyzing reports from the previous day.

The general rubbed his tired eyes and ran his fingers through his close-cropped hair as if to massage his weary brain.

But he wasn't surprised to see Hunter.

"Couldn't sleep, Captain?" he asked, knowing he too would have a hard time sleeping had he come as close to getting killed as Hunter had done.

The young pilot just shrugged. "I'm a little restless, sir," he said finally.

"Well, the doc told me that except for a few bumps and bruises, you're certified to fly," the general said. "You dodged a pretty big bullet out there today."

Jones moved aside a pile of computer data and reached across the desk to retrieve two fairly clean coffee cups. Then he pulled out a fifth of premium Scotch from a file cabinet drawer nearby.

Pouring the two cups about three-quarters full, he pushed one across the desk toward Hunter, motioning him to sit down.

"Strictly medicinal, Captain," Jones said.

Jones knew the therapeutic value of alcohol on pilots, jittery or otherwise. For his part, Hunter welcomed the fiery amber liquid.

After a few long sips, the general turned his attention back to the reams of data in front of him.

"This is the latest intelligence report from the front," he said. "It contains an analysis of photo transmissions from one of our

174

satellites in stationary orbit. One of the few that are still flying, I should say."

"You mean?" Hunter began to say.

Jones anticipated his question and nodded. "Yep," he said, dragging on his cigar. "We've been blowing up each others' satellites for the past forty-eight hours. The Sovs are doing it via some top secret SAM device; we've been nailing them with ASAT missiles launched from F-15s back over the States."

Hunter shook his head. The thought of outer space caused him to briefly remember his short stay at the Kennedy Space Center. It seemed like a century ago.

"Of course," Jones continued, "once both weapons get into orbit, the satellites are killed via remote control, using the stars to navigate and so on. It's all very technical."

"Has it come to this now?" Hunter wondered aloud. "Killing in space? Machines killing other machines? Why do they even bother with us flesh and blood types, sir?"

"Please don't get philosophic on me, Captain," Jones said, holding up his hand. "Some human still has to push the right buttons to make it all happen.

"Besides, before this thing is over we'll have guys knifing each other in muddy trenches even as our 'space invaders' are battling it out in orbit, mark my words."

Hunter drained his drink. "So, what *is* the latest situation, sir?" he asked. "Still bad?"

Jones nodded grimly, leaned back and re-lit his cigar.

"Is it getting worse?" Hunter asked.

Once again, Jones just nodded.

"Any chance it will still go nuclear, sir?"

This time, Jones hesitated for a moment. "Officially, the answer to your question is 'yes,' " the officer said finally. "Beyond that, everything else is classified . . ."

Jones poured out two more drinks. Looking at Hunter now, the senior officer was reminded of days long ago on the sweltering jungle airstrips of Vietnam, when he had flown and fought beside Hunter's father. Flying missions was *really* like a job back then. Take off. Drop your bomb load. Dodge some SAMs and be home for supper. Next day, do it all again.

Now, in this *real* war, every combat mission had to be evaluated in terms of how many young men wouldn't return, if any. And he, Jones, had the responsibility for all of them. It was no joyride taking the handling of lives other than your own, and having to live with the consequences afterward.

"Now, I do suggest you get some sleep," Jones told him, abruptly breaking up their drinking session. *"Real* sleep, I mean. You'll need it tomorrow."

Hunter didn't ask him why or what would take place the next day—part of him didn't want to know. He just stood up, thanked the general and saluted.

"Briefing starts at oh-six-hundred," Jones said, returning to his data through a haze of cigar smoke. "Be on time, Captain . . ."

"Yes, sir," Hunter said, turning to leave.

Jones had been careful not to let his voice betray his innermost feelings. That was part of it, too, he thought as Hunter walked out of the room.

The responsibility of command was not for sharing.

Hunter was the first one to report to the briefing early the next morning.

Alone in the room, staring at the large map on the wall, he realized why Jones had been so reluctant to tell him the news from the front the night before. Many things had happened in the past twenty-four hours. When Hunter had first seen the map before him, it was covered with red and blue opposing arrows slashing across the continent of Europe. Now the center of the map was dominated by just two huge red arrows that carved straight through West Germany in the north and south.

It didn't take a master tactician to determine the arrows were converging on France. In fact, they were pointing almost directly at Paris.

The original plan was for NATO to let the Soviets plow across the no-man's-land of West Germany, slowing them up with harassing actions and meeting them in full force somewhere west of the Rhine.

But now it was obvious that the Soviet tide flowing west had not been slowed down much, if at all, despite punishing losses from the slowly withdrawing rear guard forces. A strong stand by NATO had been made at the Rhine River and held back the Red Army's juggernaut for nearly twelve hours in some of the bloodiest fighting the continent had ever seen.

But it had not been enough.

Now, the entire NATO front was collapsing back toward France.

With the land war going so badly, it was clear that the combined air forces of the West had become the only effective means of stopping the Soviet onslaught. Flying a combination of strategic and tactical bombing runs, close air support, and long-range interdiction missions, it was the air forces that had so far held the Soviets from an all-out successful *blitzkrieg*-like dash to the sea.

How many missions had been flown, Hunter wondered, still studying the map. From allied fields in France, Belgium, Holland, Spain and England? How many pilots had been lost? How many airplanes?

How long would this madness continue?

There was a definite whiff of desperation in the air. The base seemed to be shrinking, as more and more NATO aircraft had come to call it home. On his way to the briefing, he saw an incredible assortment of displaced Free World aircraft had been crowded onto the tarmac, most of them arriving during the early morning hours.

Even the map in the briefing room seemed to be getting smaller, he thought. Or maybe it was an optical illusion, caused by the shrinking of the blue-colored NATO-controlled territory.

But worst of all, the cluster of chairs around the briefing room's podium was getting smaller, drawing in closer like wagons in a besieged camp. The day Hunter first came to Rota, there had been nearly forty pilots jammed in the briefing room, elbow-to-elbow in the small desks.

Jones would have the chairs removed when pilots didn't come back, and now, just two and a half days later, there were only fifteen seats left.

What was it Jones had told him about how many ways there were to die in an airplane? It seemed to Hunter that the lost pilots of the 16th TFW had covered all the bases. A pilot named Daly had been shot down by a MiG over Stuttgart. Someone named Bachman had caught a SAM on a bombing mission to Poland. Chang ditched in the Med and was never recovered. Van Dell hit the side of a mountain in the French Alps in a dense fog. O'Neil had run low on fuel and bailed out over Soviet-held Germany, only to be shot by ground troops.

And Teddy Crider, one of the guys that had flown over with him from Langley, had augered in during a raid on the city of Aachen. Of them all, Hunter had only known Crider. The rest were just names to him.

Extras in the war movie . . .

Yet despite the appalling loss of pilots, there was a small pinprick of good news which Jones brought them as soon as all of the remaining pilots had assembled.

The weary officer, halfway through his breakfast cigar, told them that although it was too early to tell for sure, it *did* appear that the strategy of hitting the Soviets' extended supply lines was slowly having an effect. NATO intelligence was hinting that the advancing Red Army might be facing an increasingly crucial supply problem in the next twenty four hours. In fact, there was even evidence, though slim and preliminary, that the Soviets had slowed the steady progress westward they had made since punching across the Rhine, because of the stepped-up raids on their rear areas.

But there was no less a price to pay for continuing this tactic.

As Jones explained it, the enemy's rear areas were, if anything, even more heavily protected by SAMs and AAA guns, as well as fighters, many of which the Soviets had drawn from their top echelon reserves based in Asia.

That was why NATO was about to change tactics.

Jones bluntly told them that the Pentagon was planning "a final push."

Final was the word that caught everyone's attention in the briefing room. *Final for whom?*

Jones explained that a sweeping counterstrike was being planned to sever the Red Army's supply lines that had so quickly extended across most of Europe. The idea was to cut off the head of the Soviet arrows that were poised to pierce the heart of France and complete the evil empire's conquest of

Europe.

Called Operation Rolling Thunder, the plan involved a massive airborne assault of key enemy points stretching back into West Germany and even beyond, to be carried out by a combined force of NATO parachute units, primarily American and British troops. But for such a bold, almost desperate move to work, three things had to be accomplished: 1)NATO had to gain absolute air superiority over the battlefield, 2) the almost-straining Soviet supply lines had to be hit in one massive blow, and with a force harder than the tactical fighters could deliver, and 3) the paratroopers had to land on their targets at the right time in the right place.

Jones told them that they had no control over points 2 and 3. But Point 1, gaining air superiority, was right up their alley.

And that's what the core of the briefing was all about: the aerial portion of the counter-attack, code-named Operation Chained Lightning. The final push in the air . . .

"Our plan calls for a non-stop fighter sweep across the entire Western Front for the next twenty-four to thirty-six hours," Jones told them. "Every NATO fighter from here in Rota all the way up to Oslo and back that can fly is going to be put in the air. They are even transitting over some old National Guard birds from the States. The objective is to draw the enemy's entire air force into a battle over France—and as we knock off their first-echelon squadrons, they'll move up their second-stringers, and then the reserves.

"If we can, we'll make them commit every plane, every pilot, and every SAM this side of the Urals to the defense of the front. If we can accomplish this, we can take the heat off the paratroopers once they are sent in, and we can clear the way for the big attack on the enemy supply lines.

"So, for us of the 16th TFW, that means flying multiple sorties—day and night if we have to—for the next couple of days. And I'm not going to mince words. It's going to be damn tough."

The general paused, scanning the pilots again. I'll never get used to this part, he thought. I'll never get used to sending young men up to die. But he knew there was no choice.

"General," one of the junior pilots had spoken up in a

slightly shaken tone, "when will the flight schedule be posted?"

"Mister," Jones answered firmly, "there *will be no* flight schedule. All of us will take off at thirteen hundred hours today, and from that point on, every man will refuel and rearm and take off again as often as possible. You will be flying up to the battle area in pairs or even independently. You will be expected to use your own judgment as to whether or not your aircraft—and you as a pilot—are capable of another sortie."

The rather bizarre orders were met with many an open mouth or involuntary exclamation for the pilots.

"Now I know this is all very unorthodox," Jones continued. "But the success of Operation Chain Lightning depends on us flying as many sorties as possible. However, you won't be helping the effort by flying a badly damaged airplane, or flying when you can't keep your eyes open.

"But I'll level with all of you. We're blowing the wad on this one. If this grand counter-attack fails, then anything can happen. Including the use of nuclear weapons. Either by us, or by them."

"What about the other part of the operation, General?" another pilot asked. "This attack on the supply lines. If all our airplanes are caught up in the fighter sweep, who's going to hit the enemy's supply lines?"

Jones took a deep breath and let it out slowly.

"The nature of the rest of Operation Rolling Thunder is top secret," he answered. "I'm sorry, but I can't tell you any more than that. We just can't take the chance of someone getting shot down with that knowledge. I don't have to tell you how badly the enemy is going to want to know just what the hell we're up to, and you can bet he'll have ways to squeeze it out of you."

The very thought fell across the room like a shadow, as each pilot saw his own private hell, created for him by his own imagination. Some things, Hunter thought, you *are* better off not knowing.

There were no more questions.

"It is now oh-seven hundred, gentlemen," Jones said formally, checking his pilot's chronograph. "I suggest you get some rest before this afternoon's mission. We're all going to need it."

One by one, as they had come in, the pilots left. Some would seek the uneasy solace of a few hours' restless sleep. Some would choose the distraction of a half-eaten breakfast that would later churn in their nervous stomachs. Some would write letters home. Some would pray.

Hunter had lingered behind the rest, watching Jones as the general began shoving maps and papers back into his briefcase, his brow furrowed as he thought about the orders he'd just given. To provide ground support to the retreating ground troops had been somewhat routine. To plan and execute a series of integrated deep strikes against the Soviet supply lines had been tougher, but not out of the realm of his pilots' training.

But this Operation Chain Lightning was different . . .

A fighter sweep was something that hadn't been used on such a grand scale since World War II. Back when Pappy Boyington and his Black Sheep Squadron had led more than a hundred planes at a time against the Japanese Zeros of Rabaul in the Pacific, bleeding them by using his Corsairs, Lightnings, and Thunderbolts to goad the enemy into dogfights they couldn't win, or destroying them on the ground with strafing runs.

At least back then, the US had air superiority: better planes, better pilots, better bases than the enemy, and more planes to boot. Now almost the reverse was true. He had better pilots all right, and probably rivet-for-rivet better planes; but there were so few of them! And fewer bases, crowded with the fragments of a few hundred squadrons that lacked the spare parts, trained ground crews, and hardened facilities to do the job right.

But worst of all, Jones had to admit to himself, was the purpose of the fighter sweep—of Chain Lightning itself. Not to win a particular battle, or even really to establish long-term air superiority over the fighting front. No, the 16th and the other NATO fighter units were simply being used as bait for the Soviet fighters.

"Goddamn flying circus," Jones mumbled to himself.

"What's all this about a circus, General?"

The older man looked up, suddenly aware of Hunter's presence.

"Nothing, Captain," the general said quietly, running his

hand through his gray-flecked whiffle-cut hair. "Just talking to myself. Happens when I haven't had enough scotch. I think it affects my brain cells."

Hunter knew better. Jones always exuded unalloyed confidence in any mission to which he was assigned, be it training an unruly group of Thunderbird candidates to bombing an enemy fuel dump a hundred miles behind the lines. Something wasn't kosher about this Chain Lightning stuff.

"What's the real scoop on this mission, General?" Hunter asked him squarely, moving closer to the briefing table. "Why a fighter sweep?"

"Like I told all of you before, Captain," Jones started blandly, "we have to draw out the enemy's reserves. Make him put everything in the air and bleed him dry."

Hunter knew he was about to cross a line between rank and friendship, a privilege that was his only because Jones and his father had been tight.

"But a fighter sweep is going to cost us a lot of airplanes, sir," he pressed. "And the Soviets have more of them left then we do. Not to mention pilots."

"You think I don't know that?" Jones snapped. "You think I don't know that I've only got about fifteen hundred airworthy fighters to put up against probably three or four thousand of the enemy's? You think I relish the thought of playing a game of attrition when the other guy's got more pieces to give away? *You think I like sending men up there to die?*"

He stopped abruptly. The two men just stared at each other. Hunter had never seen the man lose it as he had just now.

"I'm sorry, Hawk," the older man said softly, "But there's just no other choice . . ."

The anguish showed on Jones's face as he turned away from the young pilot.

"It's okay," he said. "Hell, I guess I can tell you a little more about it. Damn it, if you get shot down, it means the Sovs have a Wingman of their own; then we might as well hang it up anyway."

Hunter appreciated at the compliment, but he was more curious about the plan, edging up to glance at the maps and charts that Jones hauled back out.

Jones looked down at the cluttered table, hands holding down the folded edges of the maps.

"The supply situation is critical, Hawk," he began. "NATO command estimates one week of the basic supplies—*maximum*. One goddamn week and most of that is going to have to go to support the paratroop units they're assembling right now at a very secret location. We just haven't gotten the airlift, the materiel, or the manpower to keep the air bridge open twenty-four hours a day and the sea supply just isn't going to come together in time.

"So we've got to break their backs *now*, in the next couple of days, or else the Soviets are going to roll right down through France and kick our sorry asses into the next millennium. The question is: how to do it?"

"Do what we're doing now, bomb their supply lines to kingdom come," Hunter said, catching the strategic drift.

"Correct," Jones said. "But you and I both know that we can't do that with fighters alone. Not with the current state of affairs. It has to be one, big massive blow.

"That's where Rolling Thunder enters the picture . . ."

"We're not going nuclear, are we, General?" Hunter asked, his eyes widening.

"No, Hawk," said Jones. "But maybe the Soviets will wish we had when he sees the treatment we *do* have for him."

Spreading out the maps, the two men studied them until it was almost time to leave for the flight line and begin the first sortie of the last battle of World War Three.

Chapter 24

It was not the same Hawk Hunter who climbed into the cockpit of his replacement F-16 on that gray afternoon.

He barely noticed that the jet was inexplicably painted all white, a sharp contrast to the blue-gray color scheme of the other fighters of the 16th TFW. He did his pre-flight checklist in grim silence, mechanically preparing his plane for the impending combat. Four Sidewinders and a noseful of cannon ammo, he thought ruefully. It hardly seemed like enough to take on the entire Soviet air force. But then again, he wouldn't be alone in the skies above France.

All along the flightline in Rota, every NATO interceptor that could get airborne was being prepared for the first wave of Jones's fighter sweep. A ragtag fugitive fleet of aircraft—the refugees of a hundred forward NATO air bases—was clustered on the Spanish tarmac.

Besides Hunter and the other fourteen surviving F-16s of the 16th TFW, the American planes included thirty or so F-15 Eagles, the kick-ass air-superiority fighters that carried four big medium range air-to-air missiles as well as another four Sidewinders, plus a rotary 20mm cannon in the starboard wing. Hunter knew Jones wished he had more.

A couple of squadrons of F-4G Phantom IIs were lining up to join the fray. Thrown together from the remnants of half a dozen squadrons whose bases had fallen to the Soviet advance, some of the fierce-looking fighters had been fitted with AN/APR-38 electronic warfare pods to enable the old workhorses to carry up to three Sparrow AIM-7 radar-guided missiles as well as four Sidewinders.

The rest had already been configured as "Wild Weasel" SAM-killers, armed with the new AGM-88 HARMs (High-speed Anti-Radar Missiles), bundles of chaff, special decoy flares, and electronic jamming gear. Jones had wanted to provide the fighter sweep some protection from the Soviet anti-aircraft missiles sure to be packed in close to the fighting front, and the "Weasels" fit the bill.

Just as Jones had predicted, several Air National Guard units had been ferried over to Europe. Already stripped of their front-line planes — F-16s, F-4s, A-10s and F-15s — by the initial call-up, the only fighters the strapped ANG groups could muster were a handful of F-106 Delta Darts, a dozen vintage F-105 Thunderchiefs, and even some creaking F-101 Voodoos.

Hunter knew Jones didn't spend much time thinking about what would happen to the vintage interceptors if a flight of new-generation Soviet fighters, like the MiG-29 Fulcrums, fell in on the aging National Guard planes. It didn't matter whether he worried about it or not — he needed every fighter he could get.

The real "flying circus" atmosphere on the base was brought on not by the USAF planes, diverse as they were; but by the incredible assortment of NATO aircraft assembled at Rota for the final push. Almost every member nation's planes were represented on the field, and some of the southern flank countries had transferred their *entire* air forces of Jones's direct command at Rota.

The remainder of the Spanish Air Force was now there: Some US-built F-5s, and a dozen older F-4 Phantom IIs, as well as some stripped-down French Mirage IIIs and its later F-1 derivative. Even more basic was the tiny Portuguese contingent, flying an odd combination of subsonic A-7 Corsair IIs and stubby G-91s, a 1960s lightweight fighter of Italian design.

The Italians themselves had a few planes at Rota, although most of their air forces were still based in Northern Italy or deployed in the Med. About twenty of the diminutive G-91s, two squadrons of F-104G Starfighters, and several dozen F-104S versions, built by the Italians themselves, were sent to help with the fighter sweep. Their pointed fuselages and very short, thin wings, combined with a higher than average accident rate, had earned the Starfighter the nickname "Manned Missile."

Unfortunately for Jones, the Italians had already lost most of their Tornado interceptors over Germany, and had insisted on keeping the remaining squadron for the defense of Rome.

The Greeks, in an unusual show of cooperation with NATO, had seen fit to send most of their surviving planes. Much of their front-line air strength had been lost during a clash near the Bulgarian border. But there were still more Starfighters, some A-7 Corsair strike planes, two full squadrons of F-5 Tigers, and a handful of Mirage F-1s. Jones, knowing his history lessons well, had wisely separated the Greek pilots from the Turks, who also sent a contingent.

Turkey had the dubious distinction of the oldest aircraft on the flightline at Rota, a collection of ancient F-100 Super Sabres. These North American swept-wing jets were the first mass-produced interceptors to go supersonic, but they dated back to the early 1950s. At least the rest of the Turks' planes were somewhat newer: two squadrons of F-5s, some more mature F-4Cs, and whatever Starfighters hadn't already been shot down by the faster MiG-23s and -21s of the Soviet's southern air defense division.

Of all the NATO partners, it had been the Germans who had taken the brunt of the Soviet air assault, both on the ground and in the treacherous skies over Germany.

Dueling with the speedy Fulcrums and Flankers of the Soviet's front line squadrons, the pilots of the Luftwaffe had used their Tornado GR.3s, F-4 Phantom IIs, and even the aging F-104G Starfighters with skill against the newer Russian jets, holding their own in dogfights and on strike missions.

But the overwhelming numerical superiority of the enemy was too much to handle, and, for the second time in the century, the Luftwaffe had been whittled away to a shell of its former self. Most of the Tornados that remained after the airfields were overrun had been ferried to England; only a handful of German F-4s and Starfighters were now on the field at Rota.

The French had the biggest contingent of modern aircraft, next to the US planes. The advancing Soviet forces were within striking distance of most of their home bases from the fighting front in Belgium, so most of the *Armee de la Air* jet fighters had been split up. Half were sent to Rota in the south, the other half to the NATO air base at Lakenheath in southern England.

At Rota, there was a full squadron of the new Mirage 2000s; as well as almost a full wing of Mirage F-1s; some older Mirage IIIs; and a handful of British-built Jaguar GR.1 interceptors.

Although the French forces weren't under Jones's direct command, their Air Force Chief of Staff had agreed to participate in the Chain Lightning fighter sweep, and Jones was glad for the help. Rather predictably, the French had come in late to the war. But as soon as they saw the Red Army's murderous advance through Germany, they had thrown the full weight of their ground forces into the battle.

The rest of the assembled airplanes at Rota were the scraps and loose ends left from the hundreds of missions flown during the first days of ferocious fighting that had taken place on the continent. Here was a group of sturdy British Buccaneer low-level interceptors that had run out of fuel over France and been abruptly reassigned to Rota; there were some British Jaguars from the Gibraltar base. A Dutch Starfighter. A Canadian F-18. Four French Super-Entendard fighters stranded when their carrier went down in the Med. A pair of Danish Saab Viggens from God-knows-where.

And all of them were gassing and arming up for the big fighter sweep.

It truly *is* a flying circus, thought Hunter as he sat in the cockpit of his all-white replacement F-16, watching the various aircraft take off from Rota's six active runways. "A Goddamn *three-ring* circus."

The question was, could NATO keep it flying long enough to do any good?

Several hundred of the NATO aircraft were already airborne and widely circling the base. By Hunter's count, there was one airplane taking off every 12 seconds from each of the six runways. At that rate, and barring the ever-present danger of mid-air collision, it would take close to an hour to get all 800 airplanes in the air.

Per plan, the 16th TFW was scheduled to take off toward the end of the massive launch. Yet Hunter wondered if the Rota ground crews would make it that far. Already the strain on them was past the breaking point. In the past 24 hours, they had been called on to service the 800 allied fighters that had crowded Rota's hangars, shops, and runways. Aircraft from ten nations' air forces, in various states of repair, with different fuel, ammunition, and maintenance requirements. And there were not nearly enough trained mechanics to do the job.

Hunter was sure it was similar in other place as well. Rota was just one of four NATO bases—two others were in England, the third in Holland—where aircraft participating in Chain Lightning were based.

It was strangely ironic, Hunter thought as he continued the preflight activities, that after all the specialized training and practice and general screwing around, it would all come down to this: one last cavalry charge in the air. Almost 2000 NATO aircraft in the sky at one time, trying to draw out the enemy.

But Hunter knew the most important question of all: Would the Soviets take the bait?

His thoughts were broken by the appearance of his ground crew chief and real-life guardian angel, Blue.

"Good luck up yonder, Captain," the southerner drawled, "and let's try to bring this one back in one piece, OK?"

"It's a deal," Hunter said, shaking hands with the man.

Then suddenly, almost as an afterthought, the flight mechanic asked: "Do you think we have a chance, sir?"

From all the activity at the field, everyone from the pilots to the cooks knew that some kind of final push was on.

Yet the question almost stunned Hunter, not so much that Blue had asked it, but more in *how* he asked it. The pilot was silent for a moment, studying the crowded clusters of gauges and readouts on his cockpit console, yet not really seeing them. He was thinking about how he had asked the very same question of Jones earlier in the day during their discussion about Chain Lightning and Operation Rolling Thunder. That talk had been between two people who would participate in the upcoming battle and who would know whether it was a success or a failure almost immediately. The question from Hunter had actually been an inquiry about the logistics, the tactics, the *basics* of the upcoming mission.

But Blue's question was different. He, and the other base support personnel, had no other choice than to stay behind and await the outcome. It would be an agonizing long vigil. And in that moment, it seemed to Hunter that the totally-unassuming Blue suddenly represented freedom-loving peoples everywhere. What will happen? Will the plan work? *Do you think we have a chance?*

Hunter gave an answer in a measured, yet determined voice.

"Blue, take it from a betting man: this plan has about a one in a thousand chance of coming off," he said. "It's a long shot. The *longest* . . . . But somehow, we'll make it work . . ."

Blue's face fairly drained of all color. He wasn't expecting such a frank reply from the pilot.

"But don't worry, friend," Hunter continued. "I promise you, my wheels will be down and locked when I come back this time. Save the happy foam for the Frenchies, OK?"

Blue managed a laugh, then climbed down off the F-16's access ladder and gave Hunter a salute.

"Good hunting, Captain!" he yelled. "And Lord help the rest of us!"

With that, Hunter brought his screaming GE turbofan engine up nose to full power. He was soon shooting down the crowded runway, gaining speed and altitude as the all-white F-16's tricycle nose wheel lifted off the ground first, pointing the little fighter's tapered snout into the sky. Another hundred feet and the main gear had lifted off, too.

Hunter was airborne once again.

Chapter 25

Climbing high into the sun above Rota, Hunter tucked the landing gear under the wings and leveled off.

The rest of the 16TFW was already aloft and grouped. Hunter moved up into the formation and took his customary place off Jones's right wing. They circled high above the base like that for the next ten minutes until the rest of the NATO aircraft were airborne and grouped. Then, as one, the huge air armada set out to engage the enemy in the gray skies over France.

Much maneuvering followed as Jones ordered the "Wild Weasel" F-4 Phantoms to go ahead first, followed closely by the F-15s, the Tornados, and the smaller F-16s. His reasoning, he had explained to Hunter in the briefing room, was to send the first sweep over enemy-held territory in successive waves, leading off with the SAM-killing, radar-jamming Weasels to put a dent in the Soviets' air defense system. They would have the advantage of surprise, and even a temporary edge in numbers, until the enemy figured out what was going on. More than a hundred Phantoms, each carrying four HARM anti-radar missiles, would have the Soviet gunners thinking the sky had fallen on them, in large, high-explosive pieces.

But it would also tip off the Reds that something big was up, and bells would go off all the way from the front back to Moscow. Once the size of the NATO force was reported, the Soviets would be forced to launch all available aircraft, starting with their state-of-the-art fighters. That's why Jones wanted his heavy artillery to go in first. The allied air-superiority fighters like the F-15s, the Tornados and the dogfighting F-16s would draw the Soviets' first echelon interceptors—Su-27 Flankers, MiG-29 Fulcrums, plus the new MiG-31 Foxhounds—into battle in its opening stages.

If the NATO top dogs could hold the Reds off until the second wave of NATO fighters—launching from Holland—arrived, the Soviets would have no choice but to call up some of their reserves, thus matching the French Mirages and F1s, plus the rest of the interceptor F-4s and F-5s, with the roughly equivalent MiG-23s and Su-17 Fitters.

Following the same progression, the next wave of NATO planes—coming in from England—would include the older Starfighters, the National Guard Delta Darts and Daggers, the A-7s, and the G-91s. Ideally, they would face the East Bloc nations' less modern MiG-21 Fishbeds and Su-15 Flagons; and so on down to the scraps at the bottom of both forces' barrels: NATO antiques like the Turks' F-100 Super Sabres and the National Guard Voodoos, plus the Brits' Jaguars would be engaging MiG-19 Farmers and Su-9 Fishpots of similar vintage.

But Hunter and Jones both knew that such equivalent matchups were by no means preordained—if the Soviets held back a few flights of Fulcrums or Foxhounds, they would make mincemeat of the slower NATO fighters in the later waves. But this was a gamble and they had to reason that such rough parity would exist, if only in the first few hours of the battle.

One thing was for certain: As soon as both sides had scrambled once, the melee would be on in full swing, and more than forty years of jet fighter development would be on display, over the crowded skies of eastern France.

Then it would be every plane—and every pilot—for himself . . .

Up near the front line, the Soviet forward SAM crews were tired and tense, weary from a night of non-stop NATO artillery and mortar attacks, and worried about what this day would bring.

Usually the NATO forces would save their harassing fire for the forward trench line or the massed Soviet armor near the front. But this past night and on into the morning, the sky had been alive with American rockets, mortars, and shells screaming over the heads of the foot soldiers and into the ranks of the mobile SAM-11 anti-aircraft missile launchers, some two miles behind the lines.

The attacks seemed to come in short bursts, then fade away as Soviet long-range artillery responded. Although the American fire was scattered and sporadic, an occasional high-explosive shell or rocket found its mark directly on or under one of the heavy missile trucks, exploding munitions, missiles and men with a deafening thunderclap.

Each time, the cursing Soviet SAM crews had scrambled onto their massive vehicles and lurched the heavy trucks to new hiding places, only to have the Americans locate them again after they had set up the launch tubes and remounted the radar masts of their anti-aircraft missile batteries.

This exhausting game of hide-and-seek had lasted all night and well into the morning along the entire front-line.

It was past noontime before the skies had suddenly become quiet.

A bleary-eyed young Soviet lieutenant stared into the hypnotizing green screen of his mobile radar battery, blinking as the rotating sweep arc illuminated his tense face twice per second.

Like most of the SAM crews around the old French fortress near Verdun, he hadn't slept in almost 36 hours, thanks to the exasperating enemy attacks the previous night. Against standing orders, his captain had staggered off to sleep after ordering half the crew to stand down and get some rest. The lieutenant was left to monitor the droning radar screen.

The young officer muttered a curse and rubbed his bloodshot eyes hard with the heel of his hand, trying to relieve the incessant itching. What he needed was sleep, he thought, not more of this senseless game. He hadn't been able to string together more than 12 hours of sleep since the war began and even then he had been tired, his unit just having returned from maneuvers in the Urals a scant two hours before they were ordered to move west quickly.

Even he, a lowly junior officer, knew that the SCUD attack on Western Europe had caught just about everyone in the Red Army by surprise.

Now his gaze wandered about the inside of the control compartment on the back of the huge SAM launcher, straying from the assigned task of monitoring the radar screen.

If he could only close his eyes for a few seconds . . .

Suddenly, the radar's steady beeping changed tone, rising in pitch as the relentlessly sweeping beam detected an object in the French skies. The Soviet operator was instantly awake, horribly aware of his drift into semi-consciousness.

As he forced his swollen eyes to focus on the green arc, he realized that he must have slept through the initial seconds of radar contact. The southern perimeter of his screen was now alive with fast-moving blips—dozens of them! For a long, terrifying split second he stared at the bright spots on his screen as the sweep arc illuminated them. He had never seen so many indications before. . . . In one last terrifying second, he hoped that his screen was malfunctioning. Or maybe he was hallucinating.

Recovering his composure, he slammed down the red alarm button on his console, shouting hoarsely into the intercom:

"Multiple radar contacts! Distance forty miles! Bearing north-northeast, altitude one-hundred meters!"

The warning blared through the cracked speaker in the missile fire control compartment, rousing an enlisted technician from his own half-sleep. Cursing loudly, he flipped on the missile arming switches and opened the covers of the long tubes that extended up from the truck's flatbed at a forty-five degree angle.

Scrambling across the compartment to where the fire control officer should have been, the Soviet soldier was desperately trying to engage the SAM's targeting radar to lock the missile onto the speeding intruders.

Frustrated, he hollered back into his own intercom at the radar operator. "More power . . . Fire control *will not lock* target . . . Repeat, *more power* . . ."

The young lieutenant responded to the request immediately, cranking the output of the spinning radar dish up to the maximum as he scanned the screen again. Just at that moment, his captain burst through the door, holding his boots and clutching his pants to keep them from falling around his bare feet.

With a panicked look, he screamed for the position and range of the radar contacts, berating the hapless junior officer at the same time.

"Fool! How did they get so close? Give me range and speed of approaching targets *now!*"

The lieutenant sputtered out the information, nearly babbling. He was certain the captain would begin pummeling him in a rage. But instead, the senior man froze in his tracks, his eyes narrowing into slits when he heard the new position and altitude of the incoming contacts.

He started to reach across the radar console in front of the cowering junior officer, his hand traveling toward the intensity control knob. Contacts at that speed and altitude could only mean one thing—SAM killers. But the NATO anti-aircraft suppression flights were usually only four or six planes—here there were two dozen or more.

The captain had lived through three similar attacks by the lethal American "Weasels," surviving by turning off his active search radar quickly enough to avoid the deadly grip of the Yankee anti-radar missile's probing guidance mechanism.

This time he was too late.

No sooner had his hand touched the knob when his eyes widened in horror, watching each of the speeding blips give birth to four more faster blips. The tiny dots of light rapidly increased their distance away from their host blips, streaking down toward the center of the radar screen where the hub of the sweep arc was anchored in its constant rotation.

In his last few seconds of life, the Soviet captain realized exactly what was on the screen before him. The large blips were NATO attack planes, probably American F-4 Phantoms. The small blips were high-speed anti-radar missiles. The center of the screen was their SAM battery's position.

A silent scream rose in his throat as he futilely snapped off the power to the rotating radar dish. The incoming missiles' complex electronics had already locked on to the strongest radar signal available, supplied by the eager young lieutenant's boost to full intensity. Now two of the racing HARMs had homed in on the launch vehicle.

The Soviet captain knew there was no time to abandon the steel box that would become their tomb.

The two missiles struck the SAM launcher a split second apart, lifting the heavy truck completely off the ground in a thundering explosion. The high-explosive warheads detonated in the guts of the SAM vehicle, ripping it in two with powerful blasts that in turn set off the volatile anti-aircraft missiles stored within.

The two Soviet officers, their crew, and the entire vehicle were consumed in the yellow-white eruption that burst from the secondary explosions. Chucks of debris from the wrecked SAM site were flung in all directions, some more than a hundred yards.

When the smoke and flames cleared, all that was left was a burning mass of twisted metal, and the Soviet captain's boots, both of which had somehow survived the holocaust.

Less than a minute later, a wave of thirty F-4 Phantoms flashed over the smoking hulk, flying at a mere two hundred feet.

Captain "Crunch" O'Malley didn't even take a fleeting glance at his handiwork, needing to keep full concentration on the chore of flying nearly twice the speed of sound over the frozen French countryside.

But his weapons officer, Elvis, confirmed the kill from his rear-seat vantage point.

"Looks like we got 'em, Captain . . ." the young man drawled with characteristic understatement.

Crunch was too busy to celebrate; he knew there were more dangers in the sky.

As if on cue, the shrill wail of the F-4's airborne threat warning sounded, filling the small cockpit with its urgency.

"We've got company!" Elvis was instantly riveted to the tiny screen, calling out over the intercom as he identified the source of the radar's warning. "I've got multiple bogies at twelve o'clock, moving fast. Could be Foxhounds."

A sharp chill ran up Crunch's spine. The MiG-31 Foxhounds were big, two-seat interceptors with lots of speed and plenty of air-to-air missiles on board. All the Phantom had left after shooting the HARMs were a couple of decoy flares and several chaff cannisters to ward off the Soviet missiles.

But Crunch knew what he had to do.

"Steady, boys," he said tightly into his radio to the speeding Phantom flight stretched out on either side of his aircraft. "You know the drill—let 'em see us and then we pull a fast U-turn and make tracks . . . On my order . . ."

His voice trailed off in anticipation of the next bit of data he would receive from his back-seater.

"Not yet, Cap'n," Elvis near-whispered into his intercom, "A little closer . . . no movement yet . . . OK . . . *now!* They're breaking!"

Crunch savagely yanked the stick over to pull the shrieking Phantom in a gut-twisting high-g turn. The sturdy fighter shuddered at the strain, then bolted for the horizon with the MiGs in hot pursuit.

"Send the message, Lieutenant," Crunch shouted to Elvis over the roar of the Phantom's afterburner-boosted engine. "And let's hope those bastards don't catch us."

Hunter felt the presence of the Soviet planes several moments before they were acquired on his F-16's radar.

The larger F-15s ahead of him already had targets for the huge AMRAAMs (Advanced Medium Range Air-to-Air Missiles) slung under the fuselages of their speeding fighters. The Eagle pilots saw two sets of speeding blips appear on their screens—the ragged line of Phantoms escaping at low altitude was being rapidly overtaken by an orderly formation of faster MiG-31 Foxhounds.

In another ten seconds, the Soviets would be firing their own large air-to-air missiles at the fleeing F-4s. But the Eagle flight leader was holding a steady course toward the two flights of planes ahead, breaking radio silence to give instructions to his men.

"Fast Lane One, Fast Lane One," the deep voice crackled over the radio, "Bogies are dead ahead forty miles out. Do not launch until Weasel flight goes through."

The F-15's powerful radar enabled each pilot to target a separate MiG, and lock on with their big missiles. What's more, the AMRAAM's range had a slight edge over its counterpart, the Soviet AA-10.

Closing to the battle, the streaking Phantoms shot underneath the flight of F-15s. Two seconds later, the Eagle flight leader gave the order to fire.

"Fast Lane One, *launch!*" the lead F-15 pilot called out to his wing. "Break and engage at will!"

Still ten miles ahead, the Soviets were just breaking formation to pounce on the slower "Weasels" when their own threat warning radars went off, activated by the deadly AMRAAMs fired by the Eagle fighters.

For the moment, the Phantoms were ignored as the Soviet weapons officers tried desperately to jam the incoming missiles, relay evasive maneuver directions to the pilots, and engage the F-15s ahead of them instead of the escaping F-4 strike planes, all in the same thirty seconds. None of them succeeded in accomplishing all three before the missiles tore into their packed formation.

The lethal American rockets had closed the distance between the two groups of speeding fighters before most of the MiGs could react effectively. Like ducks in a gallery, four of the heavy Soviet fighters exploded into ugly black clouds. Two more of them collided in midair as they both swerved to avoid the attack, adding to the swirling confusion that stretched across the bleak skies above France.

A delayed-fired AMRAAM homed in relentlessly on the Soviet leader, as the pilot tried to jink his way out of the missile's sophisticated seeking beam. But it was no use. The AMRAAM impacted on the big Foxhound near its left engine intake, the explosion horribly ripping the fuselage along one entire side. The airplane blew up just as the pilot ejected, sending the smoking jet plummeting to the ground below.

Once the wave of AMRAAMs had passed, the Soviets who had avoided the incoming missiles breathed a collective sigh of relief. But the respite didn't last long. Ten seconds later, they were pounced on by the streaking Eagles as they descended on the scattering Foxhounds.

Hunter and the rest of the 16th were now close enough to join the swirling dogfight that was already in progress high above the French countryside. Several squadrons of MiG-29 Fulcrums had also joined the fray, as had a group of other NATO top-line fighters.

In seconds the sky was filled with roaring, diving, and twisting planes from both sides, dueling with cannons and missiles.

Hunter only saw the battle in a series of flashes. A British Tornado exploded as one of the Fulcrums unleashed a heat-seeking missile that disappeared into its hot exhaust nozzle. A

Foxhound was blown up by cannon fire from an F-16. An F-15 went down. Then two more Foxhounds. He saw a smoking F-16 twist away from the scene. Then a Tornado and a Fulcrum collided head-on no more than a half mile in front of him.

Everywhere he looked there were crazily zig-zagging, jinking fighters, dozens of air-to-air missiles, lines of cannon tracers, some missing, some not, explosions, fire, smoke—all of it leaving an insane spider web of contrails across a fifty square mile chunk of French sky. Cockpits on both sides were filled with the incessant wail of radar warning systems. Target radar screens went white from the effects of hundreds of jamming signals and too many targets to process.

Radio procedure was abandoned in the heat of the airborne melee as pilots screamed warnings to each other:

"Dive and roll!"

"There's two on your tail, Tango-Six!"

"Got 'em! Good kill!"

"Warning yellow, weapons hold . . ."

"Fox one . . . Fox one!"

"Tally two! Tally two!"

"Head's up Delta-Four! Foxhounds coming down from up-stairs!"

"Lock him up. Lock him up!"

"Break left and climb! Now!"

"Christ! I'm hit! I'm hit . . ."

Hunter had never experienced anything like it before. Nothing he'd ever done had even come close to it. Not the Thunderbird training. Not the simulations of Red Flag back in the States. Not even the hellish sorties he'd flown in the last few days.

It was a whole new ball game now.

Time seemed to slow as he tried to absorb the whole scope of the battle and yet block out the extraneous information pouring into his cockpit console and radio headphones. His head swiveled constantly around the small cockpit of the strangely all-white fighter as he tried to keep track of the expanding battle that had airplanes spinning through the sky like mad dervishes.

Suddenly a Fulcrum flashed in front of him. Purely on instinct he punched up his missile targeting system, and let go with a Sidewinder. There was a puff of smoke, a flash, an explosion and a cloud of debris. That quickly, one more enemy plane was destroyed. Hunter picked off another low-flying Fulcrum that happened in front of him with a long burst from his cannon.

Then he snap-rolled the F-16 to engage a speeding Foxhound above him. Locking another Sidewinder onto the Soviet jet, he stabbed the fire control button just as his own radar threat device was activated by an incoming air-to-air fired by an Su-27 Flanker that had just appeared on the scene.

Without missing a beat, Hunter mashed another button on his side-stick controller to release two decoy flares that shot off to his left. The Soviet missile took the high-intensity bait and veered off to explode when it met the flare. Executing a high-g vertical scissoring maneuver, Hunter drew the attacking Flanker high above the fray, twisting rapidly in the thin air.

When the eager Soviet pilot overshot the smaller F-16, Hunter lanced the big Flanker with a sustained cannon burst that gashed a wide wound in the Russian's upper wing surface. Flame immediately appeared at the edges of the torn metal, igniting the spraying fuel that quickly engulfed the entire tail section. The stricken Flanker plunged down through the clouds, spinning out of control.

Hunter had no time to savor the kill or even catch his breath before diving down into the dogfight again. He spotted Jones's fighter weaving through the crowded sky, unsuccessfully trying to shake a pair of Fulcrums that seemed to be locked onto his tail.

Without a moment's hesitation, Hunter tipped the F-16 over in a screaming power dive to intercept the pursuing MiGs. Still a thousand feet above the Soviet planes, he poured on cannon fire as he deliberately spun his agile fighter in a tight barrel roll along the path of his steep dive. The maneuver sent the 30mm shells arcing into the wing roots of both Fulcrums from above, severing one of them completely. Both planes broke off the attack as they wobbled and rapidly lost altitude as a result of Hunter's guns.

"Thank you, Captain," Jones's voice said over Hunter's radio, calm as if Hunter had just bought him a drink.

Then Jones sent out a warning to all of TFW16. "Keep an eye on your fuel gauges," he said. "We've got to make it back to the gas stations."

"That's a roger," Hunter replied, keying his microphone as he instantly scanned the fuel supply information displayed in front of him on his Heads-Up-Display (HUD). He was getting near the safe return level needed to make it to the tanker rendezvous.

But still the sky was full of Soviet fighters.

"Estimate enough fuel for a few more passes, then it's time to turn this tag team over to the next wave," Hunter informed the general.

"Roger, Captain," the general replied. "I suggest we screw them all up and do a burst and break at forty. Might draw some stray missiles."

"Roger," Hunter replied, knowing that Jones was calling for the old Starburst Thunderbird maneuver. "On you, break at forty."

Hunter slammed his side-stick controller forward and the white fighter shot through the swirling dogfight, joined by Jones a split-second behind him.

The two F-16s rose as one in a straight vertical climb, belly to belly only a scant twenty feet apart. Several Soviet fighters aimed missiles at the speeding pair of jets that were tearing through the smoke of the battle.

With at least a trio of missiles racing them for the clouds, Hunter and Jones kept the throttles open until they reached forty-thousand feet. Then both F-16s chopped power to drop their pointed noses at the ground below, twisting in an interlocking spiral as they descended in a blur of wings and contrails. The Soviet missiles couldn't make the nose-over with the F-16s, and they orbited harmlessly until their fuel was spent and they exploded.

The two pilots kept their spiral descent tight and fast until they both broke away to target separate MiGs in the cluster of fighters below them. Two Sidewinders flashed from Hunter's wings and they found the hot exhausts of two Foxhounds. The big jets burst into ugly, flaming balls of jagged metal and disappeared in the confusion of the furball.

Weaving again through the tangled mass of aircraft and missile contrails in the pack, Hunter and Jones were joined by two more familiar F-16s on the 16th TFW. Ben Wa and JT Toomey were soon flying alongside in a tight formation. Together, the four planes cut a wide swath through the enemy fighters, meeting any challenge with a hail of cannon fire that ripped through the airspace ahead of them like four high-tech Grim Reapers cutting down corn stalks. Six more MiGs had fallen away in flames before the lethal flyby was complete.

Jones communicated with his squadron by a wing signal that it was time to vector off and withdraw to let the next wave come through. The F-15s and the Tornados were also withdrawing at this point. Their fuel situation would become critical very soon, and Jones didn't want to risk losing any planes over the Pyrenees. He needed every one he could get. And then some.

"Let's go, boys," Jones said, warily eyeing his fuel data through the HUD., "Save some for the next crew."

Hunter reluctantly broke off the attack and veered off to form up on Jones and the rest of the first wave of fighters. Several Soviet fighters began a spirited pursuit, but they, too, were low on fuel and didn't chase the NATO planes much past the battle area.

Thus ended the first round of what would be the largest air-to-air battle of any war. Predictably, both sides called up reserves to cover for their spent first-echelon interceptors.

No sooner had the combined force of F-16s, F-15s, and Tornados left the area when the NATO second echelon line of aircraft arrived on the scene. So too just as the Soviet top-line fighters began retreating, their slightly slower, slightly less-sophisticated second-line fighter force showed up.

So far, the Soviets were following the script perfectly.

Chapter 26

The 16 TFW Falcons were 50 miles north of the French Riviera, when Hunter, Jones, and the others picked up a large flight of aircraft rising up from the Mediterranean and heading inland.

"Who the hell are these guys?" JT called out.

"I hope they're on our side," Wa added, as the large concentration of blips passed across his radar screen.

Jones knew they were.

"Let me put it this way," Jones told his pilots. "Next time Army plays Navy, bet on the swabbies."

Instantly, the F-16 pilots knew the large aerial force was made up of US carrier-based aircraft.

It was one ace in the hole that Jones had told no one about. For the past 36 hours he had pleaded with the Pentagon to assign him some Navy airplanes for the fighter sweep. He reminded the Washington desk jockeys that not only did the Soviets have a big numerical advantage in ground-based fighters in Europe, but their replacements had only to fly from the Urals or Siberia to join the battle. This point was the whole idea behind the first sorties the 16th had flown in the war—that was, destroying some of the enemy's key forward airbases, thus making it more difficult for them to receive and service their behind the lines fighters. Jones argued that Navy aircraft, while not plentiful enough to even out the odds in the West's numerical disadvantage, would certainly help a bad situation from getting worse.

The resistance from Washington was immediate and Jones knew

why. The Navy carrier groups had their hands full with battling the Soviets in the Atlantic as well as in spill-over battles around the Mediterranean, especially in the Balkans.

But before Jones had taken off, he had received a fairly optimistic message stating that there was a chance Navy aircraft could participate in one—and *only* one—mission of the on-going fighter sweep. Now, seeing the large force winging up from the western Med, the general knew that the Navy had come through.

Ten minutes later the two groups passed each other in the skies just over the French Riviera.

The Air Force pilots waggled their wings as a greeting to the Navy aviators as they thundered past, returning the salute. Despite a long-standing interservice rivalry, there were no insults exchanged as was usually the case when the friendly rivals met up. The pilots all knew that everyone was in it together now.

The final push.

Hunter's sharp eyes scanned the naval attack force as it wheeled up toward the front. A dozen A-6 Intruder attack planes, slung with heavy STARMs—Standard Anti-Radar Missiles—were leading the wave. Hunter knew their function, on this mission anyway, was similar to that of the "Wild Weasel" Phantoms—to preemptively knock out the mobile SAMs that the Soviets would surely be moving up to replace their recent losses.

Although the sturdy Intruders had no guns or air-to-airs to defend itself, a sister plane flew in formation with them to jam both ground and airborne anti-aircraft guidance signals. This particular A-6, called the Prowler, carried an airborne jamming system like the EF-111 Raven. This would keep the enemy radar operators busy long enough to allow the lightly-armed Intruders to escape.

Soviet fighters facing the main naval attack force would more likely be tangling with the formidable F-14 Tomcats of two carrier wings. Although they were probably one of the most expensive aircraft in the US inventory, Hunter knew they had proven to be worth their price tags in combat situations. A truly superior acquisition and targeting radar allowed the weapons officer to track and fire on six targets independently, while the pilot burned through the air at Mach 2 plus. Hunter could see huge AIM-54 Phoenix missiles visible under the wings and fuselages of the

Tomcats, ready to be targeted and fired on a Soviet plane while the F-14s were still almost a hundred miles away.

Following the Tomcats into battle were the smaller F/A-18 Hornets. The Hornets were newer, and designed to do both dog-fighting and ground attack, hence its dual F/A designation. Slightly slower than the speedy Tomcats, the Hornets topped out just under Mach 2, but they carried an impressive payload of Sidewinders and Sparrow radar-guided missiles, as well as a power-ful cannon in the nose.

Jones watched the Navy fliers flash past, and his relief that the Navy had joined the fight was quickly replaced by a pang of remorse.

More young lives going into the meat grinder . . .

He was already stung by the losses in his own formation of aircraft returning to Rota. A count-off immediately after they withdrew from the air battle over Verdun had told him the bad news: Three F-16s, four F-15s, and six Tornados were among the missing.

True, they had shot down far more of the enemy's planes in the twisting, turning dogfight—but they couldn't sustain that rate forever, especially since the Soviets had more planes to sacrifice and very little hesitation to do just that.

In the F-16 directly off Jones's wing, Hunter stared grimly at the spiked peaks of the Pyrenees directly ahead. The sun was begin-ning to set and the skies were taking on a frighteningly red hue.

Suddenly, it seemed as if there was red everywhere—even deep within the recesses of his psyche. He felt an anger building inside him. Sure, he had flamed six Soviet fighters in less than twenty minutes during the battle. But like Jones, he knew that, even with the Navy's infusion of power and the bravery and technical super-iority of the NATO air forces, the lopsided kill ratios would soon start to erode. Eventually, the Soviets' numerical superiority would start to work in their favor.

Hunter felt a cold chill run him through at the thought of it. A burning red fear had descended upon him. Not a fear of dying. He was way beyond that point. No, this was a *fear of defeat*. What would happen if NATO lost? What would become of the world if the allies failed to turn back the Red tide? Would freedom exist in a world where the Soviets dominated Europe and hobbled America's ability to defend herself? And how long would it be before America herself was consumed?

Hunter stared out of the increasingly red skies. He couldn't bear to watch the image forming in his mind's eye—a shattering American continent, pieces drifting away and burning with an eerie crimson glow, smoke billowing from the huge cracks in the earth's surface . . . Millions of innocent people immersed in the fear and pain of freedom lost . . .

The vision got worse. A nightmare shimmered into focus in the red skies to the west. The clouds and sunlight and smoke from the war seemed to be forming into the proud colors of the US flag. But the flag was on fire, flaming out of control . . .

"No!" Hunter shouted aloud, slamming his fist into the padded cockpit armrest and shaking the maddening vision from his mind. *"I will not let this happen . . ."*

Just then, a powerful force washed over him like a tidal wave. It was *the feeling.* The sixth sense was now coming into him stronger than he had ever experienced it before. Suddenly gone was his terrible vision of the dark specter of defeat. The red skies dissolved to reveal a shining new, blue sky image—a huge red, white, and blue banner rippling like the surface of a wave. It was a shimmering vision of Old Glory, the stars and stripes itself. Hunter knew an omen when he saw one: this was a sign of his own modest destiny.

The feeling had shown him the path—now he was ready to undertake the journey himself.

Refueling from the tankers, Jones had noticed Hunter's odd behavior.

The young pilot had had almost no communication with the tanker crew, just the minimum needed for the refueling process. And even then his voice sounded strange, lower in tone, almost *disembodied.* Before Jones could radio a message, the young F-16 pilot was off for Rota on full afterburner.

The general had learned to respect Hunter's periods of introspection, but this time he was worried. The young ace had taken a lot of chances in the day's first sortie, and Jones questioned his own wisdom in revealing so much of the desperate strategy to him. He suddenly felt as if he had unfairly burdened Hunter by telling him the grim prospects for the success of the final push.

Maybe I should talk to him, Jones thought.

"No," Jones immediately answered himself. "I've got a couple thousand other planes and pilots to worry about, and all of them probably need guidance more than Hunter does."

Back on the ground at the jammed Rota airbase, most of the pilots returning from the first sortie had landed, briefly checked their aircraft for damages, and headed off to the debriefing meetings that had been set up in the main mess hall. To save time between sorties, Jones had made arrangements so that his pilots could eat while they spoke with the intelligence officers who interviewed each flier about the enemy's aircraft, tactics, and numbers.

Hunter, by contrast, had landed the all-white F-16 on the auxiliary runway near the refueling hardstand. Displaying some rare rank-pulling, he "convinced" the flight crew to gas up the small fighter with a full load of JP-8, despite the standard operating procedure that dictated allowing the plane's hot engine to cool before pumping the volatile jet fuel aboard.

Hunter, still in his flight suit, was clutching a scrap of paper as he ran to the base's main service hangar. There he found Blue, the chief flight mechanic, elbows deep inside the radome chamber of an Italian F-104S Starfighter, cursing and muttering to himself as he extracted a faulty cable connector.

"Blue, I have to talk to you," the young pilot said.

Something in his voice, in the urgency of his tone, caused Blue to stop abruptly and stare at the young pilot. It was as if Hunter's voice was coming from deep within a well.

"I need you to rig up four of these," he continued, passing the scrap of paper to the busy mechanic. On it were sketched some wiring diagrams and a set of rudimentary brackets shaped like a rounded letter 'M'.

"What is this?" Blue asked, himself weary from two straight days of work without sleep. "I haven't got time for any science fair projects . . ."

Hunter didn't seem to hear the man's protestations as he handed him the scrap of paper.

"It's a modification for my F-16," he said. "For the Sidewinders. I need to carry more and these will do the trick. Not perfect, but I don't have time for anything fancy. I need four of them by the time I get back from the next run."

"*Four* of them?" Blue said, as he looked at the ragged drawing. He had to admit he was somewhat intrigued by the simple, yet efficient design of the system. "You can't just Rube Goldberg this thing onto wing or the fuselage, Captain. The plane wasn't built for it. It hasn't been tested—you don't know whether it'll work or not."

Hunter responded woodenly, his eyes already fixed on a point beyond the hangar wall. His voice was low, but steady. "It will work. I'll wire it together myself. I just want you to gin it up so I can do it as soon as I land again."

Blue stared hard at the pilot, the man whose life he had saved the day before. For the first time he noticed how tightly drawn Hunter's face looked in the grimy hangar interior. Then he looked back at the crude little sketch, as if he were being pulled into the project by an irresistible force.

He stared muttering again.

"Well, I guess the bracket's easy enough," he said. "We've got the stock right here. And these jumper wires seem . . ." Blue stopped in mid-sentence and looked at Hunter again. "Jesus, Captain, how bad is it up there?"

For the first time, Hunter looked away, unable to answer.

"Okay, Captain," Blue said with another glance at the paper, "I'll do it. But to make four of them, I'll need some help and I might be hard pressed to find a warm body to spare."

But Hunter didn't hear him. He was already running back out through the hangar door, eyes fixed on the flightline where his white F-16 had just finished receiving a new load of fuel and ammo, and had transformed once again into a fully capable supersonic killing machine.

One of the ground crew had already loaded the preflight tape containing the computer boot-ups, so the sleek fighter was ready to go as soon as Hunter strapped in.

He was airborne in less than two minutes. His total ground time was less than half an hour.

Chapter 27

Back at the front, the intense air battle continued, as more and more Soviet fighters were vectored into the area over eastern France to meet the increasing number of NATO airplanes.

Oddly enough, the massive, on-going dogfight had spurred the Soviet High Command to issue a panicky suicidal order: Its troops must punch through to Paris *now*, despite the heavy casualties being inflicted on them by the outnumbered NATO defenders.

It was a strange, almost laughable dictate, the first real indication that even though it still held the upper hand, the Soviet High Command, so unprepared as it was for the war, was now becoming a bit desperate. Just twelve hours before, the rapid Soviet advance had ground to a halt in many places, stalled partly because of overextended supply lines and partly because of the increasing reluctance of Moscow's East European "allies" to serve as cannon fodder for the Soviet armored units.

And wherever the *blitzkrieg* had sputtered, the dividing line between the armies of freedom and those of domination had become a trench-and-sandbag border, in some places quickly stretching hundreds of miles long.

Fighting side by side as their grandfathers had fought head-to-head, German, US, British, and French troops battled the Soviets in these instantly muddy trenches, struggling against overwhelming odds to maintain a foothold on the European continent—a foothold that once lost, would not be easily regained.

Everywhere along the battle lines, exhausted NATO soldiers

collapsed in the cold, winter mud, only to be roused when their comrades tripped over them in their own weariness. Leaning heavily on the quickly tattered sandbag walls, they sometimes fired at enemies they couldn't see; ghosts of World War I, rising up to do battle again. Real enough were the dreaded, hourly artillery barrages, the daily armored assaults, and the ever-present stench of death. On and on it went and those knowledgeable in history were more than convinced that they were witnessing the most ferocious fighting that France had seen in two thousand years of combat.

All the while, the air battle raged above.

The Soviet field marshal in charge of the attacking Red Army was relaying hourly messages back to Moscow, explaining the ferocity of the NATO air offensive, demanding more SAM batteries, more planes out of reserve, and more supplies if he was to have a chance of breaking through to Paris.

The NATO commanders were concerned as well. For them the air war was providing a distraction, but not a decisive victory. The NATO ground forces were beginning to get the rapidly spreading whiff of despair; the sense that they would eventually run out of French real estate; and that their backs could be against the sea soon.

In many places, troops on both sides were critically short of ammunition. In these places, many of the troops lay crouched in their fortified foxholes or the trenches, watching the ever expanding aerial combat overhead. From their mudholes carved in the war-torn French countryside, the air war seemed very distant and oddly thrilling—a non-stop movie reel of spectacular dogfighting by every type of jet fighter imaginable.

It was only when one of the wounded aircraft plunged down to the ground among them did the watching infantrymen realize that the battle in the sky was every bit as deadly and ferocious as their battle on the ground.

During one whole day and a dazzling night, they had witnessed the endless rolling airborne brawl that sent contrails of planes and missiles criss-crossing through the skies above them. And more than a few of them, officers mostly, had noticed that one airplane in particular seemed to be everywhere at once—diving, twisting, climbing, shooting all the way.

It was a USAF F-16, painted all white . . .

This airplane always seemed to be in the sky directly above them, as if the pilot never left the scene of battle. As if he had an endless supply of fuel, ammo, and endurance. As if he were fighting the entire battle on his own.

The pilot—who became known as The Ghost—either led a charmed life, the muddy grunts reasoned, or he must be one crazy son-of-a-bitch.

Chapter 28

Time had lost any meaning for Hunter since his vision the day before.

He flew and fought and flew again, a non-stop pattern from Rota's airstrip to the killing skies above France. Eighteen sorties so far, with no end in sight.

His jury-rigged Sidewinder modification was working perfectly. Now the strange white F-16 could carry up to twelve of the deadly air-to-airs in clusters on his wings. Many Soviet pilots had watched him fire four, then swooped in with the false confidence born of a mistaken belief that he had shot the entire wad.

Many had plunged to the ground in flames after discovering the truth.

Now as Hunter entered the battle for the nineteenth time, he saw the skies above France had become an even larger, swirling mass of NATO and Warsaw Pact planes. The relatively orderly matched waves of comparable forces had long ago been scrambled into a hopeless melee as the old and new came together in fiery duels which now spilled out in a 500-square-mile area.

Flashing into the periphery of the continuous dogfight, Hunter first saw a Greek F-5 take a Soviet missile head on and explode in an ugly cloud. Above, an older MiG-21 was flamed by cannon fire from a French Navy Mirage. To his left, a US National Guard Delta Dart was engaging a Polish Su-17 Fitter, and getting the worst of it, but a second Dart was heading for the rescue.

Hunter even saw one of the pluckier Turks try to turn his ancient

F-100 Super Sabre inside a supersonic Su-27 Flanker. Although far superior in firepower and maneuverability, the Soviet interceptor was out of missiles and kept overshooting the slower Sabre. But the Turk's luck ran out when the Flanker climbed sharply and rolled at high altitude to dive on the older NATO plane.

The cockpit of the F-100 exploded under a hail of cannon shells from the diving Flanker.

The Soviet pilot had no time to congratulate himself on the easy kill—in a second, Hunter was on him like a tiger, loosing a cannon barrage of his own that tore through the Soviet's engines and engulfed the big fighter in a fireball.

Barely twenty seconds into the furball, and Hunter already claimed his first kill.

The fight was on thicker than ever. Even the F-16's sophisticated acquisition radar system couldn't possibly identify all the targets in its broad sweep, as hundreds of blips and IFF signals filled the screen in the cramped cockpit. Hunter quickly realized that it had never been this packed before, and he knew he had to make a choice that he hadn't faced up until now.

If he tried to use his on-board computers to thread the needle through the tangle of enemy and friendly planes in front of him, the processing circuits, or the Sidewinder's own sensors, would overload and cause the missiles to detonate prematurely. With twelve of the lethal airborne torpedoes hanging from his wings, that was a chance he didn't want to take.

He took a deep breath from his mask, feeling the head rush that pure oxygen always gave him, then he switched the F-16's weapons systems from AUTOMATIC to MANUAL. He used to do this on occasion while training pilots at Nellis, often challenging the best student in the class to a simulated combat against him—without the use of his radar and acquisition computers and he had never lost.

But this was not simulated combat.

He had decided to rely totally on his instincts to fight, a decision that no other fighter pilot would dare to make. But no other fighter pilot had his extrasensory powers.

Seeking multiple targets for the Sidewinder clusters, he climbed sharply and scanned the eastern sky with his long-range inner sensors. He found his prey, flying in formation just beyond the horizon—two squadrons of MiG-23 Floggers.

With his radar shut down, he knew he was less likely to be picked up by the crude acquisition systems aboard the Flogger interceptors. Their systems were designed to intercept American SAC bombers, and they relied heavily on ground-based radars and the AWACS-like Mainstay radar planes for their target vectors.

Hunter mentally fixed their position in his head then armed his missiles.

Except for their flight leader, the pilots of the MiG-23 flight were young reservists who had just been recalled to active duty for the first time since their training at one of the Soviets' Siberian air defense bases.

Now, too intent on the upcoming fracas, they were barely watching their radar screens.

The veteran flight leader, Gregor Vladimirovitch Tumansky, was the only one in the bunch that had ever seen combat before and that was as an attack plane pilot in Afghanistan. However, he *was* intently watching his tiny radar screen, well aware that dangers lurked in every part of the compass in such a wide-ranging dogfight. He saw the flickering image of a single blip high above him, but it soon disappeared into the snowy edges of the screen as his balky radar set crackled with noise.

Taking the warning seriously, Tumansky ordered the young pilots behind him to stay in formation. There's safety in numbers, he told them again. Besides, he thought, no single enemy plane would dare attack a whole squadron, much less two squadrons.

The pilots' strained banter gave lie to their nervousness as they tightened up their positions, drawing together as if huddling from an unseen noise.

At the rear of the formation, Hunter was coming into range behind the last Flogger in line.

A sudden burst of speed from the F-16's afterburner put Hunter in range, and he quickly fired a Sidewinder cluster.

A split second apart, the three missiles literally fell off the F-16's wingtip as the special brackets released them. Since they were all jump-wired to the same targeting point, their flight path was similar. And since the bracket release created a half-second delay

213

between missiles, they all acquired separate targets in the tight formation when the Sidewinders' own guidance system took over, locating and sequentially locking in on the hottest sources available.

The three supersonic missiles were picked up by the Soviet pilot's threat warning receivers, but they had only time to set off one alarm cycle before they plowed up the tails of three MiGs in the rear of the formation. Three huge explosions rocked the sky as the fully armed fighters burst into flames.

"Stay on course!" Tumansky bellowed into his radio after confirming the kills on his radar scope. "This could be a deception to draw us away from the fight!"

Slightly shaken, the Soviet colonel once again had seen the small blip on his target screen, and once again, it had quickly moved off the edge beyond his limited range. Suddenly another missile cluster was fired at the MiGs—this one from almost a ninety-degree angle to the formation, intersecting it in midair like a perfectly aimed torpedo spread fired at a wallowing convoy. Each of the missiles again selected different targets as three more planes took the flaming one-way plunge to the muddy earth four miles below.

But this flight of missiles' deadly work was not yet through—debris from one of the luckless Floggers was sucked into the square side intakes of two following-in-line MiGs, causing them to flame out and spin down out of control.

His composure momentarily gone, Tumansky gasped aloud when five more of his planes disappeared from the screen, muttering to no one in particular, "How can such a thing happen? I saw only three missiles! Can this be the 'Stealth' the Yankees have?"

A chill ran up his spine. No wonder they couldn't see it for more than a few seconds on radar. He was about to transmit the warning to the survivors of his squadron when the rapidly moving blip sped into his radar range again, appearing on the other side of the now-ragged Soviet formation. Now the Soviet flight leader was very confused. Whatever it was, the enemy jet was *not* invisible to radar. But the pilot seemed to know how to stay out of sight—and somehow, he was carrying many more air-to-air missiles than the Soviet officer thought was possible.

Reluctantly, Tumansky knew the mystery pilot would tear the MiG formation to shreds if they stayed in a rigid box.

Even before he could bring his jaw closed to give the order, the Soviet flight leader saw yet another spread of Sidewinder missiles come into view on his screen, from the *opposite* direction from where he last saw the phantom attacker! Three more deadly darts ended the flights of three more Floggers in flaming clouds of debris.

"Break formation, and attack at will!" Tumansky called out, his voice rising sharply. "Find that bastard, *now!*"

The eager young pilots under Tumansky's command did not have the benefit of combat experience, and it showed in their amateurish pursuit of the elusive F-16.

Several times a MiG pilot thought he spotted the enemy plane near the edge of a cloud bank, and streaked off to engage without waiting for his partner to fly cover for him. Each pilot who found himself on the other side of the cloud discovered an angry Hunter on his tail, pumping round after round of cannon ammo into the hapless Soviet plane. After losing four more of his planes this way, the Soviet colonel ordered his surviving planes to pair off and *stay* paired off.

But the results were no different.

No longer content to play the Invisible Man, Hunter barrel-rolled through the MiG tag teams at high speed, almost daring the Soviets to fire their Atoll air-to-air missiles at him. When they did, the marauding ivory F-16 somehow managed to lure the speeding darts toward him while maneuvering *behind* another pair of Floggers. Incredibly, another four planes were downed by their comrades' own missiles.

Hunter had rigged the last three Sidewinders for independent firing, and he proceeded to target them as he approached the front of the now-scattered Flogger formation. Head-on, the big Soviet jets looked like malevolent insects, their pointed noses and huge air intakes looming larger than life. The combined approach speed between the MiGs and Hunter was almost four times the speed of sound.

Deftly jinking and side-slipping the agile F-16, Hunter fired the last three missiles at the MiGs in front of the pack. Then, with all the speed his afterburner could muster, he shot the white fighter straight up into the air, climbing until he could see the blue edge of the stratosphere arching above his nose.

Tumansky heard his threat warning alarm sound, and he heard the frantic cries of the two planes on either side of him as the deadly missiles engulfed their Floggers in flaming mushrooms of destruction. He heard the clicks of their radios as the transmitters melted and died forever. He heard the frightened questions from his other pilots, wanting to know whether they should turn back. At the same instant, he saw the F-16 shoot by him and climb straight into the sun.

The plane looked so small, so graceful. Without its deadly load of air-to-air missiles, it seemed almost . . . *regal*. The shock wave left behind by the F-16's supersonic climb brought the Soviet pilot out of his hypnotic trance.

He knew when he had had enough. His remaining pilots were so rattled, they would be worthless in the gigantic dogfight now only fifty miles away.

With one curt order, Tumansky regrouped his survivors and turned back toward his base.

Chapter 29

Back on the auxiliary fueling strip at Rota, a dozen fighters lined up to be pumped full of JP-8.

Of the eight hundred planes that had thundered into the skies only forty-eight hours ago, less than two hundred were now operational. Forty or so were up at the battle front, another thirty had just taken off, and many others were limping back to the Spanish base. The rest had either been shot down, crashed en route or damaged beyond all hopes of repair.

Crippled aircraft of a half-dozen nation's air forces were scattered around the auxiliary runway and in various hangars of the base's sprawling repair facility. Here a Greek Mirage was getting a new wing section to replace a riddled chunk of metal sheeting. Next to it, an Italian Starfighter was propped on a huge steel jack stand, waiting for a new landing gear strut. On the far side of the field were the burned-out hulks of six or seven more fighters that had pancaked into the crowded runway and exploded.

General Seth Jones, commander of the dwindling NATO air forces, had just stubbed out the last bitter end of a cigar, grinding it into the hot tarmac of the base's runway. More than five hundred airplanes lost or knocked out of operation. And that just from Rota alone. . . . God knows how many of those pilots had been able to bail out and make it to safety. And he was the one responsible for sending them into the madness.

He shook his head, peeling off his flight helmet to run his hands through the trademark whiffle cut. He suddenly stopped, stifling a yawn, and looked hard at his hands. They trembled slightly, even after a concentrated effort to steady them. He shook his head again, cursing silently.

Almost a dozen sorties in the last two days. Grabbing a sandwich at the debriefing tables set up in the mess hall. A precious three hours of sleep while his plane's radar was repaired was required. And all the while he was being fed new information about the progress of the other airborne operation — Rolling Thunder. It was the hinge of fate that determined whether the fighter sweep of Chain Lightning was a bold and desperate ploy or just another senseless waste of men and machinery.

In the midst of his dark thoughts about the war's progress and the appalling losses, Jones's thoughts turned back to one pilot. It was almost ludicrous to be concerned for a single man with all the death and destruction around him, but Jones knew this man was different — he was more than just another pilot.

He approached the white F-16 just as it finished taking on fuel. The pilot was looking over the side of the cockpit, checking the motion of his tail surfaces, when Jones clambered up the ladder and stepped across the wing.

"Greetings, Captain," he shouted above the whine of the idling jet engine. "Good hunting?"

Jones was shocked when Hunter turned around to face him. The younger man's face was pale and drawn, his chin carried the stubble of two days' growth, and his flight suit looked like he hadn't taken it off in weeks. But it was the eyes that startled Jones the most — two glowing embers, crackling with an eerie fire that seemed to make them burn like lasers from deep within his head.

Hunter barely acknowledged Jones's presence and continued the preflight check, tapping several gauges on the F-16's complex console.

"Haven't seen you in debriefing, Captain," Jones said flatly.

Hunter whispered in response, "No time, sir. Later."

"What about food?" the senior officer asked.

Another whisper: "Not hungry."

"And when was the last time you climbed out of that cockpit and got some sleep, Captain Hunter?"

The rising note of authority in Jones's voice cracked out like the tip of a lash.

218

"I'll sleep when I'm dead," Hunter said in a reply that was an almost frightening monotone. With that, he snapped down the visor of his flight helmet as if to shut off the conversation.

Jones was aghast. Not three days ago Hunter had told him of his first combat kill—the Yak pilot from the *Brezhnev,* and how the taking of a human life had begun to haunt him. Was this now the same young man? Had the brutality of the front line air combat consumed Hunter so quickly, so completely, wiping out the last traces of humanity?

Jones knew Hunter had already shot down dozens of enemy aircraft, many times more than anyone else in the squadron. Yet what could be left after that amount of stress and anguish passed through the young man's soul?

"How many sorties have you flown, Captain?" Jones asked, almost sadly.

This time, Hunter didn't even shrug.

Jones was getting unnerved. Although Hunter's actions were now bordering on insubordination, military manners were not foremost in his mind at that moment. Hunter's mental condition was.

"You *can't* keep pushing like this," Jones told him. "You can't take on the whole fucking Soviet Air Force.

"You can't fight this war alone."

Hunter was silent for a moment, the sun visor still masking his eyes. But Jones could see the square jaw work back and forth underneath the impassive mirrored lenses.

It was a controlled Hawk Hunter who finally replied, "General, I'll fight the whole fucking *world* if I have to."

Jones shook his head, thought for a moment then reached into his flight jacket pocket. He pulled out a small, worn leatherette-covered box and dropped it on Hunter's lap in the cockpit.

Hunter opened the battered box to find an old-style pair of sterling silver combat wings and a major's oak leaf insignia devices. Turning them over in his hand, he read the inscription on the back:

"Major James Hunter, USAF, 2-14-68"

"Those belonged to your father," Jones told him. "Right after Tet, he and I flew seventeen sorties against Charlie. Got four kills between us. I went down over Heni Bana up North—took a SAM in the tail and flamed out. And he stayed with me, orbiting around for an hour . . . strafing any of the NVA patrols that tried to approach my plane. Hung around until the Marines sent a chopper in for me. He used up so much fuel guarding me that he didn't have enough to make it back, so he ditched in the sea and the Navy boys fished him out."

Jones looked down at the son of the man he had flown with in Vietnam, recalling the bonds of brotherhood forged in the crucible of combat.

"A lot of guys said *he* was crazy, and maybe he was," the senior officer continued. "But he was my best friend. And he was the best goddamn pilot I'd ever seen . . . Until now."

Hunter flipped the reflective visor back up into the helmet and stared up at Jones. The fire in his eyes was still there, but it was suddenly tempered.

Jones put a strong hand on Hunter's shoulder, pointing toward the silver insignia.

"He wanted you to have these," Jones said. "He knew you'd earn them someday. Congratulations, *Major* Hunter."

Hunter looked up at Jones, then back at the insignia.

"Thank you, sir," his ragged voice thickening with emotion. "This really means a lot to me. . . ."

"I know," Jones said, climbing down to the tarmac. He gave Hunter a crisp salute and walked away.

Two minutes later Hunter was rolling down the smoke-blackened runway again, gracefully lifting off into the murky winter skies over Spain.

Chapter 30

Soviet Air Marshal Sergei Vladimirovich Ilyushin looked at the stack of reports on his cluttered desk.

"How is it possible," he thought, "to lose so many aircraft in such a short time."

His data told him that more than fifteen hundred Warsaw Pact fighters had been consumed in the seemingly perpetual dogfight over France.

But the losses, though horrendous, were to be expected in a war such as this, he reasoned.

The question was: Why were the Americans forcing the titanic air battle?

The Americans and the other NATO ground troops hadn't counterattacked the dug-in Soviet troops on the front lines. There had been no amphibious assaults further east on the European continent. No movement on any number of possible second fronts around the world, no indication that the war was about to go nuclear. All that was happening was this senseless airborne brawl that seemed never to end.

Ilyushin shook his head in puzzlement, his fingertips gently massaging the waxy scar tissue on his forehead — a reminder of his own flying days in the great patriotic war against the Germans. His American-made Lend-Lease P-39 AirCobra had been hit by ground fire and crashed over Kursk, putting him in the hospital with a fractured skull.

Now, for the first time in many years, the headaches had started again. What could the Americans possibly be up to? They had played a game of attrition with their expensive fighter planes, losing millions — no *billions* — of dollars in advanced technology to engage the relatively cheaper, lower-technology hordes of Soviet interceptors.

What could they possibly hope to gain?

Fifteen hundred airplanes, the air chief thought again. Before it was over he knew he would probably lose more than two thousand airplanes in this meat grinder over Paris. His communications staff had been besieged with desperate pleas from his front line air commanders, to send more airplanes, more ammunition, more pilots. Already he had stripped the rear of all reserves — completely emptying some of their Warsaw Pact "allies'" air forces to throw into the fray.

When even that had not been enough, he had called up the Soviet Union's own in-country air defense forces, sending as many of the new Foxhounds and the high-speed Foxbat interceptors as he dared. He could not afford to send them all — some had to stay to defend the Soviet borders themselves if the desperate Americans attempted a last-ditch nuclear strike with their B-1 and B-52 bombers.

Yet, he knew this was not likely. According to the latest intelligence reports, all the American SAC forces were at their home bases.

So why had the Americans pursued this apparently insane strategy?

It wouldn't matter soon anyway, he thought. NATO's crazy fighter sweep had drawn off the costly harassing attacks on the Red Army's vital supply lines through Eastern Europe. Their trains would be rolling again in no time, bringing fresh troops and tanks and materiel for the final assault. They would punch through the stubborn NATO line and capture Paris. Then the rest of the continent would fall and this crazy, totally unexpected war would be won.

He picked up another ream of reports — details on the supplies and reinforcements soon to move up to the front. The Red Army supply pipeline was now chock full of every scrap of war materiel that the Soviet Union could muster. Almost a million reservists on troop trains. Thousands of tanks drawn from the vast reserves of the Chinese border units. Plus all the fuel, ammunition, SAMs, and equipment that could be spared.

The military might of the Soviet Empire was riding those steel rails to a great battle with destiny, Ilyushin thought proudly, and nothing he knew of could stop them.

But for some reason, Ilyushin's thoughts turned back to a strange report he'd received from one of his wing commanders. It told of a mysterious all-white F-16 that had single-handedly destroyed two thirds of a pair of MiG-23 squadrons, forcing the remainder to return to their base.

A war tale, the air marshal thought. Already they are springing up! Even the Americans cannot have such a pilot or an airplane that could launch so many air-to-air missiles. And surely even if they did, he too would become a victim of the battle in the skies over France before the fight was over.

At least Ilyushin hoped so.

Chapter 31

Toomey had been hanging in the tree for more than twelve hours.

He was cold, hungry and exhausted — but at least he was still alive and, as far as he could tell, he had no serious injuries.

That was more than he could say for the Soviet pilot who was also hanging from a parachute on the tree nearby. This man was quite dead — his broken, frozen body hanging like a grotesque, discarded marionette.

Toomey wasn't sure if the dead pilot across from him was the same one who was flying the MiG he had collided with the night before. In fact, there wasn't much Toomey remembered about how he came to be hanging from the massive tree that was located he believed somewhere in the Ardennes forest. All he knew was his parachute harness and straps were the only things preventing him from plunging the last 150 feet to the frozen ground below.

He had been on his twelfth sortie, reaching the outer limits of the two-day-old massive dogfight just as the sun was setting. He had greased a Foxbat almost immediately after joining the fray, but then, somehow, he collided with a MiG-29 Fulcrum, the Soviet jet clipping off his entire tail section. He hit the ejection button a mere two seconds later, and saw that the Soviet pilot had done the same thing. His F-16 had crashed about two miles from his present position.

The dead Soviet pilot was already hanging in the nearby tree when Toomey came floating down.

It was from this strange vantage point that Toomey bore eyewitness to a particularly bizarre chapter of the massive, never-ending aerial battle.

The night skies had been lit as bright as day as nightfighters from both sides clashed in fierce dogfighting, that was now visible from the rooftops of Paris. That in itself was chillingly spectacular, leaving even a veteran pilot like Toomey awestruck.

But it was the battle that commenced at dawn and continued into the morning that left Toomey with his mouth wide open in fascination.

At first sunlight, it was as if he was watching a scene from another era. For the most part, the skies were filled with NATO aircraft that were much older than Toomey himself. Challenging the NATO planes was an equally motley collection of Warsaw Pact jets, supplemented by a few newly arrived interceptors from the Soviet Air Defense Command.

Surprisingly, Toomey saw that the older planes in the NATO inventory were holding their own with fighters of similar vintage from the dregs of the Warsaw Pact aerodromes. He witnessed innumerable battles that went on right above him. In one particularly close battle, a British Lightning, an early supersonic interceptor, flashed across the crowded sky in hot pursuit of a Polish-built MiG-19 Farmer. The speedy Lightning quickly overtook the slower MiG and pumped a Firestreak air-to- air missile up the hapless Pole's exhaust, exploding the MiG in a puff of orange and black.

Everywhere, the ubiquitous F-4 Phantoms painted with the markings of a half-dozen NATO nations were dueling with the even more ubiquitous MiG-21 Fishbeds of the Warsaw Pact. The two fighters were of similar vintage, but the Phantoms had been continually upgraded with avionics improvements and better radar systems, while the Soviets had been reluctant to make the same investment in the air forces of their East European satellites. The disparity was evident as the Phantoms clawed through the MiGs, firing Sidewinders, Sparrows, and cannon with deadly precision.

On it went—an East German Fishbed was flamed by a West German Luftwaffe Phantom in a particularly savage rolling scissors exchange of cannon fire, while a Czech MiG loosed a pair of AA-2 Atoll missiles at a National Guard Delta Dart. One of the lethal air-to-airs exploded near the F-106's triangular wing, crumpling it and sending the plane spiraling downward in flames.

A squadron of Spanish A-4 Skyhawks was doing a number on the clumsier MiG-21s, but the Italian and Greek Starfighters in the fight had been jumped by a squadron of Floggers and had taken several losses before they joined the main battle. The diminutive G-91 interceptors were also taking a beating, dwindling the already-small Portuguese contribution.

In an eerie replay of the early days of the Korean conflict, a pair of Turkish Sabres tore into a flight of Romanian MiG-15s, smoking several of the older planes.

In between watching the incredible air battles, Toomey was forced on several occasions to play dead as Soviet ground units passed right below him. The enemy troops paid no attention — to him or to their dead comrade dangling nearby. This told Toomey that the war had taken a particularly nasty turn — one in which the dead were not collected, simply because they now outnumbered the living.

As the day progressed, Toomey joined a million other combatants on both sides who caught themselves looking skyward once again.

Once the antique fighters had left the scene, a battle royal erupted at high altitudes between the newly returned F-16s and the swift Soviet MiG-25 Foxbat interceptors.

In the middle of it as usual was the crazy pilot in the white F-16.

Flying with his avionics turned back on, Hunter rolled out high above the dogfight to swoop down on a pair of the big Foxbats.

He knew the heavy MiGs were initially designed to intercept the US B-70 Valkyrie, a Mach 3 strategic bomber that was never built. Even after the American bomber was scrapped, the MiG was deployed as an air defense interceptor with incredibly high speed (Mach 3.2) and as an unarmed reconnaissance version.

The two MiGs below Hunter were not the recon versions, he soon found out.

The F-16's nose cannon spat out a continuous tongue of flame as it sent shell after shell cascading down into the Soviet planes. One took several shells in the starboard fuel supply and burst into flames below the diving F-16, forcing Hunter to fly through the debris.

The second Foxbat, getting the hint when his partner exploded, had punched his afterburners and shot off toward the horizon in an incredibly fast, but wide turn. The Soviet pilot used his primitive but effective radar targeting system to pinpoint the F-16 that had just tried to blow him out of the sky, seeking to pump off one of his two large AA-6 Acrid missiles toward the speeding American.

When the smoke from his kill had cleared, Hunter found himself on the receiving end of the huge air-to-air missile fired by the fast Foxbat. With the shrill wail of the radar threat warning blasting his ears, The Wingman executed a complex series of rolls and dives, designed to break the missile's radar lock on his plane. For extra security, he pumped his chaff dispenser release several times, and ejected two bright flares that shot far away from the F-16.

The big Acrid missile was designed to take out larger targets, like strategic bombers, and was confused by the combination of decoy flares, chaff and Hunter's evasive action. Unable to reacquire a suitable target, the missile detonated itself.

All of Hunter's concentration had been focused on evading the deadly airborne harpoon, and now he searched the skies — and his radar screen — for a glimpse of the Soviet pilot who fired it. He saw the incredibly fast blip enter the field of his radar screen just as the low-pitched warble of the threat warning system started emitting a radar detection alarm once again.

The lower pitch, Hunter knew, indicated that the Foxbat's powerful but narrow-beam targeting radar was probing the skies for him with invisible pulses.

Suddenly he knew the heavy Foxbat was directly behind him — almost three miles out — and moving at near its maximum speed of Mach 3. Sooner or later, the Russian's crude radar would lock on his F-16 and another big missile would be fired.

Hunter's computer-like brain was flying through a series of calculations even as the radar threat warning's wail notched up an octave. The Soviet pilot had him locked in. . . . The Acrid missile was seconds away from launch. Closing at three times the speed of sound, there really was no way the Soviet pilot could miss.

A supernatural calm descended over Hunter in the tiny cockpit as the seconds turned into hours. As if time were suspended, Hunter was thinking about his first combat flight instruction, back at Nellis. He could hear Jones's gravelly voice giving a dogfighting "Golden Rule:"

"The surest way to scare the hell out of a bandit diving on your six is to flip over and fly straight at him," Jones had said. "It is guaranteed to make rookies panic and grown men wet their flight suits."

Hunter knew what he had to do. Even as the threat warning siren song reached its crescendo, he snap-rolled the agile fighter and executed a punishing high-g turn that put him in a steep climb directly toward the diving Foxbat. He punched the afterburner, and the F-16 quickly reached its maximum climbing speed as the two adversaries closed on each other at an incredible combined rate of five times the speed of sound.

The Foxbat pilot had just pushed the missile release when he noticed the distortion in his radar trace. What was the American up to now? he wondered. Searching the skies ahead, all he saw was the blazing trail of the big missile streak ahead of him. The heavy Foxbat was slicing through the sky right behind the missile when he saw a black dot directly ahead of him, growing larger.

The Soviet pilot's jaw sagged in disbelief, held in place only by his oxygen mask. The crazy Yankee was *charging* the missile—and him! Before he could react, he saw the American plane deftly jink and stand the speedy little F-16 up on its wing to evade the missile's flight path as he continued the hair-raising climb.

The deadly Acrid missile zoomed past the streaking American plane, unable to acquire it from a head-on angle at that unbelievable speed, and unable to make the turn to allow the infrared sensors to lock onto the hot exhaust. The missile plunged harmlessly to the ground where it exploded near an abandoned French village.

Still the all-white F-16 was closing on the larger Foxbat, using the Soviet's speed in the dive against him. The instant the two airplanes came within range, they both opened up with their cannons. Tracer shells filled the rapidly decreasing space between the fighters as the two pilots tried to aim and fire their powerful cannons in the few seconds before their planes passed each other.

At the final split second, the Soviet flier hesitated. Surely the American would pull up now . . . A thousand yards away—now five hundred! And still the F-16 was climbing directly at him, firing away with the nose cannon. Tracer shells whizzed by the Soviet's canopy, adding to the tension. A hundred yards' distance disappeared in less than the blink of an eye. The distracted Soviet pilot had but one thought: The crazy bastard is going to ram me.

Instinctively, the Soviet pilot jammed his stick hard left to avoid the collision he felt was inevitable. Bracing himself in his diving fighter's cockpit, he shut his eyes as the roar of the F-16's engine shook his plane violently. He heard the dull thud of shells lancing his wings as the American fighter sprayed the Foxbat with 30mm cannon fire. He was sure the end would come any second . . .

But then—silence. Or at least relative silence compared to the deafening din of the past few seconds. Only the dull roar of the Foxbat's own engines rushed in the pilot's ears. The threat was suddenly gone. There was no enemy plane. No engine noise. No cannon fire. It was as if the American had simply vanished like a spirit.

Slowly, the Russian regained his composure. He leveled the big interceptor out and checked for damage. A few holes in the wings and fuselage, but no critical wounds. Radar was operable, although it showed no trace of the F-16. Now his relief turned to anger, then to furious rage. How dare the crazy Yankee play this insane game, causing him to panic and turn away?

Suddenly his threat alarm sounded again . . . Missile fired from above and behind . . .

Now, incredibly, the ivory F-16 was diving on *him*. Its pilot fired one of the deadly Sidewinder air-to-airs at the Foxbat's red-hot exhaust nozzles. There was no time for fancy maneuvering, just a burst of raw speed to escape the lethal arrow. The Foxbat rolled sharply and began to dive again.

Hunter cursed as the missile overshot the fleeing Foxbat, plunging out of sight in the cloudy sky. He followed the Sidewinder's downward track, flashing the F-16 past the big Soviet jet. Once again, Hunter was preparing to use the Foxbat's superior speed as an advantage.

Busy evading the missile, the Soviet pilot cursed aloud when he saw the F-16 fly over him in a shallow dive. He would show this cocky American what a Foxbat could do with full afterburners in a steep dive. Snap-rolling the heavy interceptor and nosing over to follow Hunter, the Soviet began to quickly overtake the slower American plane. He had the Yankee's tail section in his gunsights as the distance between the two fighters closed rapidly.

Just a few more seconds, and the American would be scattered to the four winds in a million pieces, victim to the Foxbat's 23-mm internal gun.

The screaming whine from the F-16's radar threat warning pierced Hunter's ears with its shrill one-note alarm. Calmly, he reached out and switched it off. His radar screen showed the Foxbat descending on him at Mach 3. Despite the extra thrust provided by the F-16's afterburner, the big GE turbofan was being outrun by the bigger Soviet engines in the Foxbat.

But this was exactly what Hunter wanted . . .

With a deliberate move, Hunter armed the Sidewinder missile on the jet's right wingtip. Then he gently cupped the side-stick controller in his right hand and placed his left hand on the manual override flap controls. At the last possible second, he cut the throttle back, hauled sharply up on the stick, and dropped every square inch of control surface on the F-16 to its full "down" position, all in one smooth motion.

If the F-16 could have left skid marks in the sky, they would have tracked the fighter's abrupt deceleration from almost fifteen hundred miles per hour to just under three hundred in just a few seconds. Hunter was thrown hard against the shoulder harness of his reclining seat by the impact, recovering just in time to see the dark shadow of the Foxbat pass overhead at full speed, overshooting him.

With the merest flick of the side-stick control, Hunter found the Foxbat's twin tails dead in his radar sights. He released the Sidewinder that covered the short distance in seconds and disappeared into the left-side exhaust nozzle of the diving Foxbat.

The Soviet pilot never saw the missile coming. His fingers had just tightened on the cannon trigger, when the American plane had simply disappeared. It was as if the small F-16 had stopped dead in the air, hovering like a bird of prey before striking. Unable to stop or even slow the heavy Foxbat, the startled pilot could only watch as the Yankee trickster vanished beneath him.

A split second later, he realized the American's tactic. But it was too late to maneuver. The deadly air-to-air missile from the F-16's wingtip exploded deep inside the big interceptor, blowing apart the left-hand engine and severing the left wing at its junction with the fuselage.

The stricken Foxbat crumpled like a paper airplane caught in the grasp of an invisible hand. The left wing section fluttered away in flames as the main body of the plane began a sickening wobbly spiral down to the ground, propelled by the intermittent thrust of the right-hand engine. When the plane's violent spasms finally choked off its life-giving fuel, the remaining engine coughed and died, leaving the huge interceptor to plunge to the earth by the force of gravity alone.

The last thing the Soviet pilot heard as he helplessly plummeted to the ground, desperately clawing at controls that were no longer connected to wings that were no longer connected to his aircraft, was a voice that had either come from inside his head, or from the crazy American, who may have somehow found the proper radio frequency.

At that instant, he realized in horror that he would have the rest of eternity to figure it out.

"Dos vadanya, tovarich," the strangely-accented voice echoed amid the swirling chaos inside his cockpit.

Then the blackness came.

Far below, Toomey had witnessed the intricate battle between Hunter and the huge Foxbat.

Alternately screaming and cheering during the fight, the American pilot was hoarse—too hoarse to yell down at the patrol of French soldiers that were now passing below him.

Thinking quickly, he undid his left flight boot and let it drop. It hit the last man in the patrol, square on the head, stunning him. The rest of the soldiers turned their weapons upward, ready to fire on the source of the flying boot. It was only Toomey's wide grin and animated waving that saved him from joining the swelling ranks of the war dead.

231

Chapter 32

Even as the dogfight raged over the torn countryside north of Paris, preparations were underway a few hundred miles outside of another European capital.

In the quiet woods surrounding the Greenham Common NATO air base in the north of England, sixty huge camouflage nets lay strewn in large green lumps amid the deep tracks of hundreds of huge tires. Freshly cut trees that had stood for centuries now lay at crazy angles across the rutted fields, short stumps marking their original positions.

The ruts marked a random network of tracks leading across the fields that separated the edge of the forest from the base's runways.

Just a few hours ago, the base had been a beehive of activity, ground crews and armament specialists frantically working to complete the nearly impossible task of preparing a huge airborne armada for an operation known as "Rolling Thunder."

Now all was quiet, even peaceful. The only sound was a soft wind through the trees and the rustle of leaves on the ground.

But this would be temporary.

At the end of the field, the quiet was shattered as eight huge engines coughed to life and began an ear-splitting din as they were cranked up to full power. When the sound had reached its deafening crescendo, the engines lurched forward on the empty tarmac, dragging half a million pounds of plane and payload reluctantly down the runway.

The huge tapering wings sagged almost to the ground at their tips, separated by more than 160 feet of steel skin from end to end. In fact, small wheels and struts had been added to the wingtips to support the thousands of gallons of jet fuel that sloshed in the bomber's massive internal wing tanks.

As the massive airplane gathered speed down the runway, the wing sag diminished rapidly until the small wheels left the ground, floating up several feet as the wingtips flexed. The huge fuselage trundled along the tarmac, as four sets of twin tires mounted on massive struts crabbed the plane slightly to center it on the runway. The wheels straightened out, and the engines' roar increased another measure as the heavily laden aircraft began to pick up speed for takeoff.

Slowly, but inexorably, the dark green behemoth ascended into the cloudy English sky, undergoing the transformation from balky, droop-winged bomb truck to graceful, winged warrior.

When the thunder of the bomber's engines had faded, the deep quiet descended on the base once more.

Almost a hundred miles ahead, inside the cockpit of the Strategic Air Command B-52 Stratofortress, Lt. Colonel Rick Davis of the 52nd Bomb Wing's headquarters staff was adjusting his oxygen mask and intercom microphone.

Seated in the left-hand seat of the big bomber, Davis had just received confirmation that the last plane in his formation had left the ground back at Greenham Common, and was now joining the long formation at thirty thousand feet.

Minutes later, the grouped-up B-52s reached their jumping off point just off the eastern coast of England. With a single radio burst from Davis in the lead bomber, instructions were transmitted to the navigators in each crew. In turn, the navigators fed in a series of complex targeting coordinates to their bomb-coordinator counterparts seated next to them in the cramped confines of the big bomber's innards.

Once the sixty heavy bombers had computed their individual targets and flight plans, they began to peel off the formation and dive for the deck. Davis managed to sneak a quick look at the orderly formation's blossoming, as bombers on either side rolled off on their outboard wings to plunge into the darkness below. Each had a separate target, and eventually each would take a different route to get there.

The 52nd Bomb Wing had been ordered from their SAC base in California to the tiny Greenham Common field two days after the war broke out.

Flying in pairs, they had hopped across North America to the windswept airport at Gander, Newfoundland, then on to Keflavik, Iceland. There, two bombers previously stationed at the base would fly in a huge semicircle at high altitudes, almost reaching the Canadian coast. Then they would drop down to a heart-stopping two-hundred feet above the frigid Arctic sea and race back to Iceland undetected.

Later, covered under the dark of night, the two SAC B-52s would lift off from Iceland and skim the waves over to England's rocky coast, setting down with not too much room to spare on Greenham Common's short airfield. Once the base was secured by the SAS unit, the big bombers were concealed in the woods surrounding the base. Hundreds of trees were lopped off to allow the huge B-52s to ease into the edge of the forest. Then the cut trees were propped back up in huge holes dug by British engineer crews.

From the air — or from a photo satellite's probing eye — all that could be seen was the dense green of England's woods. Even the heat signatures of the big bombers had been blotted out by covering the airplanes with a blanket of CO_2 foam.

It had been quite an operation so far, Davis thought.

It was only when the sixty huge airplanes arrived in England, jamming the woods around the small RAF base, that they had received the orders that explained Operation "Rolling Thunder." Special convoys brought secret ordnance loads up to the flight line, and the huge BUFFs — Big Ugly Fat Fuckers, as the aircrews called them with varying degrees of affection — started being loaded with a very special menu of ordnance.

For eighteen straight hours, the bomb crews struggled in the thick woods, cursing and sweating as they painstakingly loaded each bomber according to its pre-determined mission.

Finally, the long-awaited "go" order was given, and the Brits had leveled the trees from their temporary post holes and the laden B-52s had trundled out onto the runway.

And now they were in the air, headed for a date with destiny over Eastern Europe.

Colonel Davis mentally reviewed the Bomb Wing's mission, the product of an endless review of the dwindling options that faced NATO in Europe.

While the combined fighter strength of the Free World's air forces had drained the huge Soviet reserve of interceptors from the critical Eastern European corridor, the Bomb Wing had been pondering its targets.

Intelligence had been unable to estimate exactly how much reserve troop strength and spare equipment was being rushed into the front by the over-extended Soviets, but it was clear that the highways and rail lines were crowded with everything needed for the Red Army's final offensive.

And that was the key.

Because the objective behind Rolling Thunder — and, in fact, the virtual last hope of the democratic alliance — was for Davis and the big bombers to prevent that equipment and those reserves from reaching the front lines.

Davis felt himself drawing heavier than usual from his oxygen mask.

Despite the myth about combat pilots — that they were ice-water-in-the-veins bomb delivery men — Davis *did* feel like the weight of the Free World was on his shoulders. As Bomb Group Leader, the success of the whole mission while it was in the air was in his hands.

Now, as he looked out on the darkened European mainland coming up before him, he suddenly felt transplanted in time. He knew that nearly a half century before, other men had flown this route, crossing the Channel to fly over Fortress Europe in battered B-17s and B-24s. By their efforts did they fail? Was all their sacrifice and misery and terror in vain? *Dammit, didn't they do the job right the first time?*

He shook away his anger and took a half dozen deep gulps of the pure Big O. No, the men in those Flying Forts and Liberators had smited their enemies, and the planet was at relative *world* peace for nearly five decades as a result.

Until now.

As his airplane reached landfall and dashed above the countryside, Davis imagined he could see the ghosts of the men killed in those old prop-driven Forts and Liberators begin to rise up. There was nothing different here, he thought. The cause was the same — the defense of freedom. The opponent — ironically once an ally — had simply changed uniforms.

The men who died trying to free Hitler's Europe had not perished in vain. They had won *their* war, defeated *their* enemies.

Now it was time for Davis and his men to do the same.

A burst of static from his radio brought him back to the business at hand.

"Green Flight, at departure point," the message came over. "Breaking at three-four-niner . . ."

"Roger, Green Flight . . ." Davis quickly replied.

The message meant that twenty of his bombers were wheeling off to dash across the flooded Low Countries and strike at the Soviet's forward supply lines and railheads in westernmost Germany.

He entered their departure in the mission log then rechecked his own position.

He knew that the enemy's front-line surface-to-air missile installations, battered by two continuous days and nights of "Weasel" attacks, would offer Green Flight little resistance. And he himself expected only scattered threats deeper into enemy territory.

But he also knew that — despite the on-going dogfight raging just south of them — his B-52s could encounter Soviet fighters at any time, either going to or coming from the battle area. And the secrecy of Rolling Thunder had dictated that his Buffs fly without a highly visible fighter escort. The only defense the lumbering B-52s had were the twin 50-caliber machine guns in the tail — and that was no defense at all against the enemy's stand-off air-to-air weapons. So the BUFFs would have to rely on their electronic jamming gear, decoy flares, and metallic "chaff" to elude enemy fighters and their deadly missiles.

"Blue Flight at departure point," his radio crackled again. "Breaking at three-three-three . . ."

"Roger, Blue Flight . . ." Davis replied.

The bomber force had split again and now Blue Flight would veer off and eventually take a roughly parallel course across the Danish peninsula to penetrate deep into East Germany and Poland right to the front step of the Soviet Union itself. But they would not cross the line. Under strict orders from NATO's highest command, the SAC bombers were not to come within a hundred miles of the Soviet border. As throughout the entire war, no NATO bombs had fallen on Mother Russia itself. The thinking was that if the US didn't bomb the Soviet homeland, the Soviets wouldn't bomb America. It was an oddly tacit agreement between warring parties, an unspoken promise that had, so far, held up.

But Davis had no intention of coming anywhere near the 100-mile exclusionary zone. He wouldn't have to.

Tactically, his mission was actually little more than an elaborate air-launched cruise missile operation, one that he and his pilots had practiced endlessly for the past six years. In his hold he held weapons that could "think," that could be told what and what not to do. With their pre-programmed terrain-following aiming system, they were smart enough to punch out a target one inch this side of the 100-mile buffer. And if nothing else, that fact would make any Soviet planner consider the difference between the West's technological prowess and his own side's battering ram approach to things.

Forty-five tense minutes passed by.

"Approaching our flight sequence departure point, Colonel," the co-pilot called out, once again shifting Davis's concentration back to the task at hand.

"We break at four-four-seven . . . in twelve seconds."

"OK, roger," Davis answered, snapping a few buttons on his flight console and tightly gripping the steering controls before him.

The huge bomber had been on autopilot ever since they'd flown over the choppy waters of the Channel, its on-board computers keeping the Buff's nose a mere four hundred feet off the ground. But now, they would have to fly even lower, at two hundred feet, and the on-board computer was not smart enough to handle that. From here on in, Davis knew it would require all the skill that he, his co-pilot, the navigator, and millions of dollars of sophisticated equipment could muster to stay low enough to avoid enemy radar detection, while trying not to plow the B-52 into the ground.

The co-pilot cleared his throat. "Departure point in five . . . four . . . three . . . two . . . one . . . *now* . . ."

"Roger," Davis said. "Beginning departure now . . ."

Slowly, the big bomber began to descend.

Scattered across the skies of enemy-held Europe, fifty-nine other

B-52 pilots were wrestling with similar flight plans, plowing through the sluggish air just a couple hundred feet above the ground. Each one knew that it was just plain crazy — perhaps, even suicidal — to risk everything on a bunch of half-century-old bombers doing a job their designers never dreamed they would be asked to do.

But such were the times . . .

"Approaching IP, Colonel," Davis's bomb-coordinator called out deliberately over the cabin intercom.

Davis quickly scanned the mission checklist which he already knew by heart. But now the words took on a new meaning. When the big bomber reached its preassigned Initial Point, the bomb coordinator would have complete control of the aircraft.

Or more accurately, his computer would. From the mission-planning data fed into the system, the bomb control computers would synchronize the big jet's airspeed, altitude, heading and other navigational data with the pre-programmed ballistics information derived from the weapons load in their bomb bay. Then, analyzing the target coordinates, terrain contours, and wind speed and direction, the computer would spit out the precise release point for each weapon.

Every twenty seconds, the data was rechecked and updated by millions of transistorized brain cells in the bomb control computer's electronic brain.

"IP in ten seconds . . ." came the call from the bomb coordinator. "Nine . . . eight . . . seven . . ."

The young lieutenant seated at the small radar screen was at least two generations removed from the bombardiers of World War Two, who used the then-advanced Norden bombsights to aim lethal loads of "dumb" iron bombs over Hitler's Fortress. But like those leather-jacketed men of yesteryear, he was the focus of attention in the aircraft as he called off the flight control commands of the computer's readout.

"IP in six . . . five . . . four . . . three . . . two . . . one . . . *now.*"

The bomb coordinator's voice rose slightly in his excitement.

"Come right to one-one-zero and hold steady . . ." he told Davis. "Alpha release in thirty seconds . . ."

Davis nudged the big plane around in the dense air, ignoring the creaks and whines from the shuddering bomber's airframe. His only job for the next half a minute was to keep the gossamer-thin needle of the special Flight Control Indicator centered where the bomb computers calculated it had to be for an accurate launch.

Right now, the needle was dead on.

"Alpha launch in ten seconds," the bomb coordinator reported evenly. "Arming switches to 'on' position."

He reached over to click off the green safety covers of the toggles, flipping up the switches underneath.

Davis tore his eyes away from the thin white needle of the FCI to steal a glance out the thick cockpit glass. The B-52's menacing shadow, outlined by the thin moonlight, stole across the flat ground of the East German plain, rippling along like a serpent.

In its path was a double line of railroad tracks.

"Weapons doors opening . . . now."

The old bomber shuddered as the huge bomb bay doors yawned open underneath its fuselage.

"Weapons door open confirmed . . ." called the co-pilot.

"Alpha launch, *now!*"

The young bomb coordinator mashed the first button on his "pickle" firing switch. Instantly two tapered cylinders fell out of the bottom of the bomber, released from the large rotary holder suspended inside.

"Weapons away!" he yelled.

Two lights blinked on the console in front of Davis.

"Weapons launched confirmed . . ." he said.

Directly beneath them and traveling on a parallel course with the B-52, the two projectiles each sprouted tail fins, a pair of stubbly wings, and a radar-sensing port opened in each nose section.

In four seconds, the drones had found the railroad tracks. Two more lights popped on in front of Davis.

"I have a weapons lock indication," the bomb coordinator called up to him.

"Roger, weapons lock confirmation . . ." Davis answered.

At that instant, the two weapons diverged from the bomber's flight path at sharp angles, each heading in the opposite direction.

Light years more advanced than the massive sticks of iron "dumb" bombs that had rained on Nazi Germany, these two projectiles were "smart" drone-bombs. Actually, more advanced than the better-known air-launched cruise missiles in many ways, the super-drones had been preprogrammed to search for and destroy targets of opportunity. Images of specific weapons-carrying rail cars were fixed in their electronic brains, along with those of enemy tanks, personnel carriers, trucks, self-propelled guns, aircraft on the ground and even certain slow-flying aircraft in the air. Davis's B-52 carried twenty of the weapons, each laden with its own store of submunitions.

The westbound drone sliced along the railroad track, its lifeless radar eye searching the steel ribbons below for any sign of movement. The intense beam pulsed the ground, interrogating the empty tracks more than eight times each second.

Fifty miles beyond the launch point, the radar sensor detected a moving object on the rails below. Then another. Then another. It instantly flashed a message back to the B-52 mother ship: "Target located."

The drone's electronic microprocessors sent a series of signals to the munitions dispensers inside its short fuselage. Then, in a feat of remarkable electronic ingenuity, the superdrone performed a flawless 180-degree turn, reducing its speed at the same time.

In seconds, it was silently cruising above the speeding train . . .

Increasing its pulsing rate to sixteen times a second, the missile's brain calculated the speed of the train, the direction of the tracks and any obstacles such as tunnels, mountain or over-hanging trees that lay ahead. It quickly decided that an upcoming twenty-second window was the optimum time for attack.

Five more seconds passed. The tracks curved and flowed into a four-mile straightaway. The missile's computer-brain clicked and then, on its command, the drone's own weapons bay door opened.

Slowing its speed so the front section of the train would overtake it, the computer issued its next-to-final command. Instantly small rockets fired downward to propel a series of powerful explosive charges at the train's midsection of heavily laden flatcars. The warhead cannisters fell with jarring thuds on the flat beds of the cars or directly on top of the canvas-covered equipment they carried.

Starting four seconds later, and working off time-delayed fuses, the warheads ignited one by one. The lightning-quick series of blinding yellow-orange flashes obliterated the second half of the mile-long train, blowing its sections off the track in more than a dozen places.

When the drone itself was free of all submunitions, it increased its speed while another electronic circuit armed the warhead in its own nose section. Switching from a radar mode to an infrared-homing target system, the remorseless little flying bomb sought out the most intense source of heat below it, quickly plunging itself into the second locomotive pulling the now-reduced line of freight cars. Within milliseconds, the diesel engine exploded in a flash of flame and black smoke. The rest of the train immediately derailed and slammed itself into a sickening pile of twisted flaming metal.

It was over in fifteen seconds. A load of Soviet SAM battery replacements would never reach the front.

The eastbound drone carried a different load of submunitions for its assigned target. Knifing above the parallel rails, the missile's radar had detected motion below as a Warsaw Pact troop train passed beneath it, carrying a 15,000-man division of replacements to the fighting front in France.

Instantly, the drone's control processors began a patterned, sequential firing sequence. One after the other, hefty rockets were ignited, propelling a lethal load of steel flechettes downward at an incredible speed of Mach 5. The flechettes were big 120-grain steel nails with sharp tail fins that screamed downward with an eerie whistling noise.

Almost 100,000 of the deadly darts were deposited along the length of the troop train, exploding through the thin railcar roofs like they were made of paper. In an instant, thousands of Red Army reservists were horribly dispatched as the speeding spikes pierced helmets, skulls and shoulder blades, tearing through their hapless victims until they exited the train's floor, bone and blood skewered around their razor-like fins.

The superdrone, mother to the thousands of lethal baby bomblets, now activated its own targeting procedure, executing a burst of speed and a rapid U-turn to send it hurtling down the track toward the oncoming locomotive at a height of only ten feet. The train's engineer had only time to open his mouth in a silent scream before the flying bomb obliterated the train's front five cars with an ear-splitting explosion that smashed the ties, rails, roadbed, and all, sending the burning hulk of the foremost locomotive spinning into the air at least fifty feet from the rails.

Farther along the flight path of Davis's B-52, another set of the munition-laden drones sought out a column of tanks bunched up in a bottleneck on the east bank of a narrow bridge. These drones carried a smaller version of the MW-1 munitions dispenser, packed with anti-armor shape charges that fit into horizontally projecting tubes in the dispenser's side walls. Explosive propulsion charges nestled in the center of each pair of tubes were fired sequentially, expelling the shape charges in a wide distribution on either side of the drone's flight path.

In a single pass over their target, the two drones deposited more than five thousand bomblets in little more than five seconds. The results were devastating to the clustered tanks. White-hot rods of molten metal burned through the armor, turning the tanks' cramped interiors into fiery crucibles of death. More than five hundred armored vehicles were destroyed or damaged as thousands of the explosively formed penetrators found their marks in the thin top plating of the T-62's turrets. Even the charges that failed to meet a tank's top were still fatal to the enemy, since they embedded themselves in the frozen soil to become land mines, claiming still more victims as the dazed crews bolted from their stricken vehicles.

As if to seal the fate of the armored column, the two flying bombs dove into opposite ends of the narrow bridge, burrowing into the concrete before exploding and severing the span from its moorings. With tanks and troops sliding off the shattered roadway, the bridge collapsed into the river in a spectacular crash.

Relentlessly, the American smart-bomb attack continued . . .

Still more of Davis's drones found strings of tank cars, full of gasoline and diesel fuel, parked in freight yards awaiting transport to the front. They erupted in towering geysers of yellow-white flame as they were ignited by hundreds of incendiary munitions dropped from the drones. The mini-firebombs created a thousand raging fires that joined into a single huge inferno, building to a firestorm that consumed the entire rail yard.

Other drones found similar fuel dumps, aircraft parking areas, long-range radar stations, temporary troop billets, bridges, tunnels, power stations, dams—literally dozens of enemy targets were hit. The bombardment was multiplied several hundred times as the rest of the B-52 force seeded the clouds above Eastern Europe with their smart weapons, raining tons of electronically guided munitions of their wide-ranging targets of opportunity.

And even as the B-52 force was raining death on the trains, tanks, and trucks in East Europe, the F-111's based at Upper Heyford and Lakenheath had hit the Soviets' airfields and the Baltic ports. Many Soviet pilots returning from the running dogfight over France arrived to find their landing fields in smoking ruins. Some were able to divert the auxiliary fields in the Soviet Union itself, but many were forced to crash-land in fields and deserted roads. Ships docked in the Baltic ports were strafed and sunk as they lay at anchor, unable to escape the low-flying Aardvarks.

By morning, the military might of the Red Army lay scattered like crushed and smoking steel toys along the length of its supply routes. Not a single rail line or major bridge between the Ukraine and the Rhine River was left intact. Only a handful of air fields, ammunition dumps and troop billets had escaped the devastation. Nearly a half million Warsaw Pact reservists were now Warsaw Pact casualties, killed or wounded long before they could reach the front lines.

Returning to his base just as the sun was coming up, Colonel Davis, his crew, and every one of his commanding officers stretching back to the Pentagon itself, knew that Rolling Thunder—the one chance roll of the dice—had been a success.

But the strategic victory hadn't been cheap.

Twenty-five of Davis's bombers had been lost some to SAMs and interceptors, but mostly to the hazards of the low-level flight they'd been forced to make.

Two hundred and fifty of his men were gone. But they had done the soldier's job; they had obeyed orders; and they had carried out an impossible mission. That wouldn't be enough for the families of those crews who didn't make it back. Words were never enough. But still, somehow, Davis felt the ghosts of the men who had fallen out of the skies in the war fifty years before could now return to their resting places, their souls at peace once again.

Chapter 33

Back at Rota, a weary collection of men gathered on the blackened runway, searching the northern horizon.

Their eyes and hands darted at the slightest sound or flicker of light, then slumped as it faded or disappeared. Eleven F-16s had landed already, exhausted pilots coaxing the last few drops of fuel into the battered engines, struggling to bring the fighters back home from the huge dogfight. More than one pilot had pulled his emergency fuel lever to make it.

"And then there was one," General Seth Jones muttered under his breath, cursing himself again for not keeping the stray pilot in closer tow after the gigantic aerial battle had finally broken up just after sunrise that morning. Later intelligence reports would confirm that the Soviet High Command, absolutely shocked at the devastation wrought by the one-time high-tech superdrone sneak attack and fearing further assaults, had issued a recall from the swirling dogfight, ordering all its fighters back to the rear areas, some back to the Soviet Union itself.

And, at that moment, thousands of NATO paratroopers were raining down on a string of key cities that stretched back into East Germany itself. Like chopping the serpent into many little pieces, the democratic forces were, in a matter of hours, regaining all of the territory lost in the past few hellish days.

But there was yet to be a celebration at Rota.

At the end of the gigantic dogfight, Jones had last seen the lone all-white F-16 chasing a single MiG off into the horizon, and his own fuel level was so critical he couldn't dare follow.

But if any pilot could make it back, Jones knew this one could.

Clustered on the tarmac with him were other pilots — JT Toomey, just returned to the base via a French Medivac chopper, Ben Wa, and the rest — including Blue, the base's chief engineer, and the base flight surgeon. All the other planes were accounted for — they were waiting for the last one.

Another thirty minutes passed.

Then, they all heard the same noise at the same time — an uneven drone that could only come from the throat of a jet engine. A jet engine throttled back too far, as the pilot tried to feed fuel to his greedy turbine a drop at a time. A jet engine that had seen more hours of operation in the past two days than it was supposed to see in two months. A jet engine that responded to the lightest touch on the throttle, easing until the fuel was almost choked off, then coughing again as it was fed more life-giving JP-8.

Only one pilot would even attempt to land a supersonic fighter with almost no fuel, with no margin for error. Only one pilot could have made it this far.

There was never much question that he would.

The F-16 had come straight in, not bothering to circle or even ask for clearance.

Like a faltering paper airplane, the dirty white Falcon descended toward the base. It swooped down gently in short, almost flat little scalloping dives as its engine was hauled back to the stall point; then it surged forward with the merest tap to the throttle, starting another gentle dive. Ever so slowly and deliberately, the plane was coming down to meet the dark runway.

A half mile out . . . Now a quarter . . . Now closer still.

And ever so slowly, the plane was descending toward the ground. Now only fifty feet of air separated the lowered landing gear from the murky tarmac of the runway as the plane crossed the fenced edge of the field. The engine was hiccupping, starved for fuel as it tried to push the little jet along.

Now forty feet . . . another cough from the engine . . . another surge to drive forward and down. Thirty feet now . . . the runway beneath was blasted by the sporadic downwash. Twenty feet . . . another gasp from the throttled-back turbine, and then a puff of black smoke was emitted from the plane's tail. A shudder seemed to

245

shake the jet as it hung for a long second above the pitted runway, its engine rumbling.

A final thrust from the dying turbofan propelled the F-16 along the last stretch of landing strip, until finally the main gear touch the ground heavily, kicking up twin puffs of rubber smoke and bringing the tapered nose of the fighter swiftly down to compress the sturdy nosewheel strut to its maximum retraction. At the instant the nosewheel made contact with the pavement, the mighty turbo fan engine sputtered once and was silent.

The Wingman had come home.

With its engine trailing the thinnest wisp of gray smoke, the lone F-16 rolled quietly down the runway until it came to a stop directly in front of the refueling station. It took several minutes before the crowd of pilots, with the mechanic and flight surgeon in tow, reached the wingtip of the small fighter.

Jones was the first one up to the cockpit, surprising many of the younger pilots with an athletic bound onto the flat wing surface, then over to the emergency foothold. To his dismay, he found the canopy had been popped already. The pilot had already dismounted and was walking toward the fueling hoses, still wearing his heavy flight helmet.

Because the pilot still wore the oxygen mask loose around his neck, Jones and the others couldn't hear the mumbling voice as he walked briskly over to the JP-8 supply and began dragging a supply hose back toward his airplane's starboard side wing tank. Only when he got closer did Jones realize what the young man was saying.

"Got to fuel up. I'll get more ammo, too . . ."

The words barely stumbled out of Hunter's mouth before they fell off in confused slurs around his dangling black mask. Yet his stride was even and regular, carrying the heavy hose without even noticing the stunned crowd of on-lookers.

"Captain Hunter," Jones called out to the young pilot, instinctively knowing that he should keep a distance. "Captain, listen to me . . . It's all over . . ."

Hunter didn't pause or even break stride. "After fuel, more ammo," he mumbled. "Be back up there in thirty . . ."

Jones finally walked up to the younger man and forcibly grabbed his arm. He was visibly shocked by how ghostly Hunter's face had become since he'd given him his father's wings not many hours ago.

"Captain, you don't understand," Jones said patiently, standing directly in front of him, physically blocking his path to the all-white airplane. "It's all *over*—Moscow has asked for a cease-fire. *We don't have to fly the mission any more.*"

Hunter stopped abruptly. His bleary, vacant eyes tried to struggle into focus on Jones. His jaw worked back and forth beneath the beard stubble as if he were trying to understand words spoken in some foreign tongue. His hands fumbled with the heavy fueling hose as if he were unsure about what to do with it. Finally he looked up at Jones again.

"Cease-fire?" he asked haltingly.

Hunter's voice was thick with exhaustion, but his computer-like brain was racing on adrenaline, forcing the thoughts to process through the fog of his weariness.

"It's being confirmed now, Captain," Jones reassured the dazed pilot. "We received the initial burst message. Came from the Vice-President himself—the President was still airborne in the White House command plane. It was garbled somewhat, but still understandable. The Sovs want to talk. They've had it. They're licked."

"What?" Hunter asked, not quite believing what he was hearing.

Jones smiled for the first time in days.

"It's true," he said. "While we were zapping their fighters, SAC bombed their supply lines back into the Stone Age. Our troops are securing a dozen cities all the way back to Russia itself. The commie bastards don't even want to know how it comes out. They're retreating in droves. Their top brass has called it quits. In other words, we did it, Captain."

Hunter, still clutching the big hose, kept staring back at his stained, dirty, oil-covered white F-16. Its air intake, slung as it was under the pointed nose, looked like a gaping mouth, silently panting as if to catch its breath. Hunter made a half-step toward the plane as if he were still undecided about whether to continue.

Jones had anticipated his extraordinary pilot's potential burnout, and he discreetly motioned behind Hunter to the flight surgeon, who deftly palmed a small silver syringe out of his satchel. Maneuvering through the crowd of gathered pilots, the doctor approached Hunter as if to give him a firm handclasp, then quickly plunged the needle right through Hunter's flight suit into his arm.

The sharp twinge of pain from the stabbing syringe made Hunter wince and recoil, but it was as if he was in slow motion. The powerful sedative quickly found its way through his overtaxed system, and though he instinctively tried to fight it, he finally buckled. Jones, the doctor, and several others reached around to grab him under the arms to prevent him from falling to the pavement.

Just before Hunter's bloodshot eyes closed, he looked up at Jones.

"It's over, Hawk," the general said calmly. "And we won."

"We won?" Hunter repeated groggily, catching one last glimpse of his battle-scarred white fighter and then beyond it, to the piles of burned hulks and salvage wrecks that lined the base.

"We won what?" he asked.

248

Chapter 34

The Aftermath

Hunter spent the next forty-eight hours sleeping.

Yet, in a strange way, he was never more awake. He found himself immersed in strange dreams—actual living visions in which he teetered between a coma-like unconsciousness and an eerie trance that was more half-sleep and half-hallucination.

At times he rolled fitfully in the hospital bed, his arms flailing as he fought off dark demons that the powerful sedative drug had released from his subconscious. Now they roved through his nightmare, gruesome and malevolent, conjuring the lurid images that played out in his fragmented non-stop incubus.

Throughout his drug-induced fog, one cruel vision kept assaulting his tormented brain. He was high above the surface of the earth, as if he was cruising his F-16 into the stratosphere. But there was no sensation of being confined to a cockpit, or even an aircraft. He was just floating—floating along in the thin air, powerless to control his flight, like a runaway helium balloon accidentally released from a child's hand. And all he could do was watch helplessly as the planet below appeared sporadically through the dense cloud formations.

At times he was miles above the North American continent, suspended over the whirling clouds as they were driven along by the swift river of the jet stream. Below him, by some trick of the cloud's parting, he could see the entire United States stretching serenely from Atlantic to Pacific coast, and from Canadian to Mexican border. The towering peaks of the Continental Divide tumbled down to become the flat plains of the central West, then the fertile fields of the Midwest, and then the rolling knobs of the green

Appalachian chain rose up until they faded into the eastern coastal plain. It was, at first, a beautiful, nirvana-like vision.

But something was terribly wrong.

Even as Hunter was watching, an evil-looking red-and-black stain appeared in North Dakota and began spreading south and west. Terrific explosions rocked the ground below him, seeming to engulf whole states in their deadly volatile embrace. The shock waves buffeted Hunter as he hung there, unable to react except to cry out in anguish for the wounded land below.

The dark stain flowed faster with each explosion, driving farther and farther into the heartland of the nation. As more territory was consumed, new explosions erupted and added to the smoke and noise swirling across the continent.

Hunter was shocked and amazed; even in his dream state he tried to avert his eyes from the terrible scene. But strangely he was unable to do so. He watched with trancelike fixation as the explosions finally subsided. From the badlands of the Dakotas, down to the northern rim of Texas, the ground had turned inky black, punctuated only by a series of eerie, glowing pinspots that shimmered luminescently against the darkness.

Then something even more horrifying occurred.

Just as the shock waves subsided, the turbulent air was blasted by another huge explosion. This one was different from the rest, as if it were a volcanic force welling up from the earth's core itself, rumbling to a deafening crescendo that threatened to split Hunter's eardrums.

Suddenly, huge fissures gaped open in the boiling surface below, as if a cataclysmic earthquake were ripping chunks from the very continent itself and sending them sliding away.

He couldn't bear to watch, but still he wasn't able to turn away, being horrified and mesmerized at the same time. The explosions continued, opening still more wedges of darkness in the land. A huge piece of New England was split off from the continent, and began drifting out to sea. More explosions sent Texas plunging southward. The Southeast, from Maryland to FLorida, had entirely separated from the larger land mass, propelled by the mighty convulsions of the earth.

There was fire and smoke everywhere. The earth-rending explosions sent powerful shock waves up to smash against Hunter, who struggled against them like a man being swamped by a series of successive tidal waves. Their crushing force pressed against his chest like a massive weight, sucking the breath out of him, forcing him downward.

More explosions. Closer this time. The downward pull became a free-fall as the powerful waves hit him again and again. He was plunging downward faster and faster toward the fragmenting continent, his arms punching uselessly against the onrushing air that stole the breath from his lungs. Another explosion shook him violently. Now he was falling faster, screaming against the sound that seemed to draw him downward.

He was falling, hurtling down at almost terminal velocity, when . . .

Hunter's body struck the floor heavily, causing him to exhale involuntarily and then gasp for breath with heaving lungs.

It took several seconds for him to look up at the hospital bed, and the sterile white walls to realize that he had been dreaming. But everything—the sensation of falling, the noise of the explosions, the continent breaking up—had been so vivid . . .

So real . . .

Boom!

He instinctively dove under the metal frame of the hospital bed as the shock wave hit the sturdy little building, washing over and around it with the sound of the explosion. Hunter looked around as dust filtered down from a hundred crevices in the room. Whatever else it was, he thought, *this* wasn't just a nightmare.

Another explosion shook the building.

The base must be under attack! he thought, his mind racing.

Another blast, this one closer, more powerful.

He had to get up, his brain told him. He had to *fight back!*

His groggy mind attempted to cut through the last traces of the drug's fog as he forced unwilling limbs to respond with urgency. He clumsily stepped into his flightsuit, washed and neatly pressed and folded on the edge of his bed. His boots half-on, he stumbled heavily to the door, banging his shin painfully on the frame, and staggered quickly down the hall to the exit that led to the flightline.

Another explosion rocked him just as he reached the building's main door. His eyes finally cleared and saw that the puff of smoke and the spit of flame out on the runway was real enough.

That's when he stopped in his tracks, and literally pinched himself hoping now that he *was* asleep and the horror before him was just another dream.

But it wasn't . . .

Out on the flightline were ten smoldering wrecks. He squinted and realized that he was looking at ten smoking and burning air frames—the remains of ten F-16s.

Someone—or something—had blown them up.

The smoking hulks lay heavily on their smashed airframes, landing gear crumpled beneath them, their backs broken in a hideous posture of death. The shattered air intakes pointed skyward at crazy angles, their now-jagged metal mouths were frozen in silent death cries.

He turned back toward the hospital, one more time convincing himself that he was actually up and out of the building, and not still experiencing the sedative hallucination.

But it was all too real.

He turned back to the almost surrealistic scene. A pair of jeeps were parked in front of the now-destroyed aircraft on the tarmac, and several soldiers wearing uniforms Hunter didn't recognize were unloading what looked like another batch of high explosives. They called out in a strange language to each other, methodically preparing another charge and detonator for the next aircraft in line.

Hunter froze again.

He stared hard at the small blue flags perched on the jeeps' front fenders, and the light blue armbands worn by the sappers. They bore the blue field and white globe symbol of the United Nations.

What the hell was the UN doing here at Rota, demolishing their airplanes? And why were the US personnel at the base—Jones, Ben, Toomey, Blue, and the others—allowing it to go on?

Then he noticed the small cluster of Air Force personnel standing woodenly behind a hastily erected barricade of saw horses and bright yellow plastic tape. Seemingly impervious to the smoldering glares of raw hatred from the confined men, two of the foreign soldiers stood impassively in front of the group, watching them closely, with their AK-47 assault rifles at the ready.

Puzzled for a moment, Hunter looked both at the demolition team, then at the improvised holding pen. Then he lowered his head and began charging toward the last two F-16s.

A warning cry went up from one of the guards around the airmen; another raised his rifle to sight in the running pilot. Suddenly one of the confined men—it was Blue—leaped forward and struck the guard's gun just as the trigger was pulled, causing the bullet to ricochet off the ground.

For his trouble, the mechanic was leveled with a chop of the second guard's rifle butt.

But Hunter kept running, oblivious to the commotion over at the holding pen. He was on top of the startled demolition team before they knew what was happening. The two unarmed soldiers carrying the plastic explosives were quickly dispatched by Hunter's powerful punches, and they hit the tarmac heavily as their dangerous baggage was thrown to the ground in the fight.

Hunter barely had time to turn his head back toward the holding area before the savage thrust of an AK-47 rifle stock to the back of his neck crumpled him to his knees beside one of the wrecked planes.

Blue's face loomed large above him as his eyes gradually focused again. Hunter rubbed the back of his head where a painful lump was forming. He looked up at the lanky crew chief, whose face was twisted in a tight mask of barely controlled fury.

Suddenly, the mechanic was hustled away by two UN guards, dragged over to a wall nearby and instantly shot in the head.

Now an officer wearing a blue patch leaned over Hunter, a .45 automatic in his hand. The dazed pilot heard the pistol's hammer click open.

At that moment, Jones came up beside the officer, and started pleading with him. The UN officer was staring at Jones, a rock hard expression on his face. Finally, the officer nodded harshly and stormed away.

Next thing he knew, Hunter was hauled to his feet by the two UN soldiers.

All the while he was yelling out: "What the hell is going on? Who are these guys? Why are they pranging all the goddamn planes?"

"They're Finnish soldiers," Jones told him warily once he was thrown inside the pen by the soldiers. "They're the enforcers of the cease-fire, under the guidance of the United Nations."

Hunter was confused. He sat down and took a series of deep breaths, trying like hell to clear his head. "Finns? . . . UN? . . . why are they blowing up our airplanes?"

Jones looked him straight in the eye.

"Buck up," the senior officer said through clenched teeth, his tone more serious than at any other time Hunter could remember. "A lot happened while you were knocked out. Now these guys are not going to let me stay around here much longer, so I'm going to tell it all to you once and straight from the hip. Save the questions—it ain't going to do you any good to know the answers. Got it?"

Hunter nodded. "Yes, sir . . ."

"OK, here's the situation in a nutshell. The Soviets nuked the US. Started two nights ago, ended this morning."

"What?"

"It was a bolt-from-the-blue sneak attack. Everything from North Dakota down to Texas is gone. Wiped out. All our underground ICBMs are gone."

"I can't believe this . . ."

"Believe it, Major. There's more: The President is dead—assassinated. Along with his Cabinet, his family, his kids, everyone. We're not sure but we think the Vice President is running things. But someone in Washington has already tossed in the towel. That means the war is *really* over now—and we lost."

"But, the ceasefire," Hunter said, never more feeling like he was living a nightmare as at that moment. "The Soviets gave up . . . I *remember* that."

"It was bullshit, Hawk," Jones said, his teeth still clenched in silent rage. "The President got it less than an hour after the Sovs cried uncle. Two hours later, the missiles began to fall."

"Did we retaliate?"

"No," Jones answered. "Not one of our missiles got off the ground."

"But the Navy subs . . ."

"The Navy's sub launch systems were sabotaged," Jones said harshly. "I told you, not one of our missiles were launched. Someone high up in the US government called off all our defensive systems. Someone up there must have been a first-class Soviet mole . . ."

Hunter could not stop shaking his head. He felt like his brain fibers were going to burst.

Jones drew even closer to him, eyeing one of the guards who had moved closer to them. "Now there's something you are going to have to understand, right now," he said in a harsh near whisper. "There is no more United States of America. Get that? It's gone. And these boys here will shoot you, right now, if you even say those words, *United States of America.*"

"What the hell are you talking about, sir?" Hunter said. This, of all the news, shook him the deepest.

"It's called 'The New Order,' Hawk," Jones said quickly as two more guards moved up beside him. "It's the terms that the U . . . I mean, that our former country agreed to as part of the armistice . . . That's why they're blowing up our airplanes. Part of the 'peace agreement.' We have agreed to be disarmed. Both here and back home . . . These 'neutral' bastards have agreed to help things along . . ."

At that point, the two guards grabbed Jones and began hauling him away. Inexplicably, a new Mercedes-Benz pulled up, and the guards began leading Jones toward it.

"Remember, Hawk," he yelled as he was being put in the car. "It's no more. The country is gone. Don't talk about it . . . to anyone . . ."

Jones was then literally thrown into the car. Five guards climbed in with him and with a screech of tires, the car drove away, down the flightline and out of the base.

At that point, one more deafening explosion thundered across the landing strip. The last F-16 reared up off its landing gear, propelled by an orange fireball that encircled the plane's nose and wings, setting off a series of secondary explosions inside the jet's fuselage.

The interceptor's nose reared up almost vertically in an anguished breach to the cold Spanish sun. Then the crippled jet came down hard, smashing the thin struts of its main landing gear and nosewheel as the heavy fuselage slammed the ground. Sparks of flaming fuel and oil streamed from the airplane as if it were bleeding to death in the flames.

It was his all-white airplane.

Hunter felt sick as he watched the F-16 convulse in its death agony. How could this be happening? How many millions of dollars were being systematically destroyed? How could they ever be replaced?

His mind was now racing in afterburner. Had they really fought and won against impossible odds at the fighting front, only to be stabbed in the back? Had America been the victim of a deliberate, well-rehearsed plan?

It would be later before he learned all the details of the New Order: No more NATO. No more armies. No more weapons. No more flag.

No more America.

He knew in his consciousness that his country had been betrayed. Done in by an inside job. Someone up top. Hunter felt sick again, sick to his stomach that an American, one who undoubtedly held a position of trust, had been so callous — so ruthless as to sell out his own people. How many had died during the last few terrible days, just to prevent this type of tyranny? And how many innocents had died in the deadly Soviet nuclear strike?

He knew there was blood on somebody's hands.

A secondary explosion ripped through his fighter and Hunter felt a sharp pain in his heart. It was as if he was experiencing the mortal agony of the dying F-16. In a real sense, he *was* dying. Along with his airplane. Along with his country.

But even in the depths of that terrible despair; even from the dark hole of a grave that Hunter found himself hurtling through; even though he was physically and mentally beaten, the pain stopped. Suddenly, he felt something was still beating deep inside him. Something down in the unfathomed reaches of his innermost soul was stirring. Lights flashed across his psyche. He knew his dreams during the drug-induced state were no mere coincidence. And now, he knew more about this seeping horror than Jones or the other pilots, or the Finns or the Soviets. He had lived side by side with this evil, thrashing it out in his dreams even as the dreams were becoming reality.

There was a new, terrible, *powerful* anger boiling within him now.

Somehow, he vowed silently — some way, some day — he would pay back those who had taken this from him.

Part III
The Final Storm

Chapter 35

It took three days to present the entire book of testimony to the court.

As Dr. Leylah read every word aloud with conviction and feeling, the trial's justices, the witnesses, the thousands of spectators, and even the defendant himself followed along, at times fascinated, at times angry.

Hunter's own emotions swung from intense pride to acute embarrassment as he heard the re-telling of his exploits and those of his colleagues during the nightmarish days of the war.

But it was actually another thought that burned in his mind during the three days. It was the comment that Fitzie had made to him just before the second day of the trial—that America was in more danger now than ever before.

Throughout the trial, Hunter had kept an eye on the Irishman as he squirmed in his chair just behind the prosecution table, his ruddy face showing the signs of strain of someone who knew a terrible secret and could not unload it on anybody.

But it was a secret he wouldn't have to keep much longer . . .

The fifth day of the trial dawned cold and rainy over Syracuse.

Once more the throngs crowded into the Dome; once more all the principals took their appointed seats. Now that the prosecution's opening statement was finished, it was the defense team's turn.

Just about everyone assumed that one of the Finnish lawyers

would take the stand and, through an agonizing translation process, would read a rebuttal as lengthy as the one prepared by the prosecution.

So it was to just about everyone's shock when the traitor himself rose to take the stand.

The Chief Justice was the first to recover his composure, slamming his gavel down three times to silence the huge crowd. With admirable aplomb, the judge led the ex-VP through the swearing-in process, emphasizing the words ". . . *so help you God*."

Once done, the traitor took his seat, adjusted his microphone, looked out first on the crowd and then directly at Hunter and said:

"I hereby demand that this trial be stopped and that I be released immediately. If this is not done, then at noontime tomorrow, a Soviet ICBM will be launched and its nuclear-armed warhead will detonate at a height of twenty thousand feet directly above this dome."

An absolute blanket of silence fell onto the crowd. Had they heard correctly? Had the traitor really threatened to nuke Syracuse?

Once again, the Chief Justice was the first person to come to his senses. He asked the ex-VP to repeat his statement, and the traitor, reciting the sentences like a child does his school lesson, respoke the dire threat, word for word.

That's when all hell broke loose in the Dome. Some of the spectators attempted to charge the cordoned off trial area, only to be restrained by the strong arms of the Marine security forces. Others, obviously taking the traitor's threat seriously, tried to flee the place. Once again, it took a strong action by the inside security forces to push back those panic-stricken spectators, thus preventing a disastrous stampede.

All the while the Chief Justice was smashing his gavel on the table, its pounding reverberating throughout the Dome via the sophisticated public address system.

"Order!" the judge screamed. *"Order* in this court!"

It took five full minutes before some semblance of calm returned to the Dome. All the while the traitor sat in the dock, a maddening smirk on his face.

Once the place had quieted down, the Chief Justice, angry beyond words, turned to the head of the defense team and demanded an explanation.

The Finnish lawyer obediently stood up and carried a document to the Justices' bench, handing it to the lead judge. A quick, hushed conversation ensued, then an uneasy silence fell on the place as the Chief Justice read the document.

Hunter, sitting in the witness gallery, had been watching the latest development with a mixture of shock and anger. He knew the bombshell that Fitzie had talked about had been dropped. Now, he felt an uncomfortable empty feeling in the pit of his stomach as he watched the Chief Justice's face turn from angry red to ashen white.

Suddenly the judge pounded his gavel loudly twice. Then he pulled the microphone closer to him and said:

"In light of irrefutable evidence just handed to me, I hereby declare these proceedings a mistrial. . . . I am also hereby ordering the security forces both inside and outside this building to commence a safe and orderly evacuation of all citizens from this area.

"From the information just handed to me, I am convinced that an atomic bomb will be dropped on this city at noontime tomorrow . . ."

Chapter 36

Almost two hours later, Hunter, Jones, Fitzgerald, Toomey, Wa, and several other members of the United American Army Command Staff were assembled in the Dome's adjacent conference center.

Outside, a massive, not entirely orderly evacuation was taking place. By the judge's orders, everyone was to leave Syracuse as quickly as possible with the multitude of civilians going first. Most people needed no further prompting. However, huge C-5A Galaxy transports were flying into the city, picking up those civilians who had no other means of escape.

By the judge's own estimate, there were close to 150,000 people within the potential blast area. It would take all night and most of the next morning to clear them all out.

But the men meeting in the conference center could not be concerned with the evacuation. They had an even more serious problem to face.

None of them had been able to grab more than a few hours of sleep in the past few days, and their tired eyes and beard stubble showed their fatigue. Most of the men in the room poured hot coffee into their mugs, this time without the benefit of the usual liberal splashes of "medicinal" whiskey.

This was hardly time for drinking alcohol. Clear heads were needed all around.

Fitzgerald was the first to speak.

"What the traitor told us during his interrogation was the same information contained in that statement handed to the judge. It is apparent now, and without a shadow of a doubt, that the Soviet military clique now running things over there has enough hardware to launch ICBMs at this country."

Although most in the conference room knew the gist of what the ex-VP's lawyer had told the judge, the news still hit them like a lightning bolt.

"We are certain now that they gained this launch capability in two ways," Fitz continued, wearily. "First, they were able to patch together some of their own hardware left over from the Big War, not an easy task.

"Second, we have learned that the hardened SAC facilities that housed this country's own ICBM command, control, and communications system were looted during the Circle War, their critical components smuggled over to the Soviets.

"The most critical of this equipment were systems that control targeting and re-entry of the ICBMs. This system, which was developed secretly here in the US before the war, uses satellites put into orbit by the space shuttle. These satellites are incredibly advanced and in several ways. Foremost to us here right now, they can direct with incredible accuracy ICBMs launched from anywhere on the globe.

"The Soviets have incorporated this technology into their own patchwork system and come up with a launch and detonation procedure that has the ability to hit us anywhere, at anytime."

"It's Goddamn nuclear blackmail!" Toomey cried out.

"Exactly . . ." Fitz agreed, nodding his head glumly.

An absolutely stone-cold silence descended on the room.

Fitz cleared his throat and began again. "You may recall a series of secret space shuttle launches in the years right before the war," he said. "Despite what was told — or leaked — to the media at the time, those launches really had to do with putting this particular system into space. And as I said, these satellites have incredible features. Besides the targeting system, they have the ability to clearly photograph any point and anything on our continent that's bigger than a cigarette pack."

"If that's true," Jones said. "That means they can watch our every move . . ."

"But wait a minute," Toomey said, holding up his hand. "Don't these satellites revolve around the earth? If they do, then there must be times when they *can't* see us . . ."

Once more, Fitz shook his head. "They are all thousands of miles straight up, in a series of geo-synchronic orbits. This means that they can match the speed of the earth's revolution and therefore stay right on top of us, day and night . . ."

"Jesus Christ, Big Brother *is* watching us . . ." Ben said angrily.

"That's correct," Fitz replied somberly.

"But how did the Soviets know that this sophisticated system was even in place?" Jones asked. "I was working in Pentagon secret operations during those years and this is the first I've heard of it."

Suddenly everyone in the room knew the answer.

"*He* told them," Fitz confirmed, his face flushing with anger at the mere mention of the traitor. "Only a handful of people knew just how advanced these satellites were. The Vice-President was one of them."

"And he tipped the Soviets," Wa said, speaking the conclusion all of them had already reached.

"Tipped them about the system," Fitz said. "*And* how they could integrate it into their own system."

Another pall of silence came over the room.

"So he *can* make good with his threat to nuke this city," Jones asked. "Or any other place?"

"Can and will," Fitz said. "After spending so much time with him, during the interrogation, I'm convinced that he would stop at nothing. His threat today is a definite one. I'm sure they have a spy or two in the audience and in the area. If he isn't set free in twenty-four hours, they'll launch. I'm certain of it, and apparently so is the Chief Justice."

"You don't think they'll actually let him go, do you?" Ben asked.

Fitz could only shrug. "It's either that or this place gets nuked," he said. "He's even put a proviso into his threat. That is, if anything untoward happens to him, the Soviets will launch anyway."

"So in other words," Jones said, "even if we strung the bastard up right now, they'll still come down on us."

"That's correct, sir," Fitz replied.

At this point, Hunter stood up.

"Just where are they supposed to be launching these ICBMs from, Mike?" he asked.

It was the first time the Wingman had spoken at the meeting. Suddenly all eyes in the room turned to him.

"Just where the particular missile launchers are being kept, we

264

have no idea," Fitz told him. "I'm sure there are SS-20 mobile launchers, so they can be moved around at anytime.

"But as for this hybrid control center, they were quite open about it being located in the same complex as the big phased- array radar in Soviet Central Asia. It's called Krasnoyarsk, and it's in the Soviet republic of Khazakstan.

"They can control the remainder of their ICBM missiles from that one point. All they really have to do is push the button. The satellites do the rest: begin the launch sequence, flight time, re-entry curves, targeting adjustments, determine ground blast or air burst."

"In other words, they have control of the ultimate 'smart bombs,' " Hunter said. "Smart ICBMs, almost . . ."

"Yes," Fitz answered. "The satellites not only can keep an eye on all of us, day or night, in all kinds of weather, they can also steer a nuke to land on a dime."

Another damning silence fell.

"And because there are no ASAT weapons around anywhere," Jones said in a near whisper, "there's not a damn thing we can do about it."

"Yes, there is," Hunter said quickly, firmly. "We can go in and take out that radar station."

"In Central Asia?" someone asked. "How? If we can't make a move without those bastards tracking every one of us?"

Hunter's eyes suddenly began to glow. "There's one place those satellites can't see," he said.

Early the next morning, the UA Command Staff flew out of Syracuse, convinced that the city had been completely evacuated. The ex-VP, under heavy guard, had been moved back to Washington earlier.

At exactly 12:01 PM, a five-kiloton-yield Soviet-launched nuclear warhead detonated twenty thousand feet above the city.

Chapter 37

Three weeks later, Hunter was standing on the weather-beaten docks of an abandoned shipyard on the Virginia coast, remembering a dream he once had. A dream about submarines. And a port with many military ships, most long ago abandoned to the salt and rust. And talking to people he didn't recognize.

"Welcome to Newport News, Major," the man in the United American Navy uniform told him. "Such as it is . . ."

The scene at the port was right out of his dream. There was a line of former US Navy ships now rusted and scavenged for parts. Most of the shipyard and its facilities had fallen into disrepair. And he had never met the man who was now shaking his hand.

"I'm Admiral Cousins," he said. "Commander of the United American Navy."

Hunter knew the UAN was little more than a collection of armed merchant ships and some semi-reliable destroyers and corvettes. While in the post-Big War years the United Americans had, by necessity, built up their ground forces as well as their air strength, the maritime contingent had been left behind.

Once a bustling port and shipbuilding center, Newport News had been an early victim of the New Order's disarmament program. Hunter's eyes scanned the rusting hulks of Navy warships that had been sabotaged by the treacherous New Order goons, or deliberately scuttled by their crews to prevent them from falling into the hands of the Mid-Aks.

Now, more than forty once-proud ships of the line lay in ruins or on the muddy bottom of the crowded harbor, their skeleton-like superstructures protruding above the surface like tombstones. Hunter recognized the huge forward compartment of a Ticonderoga-class *AEGIS* cruiser, peppered with ugly wounds of festering rust and scale. Further on were two Oliver Hazard Perry-class frigates, both sunk deep in the silty muck. The closer of the two had rolled over on its side during a recent storm, exposing its gray belly to the harsh sun and rusting waves. Now a flock of hungry seagulls walked its barnacle-encrusted keel, just as sailors had once patrolled her narrow decks.

And somewhere below the gray waters that lapped at the dead ships and the leaning piers, Hunter knew there were submarines. Like dying sharks, the giant prowlers of the deep sea had plunged to the sea floor to meet their end. Some had been the victims of the Mid-Ak's mindless destruction after the war—torpedoes had been detonated inside the forward and rear tubes, tearing the bows and sterns open like huge firecrackers in oversized tin cans. In mortal agony, the stricken ships had turned out their innards to the sea and been lost forever.

The waters must have foamed and churned with the carnage of dying ships, Hunter thought. Oil slicks must have covered the beaches for miles. But now the water was clean—the sea had stripped the wrecks of their polluting fluids and they became like natural reefs. The waves that washed up onto the beach around the docks were white with the natural crisp foam of seawater, almost completely uncontaminated by the telltale rainbow-like pattern of oil and gasoline that used to cover the harbor's surface like a dirty blanket.

Except Hunter's sharp eyes detected a single iridescent trail of wavy color floating on the gentle waves in the harbor. It led a meandering path from the storm-battered dock out into the harbor until it disappeared under the locked door of the huge covered berth along the ruins of the gigantic shipyard complex. The nondescript building blended in with the other hulks of the harbor, its rusting sides and rippling roof giving the appearance of a long-abandoned railroad car.

But Hunter knew the building was not abandoned. He watched a thin trail of gray smoke curl upward from the smokestack near the shore side of the enormous structure. The muffled sounds of workers inside—hammers, torches, cranes and lifts—were magnified by the steel walls and roof, echoing out over the harbor like the voices of the ghost ships that rested here.

Inside the covered berth, Hunter knew, was the first part of a bold scheme to strike back at the Soviets—the first direct retaliation against the Russian soil since World War Three.

Entering the massive building past the heavily armed Marine guards, Hunter's ears were assaulted by the crashing din of hammers on steel, the staccato pounding of high-powered rivet guns, and the sizzle of acetylene torches cutting through hardened metal. Sparks flew everywhere in the dark cavern, from pounding sledges and arc welders, and from the brilliant flares of the metal-cutting torches.

It took Hunter's eyes several seconds to adjust to the relative darkness inside, until he oriented himself and made his way across the cluttered floor.

He approached a small but powerfully built man in sweat-stained Navy denims, carefully welding a massive steel hatch cover in place. A full face shield covered the man's head, its tiny slit of smoked glass reflecting the dazzling shower of sparks cascading from the welder's tip.

Satisfied at last with the weld, the man cut off the torch and turned to face Hunter. He tilted the heavy mask back to wipe the sweat from his brow.

"Hey, Hawk, old buddy," the man said furiously pumping Hunter's outstretched hand. "How you doing, pal?"

The man was Navy Lieutenant Stan Yastrewski, better known as "Yaz." Hunter had first met the Navy officer during the Lucifer Crusade, as the desperate struggle in the Mediterranean against the renegade fanatic "Viktor," had come to be called.

During the Big War, Yaz and his crew had survived the wreck of their nuclear sub, the USS Albany, off the coast of Ireland. Settling first in England, then eventually moving to Algiers, Yaz and his men became a free-lance team of military technicians and were hired out to consult on high-tech weapons being used in the madness of the New Order world. Hunter, along with a team of British mercenaries, had hired Yaz and his boys to help them tow an abandoned aircraft carrier—the USS *Saratoga*—across the Med to engage the hordes of Lucifer's armies at the Suez.

After that battle, an extraordinary series of events took place that brought Yaz back to the States, this time as a prisoner of the dreaded Circle Army. Hunter and the United American Army liberated Football City, where Yaz was being held, and ever since, the Navy man had worked closely with the United American Command.

"Good to see you, Yaz," Hunter shouted above the noise inside the building. "How's it going? We gonna be ready in time?"

"I hope so, Hawk," the sweat-streaked Navy man answered. "It may look like a Chinese fire drill in here, but believe it or not, we've been working round the clock for twenty days now. But I think we're going to get these old girls back together again."

Hunter nodded, and both men turned toward the immense steel and concrete trough cut into the floor of the massive building. Nestled inside the cradle, surrounded by hundreds of workers, were two enormous, but somewhat battered U.S Navy Trident submarines.

"I've been involved in crazy plans before," Hunter yelled to Yaz. "But this has got to be the craziest. . . ."

Yaz's team of ex-submariners had been hard at work ever since they received word from Jones that the two oddly configured subs had to be refurbished and modified—damn quickly.

The subs, the USS *Theodore Roosevelt* and the USS *Ohio,* had both been in dry dock when the New Order came down. When Newport News was overrun by the Mid-Aks, the two boats had had the guts of their missile launching systems stripped out by reason of some unknown, hare-brained Mid-Ak directive. All that remained of the boats when democratic forces retook the area were the two hollow shells. But fortunately, their propulsion systems had been left intact.

The fledgling United American Navy took command of the boats and had actually put them through sea trials, although with no weapons aboard, the maneuvers were purely for training, and, truth be known, somewhat recreational.

But as it turned out, the massive hollow subs were just what the United Americans needed to carry out their bold plan. The huge empty missile bay behind the conning tower on each ship was now being converted into an equally huge cargo hold. Even now, as Hunter and Yaz talked, Yaz's shipfitters were fashioning hatch covers for the compartments, all the work being done hidden in the massive shelter, away from the ever-prying eyes of the Soviet-controlled geo-synchronic satellites.

Yaz led Hunter to his makeshift office in a quieter corner of the facility and produced two cups and a steaming pot of coffee.

"I couldn't believe it when I heard about what happened up in Syracuse," Yaz said, handing a cup of joe to Hunter. "Is everything really gone?"

Hunter nodded grimly. "Just about," he said. "The warhead itself wasn't very large. But it was the airburst detonation that really did all the damage."

"Those bastards," Yaz said through gritted teeth. Then he added: "But I have to give everyone involved in that trial some credit. At least we didn't give in to their blackmail."

Hunter took a gulp of his coffee. "I agree," he said. "Mr. Benedict Arnold is locked up so tight Houdini couldn't get him out. But, to tell you the truth, I'm not so sure that history will think losing an entire city in return was such a noble gesture."

"Do they expect any more launchings?" Yaz asked nervously. "I mean, if they ever knew what we were up to here . . ."

Hunter slowly shook his head, and for the first time in a while, he actually allowed himself a grin. "No, we don't think anything will come over," he said, adding, "not any time soon, anyway . . ."

Yaz's eyes brightened somewhat. "You seem pretty sure about that," he said.

Hunter took another swig of coffee. "It's just about the only damn thing I *am* sure of these days," he replied.

"Well, fill me in," Yaz prodded him.

Hunter shrugged. "It's simple, really," he said. "One of our decontamination teams went into Syracuse seven days after the blast, took a bunch of readings, even recovered small parts of the ICBM re-entry booster.

"We ran some tests and found out that not only was it a liquid-fueled booster that delivered the warhead, but that the fuel used was a mixture. Some old stale stuff, with a little bit of new stuff . . ."

Yaz knew enough about ICBM boosters to get Hunter's meaning.

"So they're mixing their fuels," he said. "Dangerous business. Very tricky . . ."

"And very experimental," Hunter said. "You know it takes weeks to mix old stuff with new stuff. Just about a drop at a time, as I understand it. You never know how much or how little and the only way to test it is to fire it."

"So," Yaz said, pulling his chin in thought. "We've got to figure that although they hit upon a working formula, it will take them some time to mix another batch."

"That's right," Hunter said, draining his coffee. "Minimum four weeks, with a few days for refueling. Now we've got to assume that they've been working on it now for three weeks."

"So we've got just a little over a week to do something about all this," Yaz concluded.

"Bingo," Hunter said. "It's going right to the wire. And I can't imagine them *not* hitting Washington with their second strike."

"Those sons-of-bitches," Yaz said, turning to refill his coffee cup. Then he pointed to the two subs.

"Well, if everything goes right," Yaz told him, "we'll be ready to launch in forty-eight hours."

"I'm really glad to hear you say that," Hunter said, pouring himself another half cup. "You know we could never have even considered this mission if it weren't for you and your guys."

"Are you kidding?" Yaz said. "We're just glad we could help. I mean, if you can't chip in when the alternative is Soviet missiles raining down on you, well . . ."

Yaz's voice trailed off for a moment.

"But let me ask you a question, Hawk," he continued. "I'm sure we'll have the delivery wagons in shape. How about the cargo?"

Hunter instinctively lowered his voice.

"It's on the way," he said. "All in pieces. Some being carried by truck. Others by railcar. They're all taking different routes, nothing that can be tracked directly to this place."

Yaz nodded, at once comprehending the enormity of their task,

271

as well as the danger.

"It's going to be one hell of a tight fit," he said, leaning back toward the work area. "For *both* subs. We'll be lucky if we can find an extra place to put a blanket down and go to sleep."

"I know what you mean," Hunter said. "But the way things are going, I don't feel much like sleeping anyway."

Chapter 38

Eight hours later, Hunter and Yaz were standing back in the same spot, once again drinking thick, black coffee.

The pilot had just put in an overtime shift, helping Yaz and his guys weld the last components of the *Ohio*'s cargo hold in place. Now, they watched as a huge crane mounted on the dock next to the sub's cradle swung into action.

"The moment of truth," Yaz said anxiously. "I just hope my calculations weren't off."

The big mechanical arm reached over to what seemed like a disorderly jumble of green metal, or more accurately, pieces of a huge model airplane. Like a robot arm grasping pieces of a child's toy, the huge claw picked up a tapered wing and delicately lowered it into the yawning cargo hold of the *Ohio,* where it was carefully secured by a crew of stevedores, and padded to receive the next piece.

A fuselage section went in next, then an entire landing gear assembly. Then an engine. Then another part of a wing.

On the other side of the building, another crane was lowering similar components into the hold of the *Theodore Roosevelt.*

"There are one-million, two-hundred and thirty-two-thousand, four-hundred and eighty-three separate pieces to a B-1B bomber," Hunter told Yaz, reciting the figures by heart. "Not counting the forty-eight miles of electrical wiring.

"The question is, can it all fit into the cargo holds of these two subs?"

* * *

The supersonic B-1 bomber had been part of the five-plane *Ghost Rider* flight that had served the forces of freedom in the great battles on the North American continent after the war.

The Ghost Riders were a unique group of airplanes. Their fuselages were jammed with literally tons of sophisticated electronic jamming and masking gear. When linked by computer and flying under the right conditions, the five airplanes were able to cover up one-hundred percent of their "signatures."

In short, when the Ghost Riders were "in system," they could become invisible to radar.

But now, the *Ghost Riders* were no more.

They had to be sacrificed for this mission, a decision that Jones and Hunter painfully had to make. One of the Ghost Riders, Ghost #2, had to be gutted of all its intricate masking electronics, thus forever breaking up the integrity of the Ghost flight.

Once this sobering yet crucial operation was completed, a whole new set of avionics and weapons systems had to be fitted into the swing-wing bomber, again in record time. This equipment too was sadly cannibalized from the more modern fighters—the ultra-sophisticated F-20s, mostly—in the United American Air Corps inventory.

A highly advanced video broadcast system was also shoe-horned into the plane's cockpit, this at the special request of Hunter.

Then, once it was certain that everything fit, it all had to be taken out again, and the airplane itself dismantled and packed, and then secretly shipped via forty-five different routes and vehicles to Newport News.

In all, a dozen airplanes had to be scrapped or disabled to provide the needed equipment for the mission. Twelve airplanes that would likely never fly again . . .

Eighteen hours after the loading operation began, the last pieces of the disassembled bomber were loaded into the gaping cargo holds of the huge submarines.

Once done, steel I-beam supports were guided in across the top of the holds, and inch-thick steel plates were laid in on top of the bomber pieces. The *Ohio* wound up with the most room left over—this of course was by design. Into its hold, several pieces of earth moving equipment were secured—a small grader and one of the portable cranes were crammed into the crowded cargo bay that had once held two dozen Trident D-4 nuclear missiles.

Hunter tracked down an exhausted Yaz, thanked him and ordered that he and his men get no less than seven hours sleep. The next day would be devoted to the task of fitting the massive hatch covers onto the converted submarines' decks and making the final launch preparations.

"That was the easy part," Hunter thought to himself before leaving the huge building. "Now, it really gets tough . . ."

Chapter 39

General Dave Jones lit his fourth cigar of the morning, and took a swig of cold coffee.

He was seated before a large video monitor encased in a sturdy black-green box. A smaller box underneath it contained a small computer screen and a keyboard, which Jones was using to punch in coordinates from a small pile of maps and photographs spread out on the table in front of him.

Periodically, he glanced up at the video monitor to examine the picture gradually taking shape, and, if he approved, he would store the information away in the computer's memory.

Once every thirty minutes, he would relight his stogie, warm up his coffee, and stroll over to the office window and look out on the seemingly empty, rusting shipyard nearby.

"Perfect," he would think to himself just about every time. "Looks like there isn't a soul out there . . ."

Like Hunter and the others close to the mission, Jones had taken up residence at Newport News; specifically in the former digs of the yard's one-time commander. It had taken him a day and a half to move all the equipment he needed down from Washington, and another half day to get it up and working.

Only then could the down-and-dirty mission planning begin in earnest.

The target was the phased-array radar complex at Krasnoyarsk, the place identified as the location of the Soviets' control center for using the sophisticated weapons-targeting satellites. It was in the middle of Godforsaken Khazakstan, a place not too far from equally Godforsaken Siberia.

Jones's equipment—the video monitor, the keyboard and the hefty computer—were all part of the formidable MAPS, or Mission Analysis & Planning System. Developed before World War Three, the system employed sophisticated digital imaging technology and a powerful computer platform to allow pilots and mission planners to plot each leg of their battle sorties on the computer screen.

Constructing computer images from pre-war satellite photographs, topographical maps, and other sources, the MAPS computer automatically calculated fuel consumption, optimum weapons load and selected each turnpoint for the mission planner, plotting the coordinates and vectors for the pilot or navigator.

More importantly, the system analyzed the known defenses and enemy radar screen coverage, highlighting areas where the attacking aircraft would be vulnerable to SAMs or ground fire.

Best of all, the MAPS provided a simulated radar readout from the compiled data for any given point on the flight path. Complex software and hardware tools allowed a pilot to "preview" his radar screen over the target even before he left the ground. And the information was stored in an optical memory disk cartridge that could be inserted into the plane's cockpit console for playback during the mission.

It was for the installation of this MAPS hardware that the Ghost Rider ships had been stripped.

Jones was just configuring the system to show enemy radar coverage along the Soviet northern border and down to the target when Hunter walked in, carrying a bag of sandwiches and four bottles of beer.

Punching several buttons to select the widest view possible, Hunter settled down just as the big video screen was filled with a bright red map of the Soviet Union. Large pie-shaped blue wedges fanned out from selected locations inside Soviet territory, showing the range of the known radar sites.

The largest one indicated was at Krasnoyarsk.

"How are things down at the marina?" Jones asked without taking his eyes off the video screen and keyboard. "Will our bird and our fish be ready on time?"

"The bird has been carved and stuffed," Hunter said, chomping a

277

tuna-and-chicken sandwich. "The fish will be ready by tomorrow morning."

"Yaz and his guys did a great job," Jones said, never taking his eyes off the computer screen.

Hunter took a long swig of the bathtub beer. "How's your end going?"

"We'll know in a minute," Jones said, taking bites of his own sandwich, and washing them down with beer. "Just as soon as the computer finishes drawing the latest picture."

As if on cue, the video monitor flashed once, indicating completion of the radar mapping. Hunter let out a low whistle as the blue cones appeared to shroud the entire periphery of the Soviet Union.

"Goddamn," he exclaimed. "According to this, the whole damned country is sealed up with SAMs."

Jones studied the video image and pulled his mouth down in a frown. "Remember, although we're basing this on satellite photos that were snapped before the Big War, I think we have to assume that the Sovs have kept most of them in operation."

Hunter studied the computer image closely. "If I didn't know better, I would say, judging by this, it would seem as if there was no way to get in without them spotting the airplane."

"Or so it would seem at first glance," Jones replied. "But look carefully at the northern frontier. This is really what we are keying in on. See it?

Jones pointed to the screen, and Hunter looked even closer. Some nine hundred miles northeast of Moscow, there was indeed a small triangular area near the northern coastline that appeared to be uncovered by one of the many blue cones that interlocked around the entire country's perimeter. The powerful Soviet radars based in Moscow scanned most of the northwestern corner of the country, including the area due north of the clear spot, nearly up to the North Pole. The corresponding radar site at Peckora fanned out toward the northeast, leaving a sliver of clear on the screen.

"It means we've got to go in closer than I'd like," Jones offered, "but it's really the only option I see."

Hunter stared at the video image for a long moment, finally nodding his concurrence with Jones's analysis.

"And egress from the target area?" Hunter asked, falling into the formal terminology used to describe getting the hell out of someplace you've just nailed with tons of high explosives.

"Ah, yes, the egress," Jones intoned. "Well, as you can see from the close-up,"—he stabbed a few buttons on the keyboard to zoom the image up to a smaller section of the picture—"there is a very narrow window to try and shoot through, if for some reason the missile fails to take out the Krasnoyarsk radar. It's right here."

Jones traced along a narrow wedge that followed the southern edge of the Krasnoyarsk radar's cone until it met the northern edge of a radar site near Vladivostok. Ominously, the two radar ranges overlapped somewhere over the Sea of Japan.

"Of course, if all goes exactly according to plan, we could egress due east in the Goodyear blimp, right over the chunk of real estate the Krasnoyarsk radar is covering," Jones said blandly. "But I've already laid in an alternative course just in case."

Hunter nodded again, recognizing the importance of a contingency plan.

He spent time with one more beer and another sandwich, watching as Jones continued to punch more buttons on the computer keyboard. Within two minutes, he was able to call up what appeared to be a close-in aerial shot of the Krasnoyarsk facility.

Actually, it was a digitized simulation compiled from satellite photos and map coordinates. A thin white line traced a jagged path across the screen, each turnpoint labeled with a string of numbers that Hunter knew represented altitudes, speeds, and vectors.

A white "V" shape highlighted a spot on the map some twelve miles northwest of the Krasnoyarsk radar itself, which was distinguished with a large red "X" that bisected the narrow radar building dead center.

"There it is," Jones pronounced, entering the image into the computer's memory. "Almost as close a shot of them as they have of us, the bastards."

Hunter was studying the image at the same time, committing it to *his* extraordinary memory banks.

The target work continued, with Hunter taking the place behind the huge computer video board.

Swiftly, he tapped a series of keys that instructed the computer to construct both a visual and a radar screen image of the target area at the weapons release point. When completed, he made sure to save it on the optical disk, so they could play it back during the mission.

But before he did, he made a vivid mental image of the radar picture and filed it away in his own brain. This way, even without the aid of the on-board computers, he'd know when to release the payload.

"Well, Hawk," Jones said after reviewing everything stored in the mission's computer's memory, "that should be about it. We've laid in the entire course except for the first fifty miles. Since we don't know the exact point of takeoff, we'll have to play that by ear until we link up with our flight plan. But that should be the least of our worries."

"Did the ordnance arrive on schedule?" Hunter asked.

"Being delivered right now," the general explained. "AGM-130 Strikers—the biggest non-nuclear bang for the buck available in what's left of the Free World's arsenal. As you know, it's got a hell of a TV camera built into the nose of an infrared guidance system. It drops like a dumb bomb, but we can monitor its flight on one of the TV screens and 'fly' it in with a joystick."

Hunter nodded in agreement, though somewhat ruefully.

"The big drawback," Jones continued, "is that the damn bombs weigh about three thousand pounds apiece, that's with a full conventional high-explosive warhead. So we've got to get within twelve miles to drop it on the target."

"I'm not worried about that . . ." Hunter said frankly.

Suddenly Jones turned and looked at him.

"Goddamn it, Hawk," he said, "I've been rattling on like a bunch of us are flying in with you . . . I'm sorry about that."

Hunter shrugged. He really wasn't bothered by the comments. Not much anyway . . .

Everyone involved in the mission planning knew that the B-1 could probably be launched, flown to the target and ordered to dispense its weapons, all via radio and computer-generated commands.

But the computers couldn't take into account all of the intangibles that inevitably arose during critical missions such as this one. These unforeseen dangers would have to be dealt with as they popped up and only a human could do that. Yet, the cold hard statistics dictated that the chances of the airplane returning safely from the mission were slightly less than one hundred to one.

That's why Hunter was going on this one alone.

Sort of . . .

Actually, the mission called for at least a crew of four. Whereas Jones, Toomey, and Wa were, next to Hunter, the best pilots around, they would have been the natural choice to fly the mission with him. But again, common sense dictated that you didn't send your four best pilots on a suicide mission.

So Hunter had come up with the next best thing.

In one night he had designed and linked the elaborate system of TV cameras and screens for set-up inside the B-1's cockpit. He also installed a long-range computer/radio control system which was hitched to the airplane's myriad of flight systems.

Once the mission was underway, Jones, Toomey, and Wa would take their places behind a bank of similar video cameras and screens inside the CIC of the USS *Ohio*. The broadcast cameras would be hooked up to those TV screens inside B-1 cockpit, and vice versa. The controls in front of them on the sub would be radio linked to those on the airplane.

In other words, when the time came, they would serve as the flight crew — assisting in flying the plane, locating and evaluating the threats, preparing and eventually launching the weapons — all without leaving the comparative safety of the USS *Ohio*.

It would be the next best thing to having a crew on hand.

Chapter 40

Less than twenty-four hours later, a small group of men assembled inside the grimy repair shed at the Newport News shipyard.

The stern of the black cigar-shaped USS *Ohio* lay awash in the sunken cradle in front of them, now lowered to sea level. The bright streaks of weld marks still showed on the massive cargo hold hatches behind the conning tower as the big submarine prepared to inch its way out of the covered repair berth.

As the powerful turbines came to life, spinning the giant propellers that churned the water behind her, the huge submarine began to ease through the enormous doors and slide into the harbor, just as the *Roosevelt* had done an hour earlier.

Now, as the towering bow of the USS *Ohio* began to slip away from the cluster of men in the building, one of them spoke.

"Shouldn't we say something?" a voice in the back said. "After all, the ship is being commissioned again—you know, this is her second maiden voyage."

"Indeed, you're right," Mike Fitzgerald replied. He had overseen the delicate operation of bringing the bomber's weapons to Newport News. Now he would stay behind and monitor the mission from Washington. "A proper launching ceremony she deserves, too."

The ruddy Irishman produced a half-empty bottle of Scotch from his duffle bag, and at the last possible moment, hurled it at the rapidly retreating bow of the submarine. It crashed against the side of the ship, shattering and splashing its contents across the weathered name, "USS *Ohio*," stenciled on the stubby bow.

"Godspeed to you, lads," Fitzgerald called out as the sub sped down the ways into the dark water.

The dark form of the submarine bobbed slightly as it left the darkness of the shed doors behind and entered the twilight world beyond. For a time, the men on shore could see the black conning tower against the evening sky, until it slipped silently beneath the waves.

Chapter 41

Six days later

Ed Patrick hated the cold.

He had hated the frozen ground and the six-month night of the Aleutian Islands when he was stationed there before the Big War to build secret airfields on several of the barren rocks. And he'd hated the bone-chilling, raw, devouring wind that blasted the Korean peninsula when he was there building roads and bridges for the American forces in the Eighties. And even when he volunteered for duty in World War Three, he had wound up on the icy tundra north of Thule, Greenland, helping construct a new radar base.

And now he was fifty feet beneath the polar icecap, well north of the Arctic Circle, stamping his feet and shivering under his insulated parka, waiting for his grader to be unloaded. His breath crystallized in the frigid air, punctuating his speech with the tinkling of ice particles. Spit crackled audibly as it froze and snapped before hitting the icy floor.

Just once, he asked himself, why can't the Seabees build an airfield on Aruba?

Patrick wasn't with the Seabees any more, at least not technically.

True, he had volunteered his services when the balloon went up in World War Three, and he was admitted back to active duty under the Naval Reserve Veteran Program. Despite the fact that he was past sixty, the Navy's Seabees had allowed him to deduct his eighteen years of active duty from his age, making him eligible to rejoin one of the elite Construction Battalion units, where his experience at construction under combat conditions had quickly made him an invaluable commodity.

But after the Vice-President's phony armistice was declared, the Seabees were disbanded along with the rest of the nation's military units. After months of freezing isolation in Greenland, he and some of his crew had hitched a ride back to the States on a tramp steamer. On the shattered continent, they had found more than enough free-lance construction work to keep them busy.

In fact, it was Patrick and his crew that had helped Mike Fitzgerald rebuild the Syracuse Aerodrome into a bustling "truck stop of the skies" after the New Order took over. So it was only natural that Fitzgerald would look to the elder Irishman when they needed a construction crew for "a bit of ice-scraping," as it was first described to the ex-Seabee.

"Fitzie, you bastard," Patrick growled under his breath, looking up at the vaulted ceiling of the huge, secret ice cave. "If I ever get out of this damned deepfreeze, I'll kick your Irish ass back to County Cork!"

But Patrick's grumbling was more than half in jest. He knew the stakes involved in the desperate operation that the younger men were about to embark upon, and he knew they needed his help to carry it out. And he was more than ready to do his part.

If he didn't freeze to death first . . .

The top-speed voyage had brought the two submarines carrying Hunter and the others plus the unassembled bomber to a point just under the lip of the polar ice cap, in the northern reaches of the Soviet Union. Traversing the Atlantic and the Arctic Ocean in just five days, they had carefully made their way to the spot that corresponded with the gap Jones had detected in the Soviet radar coverage.

Once in position, the huge subs had inched their way along the underside of the massive ice formation, pinging with their powerful sonar upward to probe the inner structure of the glacier-like mass.

After several hours of searching, the sonar echoes traced out the pattern they were seeking in the ice above them. A huge glacial cave that had been secretly carved out years before the Big War as part of a joint "black program" between the CIA and Naval Intelligence.

Back then, the cave was used to allow US Navy subs sanctuary well within the territorial limits of the Soviet Union. Fitzgerald had accidentally become privy to secret documents referring to the cave several years before, and now, that stroke of good luck seemed downright serendipitous: The hiding place was an almost-perfect jump-off site for the crucial bombing mission.

Once the coordinate point was found, the *Ohio* patrolled along the length of the cavern underneath the ice shelf, sonar mapping the entire inner structure of the huge cave.

Finding a weakness in the ice at the far end of the shelf, the *Ohio*'s crew brought its blunt nose up to contact the ice at its thinnest point. By using the power of the ship's engines and releasing ballast, they rammed the jagged ice shelf repeatedly, opening a wide gash in the long frozen-over floor of the ice cave.

Once the opening was wide enough for the big sub's conning tower and cargo hatch, the ship surfaced on the icebound lake they had created inside the yawning cavern of ice.

Two hours later, the *Roosevelt* repeated the maneuver, popping up some five hundred feet from the *Ohio*.

Securing the wallowing subs to the shifting ice mass was no easy feat, as the thickened seawater-slush froze and rethawed between the hulls and the ice shelf. It had taken both crews more than three hours just to unload their portable cranes so that they could in turn unload the rest of the equipment.

Once the *Roosevelt* was empty of its cargo, its captain and a skeleton crew departed the ice-covered hiding place and headed back for Greenland, its part in the long-range mission complete.

Now, just the principals remained, living, eating and sleeping in the *Ohio* while Mike Patrick's grader began the long process of carving a smooth runway along the nearly mile-long length of the ice cave, one which would gradually ramp uphill toward the narrow crevice at the far end.

Meanwhile, the UA engineering crew were assembling what looked like a jumble of dark green metal slabs and tubes brought up from the depths of both subs' cargo bays. Even though the engineers had carefully planned the position of each piece in the holds to allow a reverse sequence for assembling the big bomber, it would be a massive and complex task.

A task that would ordinarily take weeks of effort in a well-equipped repair hangar *had* to be completed in less than forty-eight hours. In subzero temperatures. Inside the fragile eggshell of the ice cave.

Meanwhile, inside the relative warmth of the submarine's wardroom, Hunter and Jones were plotting the last calculations on the MAPS computer, linking their present position to the course they'd already laid in back at Newport News. JT Toomey and Ben Wa looked on, making notes and carefully watching the screen while Jones reviewed the flight plan to the target area.

As the defensive systems coordinator for the mission, it would be Toomey's responsibility to remotely operate the complex AN/ALQ-161 avionics package and jam or evade incoming threats. Even while hurtling through the air at near supersonic speeds, the big bomber's electronic countermeasures (ECM) system was supposed to be capable of automatically detecting, identifying and jamming multiple enemy search radars, and monitoring the threat to make sure the jamming worked.

Toomey knew he would probably be busy at his sub console toward the end of the B-1's flight, sifting through the thousands of signals processed by the threat receiver, and designating appropriate jamming signals to counter them. In addition, there was a separate tail warning system that would alert him to a missile or fighter approaching the swing-wing bomber from behind.

Besides the jamming electronics, Toomey would control the bomber's decoy flares and chaff dispensers. To supplement the existing chaff cannisters embedded in the fuselage behind the cockpit, he had supervised the installation of a large chaff pod under the right wing, well outboard from the main engines. Several miles of the hairlike, metal-coated fibers were tightly wound in the cylinder, ready to be spun out and cut at the touch of a button. Should a radar-guided missile detect the false radar image created by the metallic "tinsel," it would be diverted from the bomber itself.

Despite all this, Toomey knew that Hunter's best defense for the hazardous flight would be a combination of stealth and speed.

Flying a low-level, terrain-hugging course at speeds near Mach 1, the big aircraft could get below most of the Soviets' radar coverage, and jam the rest that got in their way. And a host of radar-absorbing materials on the bomber's airframe would help reduce their radar profile to less than 1/100th that of a conventional B-52.

But Hunter had anticipated the unexpected, so Toomey had an additional defensive ace up his sleeve. *Six* aces, to be precise — six sleek AMRAAMs (Advanced Medium Range Air-to-Air Missiles) were stored inside the aft weapons bay of the B-1. Controlled from Toomey's remote radar console, the deadly airborne torpedoes could be spun out of the rotary launcher and fired at an intercepting fighter from a range of more than thirty miles.

Ben Wa, on the other hand, had the task of the offensive systems operator: he would remotely control the delivery of the critical payload to the target. The AGM-130 rocket-powered glide bombs could be launched from his TV console, which also contained the low-light television screen on which he could monitor the images transmitted by the bomb's six-inch TV camera. A similar screen was part of the TV bank inside the cockpit of the bomber itself. By operating a small tracking handle, Ben would be able to control the bomb's on-board rocket boosters to actually "fly" the weapon right into the target shown on the TV monitor.

Also at Wa's station were the remote controls for the AN/APQ-164 multimode offensive radar system. In addition to probing the target area, the radar's advanced phased-array antennas were used to control the big bomber's altitude during the automatic terrain-following system's operation.

Several times a second, the radar pulse would interrogate the ground below for approximately ten miles ahead, and the sensitive receivers would convert the data almost instantly to a CRT image of the approaching terrain for both Wa and the pilot. It was all simultaneously fed into the flight-control computer to maintain the plane's constant height above the contours of the earth below.

It was this feature that enabled the huge form of the B-1 to dive within two hundred feet of the ground below and dash along at Mach 1, popping up to avoid major obstacles and diving down to stay under the protective ground clutter that would shield the bomber from enemy ground-based radar and fighters alike.

Fidgeting in his chair, Wa looked again at the MAPS printout and the initial leg of the flight plan.

As for Jones, he would serve as Hunter's long-range co-pilot and navigator. As such he would help Hunter to any degree possible with the flying of the mission, plus he'd be able to chip in and assist

Toomey and Wa in the event that they were overwhelmed at some point.

It was more than twenty hours later that Hunter found himself on the floor of the ice cave, huddled underneath a tarp that draped over the B-1's wingroot and hung down to the ground. The makeshift shelter was barely keeping in the scant warmth of a portable heater, powered by thick cables from the submarine.

The blasting heater made the temperature inside the tarp about ten degrees Fahrenheit. Not exactly balmy, Hunter thought, until he considered that the temperature outside the shelter was almost thirty degrees below zero.

For nearly four hours, he and a couple of Patrick's workcrew had been connecting the maze of wiring that served as the nerves and veins and arteries of the big bomber. Like some huge mechanical bird, the B-1 stood mute on the frozen surface, awaiting the spark of life from the four powerful GE turbofan engines, which would in turn generate the electrical power to run the bomber's internal organs.

Literally hundreds of wires, cable trunks, and sensors made up the bomber's complex nervous system, and each connection had to be identified, securely mated, and tested. Working together, the three men had accomplished almost half the seemingly impossible task.

But even as they struggled to connect the bomber's eyes and ears, she was already drinking in a hefty draught of volatile nutrients. Jet fuel, thickened with the bitter cold, was now being pumped from the special holding tank in the submarine to the two fueling ports and eight pumps of the B-1's integral "wet wing" fuel system, filling it with almost 200,000 pounds of the precious liquid.

Firing up the engines would be next. Now silent, the four augmented turbofan engines would eventually cough to life, inhaling the frigid air of the ice cavern and blasting out more than 120,000 pounds of thrust in four fiery torches from the gaping black nozzles, which currently sported a fine coating of delicate rime.

Further ahead, under the green tube of the B-1's fuselage, Wa was supervising the installation of the two AGM-130 Striker glide bombs in the after weapons bay, as Toomey helped load the defensive air-to-airs in the forward bay's rotary launcher.

Jones was up in the cockpit, communicating with the other members of the work details using the plane's intercom, powered temporarily by a thick cable from the submarine's auxiliary power unit. Checking the cockpit flight controls, the offensive and defensive weapons system, and the rest of the bomber's complex circuitry, the senior officer was gradually bringing each system on line with the standby power from the submarine.

And more than four thousand feet away from where the bomber was being assembled by the team of freezing, feverish workers, Patrick's crew of ex-Seabees were putting the finishing touches on the nearly mile-long, slightly sloping ramp that was to serve as the B-1's takeoff runway. All that remained was to break the thin shell of ice that now separated the interior of the cave from the cold Arctic surface, and the imprisoned green bird of prey could break free from the ice to deliver its deadly payload.

Patrick was gunning the engine of the land grader, shoving nearly a quarter ton of ice in front of its blade to help clear the furthest end of the ramp. Even the roar of the grader's diesel couldn't drown out the ominous creaks, groans, and cracking sounds from the blue-white ice of the giant cavern itself.

The grizzled Seabee had seen more than his share of frozen wastelands, and he knew the fickleness of the shifting plates of the jagged icecap. What seemed to be a solid mass of smooth ice underneath him was actually a dangerously fragile mixture of frozen seawater, arctic snow, and crystallized moisture, ready to split apart and become one with the gray water below, or the white icefields above in a second's terrible fury.

Every minute they spent in the ice cavern was on borrowed time, as the wind and weather above pressed down on the arching roof, and the mighty ocean heaved and strained against the thin floor. More than once, Patrick had seen the thirty-foot-thick ice shelf ripple with the motion of an errant wave, or shudder at the impact of some far-off iceberg.

But he knew that the men on the other end of the ramp were working as fast as they could, frantically trying to reassemble one of man's most advanced mechanical marvels under near-prehistoric conditions. He only hoped it would be done in time.

More freezing hours passed. Finally the project was nearing

completion.

Now up in the cockpit, Hunter watched through the sloping forward canopy as the last of Patrick's Seabees drove the grader off the top of the long, upward ramping runway in front of the plane. The heavy equipment was to be left inside the ice cave, probably never to be used again.

As Yaz's crewmen started to dog down the huge cargo hatches, Hunter's thoughts turned to the task ahead of him.

Through the frost crystals on the front canopy, he could see the narrow horizontal slit in the ice cavern at the far end of the nearly mile-long ramp they had constructed. Frozen light from the weakened Arctic sun shafted in through the crevice, casting an eerie blue glow on the surrounding ice. Outside, he knew this part of the world was bathed in near-twilight this time of year. It would give the B-1, which would be flying without any external lights, an additional blanket of cover.

The opening Hunter had to drive the bomber through was just under 160 feet across—enough for the B-1's wings to pass through at their maximum extension of fifteen-degree sweep, with maybe six feet to spare on either side. He knew that his was not the first airplane to take off from the clandestine ice cave—Fitz told him that the CIA once flew light-weight OV-1 Mohawk recon-observation airplanes from the place—ones specially adapted to flying in the frigid arctic weather. They had been used to trip the Soviets' northern frontier radar net, then dash away, no doubt giving fits to the isolated Soviet radar operators.

But there was a world of difference between a small, two-prop Mohawk and the B-1 supersonic swing-wing bomber. But a larger opening was out of the question—cutting the crevice any wider might cause the whole ceiling to collapse, or the shifting floor to give way.

However, getting out of the small opening was just one of the problems Hunter expected to encounter on take-off. He knew it would be difficult just to guide the big bomber along the slick, packed-ice surface, especially under full power on takeoff. A half-inch mistake of the throttle or control stick could send the green monster careening off the narrow ramp to be smashed on the jagged ice below, or crush a fragile wingtip on the crusted edge of the cave opening.

So he knew he had to make it happen on the first try. There would be no aborts once he punched the four powerful afterburners . . .

Eight more hours passed.

Finally, the work was completed on the bomber. At just about the same time, Patrick christened the runway of ice as being ready.

At this point, Hunter, JT, Ben, and Jones gathered for one last meeting, went over all aspects of the mission once again, then feasted on some stale sandwiches and water made from melting the Arctic.

Hunter was three bites into his sandwich when he closed his eyes just to give them a rest. So much had happened over the past few weeks, his head felt like it was caught up in a perpetual swirl: the raid on Bermuda, the hypnotic testimony session, the trial itself, the nuking of Syracuse, the endless preparations for this mission.

It was enough turmoil for a hundred lifetimes. He promised himself that after this was over, he was going to take some extended R&R and do what he had vowed to do right after the Panama operation. That was to find his only true love, Dominique, wherever she was. Maybe he would even ask her to finally settle down and . . .

Next thing he knew, JT was shaking him awake. He had unintentionally slept for three hours.

It was now time to go . . .

The last crewman was aboard the USS *Ohio* when Hunter finally fired up the B-1's engines for real.

It took more than forty-five minutes for the cold turbines to power up to their optimum speeds under full oil pressure. Another thirty minutes was devoted to Hunter's checking his cockpit avionics against those readings in the remote-control room deep within the *Ohio*. A few minor problems were ironed out, and the MAPS device recalibrated for the final time.

At that point, there was nothing else to do but take off and get the damn thing over with.

With JT, Ben, and Jones seated at their remote-control console Yaz and Patrick were the only ones to stay up on the big sub's conning tower weather bridge to watch the B-1 take off.

Yaz flashed a "thumbs up" sign to Hunter as he nudged the B-1 forward along the improvised flight line, but Patrick stood watching, hands clenched tightly against the railing, straining to listen with his entire body for any sound from the ice.

But he couldn't hear the creaks and groans from the densely packed ice now. The steady whine of the B-1's idling engines became a deafening roar as the four GE turbofans spat out their fiery exhausts a mixture of red-hot flame and billowing white vapor clouds in the frigid air. Their thundering blast rocked the sub and the men on deck as it echoed in the closed cave. His ears useless, Patrick nevertheless could almost *feel* the ice mass shuddering.

"The engines!" he hollered above the noise to Yaz. "The damned vibrations'll rip this place apart!"

"Too late now, Pops," Yaz screamed back, "He's already committed to go!"

The two men watched, unable to speak, both being pounded by the howling engine roar.

The B-1's wings swung outward toward their full extension even as the plane began to gather speed toward the narrow beam of light at the far end.

Within a matter of seconds, the bomber was traveling at almost a hundred and fifty miles per hour, straight as an arrow toward the opening. The wheels seemed locked into their tracks as the big bomber gained the acceleration it needed for takeoff.

"Time for afterburners, Hawk buddy," Yaz said through clenched teeth, his hands clasping an imaginary control stick in front of him, as if he were trying to fly the plane himself. Without the extra punch of power, the airplane would never break the lock of gravity.

The screaming engine noise was notched upward an order of magnitude as all four afterburners sent the bomber hurtling along. But suddenly a new sound was heard over the jet's thunder. An ear-splitting explosion echoed through the cavern, and an ominous crack appeared in the floor of the cave near where the bomber had been assembled.

The men on the submarine's bridge watched in horror as the crevice continued to grow, chasing the speeding bomber along the runway. A deep rumbling welled up from the ice mass around them, drowning the roar of the engines. More cracks opened in the ice floor, spreading across the makeshift airstrip scant feet behind the plane's path as it continued to rush toward the bright slit at the end of the ramp.

Now they could actually see the ice of the floor buckle and ripple before them.

Jagged frozen chunks began heaving themselves up as the green-gray seawater rushed through the crevices between them. The grader they'd used to clear the runway quickly disappeared into the dark water, followed by leftover fuel barrels and empty electrical wire spools. At the same time, ice stalactites were shaken loose from the ceiling, and plunged downward like white daggers toward the green blur now nearing the opening.

Miraculously, none struck the bomber.

Finally, one of the ice daggers tore away from the ice roof with a huge chunk of ice connected. It struck the runway just behind the jet's moving tail section and opened a gaping tear in the packed-ice floor. The massive block of ice had been the keystone of the crazy-quilt structure that formed the cavern's ceiling, and its sudden dislodging sent shockwaves rippling throughout the cave.

First one fissure appeared in the ceiling, starting to slice over to the top of the runway. Then another dashed down a wall to join the disintegration of the floor. Finally, the huge arching cavern roof began to give way, sending huge blocks of ice smashing into the churning seawater and ice that floated below. Several ice boulders struck the exposed hull of the submarine.

At that moment, Yaz knew it was time to get the hell below and get the *Ohio* down to safety.

Patrick was the last one on the bridge. He glanced back over his shoulder to see the green arrow-shape of the B-1 shoot out of the mouth of the ice cave, wings barely clearing the narrow window.

Then the plane was gone from sight.

Chapter 42

In the elaborate bunker deep beneath the Krasnoyarsk radar building, Soviet Air Marshal Alexsandi Petrovich Porogarkov lit a cigarette and looked about him.

A dozen radar consoles lined the smart, bright red walls of this main control room, their sparkling TV screens dwarfed by the mammoth black cabinets that contained their elaborate supporting hardware and electronics. He checked a bank of LED indicator lights on his own desk-top console and was reassured to see that all twelve of the radar screens were in operation now, each one of them attended by two crack technicians.

He leaned back and took a deep drag on his cigarette. All was correct with his world at the moment — even the music. A constant symphony of duo-tone beeps and blips intermittently echoed through the room, filling it with a forceful, yet pleasant chorus of sounds.

Above it all was the sterling banner of the Red Star — the near-secret, elite ruling party that had guided the Soviet Union since the beginning of World War III.

There is an inherent simplicity in smaller numbers, Porogarkov thought, not for the first time. Whereas before the war the Soviet Union's Communist Party was a bureaucracy bloated beyond all recognition, the new Party, the Red Star, was small, manageable and common-sensical. For in his mind, of the many positive things that resulted from the Soviet Union's "victory" in World War III, the best of all was the thorough cleansing of the old Kremlin ruling clique. In fact, he knew this purification was the *real* reason the war was started in the first place. No sooner had his confederates launched the surprise Scud missile attack on western Europe, when the precarious dominoes in the Politburo came crashing down. Even before the Scuds had hit their targets, the reformers in the Kremlin were gone. Assassinated. With them went *glasnost, perastroika* and all the rest of the obscene Western-style fads.

Yes, even before the deadly gas from the Scuds had scattered more than a few feet, the *original* communist ideal was firmly back in place in the Kremlin. Now, a handful of years later, under the banner of the Red Star, that ideal was stronger, leaner, more enduring.

Only now did he truly believe he would see the Red Star banner flying over the entire planet in his lifetime.

Porogarkov had known this place when it was little more than a crudely constructed radar station.

Based on thirty- or forty-year-old designs stolen from the West, it had been built by Soviet engineers from available Soviet equipment. At that time, before the Big War, he remembered touring Krasnoyarsk and seeing more than half of the radar stations shut down or only partially operable. Back then there was an absence of trained operators so acute the station commander had been forced to man some of the stations with untrained, unqualified recruits.

At one time, only one in four of the enlisted men assigned to the place had had any radar experience. Alcoholism was rampant. The console crews were little more than repetitive sets of bloodshot eyes staring past the screens into nothingness, and shaking hands nervously fidgeting with the dials on the bench.

But all of that changed with the coming of Red Star.

His own life had changed too—dramatically so. Once he had been little more than an assistant to the deputy air defense minister, a petty functionary who couldn't even get an extra book of meat ration tickets. Now, since the dawning of Red Star, he *was* the air defense minister—a very important person in a very important position. He now had power and prestige of the kind he had only dreamed of before—a luxury apartment in Moscow not far from the Kremlin, as well as a *dacha* on the Black Sea. His wife could shop at the exclusive stores where there were no lines, no shortages, and plenty of pre-war quality goods. His mistresses could do the same.

He lit another cigarette and reveled in the ever-budding glory of Red Star. *They* had defeated the United States, forced its disarmament, presided over its break-up, enforced the New Order. *They* had kept the mish mash of America's countries and states on edge for the last few years, all of it part of the plan to buy time. Time for their scientists to reactivate the warhead-targeting satellites. Time for their scientists to refurbish their remaining ICBMs. Time to plan, with an intelligent step-by-step approach, the eventual conquest of the entire globe.

And once that was accomplished, Porogarkov told himself without a hint of false modesty, Red Star would rebuild a space shuttle, reconquer space, and eventually go to the Moon and Mars.

Nothing could stop them now.

Not even the news that the former US Vice-President had been kidnapped and returned to America.

This too was part of a plan. The American turncoat had long ago worn out his usefulness — his role had simply been another device to buy time. And with his capture came an opportunity to send the Americans a message. No more would the Soviets be forced to infiltrate entire armies halfway around the world, or pay out enormous sums of money to every two-bit hooligan terrorist who promised to make things hard for the United Americans' shaky provisional government.

No, the days of the shotgun approach were gone. The Soviets' *new* message — the firm bold message of Red Star — had arrived in an air burst twenty thousand feet above the city of Syracuse.

Porogarkov had only seen the American traitor once, when the man had visited Krasnoyarsk not six months after his act of betrayal. But even before the Big War, there had been inside, deep rumors of the American's collusion with the Red Star fringe elements of the Politburo. The logical payoff had come in the form of highly sophisticated satellite software technology the Vice-President had somehow managed to squirrel away in Finland before hostilities broke out.

Now, not fifty meters from where Porogarkov stood, the very last of that same high-tech booty was finally being fully installed.

As air defense minister, he was privy to all aspects of the First Launch, as the bombing of Syracuse had come to be called. In many ways the operation had been a test firing; the liquid fuel mixture had been critical, but so had been the correct interaction between the equipment installed at Krasnoyarsk and the orbiting satellites. All things considered, not only had the First Launch gone off flawlessly, but it had answered many questions. Now, with only a few more adjustments to make, the Red Star technicians had transformed the Krasnoyarsk station into a military command center like no other in history. Not only would it be able to cover ninety percent of the Soviet Union with an early-warning radar screen and look in on any part of the US via the astoundingly advanced American-built spy satellites, but it would also be able to independently target any of the Red Star ICBMs with pinpoint accuracy to any spot on the globe.

It was a simple concept. Manageable. Sublimely so.

In this, Porogarkov saw the beauty of it all. For from this isolated Central Asian outpost, Red Star *could* control the world.

At the far end of the building, Captain Nikita Mursk had just reported for duty.

Refreshed from a good night's sleep and a hearty meal of delicious food, the young Red Star officer began his duty shift as he always did: making the rounds in the complex's defensive radar section. Walking around the large, terminal-filled room like a benevolent schoolmaster looking over the shoulders of his students, Mursk saw that most of the radar scopes yielded nothing but the shapeless masses of huge weather systems that reeled across the Asian continent, blotting out huge areas. On others there was an occasional blip from a military flight, with its authorization code duly noted alongside the dot on the screen where it appeared.

All seemed to be normal.

Except for the last screen . . .

This station's radar scope, manned by a sergeant named Vasilov, showed more of the same weather patterns and identified flights. But Mursk noticed the young man was staring at a certain point near the northern border's coastline.

"Anything to report, Vasilov?" Mursk asked, scanning the young man's console without waiting for an answer.

"Nothing, Comrade," the well-groomed, muscular enlisted man

began, his voice quavering only slightly. "At least it appears to be nothing . . ."

"Explain, Sergeant," Mursk said calmly. "Don't hold back."

"I saw a large blip appear in the middle of the White Sea, sir," the man replied. "Only for a brief moment. It was moving very fast. But now, I see no such indication."

Mursk half-listened to the radarman as he watched the screen. The area Sergeant Vasilov had pointed to was on the edge of the dense Arctic pack ice in the White Sea. For the most part Mursk was certain, beyond question, that no aircraft could just simply appear and penetrate the zone undetected.

"Probably just a case of atmospheric distortion," Mursk said confidently, dismissing the enlisted man's concern. "Anything else?"

"Nothing, sir," Vasilov said, returning to his regular position at the console. "Only some ground clutter farther south."

Mursk gave the man a comradely pat on the back. "Carry on, Sergeant," he said.

Chapter 43

Hunter checked the mission clock and saw it was already at four and one half minutes.

So far, so good.

Time seemed to be moving extra fast ever since he'd burst forth from the hidden ice cavern base. It was only a second after he had punched in the big bomber's afterburners that the deafening roar of the engines diminished all at once to a distant rumble. This told him that his power plants were working well.

Wing configuration came next. Upon leaving the cavern, the big bomber's wings were fanned out to their full extension as it shot skyward on a steep angle. After only seconds in the air, Hunter had grasped the large wing-sweep lever to his right, pulling it up almost halfway. Immediately, giant ball-screw assemblies in the wingroots smoothly cranked the tapered wings in toward the slim fuselage at a twenty-five-degree angle, and the B-1's rocketlike rise increased another notch.

Ten seconds into the flight, he knew that the heavy bomber was climbing at a rate of more than two thousand feet per minute, slicing through the frozen skies at almost four hundred miles per hour.

"Quarterback to base," he had called into his microphone. "I'm up and still climbing. At fifteen hundred feet now at mark . . ."

"Roger, QB," came Jones's reply. "Activate on-board sensor and monitoring systems . . ."

Hunter had reached over and punched a series of switches on a computer-driven TV transmitter that had been installed on his right side where the co-pilot's seat would normally be.

"Sensor and monitoring systems on," he reported, as he watched the four, side-by-side TV screens facing him on the front console blink to life.

Almost magically, the color images of Jones, Toomey, and Ben materialized, each on his own TV screen. The fourth screen, designated "mission master" would display all data—fuel load, time to target, potential threats, and so on—deemed important by the mission computer.

"This is very strange," Hunter admitted as he looked at the three video talking heads. "I actually feel like it's getting crowded in here."

"Imagine what it looks like to us back here," Toomey said, reaching up to tap the lens of the TV camera devoted to his station. "You look like Buck Rogers, or Captain Midnight."

"We have communication link-up integrity confirmation," Jones told Hunter, confirming that the video link-up between the B-1 and the sub's mission control center was being properly scrambled and dispersed, making it practically impossible to be monitored by the Soviets.

"OK, guys," Hunter said, finally taking his eyes off the images of his friends on the TV screens, "glad to have you aboard. But now it's time to go to work . . ."

The big plane's altimeter display to the right of the center CRT screen had barely clicked over to five thousand feet when Hunter eased up on the B-1's fighter-like stick control with his right hand and quickly backed the four throttles down from full afterburner with his left.

As the bomber leveled off, several high-speed fuel pumps rapidly began transferring tons of JP-8 among the network of fuel cells in the internal circulatory system of the airplane, maintaining a balance with the ever-shifting delicate center of gravity.

Hunter monitored the fuel exchange on his console, and was heartened to see that everything was in order.

"Let's get a position fix, Ben," he said crisply into the microphone in his oxygen mask, "and then let's get back down on the deck. No sense loitering around up here."

"Roger, Hawk," Wa answered from his station. Without delay, he began deftly flicking switches and reading in-flight data to the inertial navigation system, coaxing the complex computer to establish the B-1's exact position and calibrate the coordinates with the MAPS readout on his display screen. After a few moments of activity, the proper series of characters, beeps and flashes appeared on the flickering screen.

"It's a go," Ben reported, his TV image flickering slightly. "Heading one-zero-zero, maximum warp. . . . Head for the tall grass and let's meet up with our plotted course about six klicks over landfall. You'll have to tell us where the hell the land begins and the icepack ends."

"Roger, Ben," Hunter replied. "Doing a visual terrain check now."

Hunter turned away from the TV screens for a moment and looked down at the frozen, barren expanse of jagged ice fields below him, trying to pick out the coastline where the frigid tundra met the jagged icepack of the White Sea. Within seconds, his extraordinarily sharp eyes detected a dark outcropping of black rocks, blasted free of snow by the howling Arctic winds, and he knew that it marked the edge of the Soviet landmass.

"OK, I've got the shoreline dead ahead," he called back to the trio. "Ben, let's go down to two hundred feet."

He checked his other console readings, then nudged the big control stick forward to nose the B-1 over in a deep dive toward the ground. Back in the sub, Jones simultaneously pushed a button which activated the airplane's wing sweep lever all the way up until it locked, bringing the giant wings in toward the fuselage at their full retraction angle of sixty-five degrees.

"I have wing lock confirmation, here," Jones radioed Hunter.

"Ditto wing lock confirm here," Hunter answered, seeing the appropriate light come to life on his console.

Gently, the Wingman eased the B-1's stick up and the bomber gracefully leveled off as it flashed over the coastline just under the speed of sound. Once again coordinating via the TV with Wa, Hunter set the plane's terrain-following radar guidance system to full automatic, and locked the altitude setting at a scant two hundred feet above the ground. Once the B-1's flight control computers were thus set, the complex navigation program would automatically raise and lower the big bomber's flight path to maintain that two-hundred-foot altitude.

"Anything on the scope, J.T.?" Hunter asked Toomey.

"Nothing . . . yet," Toomey's voice was steady as his eyes remained glued to the small CRT screen.

It displayed straight horizontal lines, indicating various radar frequencies that might be used by the Soviets' ground controllers to probe the skies for intruders. As of that moment, no threat was indicated.

"Intersecting MAPS plotted course in ten seconds," Jones said crisply, punching buttons on his console to overlay the earlier MAPS coordinates on the B-1's real-time CRT projection.

Slowly, the white icon that represented the bomber was tracing a path toward the gray bar that showed the plotted course almost due south. In less than three blinks of the screen, the outline image of the plane joined up with the chosen path and remained locked on it.

"MAPS course locked on, altitude two hundred feet, airspeed six hundred knots, fuel load one-hundred-fifty-thousand pounds," Jones announced. Hunter could see that the general had lit a cigar and was puffing away furiously.

"Roger that, base," Hunter responded. "Could I have a status check on the rest of the systems?"

"Offensive systems A-OK," Wa responded immediately. "Terrain avoidance locked on, bomb load unarmed and intact, forward weapons bay secure."

"Defense systems, check," Toomey said tersely. "No threat indicated, air-to-airs on standby, after weapons bay secure."

"OK, gents, this is the real thing," Hunter began.

Hunter started to reach for the four throttle levers to the left of his seat, but he paused for a moment. Instead, he reached up to his left breast pocket beneath his flight suit and felt for the American flag that he always kept there. It had brought him good luck so many times before—he hoped its charm would continue.

Then his eyes darted to the MAPS display projected on the small CRT in front of him on the B-1's cockpit console, seeking out the thin red 'X' that marked the Soviet radar complex.

Tapping the flag three times gently, Hunter punched the throttles to full military, and the big green bomber suddenly lurched ahead through the cold sky, speeding ever closer to his destination.

Chapter 44

Time passed

The dark green shape of the B-1 shot through the deep twilight over Soviet Central Asia, pushing its huge shadow along the flat, barren ground only two hundred feet below.

In less than two hours, Hunter had traversed some twelve hundred miles straight through the heart of Russian airspace without being detected. The feat, though on the face of it fairly incredible, was actually the result of the close video teamwork between himself and the three officers back in the mission control center of the USS *Ohio*.

To help him fly safely at that altitude, Wa had been typically alert, calling out terrain features in his path that were detected by the guidance system. Once warned, Hunter was able on most occasions to manually compensate for the plane's automatic tendency to pitch up several hundred feet to avoid ground obstacles. And by keeping the big bomber as low as possible, they had already avoided a few Soviet ground-based SAM sites and even a couple of transport planes lumbering across the desolate skies.

Toomey had been silent, except to relay information from his screen about the potential threats. Whenever possible, Hunter had simply diverted the plane's flight path around the missile sites' effective radar range, not wanting to give away the bomber's presence by forcing Toomey to remotely switch on the high-powered jammers of the defensive system. That would be risky. Because although the powerful electronic "noise" would surely drown out the Soviets' radars, it would also be sure to tip them off that there was something out there.

Better to rely on stealth and speed, Hunter reasoned, until absolutely necessary.

Suddenly, Jones hollered out an alarm.

"Jesus Christ, Hawk! *Look out!"*

Hunter, busy rechecking the MAPS coordinates on his CRT screen, looked up just in time to see a giant spiderweb looming in front of the big bomber. Gray steel and black wire rose like a huge fence that threatened to trap the B-1 like a trawling net.

Even before Hunter could react, he felt the B-1's nose pitch violently upward, accelerating to respond to an instantaneous command from the bomber's navigational system. The sensitive probes of the bomber's phased-array antenna had detected the thin skeleton of a high-tension power line support tower built after the war and therefore not included in the MAPS data. Immediately the onboard terrain guidance system put the B-1 into a drastic climb to get over the maze of wires.

But while the airplane's avoidance gear had done its job and saved the airplane, it was not without cost.

First of all, the rear portion of the B-1's left side tailplane stabilizer slashed through one of the electrical wires, tearing a large gash in the small wing's skin, and carrying away several important static dischargers located there. Suddenly the rear end of the airplane was rippling with hundreds of small electrical shocks, caused by the loss of the discharge units. But even more serious, in climbing to almost a thousand feet in the rapid ascent, the huge shape of the bomber was now visible to the Soviet radar crews on the ground.

"They see us!" Toomey yelled sharply over the intermittent screech of the radar threat warning. "It's a search radar—narrow-beam scan. . . . Take her back down, Hawk, before they lock on us!"

They had appeared on the radar screen at a nearby auxiliary SAM station only for an instant. But before Hunter was able to wrestle the big plane back down to two hundred feet, the B-1's radar warning signal began to howl both in the sub's command center and in the airplane cockpit. At the same time, Toomey saw two thin pencil beams on his screen begin to tighten around a single point along the line.

"They've locked on to us!" he snapped, as he turned the dials of his defensive countermeasures system to transmit a strong remote-control barrage of electronic energy over a corresponding band to thwart the Russians' radar. "Commencing jamming now . . ."

Even as Hunter rolled the big plane over to dive for the ground, Toomey could see the electronically imprinted flash on his screen. He knew it was the resulting fire on the horizon as a huge Soviet anti-aircraft missile blazed off its launch rails to streak after the suddenly exposed bomber.

"Missile launch! SA-2!" Toomey said tightly, frantically twisting his dials to jam the ground controllers' uplink signals. "Take evasive action!"

Hunter was already reacting. He didn't need to be told twice that the deadly "telephone pole" SAM was headed straight for the B-1.

"You can't outrun it, Hawk, so aim *right for it,*" Jones said, looking up at Hunter through the TV screen. Hunter immediately hauled the control stick sharply over and turned toward the glowing rocket.

"Aim right for the Goddamn thing, Hawk . . ." Jones repeated, a little more anxious now.

Hunter continued the maneuver, forcing the shuddering plane into a sixty-degree bank. Suddenly the glowing missile shot directly under his right wing. Due to Toomey's jamming, the missile's guidance system was left with nothing to aim for. But unluckily, the SAM's on-board self-destruct system picked that moment to detonate.

The near-miss explosion nearly tipped the B-1 completely over—it was only Hunter's quick action and extraordinary skill as a pilot that kept the bomber from plowing into the tundra.

The four TV screens began to blink incessantly as Hunter fought to control the airplane. Finally, he leveled it out and the TV screens refocused.

"Hawk, *you still there?*" JT yelled.

"I am," Hunter answered, looking over his left shoulder. "But I'm not so sure about the left wing . . ."

His control board computer TV screen was blinking crazily, telling him that he had sustained damage to the port wing's leading edge slat guide rails and the slat drive shaft, both critical steering mechanisms for the big airplane.

"What's your condition, Hawk?" Jones asked soberly.

"The port wing's frontside is ripped up," he reported. "It also looks like the tip fairing is gone."

"I'm not getting any fire indications," Wa reported. "Slight leak through the fuel vent tank. Could get worse . . ."

"Whatever the damage, you've got to get the hell out of there before they lock in on you again," Jones told him.

"I hear you, General," Hunter said.

With that he immediately punched all four throttles down to the afterburner stops and the B-1 leapt forward as if propelled by a cannon blast. The sudden burst of speed drove him deep into his seat as the view outside the cockpit became an unrecognizable blur.

It was only after Toomey gave the "all clear" signal that Hunter began to decelerate to full military power, shutting down the fuel-greedy afterburners.

"Looks like it's still holding together," Hunter said, quickly scanning his control board and glancing back at the injured wing. "We were lucky."

The general waved away the statement with a static-filled swirl of cigar smoke.

"You still got a long way to go," he said. "And now they know you're there."

"Anything on the screen, JT?" Hunter asked.

"Nothing. They lost us after that little dash." Toomey's video image was tight as Hunter watched his friend continue to scan the video display.

The silence from the radar threat warning was a welcome relief after the high-decibel shrieking faded out.

"But now they know that you're not just some fog or atmospheric interference," Jones said soberly. "And judging by the MAPS display, even if you jink and jag the rest of the way, the SAM sites get thicker from here on in. Not to mention fighters . . ."

"OK," Hunter said, "I think it's time to give these bulletheads something to chase."

With that he reached over to the wounded B-1's radio transmitter, flicked a series of switches and watched as a yellow light glowed for several seconds, then blinked off.

"Now let's just hope they take the bait," he said grimly.

Chapter 45

Fifty-two thousand feet over the frigid waters west of the Bering Sea, a lone B-52H Stratofortress sliced through the blackness of the night skies, leaving eight ghostly contrails behind its tapered wings.

The navigator had just relayed a position check to the pilot, and the bomb coordinator had rechecked his console to confirm the bomber's readiness.

Minutes before a yellow light on the pilot's cockpit display flashed six times, illuminating the dim interior of the bomber with its amber glow. Now a sharp wail burst from the radio receiver.

"That's it," the pilot said to the co-pilot. "Priority signal received and confirmed . . ."

The pilot reached over and toggled a series of switches, shutting off the light and the alarm.

"Pilot to crew," the bomber's commander then called over the airplane's intercom. "We have just received the incoming priority signal confirmation. Everyone knows the drill. We can assume that Soviet interceptors have already been scrambled, so we'll dive for the deck as soon as our birds are away. Hang tight — it will be rough riding for a while, especially when we start to pull out. But I promise you a smooth ride home."

With that, the Stratofortress's bomb coordinator flicked open the safety covers of the bomber's weapons control switches and deliberately clicked down the two toggles on the left-hand side. Instantly, red "Armed" lights came on above them. A similar action brought the massive bomb bay doors swinging down to their full open position.

A confirming light appeared on the pilot's cockpit display.

"I have arming lock confirmation," he called into his microphone. "Ditto bomb bay open confirmation."

"Roger," came the message back from the bomb coordinator. "My confirms also 'green,' sir."

"OK," the pilot said, checking his position one last time against the mission checklist. "Drop 'em . . ."

Instantly the bomb coordinator flipped another series of buttons, activating the very special load of weapons that had been stowed in the B-52's massive bomb bay.

"Payload away!" he called into his microphone, mashing his "pickle" button twice.

At that moment, two heavy cylinders tumbled off the big jet's bomb racks, dropping through the open bay doors into the freezing slipstream of the big bomber's flight patterns.

Almost immediately, both cylinders sprouted short, stubby wings as each drone's tiny turbofan motor coughed to life and propelled it rapidly ahead of the bomber. Soon, the two vehicles established parallel flight paths some five hundred feet apart.

Each missile, technically termed a "self-propelled decoy unit," was specially designed to mimic the radar and infrared signature of the huge B-52 that had given birth to it in mid-flight. Along the barrel-shaped fuselage and stubby wings of the decoy, dozens of radar-reflective pods bounced the searching beams of the Soviet radars back with great intensity—great enough to make each little drone appear to be a full-size bomber headed for the Soviet mainland . . .

Even as the high-tech decoys began their one-way journey, the bomber that had launched them was engaged in a death-defying maneuver to escape and reverse direction.

Against the protesting shrieks of fifty-year-old metal in the sagging wings, the pilot had plunged the Stratofortress in a hard, diving turn that exceeded the plane's maximum safe angle of forty-five degrees. The shuddering monster groaned as eight powerful engines combined with sheer gravity to force her downward toward the frigid blackness of the sea below at a terrifying rate of more than five hundred miles per hour.

Lights were flashing intermittently, and multiple stall warnings sounded as the big bomber continued what would seem to be her death plunge to the sea. But as they entered the relative warmth of the lower altitudes, the thicker air began to flatten out the steep dive.

Gradually, responding to the pilot's firm pressure on the yoke and the increased lift, the huge Stratofortress leveled out at a mere three hundred feet above the wavetops.

Like a gray ghost ship, the B-52 whispered along through the freezing spray, rapidly increasing the distance between herself and the drones she had just launched. The dull moonlight was reflected in the off-white surface of the wings, each of which carried the telltale identification letters UAAC on its topside.

A hundred miles to the east, another B-52 had completed a similar missile launch and diving escape. And a hundred miles to the west, the same.

All in all, ten of the hulking bombers had launched a total of twenty self-propelled decoy units. Now, all of them broke away and headed back to their bases in Alaska.

Chapter 46

"It was right here, Captain," Sergeant Vasilov exclaimed, pointing to his screen. "Now it appears to have vanished."

For the second time in two hours what looked like a solid radar contact had appeared momentarily in the pulsing sweep of the radar's scanning bar which covered an area some two hundred and fifty kilometers to the west of Krasnoyarsk.

Captain Mursk had dismissed the first reported contact as typical interference, or even the product of Vasilov's nerves.

But he was now becoming very uneasy about the second event.

After calling out to all his operators to be extra alert, Mursk walked away from the bank of radar consoles to an isolated corner of the vast Defensive Systems room. He needed time to consider his next course of action.

His instincts were telling him that something unusual was passing through their airspace and possibly heading for the massive Krasnoyarsk complex itself. In the old days, before the emergence of the forward-thinking Red Star, he would have definitely sat on the information, not daring to alert his superiors unless something solid happened.

But things had changed. No longer would a Soviet officer be punished for tripping the defense alert system only to later find out it was an honest mistake.

Deciding his course of action, Mursk reached for a special red phone on the central control console and punched in a special code. Within seconds he expected to be talking to the commander of the nearest Red Star air base.

But even before his connection went through, the control room's radio crackled. Piped through the PA system, it was an excited report from an officer at an isolated air defense battery. A missile had been launched at a possible radar contact—unsuccessfully as the missile had been interfered with by airborne jamming. Mursk quickly checked the control room's main screen and saw the report had come from an area that corresponded to the place on Vasilov's radar screen where the phantom contact had been spotted minutes earlier.

Mursk felt his mouth go dry. He knew the radar contacts and the SAM launching could mean only one thing—an enemy aircraft was heading for Krasnoyarsk.

Quickly, Mursk redialed the commander of the large air base located several hundred miles east of the massive radar station. Within thirty seconds he was talking to the man.

"This is Krasnoyarsk reporting," Mursk began formally. "We have radar contact at—"

"Yes, yes! Of course," the air wing commander told him brusquely. "We already know of the radar contacts. . . . They have been on our screens for several minutes now."

"But the interceptors must be . . ." Mursk continued before he was abruptly cut off again by the commander.

"We have already launched the interceptors, Krasnoyarsk!" the shrill voice rang through the earpiece's receiver. "They are now being vectored to meet the American bombers over the ocean!"

Mursk was shocked. "The ocean? But my contact was . . ."

"Krasnoyarsk," the commander replied. "Our radar contacts show twenty American bombers less than five hundred miles from the Kamchatka peninsula. They are flying in groups of two along the high-altitude tracks of the old SAC alert routes we used to see before the war.

"All available fighters have been ordered to intercept."

And with that, the air base commander hung up.

Chapter 47

"Are you sure you had a positive contact, Mursk?"

Air Marshal Porogarkov was pacing the gray floor of the Krasnoyarsk radar station. Next to him, Captain Mursk was reviewing a replay of the two radar contact indications picked up by his sergeant's radar console.

"We had two events, sir," Mursk told the air marshal, pointing to the radar replay review screen. "One there. The other . . . right there . . ."

Mursk replayed the tape for the air marshal. "Both were only on-screen for a second, sir," Mursk said. "At extremely low altitudes. But I felt we couldn't take the chance . . ."

Porogarkov watched the replay a final time and slowly nodded his head.

"Good work, Mursk," he said. "You were correct in calling for the fighters. But apparently there *is* a larger threat coming in from the east as picked up by Irkutsk."

They both stared at the radar screen for a long moment, then Porogarkov said: "I must call Moscow right now and tell them of this."

With that, the senior officer gave Mursk two hard, complimentary slaps on the back, then he rushed to his office and the special phone line to Moscow.

"How things *have* changed," Mursk thought.

The air defense minister was back just a minute later.

"Moscow has ordered the commander in Irkutsk to deal with the threat over the Bering Sea," he said, his voice a mixture of concern and agitation. "However, there is a reserve squadron of fighters still on the ground. Only a few airplanes — a MiG-31, two MiG-25s, and the rest are old MiG-21s from our reserves — with trainee pilots. They'll be released to us once the situation in the east is evaluated."

"But what if it's too late, sir?" Mursk asked.

Porogarkov turned and stared at the younger officer. He had no answer — so he simply shrugged.

Suddenly, for both of them, it felt just like the *bad, old* days . . .

High above the Bering Sea in the cockpit of his MiG-29, Soviet Colonel Artyem Ivanovich Mikoyan was locking a pair of targets into his modern fighter's tracking computer.

He knew the others in his flight were doing the same. They were more than two hundred miles off the Pacific coast of the Soviet Union, two squadrons of Soviet fighters in all, tracking a series of solid radar contacts at high altitude.

The blips on their screens represented the invading American bombers, undoubtedly the decrepit B-52 dinosaurs, hoping to bomb the valuable combat control center at Krasnoyarsk. No matter, Mikoyan thought to himself, they will soon be deep beneath the sea.

His interceptor was one of the few Soviet Fulcrums to survive World War Three, or "The Second Great Patriotic War," as some in Red Star had begun to refer to it. The twin-tailed fighter packed a full load of heat-seeking and radar-guided missiles under its wings, and he had orders to attack and destroy the invading Americans "at all costs."

As he closed to within range, he launched one of his radar-guided AA-7 missiles toward the two targets that appeared on his pulse Doppler radar's display. A second later, his wingman had launched a similar missile. Intent on personally observing the kill, he increased his speed another notch to follow the streaking missiles.

He kept watching the tiny display, expecting to see the huge bombers begin their pathetic attempts to evade the deadly missiles, but instead he saw only the monotonous track of the hulking American planes, steadily boring into Soviet air space, oblivious to the airborne darts that sped toward them.

Could it be, Mikoyan thought, that he had caught the Americans napping?

His thought was confirmed as he observed both his own missile, as well as his wingman's, draw closer to the plodding radar blip that appeared on his display.

Another second, and there would be a direct hit.

The nearest target blip suddenly brightened significantly, as if a burst of energy had infused it. The surge attracted both his and his wingman's missile to it, and the target disappeared in a spreading blossom on his display. A cry of jubilation echoed through his headset as his wingman cheered the kill.

But Mikoyan sensed something was wrong.

What had caused that sudden energy boost in the first bomber? And why was the remaining American still tracking the same course as though nothing had happened? Ignored by the missiles, it had just continued along without diverting, and without changing course or speed.

Quickly cutting off his partner's celebration, he ordered the other pilot to break off and intercept the American plane along with him. When he punched down his throttles, the huge engines responded instantly, catapulting the sleek Fulcrum ahead at better than Mach 2.

Mikoyan was determined to get within visual range of these insane Yankees. He could always make the second kill with infrared-seeking AA-6 missile if need be.

But he had to find out what madness drove this suicidal American.

Mikoyan's suspicions deepened as he closed the range. At forty miles and coming up rapidly on the slow-moving B-52, he still detected no jamming signals, no evasion, and no threat warnings. Only the steadily increasing hum and buzz of crackling static in his radio headphones. As a precaution, he keyed in the target data and began preparing his heat-seeking air-to-air missiles for launch against the curious target.

As he closed the range further, Mikoyan was dismayed to find that he couldn't make out the silhouette of the huge bomber, even though by now the full moon shone brightly off the ice-flecked surface of the Bering Sea below. His radar scope certainly detected it, as the tiny display mushroomed with a huge target blip.

His missile guidance system bleeped out a shrill alert, indicating that his missile target guidance system had acquired a positive target. Still, wanting to get closer, Mikoyan waited until the last possible second to launch the deadly heat-seeker. Although his display indicated a target of immense proportions, he could not see anything in the frigid skies over the gray ocean.

Mikoyan reluctantly punched the missile "fire" button, confident that his air-to-air could find the target even if he couldn't. The tapered missile shot off his left wing toward the target that he still couldn't see, and it quickly found a strong infrared signal that beckoned it along faster.

Unfortunately for the Soviet pilot and his wingman, the missile found its mark all too well. As it detected the presence of the IR seeking signals from the AA-6 missile, the tiny American drone suddenly erupted in white-hot flames. Phosphorous flares spewed out their blinding light and fiery jets flamed out from the ports on the drone's wings.

The missile immediately locked on to the drone's heat, and it quickly impacted the little decoy, disappearing inside the flaming ball in the sky.

For a split second, Mikoyan finally saw the target of his missile attack, as the glowing meteor erupted across the black sky. What he would never know was that the tiny drone had actually exploded, its huge warhead of TNT sending metal shards out for hundreds of yards in all directions.

There was no escaping the shower of brilliant sparks that arced in all around his plane. Both Mikoyan and his wingman were flying directly through the deadly hailstorm of shrapnel, wings and canopies absorbing the flaming debris that pelted them furiously. And the gruesome sound of jagged metal chunks being sucked into the MiG's powerful jet engines filled the cramped cockpit of the Soviet fighter.

At least one of the fiery shards was expelled by the whirling turbine blades into Mikoyan's primary fuel line that fed his airplane's left engine its volatile mixture. A single spark ignited a steady stream of burning fuel, which in turn was inhaled by the rattling jet engine, and literally blow-torched out the exhaust nozzle of the stricken Fulcrum.

There was no time for Mikoyan to cut the fuel supply, no time to radio his wingman for help, no time even to pull the ejection handles in the front of his seat.

He had only time enough to realize that he was already a dead man . . .

Ten thousand liters of explosive jet fuel was instantly touched off, transforming his fighter into a white-hot fireball that turned the blackness of the Pacific night into a ghastly backdrop for the Fulcrum's mini-nova eruption. The brilliant fire glowed for several terrible seconds, hanging in the cold sky, before plunging to the ocean like a spent meteorite. Mikoyan's cremation was complete before the wreckage struck the ocean.

A total of twenty Soviet fighters were lost attacking the drones that night over the Bering Sea.

Chapter 48

It was only after the third radar event was picked up west of Krasnoyarsk that Air Marshal Porogarkov called the nearby air base commander and threatened to shoot him if he didn't release the reserve fighter squadron.

Despite the man's pleas for reconsideration, based on now solid evidence that some kind of an American attack force was approaching from the Bering Sea, Porogarkov refused to change his order. The base commander would face a firing squad if the reserve jets weren't scrambled immediately.

Ten minutes later, a flight of six Soviet fighters lifted off a dimly lit runway and sped toward a point in the sky a hundred miles west of Krasnoyarsk.

"Picking up multiple bogies at high altitude." Toomey's voice was steady as he called out the alert to Hunter in the B-1's cockpit. "They've got search radars on wide scan . . . they haven't found us. Yet."

"Damn!" Jones exclaimed from his TV screen. "Maybe they didn't take the bait over the Bering after all!"

"We've come this far without them finding us," Wa said hopefully. "Maybe it's just a routine patrol . . ."

"Don't bet on it," Hunter responded grimly, his unique inner senses detecting the enemy airplanes just seconds before JT's radar. "These guys never just fly around for fun. If there are any interceptors up here, they're definitely looking for us."

Two tense minutes passed. The B-1 was now only eighty-five miles away from the target.

"Any positive ID on the bogies, JT?" Hunter asked.

"Looks like three Foxbats — no, wait — one's got a different signature. . . . It's a Foxhound!" Toomey replied tightly, remembering his air duels with the tough Soviet MiG-25s and -31s during the war. Both were super-fast Mach 3 fighters that carried lots of firepower — usually big AA-6 air-to-air missiles. And both had a fairly sophisticated look-down/shoot-down radar to search out and destroy their prey.

"What about the others?" Hunter asked, instinctively nudging the big, battered B-1 a few feet lower, in a effort to closer hug the hard ground below.

"Can't tell for sure, Hawk," Toomey said after checking his scope. "Single-engine jobs, well behind the first group, about Mach 1.5 speed. . . . Maybe MiG-21s."

Hunter was scanning the MAPS plot on his small CRT screen, reviewing the remaining course to the target to see if there were any alternate routes in case they had to engage in evasive maneuvers.

No sooner had the B-1's sleek nose section risen slightly to clear some terrain feature below, when the cockpit radio crackled again.

"Narrow-beam scan! Tracking radar signals!" Toomey's alert confirmed Hunter's apprehension. "One of the bastards found us! Should I commence jamming on guidance frequency?"

"No, wait!" Jones called out at this point. "If we light up the jammer, the others will pinpoint our location. Save it until we get a positive missile detect signal. But start jamming the hell out of the VHF signals — we don't want them reporting our position to each other or back to their base."

"Roger . . ." Toomey went to work on the countermeasure scope, sending out powerful jamming signals on the VHF transmission bands he'd monitored the Soviet pilots using. With their radios spewing forth an ear-splitting blast of crackling static, the Soviet pilots knew the American was out there somewhere, but they couldn't locate him.

The B-1 screamed along below a thirty-mile ridgeline, hidden from the clawing fingers of electronic energy emanating out of the Soviet planes desperate to find them. Hunter checked the MAPS display and saw he was now just fifty-five miles from the target.

Suddenly the protective ridgeline curved to the left, directly in front of the racing bomber's path. Even before Wa's shouted instruction reached his ears, Hunter had disengaged the autopilot to haul the big bomber's stick back to raise them up over the ridge.

Hunter knew that if he had let the terrain avoidance gear take its normal course, it would raise them up several hundred feet above the ground — easy bait for the speedy Soviet interceptors. Instead he had no other choice but to attempt to clear the ridge at a lower altitude, perhaps avoiding detection a little longer. Keeping one eye on the terrain display on his second CRT, and the other on the altimeter reading, he twisted the B-1 to one side and powered it over the ridge at a steep angle.

The howling blast from the bomber's four engines shook the ground just fifty feet below. Once the bomber was clear of the ridgetop, Hunter pushed the stick forward again to force the big plane down to the protective terrain below.

But there was no time to congratulate himself for the maneuver's success, as Toomey clipped out another warning.

"Missile alert!" JT yelled so loudly his TV image actually became scrambled for a moment. "They must've tagged us just as we crossed the ridgeline. Signal indicates tracking radar now."

Hunter had only seconds to react before the low wailing of the threat warning blared out an octave higher, filling the narrow cabin with its shrillness.

"Missile lock signals now . . . He's launched one!" Toomey hollered above the sound of the threat warning, as he hurriedly attempted to jam the missile's guidance signals.

"Must be the damn Foxhound," said Jones. "He closed that distance in a couple of seconds."

"The Foxbats won't be far behind, either," Hunter reminded them. "Can you jam the missile, JT?"

"Negative jam, repeat, negative jam." Toomey's voice was slightly rushed now. "Break left and climb, Hawk! It's a heat-seeker — Ben, blow off some flares!"

Wa punched a button on his console that immediately ejected two high-intensity decoy flares, one from each side of the aircraft. The white-hot phosphorous mini-rockets resembled brilliant fireworks shells that arced swiftly out a hundred yards and burned with a blue-white fire. In slow motion freefall, the small flares presented a hot target larger than the bomber itself.

Even before Hunter heard Toomey call for the break and climb, he had planned the evasive maneuver he intended to take. Hauling the big bomber's stick up and to the right, he forced the B-1 to climb on a hard bank, snapping the big plane around like it was tethered on a line. The banking turn continued until he was near one thousand feet.

He took several deep gulps of oxygen and tapped the flag in his pocket.

"C'mon, baby," he whispered. "Don't give out on me now . . ."

The Soviet missile had been fired at maximum range, and the first target it encountered was the brilliantly burning decoy flare Wa had launched off the bomber's left side.

Like a mute airborne attack dog, the big AA-6 missile lunged for the flare, which was now descending in a slow spiral toward the ground. The air-to-air detonated on contact with the heat source, exploding in a yellow-white fireball.

By the time he saw the missile's flame, Hunter had already leveled out of the punishing turn he'd forced on the ailing B-1, and now he rammed the stick forward to dive back down *under* the attacking fighters. The bomber screamed back down in a steep dive, passing below the sharp ridgeline they had risen above earlier. Hunter cranked out the bomber's wings to provide more lift at the lower altitude, but he didn't level off again until the altimeter warning sounded, indicating that he was back below two hundred feet.

By doubling back on himself, Hunter was trying to use the Soviets' greater speed to their disadvantage. The tactic worked, as evidenced by the deafening thunder that enveloped the B-1 as the three front-line Soviet interceptors roared past overhead.

"Okay, JT, let's give those bastards a kick in the ass," Hunter growled as he prepared for the next maneuver.

He tightened his grip on the stick and flashed a glance at the CRT display showing the Soviet fighters' positions. "Say when ready, JT."

Toomey had previously configured his radar screen to accommodate the B-1's defensive air-to-air launches, and he quickly prepared

321

the deadly rockets, still nestled snug in their rotary launcher suspended inside the aft weapons bay. The red "Ready" lights confirmed the procedure.

"Missiles ready. Commence attack maneuver . . . now!" Toomey shouted.

Hunter did so and was instantly thrown back into his seat by the airplane's violent motion.

He had pitched the bomber up sharply in a rapid climb, cranking the wings in toward the fuselage as the B-1 shot through the thin air to rise above the racing Soviet fighters. The steep climb leveled out at five thousand feet, where Hunter called back to Toomey to fire when ready.

Toomey had already found the trio of Soviet fighters on his scope, and the tracking signals of the B-1's powerful search radar illuminated their positions for the missile guidance system. When three small cursors appeared beside the white "enemy aircraft" icons on the scope, he mashed the fire control "pickle" three times.

"Missiles away!" JT said loudly.

At the same instant Hunter could hear the rotary launcher smoothly pump three of the lethal torpedoes out of the open weapons bay. The big AMRAAMs fell into the bomber's slipstream and quickly armed themselves. When the complex guidance circuitry came alive in the missiles' warheads, they ignited their small rocket motors and shot away from the B-1 toward the fleeing Soviet interceptors.

The two outboard AMRAAMs worked as advertised. Each selected a separate target, fed in by the attack computer seconds before launch from the B-1's weapons bay. Each missile's solid fuel propellant drove it toward the selected target at better than Mach 3.

And each missile came within twenty yards of a Soviet MiG-25 Foxbat before erupting in a blinding flash of high explosives and jagged metal, engulfing each Soviet plane in a destructive fireball.

But the center missile was a half-second late in reaching its target—the MiG-31 Foxhound leading the squadron. When the squadron leader heard his own missile warning alarm go off, he punched the powerful engines to full afterburner, shooting the interceptor forward like a bullet from a gun.

Major Mikh Iosifovich Guryevich saw his wingmen perish in the unholy flames of the AMRAAMs' explosions, and he felt the buffeting of massive turbulence behind him. The missile intended for his plane had been detonated by the other two explosions, and only his incredible speed had saved Guryevich from the fate of his comrades.

Anger burned within the Soviet pilot as he saw the flaming wreckage of two planes cartwheel crazily to the ground. He didn't know how the Americans had done it — launching missiles from one of their B-1s — but Guryevich was determined to exact revenge for the death of his pilots.

He quickly snap-rolled the speedy Foxhound around to give chase to the wily American.

"Two away!" Wa called out jubilantly, watching the icons disappear from Toomey's scope. "One to go."

"Yeah, but that's the deadly one," Toomey responded grimly. "Hawk, we missed the Foxhound, and he's coming around. Range twenty miles."

Hunter wasted no time in reacting. He punched the B-1's throttles down past the stops to full afterburner, and the big bomber streaked through the sky directly toward the oncoming Soviet fighter.

Guryevich checked his radar scope and couldn't believe his eyes. The insane Yankee was coming straight at him. . . . In the blink of an eye, the range between the two planes closed at a combined speed almost four times the speed of sound.

There was no time for the Soviet pilot to check his radar again before the menacing green shape of the B-1 filled his cockpit canopy. There was no time to launch a missile or even squeeze the trigger to spray the big bomber with his internal gun. The only thing his brain commanded him to do was to break away — to escape the mad rush of this crazy American.

Guryevich swung the MiG's stick sharply down and to the left to dive out of the path of the huge green bomber, dropping his plane down as the B-1 thundered overhead, smashing his smaller plane with the jetwash from its four powerful turbofans.

By the time he regained control of his fighter, the B-1 had disappeared over a ridgeline to the east.

"Damn this lunatic . . ." Guryevich thought. "Doesn't he know I will certainly catch him?"

The puzzled Soviet pilot rammed his throttle down again to pursue the spot on the horizon where the American bomber had vanished.

"Guess he's never played Chicken Kiev, General," Hunter said grimly, turning toward the bank of TVs facing him. "Ready on my signal, JT?"

"Ready status confirmed," Toomey answered, quickly preparing another AMRAAM for launch, already sensing what Hunter had planned.

"Okay," Hunter said evenly, "just keep your finger on the launch button, and let me know when that bandit comes close enough to nail."

"Fifteen miles . . . Picking up tracking signals . . ." Toomey began, his voice trailing past each sentence as his sunglassed eyes remained locked on the defensive systems scope. "Pump some chaff out, Ben."

Wa obliged by pressing the "Chaff Release" button sharply, knowing it would send two half-pound bundles of the tinsel-like metal shavings into the air beyond the bomber. The dense clouds of chaff would appear as huge blips on the Soviet fighter's radar screen. It would distract the pilot, perhaps only for a fraction of a second.

But it was all the time Hunter would need.

"Ten miles . . . We've got a missile alert!" Toomey called out as a threat warning started its rising-pitch song, which was rapidly reaching a crescendo as the Soviet prepared to launch a deadly AA-9 missile at the fleeing B-1.

"Five miles . . ." JT said, his screen once again going briefly to static. "He's going to launch in a second . . . Missile lock now! *He's firing . . .*"

Hunter had simultaneously yanked all four throttles all the way back past their full afterburner position to a near stall, at the same time pushing the wing sweep lever down hard, cranking the big wings out to their full fifteen-degree swept out position. A split second later, Hunter had dropped full flaps and lowered the landing gear and weapon bay doors.

The result was a dramatic decrease in airspeed, as if the plane had simply screeched to a halt in midair. The "enemy aircraft" blip on Toomey's screen disappeared momentarily as it streaked through the center of the sweep arm, indicating it had passed the B-1 overhead.

The Russian pilot was at first annoyed by the huge chaff clouds that spread across his radar screen, momentarily interfering with his weapons lock on the tail of the American bomber. He wasted several precious seconds waiting to zoom clear of the metallic mess before re-targeting his missile.

His annoyance quickly turned to dismay as the large silhouette of the green bomber suddenly filled his whole canopy, as if the B-1 had been instantly increased to giant proportions. The distance between the two planes had been slashed to nothing as the Mach 3 speed of the MiG had brought it to a near collision with the tail of the stalling bomber.

Guryevich's finger was still pressing the missile's release button when he shot like a rifle bullet over the top of the fluttering plane that appeared to hover in midair. The missile leaped off his wing just as the B-1's green blur disappeared beneath the streaking Soviet Foxhound. Unable to acquire a target that was now behind it, the missile whizzed off toward the horizon and exploded harmlessly.

The Soviet officer knew he had been tricked again. But this time there would be no chance to even the score with the bold Yankee air pirate. Even the crude Soviet radar threat warning couldn't fail to pick up a ten-foot air-to-air missile being launched from the B-1 at point-blank range less than a hundred yards behind his speeding fighter.

Even before he could turn to look back, the huge AMRAAM impacted the rear of his canopy. In a heartbeat, the Soviet airplane and its pilot were obliterated.

Large and small pieces of the shattered Foxhound went cartwheeling across the sky, some drifting back to earth, some falling directly into the path of the slow-moving American bomber.

"Got him!" Wa cried out as he saw the explosion blossom across his TV screen.

A second later they all heard the staccato rattling of metal shards striking the topside of the B-1's fuselage as the big bomber flew right through the cloud of debris that had only a second before been a Soviet fighter.

Hunter had to rapidly accelerate the big bomber to prevent a stall, punching all four throttles up to full military before he reclosed the landing gear and weapons bay doors. Despite the lightning-quick maneuver, the bomber still collided with a large piece of what had been one of the enemy fighter's engines.

Hunter felt a shudder run through the entire airplane, complete with a creaking groan.

"We ran right into the wreckage," Hunter reported over his suddenly static-filled radio. "It sounds like half his Goddamn airplane bounced right on top of me."

Instantly all three of the remote-control crew members started scanning their consoles for damage evaluation.

"I *do not* have FOD to the engines," Toomey said through a gasp of relief.

"Confirm Foreign Object Damage is negative," Hunter called back, rapidly scanning his instrument panel and pressure gauges to confirm normal engine operation, even as he raised the landing gear. "But I can hear a hole in the roof about halfway back, and it is definitely affecting the flight controls."

No one bothered to ask Hunter if he thought he would be able to still control the big airplane. They knew if anyone could keep the B-1 aloft, it was Hunter.

"And now we're out of bullets," the pilot added grimly. Greasing the four enemy airplanes had taken all of his enormous flight skills, and his body was shimmering with the solid feeling of success.

But he knew he had a lot of problems.

"Any sign of the other bandits, JT?" he asked, after a few deep gulps of oxygen.

"As of now, I've got negative radar contact, Hawk," Toomey responded after checking the TV scope in front of him.

Hunter checked the MAPS display. He was now thirty-two miles from the target.

Chapter 49

Captain Mursk read the computer screen message twice before he was able to absorb it all.

Once he had, however, he immediately transferred the message to the air marshal's screen, then sprinted over to his superior's desk.

"Is this an accurate report, Captain?" the air defense minister asked, slightly startled.

"It has to be," Mursk answered. "It's being confirmed throughout the network."

Porogarkov read the message one more time. In a nutshell it stated that an American bomber was just minutes away from entering the immediate airspace around Krasnoyarsk, after having destroyed four scrambled interceptors fifty miles from the radar station.

"Then it will be here in a matter of minutes . . ." the air marshal said, more to himself than to Mursk. Instantly he knew that whatever had happened out over the Bering Sea had been a ruse.

"Our SAM crews have been alerted, sir," Mursk said, his voice also a little shaky. "Plus there are still six reserve interceptors tracking the enemy airplane."

Porogarkov immediately started punching buttons on his console. An instant later, a klaxon began blaring inside the entire radar station. Large shutters automatically lowered in front of all windows and exposed doorways. A recorded announcement broadcast via a continuous loop track, ordered that all personnel should to go the station's deep underground bomb shelter immediately.

Mursk turned toward the exit, then stopped.

"You *are* coming, sir?" he asked Porogarkov. "The SAM crews will handle the intruder."

"No, Captain," the senior officer said. "You go . . . there are things here I have to do . . ."

"But, sir—"

Porogarkov waved away the younger man's protests. "Go, Captain . . ."

"But I will stay with you, sir."

Porogarkov's face turned crimson. "Captain, this is an order," he said: "Go to the shelter . . . immediately."

The air marshal turned back to his console and punched in a series of red buttons, all of which produced a glowing amber light on his screen. Mursk took one look at his superior's action and felt a chill run through him. The senior man was arming at least a half dozen SS-19 ICBMs that were located at a refurbished Red Star base near Leningrad.

Porogarkov pushed another series of buttons, and a low whine began to emanate from his console. Mursk knew this was the "in-system" signal for the weapons targeting satellites—at the speed of light, tracking and targeting information was being relayed between the high-orbiting satellites and the mini-computers within the SS-19s themselves.

"Sir, the fuel in those rockets . . ." Mursk began to say.

Porogarkov's pistol was out of his belt in a second.

"Captain, I will say this one last time," the marshal hissed at him. "Go to the shelter."

"But, sir," Mursk foolishly protested. "There's no way of knowing whether the fuel mixture in those rockets is adequate. Our technicians needed one more week to re-confirm the First Launch mixture . . ."

Porogarkov fired one shot—into the air. But with the blaring klaxon, the constantly repeating air raid warning and the general confusion inside the control room, the gunshot was hardly heard.

"The next one will be aimed at your heart, Captain," Porogarkov said.

Finally, Mursk turned to go. That's when he heard the air marshal mutter: "How do they do it? These *damn* Americans! How could they have flown a bomber halfway around the world and through our outermost radar defenses, without us seeing them?"

For the first time in a long time, Mursk had no ready answer.

"Starting bomb run checklist now . . ."

With that, Wa began rattling off a long list of procedures that eventually would transform the fat, lifeless cylinders in the B-1's forward weapons bay into the lethal bombs that could "fly" with deadly accuracy to the target now being programmed into his offensive systems computer.

All the while, Hunter's arms were straining just keeping the bomber steady. He had shut off the automatic terrain avoidance gear after being hit by the flying wreckage — its computers were not sophisticated enough to handle a B-1 with a cracked back, a chopped-up left wing, and a shredded tailplane, flying only one hundred feet above the ground.

Only a pilot — a *human* pilot — could do that.

"I read twenty plus one to target," Jones told Hunter over the now very-shaky TV monitors.

"Roger," Hunter said, in between checking off the bomb run procedures with Ben.

At that moment, Hunter felt a very familiar tingling in the back of his head. An instant later, JT's voice crackled from the cockpit speaker.

"I got two bandits!" he yelled. "About eleven miles behind you. Looks like a pair of MiG-21s. They are riding high at Mach 1.2."

Hunter shook his head and gritted his teeth. He didn't need this. The B-1 was in bad enough shape as it was. But within twenty seconds, it would be in the range of yet another barrage of enemy AA-2 Atoll air-to-air missiles.

In the cramped cockpit of the lead MiG-21, the young Soviet trainee was flying at top speed, hugging the rugged terrain as near as he dared to close the distance to the American bomber.

The B-1's dark shape loomed before him, silhouetted against the fiery glow from the bomber's four exhaust nozzles. Trying his best to remember his lessons, he locked in the targeting coordinates for his one and only Atoll missile, suspended from the fighter's fuselage.

At this range, he believed nothing could prevent the deadly explosive dart from penetrating the bomber's innards, drawn into the heat of the flaming exhausts.

The Soviet pilot pushed the missile release trigger on his control stick. The Atoll missile screamed out from under his airplane toward the B-1's tail at twice the speed of sound.

The B-1's automatic tail warning system was alert, scanning the skies behind the speeding bomber with an unblinking infrared eye, watching for a "hot spot" in the cold skies of Soviet Central Asia. When it detected the fiery plume of the Atoll, it triggered a pair of red "warning" lights on the consoles of both Hunter in the cockpit and Toomey back in the sub. Simultaneously, the system independently launched a pair of decoy flares and several chaff bundles in a last-ditch effort to draw the missile off its target.

Instantly Toomey was hollering for Hunter to begin evasive maneuvers.

"It's not falling for it," Toomey reported grimly as his instruments told him that the heat-seeking missile was ignoring the glittering chaff, deviating only slightly toward the super-hot light of the white phosphorous flares.

Hunter was already reacting to his own warning light. He took a quick look at the threat display on his CRT screen; he would have only one glimpse to tell him where the missile was coming from, and he would have to decide in the next two seconds how he was going to escape it. As if time were moving in slow motion, Hunter stared at the tiny screen, waiting for the refresh of its blinking scope trace.

There it was — as he had guessed, launched from low and to the left.

Hunter quickly yanked the bomber's control stick back all the way as he floored all four throttles to full afterburner. The big bomber protested with groans from the battered wings and roars from the engines as it attempted to respond to Hunter's commands that literally attempted to stand the huge plane up on its tail in midair, momentarily past the maximum safe angle of flight programmed into the bomber's flight envelope.

It was a maneuver Hunter had perfected in his F-16, and it served him well in the larger bomber. The B-1 reared up like a bucking bronco, its wings flexing dangerously at the high-g stress. Multiple stall warnings sounded in the cramped cockpit as the plane strove to remain in the air, struggling against the principles of aeronautics to meet Hunter's demands.

Just as the B-1's forward motion had almost stopped, the sixty-pound warhead of the streaking Atoll missile detonated, confused by the sudden shift in its selected infrared heat source—the B-1's right outboard engine. The powerful explosion rocked the upright bomber like a paper airplane, and although the deadly cloud of spreading shrapnel and debris was mostly directed away from the plane, several large flaming pieces impacted on the bomber's starboard wing. At the same time a ragged hailstorm of metal pellets, some of them searing white-hot, struck the exposed topside of the B-1's fuselage as it was buffeted by the explosion.

All at once, lights flicked off and on in the tilted cabin. Console displays and computer screens flickered out as power supplies failed in the complex systems. The explosion-rocked bomber shook like it was being electrocuted as it began to tumble, out of control, toward the hard earth below.

It was only by the quick combination of Hunter in the bucking cockpit and Jones at his remote-control console that prevented a massive flameout from stalling all four engines. Wrestling the uncooperative stick forward again, Hunter once again rapidly slammed the four-throttle handle down to full military to give the fluttering bomber some forward airspeed to restore control.

Jones pushed a button that cranked out the tapered wings to their full extension to prevent a fatal spin, and slowly the green heavily smoking bomber regained altitude and settled its nose into a more horizontal track.

Already Toomey and Wa were pushing buttons and twisting dials, trying to bring the wounded bomber's systems back on line. Wa particularly continued to struggle with both the MAPS display and the bombing computer, both of which had failed during the attack.

At last, Jones asked the critical question: "Can you still hold her, Hawk?"

"Affirmative," Hunter yelled into his radio, the noise inside the battered airplane being so loud he could barely hear the straining engines. "Where the hell are those two bandits right now?"

331

"They've circled out a mile or two after launching the missile," Toomey answered, adjusting his sunglasses. "My guess is they didn't want to pick up bits and pieces of your remains if that missile had gone where it was supposed to have gone."

"Can you jam him up?" Hunter asked, "Prevent him from popping us again?"

"Not unless the system comes back up on line," Toomey said in a flat tone, "It may not be for another four minutes."

"By that time, we'll be on target," Jones said grimly. "And there's not a Goddamn thing we can do about it."

As if to confirm Jones's pessimism, the menacing shapes of the two delta-winged MiG-21s flashed in front of the bomber's cockpit just a few hundred yards ahead, as if they were inspecting their prize. Hunter quickly noticed that neither airplane was carrying any more air-to-air missiles.

But it didn't really matter. He knew that while the B-1 still had close to full engine power, the speedy MiGs could easy keep pace with him, blasting him out of the sky with their pod-mounted GSh-23 twin-barrel gun, slung between the forward airbrakes.

"JT!" Hunter called out. "What's our defensive status?"

"Jamming system is gone. It's busted," Toomey responded, glancing at the blinking console lights.

"You're twelve miles from target," Jones told him, through his flickering TV screens.

"Ben!" Hunter called out sharply, his voice shaky from the incredibly rough ride. "What's our weapons delivery status?"

"Bad, Hawk," Ben replied firmly. "The bomb computer is completely greased. Ditto our back-up here. As of this moment, I can't even launch the bombs on Krashnoyarsk."

"Keep trying to reset, Ben," Hunter ordered, as he scanned the width of the horizon, searching for the MiGs.

As if on cue, a stream of tracers suddenly poured across the B-1's green nose—a deadly cascading rainbow arcing right in front of Hunter's face ripping up the first few feet of the bomber's nose.

"Jesus Christ!" he yelled. "They've got the range now. What's the distance to target?"

"You are at eight and a half," Jones told him quickly.

Hunter stared up through the B-1's cockpit and saw that the MiGs were flying directly above him, like cowboys riding herd on an unruly steer. He knew that another strafing pass was inevitable.

Suddenly, Hunter deliberately reached down on his center console and activated the B-1's landing gear doors, opening them to lower the bomber's wheels. Back on the sub, Jones, Wa, and Toomey immediately recognized what Hunter was doing: lowering one's wheels during an engagement was considered the universal signal of pilot surrender.

"Hawk, you can't be—" Wa said incredulously. "You're not going to—"

Suddenly, Wa's TV screen blinked out. He turned to Jones and Toomey and saw their screens too had instantly been flooded with static.

All three men desperately punched their back-up TV transmission buttons but to no avail. From that point on, all communication with the bomber was lost.

Chapter 50

Air Marshal Porogarkov checked his console screen for the last time.

The six amber lights on the control board had now turned a dullish orange. This told him that the warheads atop the SS-19 ICBMs were fully linked and locked on with the orbiting targeting satellites.

With one long, slow deep breath, he punched six more buttons. One by one the orange lights began to glow red.

That confirmed it—the six ICBMs, each carrying a small 1.5-kiloton nuclear warhead, were on the way to independently selected targets on the East Coast of America.

Porogarkov felt a chill, even though the control room was now very, very hot. He was past thinking about how many lives he had just condemned to death. He was past thinking about what this would do to the ultimate goals of Red Star. His own goal was that if the American bomber attack was successful, he wanted to be sure that Red Star massive retaliation was on the way before the intricate satellite-to-warhead system was destroyed.

His act done, Porogarkov quickly walked to the main hall of the now-deserted radar station.

Once there, he switched on a nearby security radio and quickly dialed in the frequency he knew was used by the fighter planes charged with protecting the region.

Within thirty seconds he had learned that the American bomber—the trainee pilots claimed it was a B-1—had been severely damaged and had lowered its landing gear and flaps in an apparent attempt at surrender.

Porogarkov's spirits suddenly were soaring. If the American bomber wanted to surrender, then perhaps Red Star would survive this incident after all!

He instantly began doing calculations in his head. He was very familiar with the little-used airstrip right next to the radar station — he had landed in his own airplane there many times. Its runway was extra long, due to the needs of the huge An-22 and IL-76 cargo jets that had flown in the majority of the materials used to upgrade the Krasnoyarsk station.

He knew the B-1 didn't need a very long runway to land. Could it be possible that not only would the valuable station be spared but this his forces would also *capture* an American bomber?

Manipulating the bank of switches near the station entrance, he was able to lift one of the protective shutters that covered the huge, six-inch-thick plate glass windows of the station's main building.

Now he had a perfect view of the airstrip.

A quick shudder ran through him as he heard the base's SAM group leader order his crews to lock on to the approaching American airplane.

"No!" he screamed involuntarily, quickly yanking the microphone from the radio set. The last thing he wanted now was for his missile crews to shoot down the surrendering bomber. The airplane would be much more valuable to Red Star intact — both technologically and propaganda-wise.

A quick call to the base defense commander and the SAM crews were quickly put on stand-by.

Another minute passed. Now Porogarkov could just barely make out the outline of the approaching American bomber, its smoking dark silhouette casting a ghostly image in the twilight sky, the two MiG-21s, their exhausts flaming, riding on either side.

He reached for the phone again. In a matter of seconds he was talking with one of the trainee pilots.

"Is he still intending to surrender?" he asked the young man.

"Yes, sir," came the nervous reply. "He has no choice, sir. His airplane has sustained damage to both wings, its tail and its mid-section. His engines are smoking heavily and we can see he is having trouble just controlling his level."

Of course Porogarkov knew that there was a chance the American would simply dive into the radar station. In fact the airstrip defense commander was quickly on line expressing the same concern.

"Not to worry, Comrade," the air marshal said, knowing the Americans' long-standing policy against "one-way" bombing runs. In fact, he knew that a great amount of their bomber technology ever since World War II — durable engines, high fuel capacity, in-flight refueling exercises — had been geared around bringing the crews *back* from long-range bombing missions.

"These Americans never go on suicide missions," he said confidently. "They feel that life is much too valuable."

In a strange way, Porogarkov felt a little envious of the American behind the controls of the slowly approaching airplane. He knew that if the positions were reversed, Porogarkov would have been expected by his superiors to give up his life to destroy the target.

"He is starting a turn for landing . . ." one of the MiG pilots called out.

"Stay with him!" Porogarkov immediately called back. "Stay right beside him and make sure he lands."

The air marshal could clearly see the American bomber now. It *was* a B-1, probably one of the last ones left, he thought. He was looking forward to finally getting to see the insides of one.

The airstrip landing lights began to blink on, giving the American a clear view of the strip. Briefly, Porogarkov's mind flashed back to the six ICBMs he knew were at that moment streaking through the upper atmosphere, heading for their targets. All the better, he thought.

With this last gasp, the Americans would finally be finished.

Chapter 51

The B-1's wheels hit the Soviet airstrip hard, violently bouncing the airplane once, then a second time. Tortured screeches of metal and rubber filled the air. Finally, after the third contact, the battered, smoking American bomber was down for good.

Porogarkov was running now. Out of the radar station's main entrance and toward the end of the runway about two hundred feet away. Already a dozen jeeps and troop trucks were tearing out onto the landing strip, racing madly in an effort to keep up with the fast rolling bomber.

The two escorting MiGs, their pilots now certain that the bomber was down, pulled up and streaked over the base, one of them brazenly performing a celebratory barrel roll.

The B-1's engines quickly reversed and a shredded parachute was released from his rear end—both acts in effort to slow the big plane's roll. Porogarkov reached the end of the runway at this point, out of breath but jubilant. The B-1 *was* slowing down and soon enough it ground to a halt right in front of him, not 150 feet from the main entrance to the radar station.

He cautiously approached the airplane, opting to wait for the security troop trucks to arrive. He was amazed at how much damage the bomber had sustained—both its wings were in tatters, its portside tailplane was hanging by only a few bolts and wires, and its mid-section looked as if some gigantic fist had battered it several times.

Each of the bomber's four engines were smoking heavily and

337

small fires had broken out on two of the afterburning nozzles. Still Porogarkov knew the chance of an explosion caused by ignited fuel was remote. Even as he was running toward the airstrip he had seen two long plumes of vented fuel burst out from the back of the airplane, its pilot obviously not wanting the battered aircraft to explode on landing.

In fact, he had seen more than a dozen pieces of the airplane fall off during its approach, leading all the more to his amazement that the airplane had actually landed in relatively one piece.

The security forces were now on the scene and the bomber was quickly surrounded.

Once Porogarkov was certain the area was secure, he motioned for a dozen of the soldiers to follow him.

Reaching the bomber's rear compartment entrance, the air marshal sent in two soldiers ahead before climbing into the aircraft himself.

If anything the interior of the airplane looked worse than its outside. The compartment was filled with acrid smoke, many small fires were blazing away and it seemed like every electrical wire was sparking brilliantly.

He and the soldiers slowly made their way up to the airplane's forward compartment, the air marshal taking his own pistol out just in case the Americans gave a struggle.

The two soldiers were the first to reach the cockpit. Instantly they turned back toward him, two identical expressions of mixed confusion and horror written across their faces.

Porogarkov brusquely stormed into the cockpit, his head filled with wild ideas of how the Red Star would honor him for this moment.

But an instant later, he understood the look of haunted disconcertion in his soldiers' eyes.

The cockpit was empty.

"Search the airplane!"

Porogarkov heard the words, but it was as if someone else had yelled the order.

That's when everything started to happen at once. His eyes had fallen into a LED display which was ticking off in seconds. When it finally reached 001, he was startled to hear the bomber's engines suddenly come to life again.

At the same instant, another more pungent odor filled the cabin. The astounded soldiers, not knowing the origin of the smell, instinctively held their noses.

But as an old weapons officer, Porogarkov knew the aroma well—it was the result of two fusing agents being ignited.

In other words, bombs on board the airplane were, at that second, being armed.

A moment later, the B-1 suddenly lurched forward in a bizarre, bumpy taxiing motion. A multitude of lights came to life on the bomber's control panel. Bells, buzzers, and shrill warning signals all started blaring at once. Shocked and unable to move, the air marshal and his dozen soldiers were thrown against the cabin wall as the B-1 crawled forward, its engines screaming in low-acceleration pain.

Then, in his last living moment, Porogarkov heard the distinct loud sizzling of two weapons just micro-seconds before detonation.

Three seconds later, the B-1, its speed up to 25 mph, slammed right through the main entrance of the radar station, the pair of high-explosive glide bombs in its mid-section detonating at the same instant.

There was a quick flash of flame, followed by a tremendous explosion—so powerful it knocked down the remaining airstrip security troops who had watched in horror as the B-1 suddenly pitched forward into the building.

A series of devastating secondary explosions followed, their combined violence producing an enormous mushroom cloud that rivaled the detonation of a small nuclear device.

When those Soviet security troops lucky to survive the blast came to, they saw that absolutely nothing was left of the bomber or the Krasnoyarsk radar station. . . .

Chapter 52

No more than a hundred people saw the six streaks of light flash across the sky high above the American northeastern seaboard.

The small number of witnesses was due to the fact that most of the New England coastal areas had been evacuated shortly after the Big War, when the murderous Mid-Aks briefly held the area.

However one person, a Down Mainer fisherman named Frank Dow, got a fairly close look at two of the Soviet ICBMs. He was twenty miles off the coast of southern Maine when the objects crashed side-by-side into the ocean no more than one thousand yards from his fishing boat, their violent re-entry creating such a tidal disturbance his craft was very nearly swamped.

Neither exploded.

Dow had no idea what the missiles were or where they had come from. In fact, when he first saw the streaks approaching him as he was beginning to haul in his daily catch, he thought he was about to be abducted by UFOs.

Once he was certain that his boat was out of danger of sinking, he quickly marked the approximate location of the crash on his sea chart and then hastily left the area, leaving his catch and his nets behind.

A South African criminal named Rook also witnessed one of the ICBMs re-entry up close and first hand.

Hiding out on a small island off the coast of the old city of

Portsmouth, New Hampshire, Rook had been awakened from a deep sleep by a monstrous crashing noise. Rousing himself from his log cabin hide-out, he ran to the beach and was amazed to see the smoky remains of the huge SS-19 missile sticking straight up in the sand just at the high tide level.

Rook, a former Circle Army mercenary who was also an airborne explosives specialist at one time, knew the object was a Soviet intercontinental ballistic missile and figured quite rightly that it contained a nuclear device inside.

Yet he also knew that whoever had fired the missile had done so incorrectly. The object sticking out of the sand was very nearly the entire missile — launch stages, warhead, everything. The missile had not separated in the upper reaches of the earth's atmosphere as it was supposed to. It had landed, virtually intact, on the beach.

It was just a guess, but he theorized that if the missile's fuel mixture had somehow been tainted — or not blended together properly in the first place — it would have prevented the ICBM from reaching its all-important "critical escape altitude," the point at which the timing mechanisms for the breakaway stages and the warhead arming systems were activated via altimeter controls.

But Rook also knew that just because the missile had landed intact that didn't necessarily mean it still wasn't about to explode.

Quickly packing his things, he set out in his small unpowered boat and rowed toward shore, upset that he would have to find yet another place to hide.

No one saw the other three SS-19s crash to earth.

One landed in a lake in western Nova Scotia. Another did a belly landing on an abandoned seaside vacation area in northern Massachusetts called Plum Island.

The sixth and final ICBM had plowed itself into the side of a New Hampshire mountain used in pre-war days as a ski slope.

Inside these three SS-19s, as in the others, the warheads had survived their less-than-auspicious re-entry. And battered though they were, with the right amount of technology, all six of the 1.5-kiloton nuclear devices could one day be repaired.

Chapter 53

Hunter knew at least three of his ribs were broken.

He tried to turn over on his side, but couldn't—the pain was too intense. He reached up to his right shoulder and found that this too was hurt—most likely it was separated.

Carefully, he tried to wiggle his toes and was relieved to find them responding, though remotely so. He held first his right hand, then his left in front of his face. Both were badly scraped and cut, but apparently free of broken bones.

He felt his face next, checking to make sure his nose, ears and jaw were still attached. They were. A quick reach between his legs also brought a spark of relief—he was sore there, but still intact.

He reached below him and felt the remains of the rubber life raft that he had used to break his fall. It was in tatters, instantly deflated when it—and he—hit the cold, sharp rocky tundra going no less than 60 mph shortly before the B-1 set down on the Soviet airstrip.

Jumping from the moving airplane had actually turned out to be the easy part. The complications happened minutes before when he had to quickly program the B-1's on-board computer to land the bomber, taxi it to a stop at a precise spot down the end of the runway, and shut down, only to have its engines fire up again exactly one minute later—the time it would take to arm and fuse the two glide bombs in its forward weapons bay—and smash into the radar station.

But he knew the plan had worked. Even through groggy and blood-misted eyes he had seen the Soviet complex explode in a mini-mushroom cloud.

"We got 'em, guys," he had coughed in a brief moment of congratulations.

But he knew he was in real trouble.

He couldn't move — not right away anyway. And if he had been able to, where would he go? If there were any Soviets left breathing at the base, he was sure they would kill him. And there was certainly no friendly faces for at least a thousand miles around.

Or so he thought . . .

He closed his eyes, for what he thought had been just a minute. But when he woke, it was almost daylight and the first thing he saw was the barrel of an AK-47 just an inch or two from his nose.

Next thing he knew, he was being put on a stretcher, while, at the same moment, someone was injecting something into his arm. He was suddenly overwhelmed with an extraordinarily pleasant, though highly narcotic feeling. He would later learn that he'd been injected with enough morphine to make a horse giddy for a week.

Over the next few days, he had only vague memories of fuzzy faces and bitter soup being forced into his mouth. He remembered being in a log cabin for at least two nights. Another night was spent in a tent, covered in thick blankets. He was constantly re-wrapped in bandages from head to toe, and was injected with the potent painkiller at least once a day.

It wasn't until he heard the sound of waves crashing against a shore that he was able to rouse himself from the heavy drug-induced haze.

It was morning and he was in a camp of some kind, placed very close to a roaring fire. He was surprised to find another person clinging to him tightly — almost intimately.

Rolling to his side for the first time in days, he came face to face with a pretty young girl who was of obvious Mongolian extraction.

She smiled to reveal a perfect set of glistening white teeth. "Stay warm," she said with some effort. "We hug. You stay warm."

He was in no mood to argue. They hugged. They stayed warm.

The sun — bright and warm — was overhead when he woke again. The girl was gone, but a soldier was sitting nearby. Hunter managed to raise himself up on his elbows, surprised that the pain in his shoulder and in his rib cage was now only a dull throb, and not the stinging stab he'd felt for days.

"Where the hell am I?" he asked, his voice husky and coarse from days of non-use.

The question somewhat startled the soldier next to him. But a smile quickly came to the man's face.

"You . . . near Vladivostok," the man said in very rough English. "You . . . are feel better?"

Hunter nodded, for the first time realizing the man was wearing a standard Red Army infantry uniform.

"Am I your prisoner?"

The man smiled. His teeth too were near perfect. "No . . ." he said shaking his head. "You are guest . . ."

"Guest?" Hunter was puzzled. "Who are you?" he asked.

The man looked at him and thought a moment. Then, through a great smile he said: "I am Soviet soldier. My comrades and I save you. From Red Star . . ."

Now Hunter was just plain confused. By all rights, this guy should consider him his enemy.

Their small conversation was interrupted with the arrival of about a dozen more men and several women. All were wearing standard Red Army combat outfits and all were armed with AK-47s. Nearby, Hunter spotted several T-80 tanks, a few BMPs and a mobile SAM launcher.

A hurried conversation in Russian commenced between the troops, complete with numerous hand gestures, some directed back at Hunter and others out toward the sea.

Then one of them came over to Hunter and carefully lifted him to a sitting position. He pointed off shore, directing Hunter's eyes to a vessel about a half mile away.

Hunter forced his eyes to focus until he could make out the distinct shape of a submarine. He felt a great leap of excitement when, upon closer inspection, he was able to make out the red maple leaf symbol of Free Canada painted on the conning tower.

Time passed and finally a boat was launched from the sub carrying a squad of Free Canadian sailors to shore. Brief greetings were exchanged, and in the span of ten minutes, Hunter was strapped into a large stretcher and carried aboard the small launch.

Although he barraged the Canadian sailors with questions—

where he was, where they came from and so on—they said very little. Apparently, they weren't quite sure who *he* was and where *he* had come from.

Finally, when it was apparent that he was to be carried to the sub, he yanked on the sleeve of one of the Canadians and said as forcefully as possible: "These guys—and girls—saved my life. I've got to at least thank them . . ."

The Canadian nodded and called the leader of the rescuers over to the boat. Hunter reached up with a bandaged hand and gripped the man's shoulder.

"Thank you," he said, tears almost filling his eyes. "Thank you for my life . . ."

The Soviet soldier grinned and nodded. Hunter had no way of knowing whether the man understood or not, but it appeared that he was getting the general idea.

Hunter just couldn't go before he asked one last question. Leaning up to see that the beach was now filled with Soviet soldiers, he looked up at the man and said: *"Who are you?"*

The man thought a moment and smiled broadly. "Me . . . a 'good Russian' . . ."

With that, the boat was launched and Hunter was carried off to the Free Canadian sub.

Chapter 54

Three weeks later

The small courthouse just outside of Washington DC was packed.

Hunter, his ribcage, shoulder, face and hands still heavily bandaged, did a quick head count. By his calculations, there were 105 people crammed into a room built for 35 at the most, and that didn't include the dozen or so video cameras taking up space right next to the judge's bench.

The second trial of the ex-VP was finally at its end. All of the testimony had been presented, witnesses questioned, rebuttals and final summations delivered. To no one's surprise, the traitor had been found guilty on all counts — including the new charge of attempted mass murder resulting from the nuclear explosion over Syracuse.

This day, the last day of the proceedings, was reserved for the sentencing.

The Chief Justice entered and quickly gaveled the room silent. Then he turned and looked at the defendant standing in the dock, looking small and frail.

"Sir . . ." the judge intoned gravely. "You stand before this court, and before this nation, accused of the highest treason. Your act of betrayal has caused the death of millions and quite nearly destroyed this country. You have shown not the slightest remorse for your actions: indeed, with your obscene attempt at disrupting these proceedings by having your confederates detonate a nuclear device over the city of Syracuse, you have expressed an outrageous contempt for this trial as well as for the ideals of this country that we hold so dear.

"It is within the power of this court to pass upon you a sentence of death for these crimes, as many here have suggested. But although it is certainly richly deserved in light of your actions, this court has been persuaded that more fitting punishment can be meted out.

"Therefore, you will serve as a lasting example for all Americans of the consequences of war and peace, of freedom and slavery, of justice and tyranny, of crime and punishment, and of life and death.

"Sir, this court finds you guilty of high treason and other crimes against the United States of America, and pronounces the following sentence:

"You will henceforth and without reservation be imprisoned in solitary confinement for the rest of your natural life.

"These proceedings are closed."

The cheering, both inside the courtroom and out, finally died down after thirty minutes or so.

The prisoner, his face an ashen white as if he were for the first time realizing the magnitude of his actions, was manacled hand and foot and brought to a security van which had parked in back of the courthouse.

As this van drove away, it was pelted with eggs, rocks, small packets of paint and saliva — all of it aimed at the traitor who would now be flown to a specially built military prison located in the bleak Arctic outreaches near Point Barrow, Alaska.

Hunter was riding close behind in another security van, along with Ben and JT. The two pilots would fly escort for the big C-141 that would carry the prisoner on his twelve-hour flight to prison. Hunter, unable to fly for at least a month, was along for the ride to the airport.

On the way, he recounted for his two friends, news he had just received from the Free Canadian Defense Ministry, confirming what the skipper of his rescue sub had told him during his trip across the Pacific.

When the Soviet soldier told Hunter that he was a "good Russian," it was no idle boast. Unknown to the United Americans or

347

the Free Canadians, there were two factions now vying for power within the Soviet Union. One, the Red Star, was the entity responsible for starting World War III in the first place. They had also engineered the New Order, and with it the many wars that had swept the American continent ever since. Finally, it was they who detonated the bomb over Syracuse, although it now seemed like the timing of that act had less to do with the ex-VP's capture as the traitor had led them all to believe.

The "good Russians" were anti-Red Star. Original backers of *glasnost*, what they lacked in technological means they made up for in determination and courage. A raiding party of Good Russians was about to hit the Krasnoyarsk facility when they saw the B-1 roar in and do the job for them. It was they who found Hunter, treated his injuries, carried him hundreds of miles to the sea, where a friendly ship captain contacted the Free Canadian sub which was in the area on a routine recon patrol.

Hunter was the first to admit that the concept of an army of "Good Russians" was a hard one for him to grasp at first. Yet he embraced it rather quickly. Having one's life saved tended to speed up the acceptance process.

Just what lay ahead between the United Americans and the Good Russian Army was anybody's guess. Obviously they shared some of the same goals, but he couldn't imagine seeing eye-to-eye on everything. Also, while the destruction of Krasnoyarsk had eliminated Red Star's nuclear weapons' launch capability, it hardly put an end to the secret movement. These "bad" Russians were too highly advanced, too firmly entrenched for that.

However, it heartened Hunter's psyche in knowing that the UA and its precious few allies were no longer completely alone in the fight against the forces of human slavery.

Maybe there was some hope yet. . . .

The ride to the former National Airport took about forty minutes and when they reached the terminal building, they were all surprised to see the place was mobbed with citizens hoping to get one last shot at berating the ex-VP.

In order to avoid most of the unruly crowd, the two security vans drove right out onto the tarmac, stopping about a hundred feet from the already warmed-up C-141.

Hunter bade a quick farewell to JT and Ben, promising to meet them two days later at their favorite Washington watering hole for an unadultered day of boozing and skirt-chasing.

Then Hunter slowly climbed out of the van, wanting to get a better look at this last historic event — the ex-VP's departure. About three hundred citizens had spilled out onto the field and were now surrounding the prisoner's van. The security personnel at the airport, made up almost entirely of Football City Special Forces, quickly sized up the situation and, as courteously as possible, created a path through the crowd by linking arms and lining up in two rows that stretched right up to the C-141.

The prisoner was at last taken out of the van and immediately a roar of derision and obscenities arose from the crowd. More eggs and packets of paint were thrown, spattering on the prisoner and his guards alike. Moving slowly due to his manacles, the ex-VP looked dazed at it all, as if he had just awoken from a nightmare to find out it was all true.

Hunter found himself leaning against the prisoner's van for support — his ribs hurt the most after standing for long periods of time — watching the scene with a mixture of fascination and historical perspective. The traitor was finally getting his due.

But suddenly he felt a very familiar feeling wash over him.

Something was wrong. *Very* wrong . . .

The prisoner was about halfway to the C-141 when Hunter started moving into the crowd, scanning the sea of angry faces. Every one of his senses was buzzing at this point, anticipating something still unknown.

The catcalls and screams grew louder as the crowd pushed in farther toward the prisoner. Some were literally trying to grab the ex-VP around the neck. The Football City Special Rangers were now having trouble being so respectful toward the crowd. Individual pushing matches between the soldiers and the citizens instantly escalated into near mini-riots.

Yet in the middle of it all, Hunter's extraordinary senses were now aflame — telling him, *warning him,* that something very wrong was about to happen.

Moving as fast as his bandages and the surging crowd would let him, he tried to catch up with the small phalanx of soldiers now surrounding the ex-VP. All the while he was looking intently into every face in the crowd.

Could it be that . . .

Suddenly, he saw a familiar face—a *very* familiar face.

It was Elizabeth.

She was standing about ten feet from the prisoner's position, wearing a long dark coat and hood. Yet she had looked up momentarily—just enough for Hunter to see her unmistakable features. That's when he saw the glint of metal in her hand.

He was about to cry out—but it was too late.

As if in slow motion, he saw Elizabeth leap through the cordon of soldiers, raise a pistol and, without hesitation, pump five shots into the ex-VP's stomach and chest.

There was an instant of stunned silence, then absolute pandemonium broke out. At once, half the soldiers picked up the prisoner and literally dragged him to the C-141, while the other half pounced on Elizabeth.

Almost as stunned as everyone else, Hunter moved forward, screaming: "Don't shoot her! *Don't shoot* . . ."

He was relieved when he heard no further gunshots—but the sound he *did* hear was almost as startling.

Above the screams of the crowd, above the shouts of the soldiers as they subdued Elizabeth, and even above the ear-piercing whine of the C-141's engines, he heard her distinctly frightening laugh. . .

THE END